Prospect Heights Public Library

D1479087

ORIANA

ORIANA

a novel of Oriana Fallaci

Anastasia Rubis

Delphinium Books

ORIANA

Printed in the United States of America

For information, address DELPHINIUM BOOKS, INC.,
16350 Ventura Boulevard, Suite D
PO Box 803
Encino, CA 91436

Library of Congress Cataloguing-in-Publication Data is available on request.
ISBN 978-1-953002-36-5

24 25 26 27 28 LBC 5 4 3 2 1
Jacket and interior design by Colin Dockrill, AIGA

For Kassandra and Yanni, who make my life full

Chapter 1

2003

GO AWAY. The handwritten sign is taped to her doorbell.

For some inexplicable reason, she has agreed to see him and cracks open the door of her townhouse. He is ridiculously handsome, the Hollywood producer. Early thirties, she guesses, an irresistible age in a man. Warm playful eyes, messy chestnut curls.

"Come in," she says. "You might be the last person I ever speak to."

The producer looks confused but recovers quickly. He's much younger than she expected and bounds in on long limbs. "Ms. Fallaci, I'm a huge fan, honored to meet you." He holds out an expensive-looking bouquet of white roses.

For a moment she stands stricken in the foyer. "How did you know?"

"Know what?" His expression is open and curious.

She accepts the flowers, caught for a moment in the plumpness of a creamy bud. "Alekos used to give me white roses." Her heart does a little skip, saying his name out loud, though so many decades have passed and she has turned into a bony old woman.

"I didn't know." The producer's features settle into a tiny frown. She sees him furiously trying to figure out if his roses are a nice coincidence or if she is going to cry. No way, Mr. Hollywood, Oriana Fallaci never cries.

He is here to discuss a movie that she doesn't want to make, but his title, Chairman of 20th Century Fox, and some instinct have made her agree to the meeting. She had a gut feeling she would like this man, and now that he's good-looking with a friendly, exuberant air . . .

How long has it been since she let a young man into her home? The three-story townhouse of white brick sits on a tree-lined street of the Upper East Side a few blocks from Bloomingdale's. It is worth five million now. She's proud of her Manhattan real estate. Bookcases in every room, the ivory carpet cozy but worn. A mahogany staircase leading up to her bedroom and down to her study, the two rooms she lives in. On this floor, the formal living room with its antique (old lady?) furniture, stiff and unused.

She has prepared herself for him with a deep red manicure, spritz of Joy, black silk dress, accessories of course: Ferragamo scarf to hide the wrinkles on her neck, ring on each hand, sapphire and ruby. Long ago, when she jetted around the world on assignment, she dressed like a man, strictly pantsuits. At Lutèce once, a stuffy French restaurant in New York that critics swooned over, she was turned away for wearing pants, the last time she dined there. And to the emperor of Ethiopia, who tried to decree her attire for an upcoming interview, she said, "I come in pants or I come in the nude." Today, all women wear pants, so she chooses dresses—there is still pleasure in going against the grain. Her hair is in a bun at the nape of her neck, thinned from the poison they dripped into her veins until she said *basta*, enough. On her feet, felt slippers, like the heroic housewives of her mother's generation. It takes an hour to dress in the morning, the pain unbearable until she swallows a pill.

"Come, I'll fix you something to eat," she says, leading the way to the galley kitchen. "You're too skinny." She is aware she's flirting with him—the challenging tone, sardonic glance—and it's disorienting for a moment, transforming her into a younger self.

The producer wears a charcoal blazer over black shirt and jeans, fashionable in his business, she knows, along with other modern touches: Stubble beard, citrusy cologne, leather messenger bag of good quality, maybe Prada—she scans for the triangular logo and it is. His movements are bouncy and loose, matching something unselfconscious in his personality. She's jealous of his youth and lightness, as if nothing could go wrong, as if nothing ever has. Happy-go-lucky, that's what he is, an adjective no one could apply to her.

"This is *cotechino* from my region," she says, slicing up a short red sausage at the counter. "Toscana, you know? You've never had sausage like this."

"I'm kind of a vegetarian."

"Not today." She fries it up, peppering him with questions about his fast rise at Fox because of some blockbuster movies. His education at Columbia, philosophy, but he dropped out . . . interesting. Exquisite to look at, he could be an actor himself. Nothing special about his brown eyes, but they crackle with light and good humor. His vocabulary is casual, his manner unassuming, but he's intelligent. She sees it in his quickness, the way he seems to catch meaning in the air, effortlessly. "*Cotechino* is always paired with lentils," she says, serving him on a Vietri ceramic plate popping with color. "Eat."

He sits on the lone wooden stool and eats.

Although it's barely noon, she pours Dom Pérignon into two crystal flutes. Lights a cigarette. "You like it, Dennis Brady?" He has a nice name. She likes saying it.

"Mmm." He devours the *cotechino* like a good carnivore, and she lets out a throaty laugh. "Aren't you eating?" he says, his mouth full.

"Difficult these days. I get my nourishment from this." She toasts him with champagne.

"Cancer, right?" he says with the frankness of a six-year-old that startles her, then brings welcome relief. People tiptoe around the word. In Italy it's taboo, so she went on television and said *I have cancer, cancer.* What a breath of fresh air with this boy, not to hide her illness or be pitied.

"My doctor at Sloan has officially given up on me." She hasn't admitted this even to herself. "*How are you still alive?* he said last week, studying my X-rays. *I'm stubborn*, I told him, *I never give in.*" Dennis Brady's face ripples with concern but she fends it off. "It's an underrated virtue. You can get through a lot of life on stubbornness."

The roses get stuffed in a vase, she'll deal with them later, and they go down one flight to her study. He admires her antique American flag from Argosy on East 59th, where she buys her cherished first editions. The Vietnam combat helmet displayed on her bookcase, the certificate for taking part in a U.S. bombing mission, her framed photographs with Golda Meir, Indira Gandhi, Robert Kennedy, Arthur Miller, Walt Disney.

He runs his fingers along the spines of her own books, editions in English, French, German, Arabic—twenty-three languages.

"I don't know why you're here," she says abruptly. "Sit." He sits on the burgundy leather chesterfield. She turns on the Tiffany lamp on the side table to see him better. "I've never sold the rights to any of my books. No one touches my babies."

He reaches into his messenger bag and takes out *A Man* with the shiny silver jacket that never fails to impress her, the stark purple letters. It's the best title she's ever come up with, direct and full of punch. "This was on my wife's bookshelf," the producer says, with a strange hitch in his voice. "I read it last winter. It's never left me."

"Why?" She narrows her eyes at him.

"It's a great love story. Like *Out of Africa* or *Reds*," he says. Easy there, she thinks, watching him launch into salesman mode. "Like all great love stories, there's something impossible about it. Tragic."

The way Mr. Easygoing pronounces *tragic* raises her antennae. Maybe there's a deeper quality she hasn't given him credit for. "I have always had a tragic life," she says, getting up stiffly from the wooden bench, which oddly eases her back pain these days. Bones warming, she moves with her usual feistiness to her oak desk. It's awash in manuscript pages, stained espresso cups, a butt-filled ashtray, and of course her manual Olivetti typewriter. She's never gone electric, though now she can't find a damn repair place when a letter sticks. One framed photograph sits on her cluttered desk, and she brings it to her guest. "Alekos and I on the day we met." She tries to sound offhand, staring at her impossibly young self, at his image frozen forever. The attraction emanating from both of them, their connection visible already.

The producer holds the photo delicately, with a surprising flicker of emotion.

"Are you married?" she says.

He hesitates. "I was."

Ah. Divorced, she concludes, and not his choice. "Then you understand me," she says. "Love doesn't stand up to scrutiny. Don't put it under a microscope. Or a camera, in your case." She tucks a stray hair into her bun. "You remind me of him." He does. The five o'clock shadow, athletic pulse of his body.

Her blue-gray almond eyes have always been her best feature—this morning, she has painted on a curl of black eyeliner—and she fixes them now on her guest. "*Allora*. You are proposing a movie I never wanted to make, but in the future I *may* want to make. You're rushing to buy the rights because next month I might be dead." He shifts awkwardly but doesn't deny it. "I don't have time to consider your proposal now," she says. "The only reason I'm seeing you is that you tortured my assistant. I respect that, by the way."

"She said you're under pressure." The producer leans forward with concern. "You're getting death threats?"

"I have a target on my head." Her recent book about 9/11, an unapologetic warning against Osama bin Laden and his followers, has been wildly controversial.

"I didn't mean to bring it up." The producer rubs his hands along his thighs.

"Why not? You might upset me? You'd never make it as a journalist." The phone rings. "Good morning," she says into it, curt. "Yes I'm fine. Thank you." She hangs up. "The police check on me every day. I'm being followed, sued, they're trying to ban my book." She levels her gaze at him. "I'm a nasty woman, you see. A woman who says and does what she wants."

"That's what I want to make, a movie about a strong female protagonist."

"Maybe you should start with someone who doesn't say *shit* or *fuck*."

They share a laugh.

"Don't you want everyone to know your story?" he says.

"No. I'm very private." She drags on her cigarette. "Who would play me?"

He names baby actresses she's never heard of. Why is he so interested in her, she can't make out. His last three movies, she's researched him, have recycled comic book heroes, nothing she would ever go to see. Her gaze drifts back to the photograph, she and Alekos on that bright August afternoon. Photographs were such devils. The image lifts her briefly, filling her with a warm glow, then drops her in midair, punching her in the throat. The longer she stares, the more unreal he becomes, as if he never walked the earth or is from a distant lifetime. The best thing happened to her, but it was so long ago, it seems never to have happened at all.

"You know," she says, interrupting as the producer is describing Jennifer somebody who won an Oscar. "Just before I met Alekos, I was at the height of my profession. But when I looked down from my mountaintop, it was as if I'd climbed the wrong mountain. This is it? I was a woman alone, you see. Men don't face that."

She doesn't say that in bed at night, she had felt adrift in the universe, connected to no one. Worrying *who is going to love me?* She had reached her forties by then, convinced there was something wrong with her. She didn't arouse tenderness even if she was hungry for it, even if she felt beaten down at times and longed for a man to lean on.

Then Alekos came along, wild and needy and ten years younger. She could still feel his mouth on her skin, the way he took her with gentle insistence. Every woman should be loved by a younger man.

"Before Alekos, I doubted that love existed," she says. "I hated love."

"That's a good title," the producer says. "*She Hated Love.*"

"It's a terrible title." He has got her chatting, the trick she always used with her subjects. Get people talking about themselves and they'll drop their pants.

Oddly, she doesn't give a damn. She likes the producer's lanky masculinity filling up her study. He is good company in this room where she toils to put words on the page. Most crucially, he's distracting her from the unspeakable task of getting ready to leave this earth. Finishing her last book, organizing her archives. Attending to business she's never really cared about—wills, royalties, legal issues with her publisher.

She doesn't want to go. She loves life, even when it's cruel and gives her suffering.

"More champagne?" she says.

They clink glasses. He has caught her at a moment when she's sleepless at four in the morning, turning over the pieces of her seventy-three years. What she did. What she should have done but didn't. What she deserved but didn't get. Her wins, ooh, she likes winning, and her damn sorrows. How she hates people who proclaim, "I have no regrets." She has plenty. She torments herself with her mistakes. Most of all this: no child. An Italian woman without Sunday gatherings of *la familia*. A true fiasco, she feels it intensely now, the failure to fulfill her biological purpose. She has missed out on the pleasures of inhaling a baby's scalp, carrying a bundle on her hip, cheering on first steps. Now, when she dies, she will *really* die, leaving no trace of herself behind. The looming void ahead, the nothingness, terrifies her, though she would never admit it. She has made a career of being insanely brave, tough as nails.

How has she ended up so alone? Traveling back in time to extract some meaning doesn't work. The pieces of her life have passed so quickly—this decade, that decision— they're so cruelly faded, she can hardly recapture their details or essence. Only sometimes, only briefly. In the end, there is so little to hold on to.

For damn sure she has never fit into any conventional box or let anyone else define her, telling her what she can and cannot do. Late at night, rewinding her choices, she has concluded only one thing: We are not here to make sense; we are here to have guts and to act. To do something with our lives. Have an adventure.

And that she has done.

If the charming producer wants her story, her story with Alekos, maybe she'll give it to him. Her version, of course. *I am the boss, I decide.* A movie might be her chance to set the record straight, to have the last word, she's always satisfied by that. Just recently, some imbecile had the gall to write *Fallaci was never truly in love with Greek patriot Alexander Panagoulis. Though she claims he was her great love, he was only her fantasy hero.*

They only did this to women, denied them authority even over their own hearts.

The producer is watching her, calculating if in an hour, he can get out of here with her signature on a contract. He's wonderful and awful to look at, the same age as Alekos when she fell off the cliff.

She wets her lips with a sip of champagne. "I almost didn't go to Greece that day," she says. "Thank God for my enemies."

"Your enemies?" He angles his head.

"Come on. You must know this by now," she says, her tone brash, flirtatious again. "Life is full of enemies." Her voice turns gravelly, saying this last almost to herself. "They push you harder to win."

Chapter 2

1973

Oriana Fallaci hunched over her desk doing what she did best: taking a drag of her cigarette, setting it down on her typewriter over the burn mark, and attacking the keys.

Attacking any bastard who dared insult her.

Dr. Kissinger. You accuse me of distorting your answers. Do you remember I taped our interview, with your permission? I have told Time, Newsweek, *and the networks I can release those tapes, to help your recollection.*

Laser-focused, she reread her telegram. Fought the temptation to change the salutation to *Dear Icy Evader. Dear Pompous Little Professor*. Release her tapes, her prized interview tapes? Never. But Icy didn't need to know that.

It was a sweltering August afternoon in the center of Florence. Fans whirred, papers rustled on desks, the windows were thrown open to the muffled sounds of afternoon siesta and the city emptied out for *Ferragosto* holidays. A mixture of perspiration, too much cologne, and heavy cigarette smoke thickened the air.

Oriana yanked out her telegram and walked it across the newsroom. "Send it to Henry Kissinger at the American embassy in Paris," she said to Lucia, the alert young secretary with waves of auburn hair. "Where he is once again holding peace talks with North Vietnam that will fail to bring peace."

Ciao. She jutted her chin at her editor, Tommaso Giglio,

through the door of his private office. He was his usual calm, cultured self, on the phone, swiveling in his chrome and leather chair, facing Florence's best street, the café-lined Lungarno Vespucci running along the Arno River. Back at her desk, she threw her legs on top, crossing them, and lit another cigarette, briefly approving the wedge sandals and pencil pants hugging her thin silhouette. She was forty-four but didn't look it. In fact, she could feel the libidinous glances of male colleagues this minute, mixed, of course, with the complicated soup of *Who the fuck does she think she is?* Female success pissed people off. It was not at all revered like male success, a lesson she'd learned early. Too bad. She would never downplay hers.

Her gaze swept over the all-male newsroom save Lucia and the cleaning woman reaching into corners with her feather duster. Always men surrounding her in this profession. The irony was she preferred men, or rather she'd learned how to be one of them, more than women.

From a messy stack on her desk (she was messy), Oriana took the latest *L'Europeo,* the weekly news magazine where she'd been a correspondent for—Christ, how long was it—nineteen years. *L'Europeo* was every bit as good as *Life*, with a mix of hard and soft stories covering politics, society, and the arts. Her interview with King Hussein of Jordan was on the cover. She made a noise of satisfaction seeing her name in bold above the headline. No matter how many times she published her byline, it seemed a miracle to her, and she had the complicated reaction of disbelief and wanting to give herself a hugely deserved pat on the back.

Skimming her piece, she approved the sharp wording, stopping only once to think no, a different adjective would have better described the king. She remembered how dejected Hussein had looked a month ago at his palace in Amman, so small in his grand armchair, his feet barely touching the ground. She kept forgetting to call him *Your Majesty*. "Are you losing power, sir?"

She hit him with the impertinent question early, as usual. The king was in the news, central to the conflict between Palestine and Israel. She always interviewed leaders at the moment they became critical on the world stage, asking questions everyone was desperate to know. It took meticulous research; she killed herself to be informed. Of course, she asked personal questions, too. King Hussein would have rather been a pilot or a lawyer. He hated being king.

Sticky from heat, she flicked back her hair—long, ash blond, and parted in the middle. What a relief not to be running to the hairdresser as she did in the 1950s and '60s, when she was interviewing all those vacuous Hollywood stars. The "women's topics" she started with.

"*Ciao*, Oriana." Mulotti breezed into the newsroom. The young upstart wore a tan safari jacket with a wide tie and flashed his predator's grin. "What a surprise, you here with us, *international superstar*."

She rarely came in, it was true. She was flying off to Germany tomorrow. She gave him a look anyway.

"This is what *Newsweek* calls you." Mulotti waved the rolled magazine in his hand.

"Give me." She flew up and grabbed it from him. "Is this my copy? Why didn't they send me one?" There was her picture, decent, still juice in her. Her eyes raced over the text. Not bad. *Greatest political interviewer of her time. Spitfire. Never intimidated by those in power.* They even quoted her correctly. *Presidents and kings are no better than us, no more intelligent or competent. In fact they're often stunted and inept. Why should I bow down and tremble before them? On the contrary, I give them hell.*

Newsweek. A profile of her, though only a paragraph. She couldn't believe it.

Mulotti was jealous. She could feel it with her intuition, and when she glanced up, there it was on his face. His tanned face, from a holiday in Sardinia or Ischia or who knows where. "It took me two decades to get here." She wagged the magazine at him. "I've had to work twice as hard as a man. But I'm thrilled. You know why? It's made me better."

He gave her the wolf grin. "Let me buy you an espresso."

"Finally you have a good idea. Medium sweet."

He summoned the coffee boy with the swinging brass tray making his daily rounds from the corner café. Oriana leaned back on her desk and toasted Mulotti with an exaggerated gesture before downing her espresso. Why did the little worm have to land here, at her magazine? Damn Italy and its nepotism. No shortcuts for her—of course not.

"Tell me, Oriana, how much do the Americans pay when they translate your articles?" Mulotti said with a wink.

"None of your business."

"I want to do the same one day."

She scoffed. "Good luck." The little prick had no idea what it took, the effort she'd exacted from herself. Something in his demeanor made her ask, "What are you working on?"

Mulotti was making a show of generously tipping the coffee boy. "I'm leaving for Athens to meet the Greek who just got amnesty."

"What Greek?" Her antennae shot up, watching him expand his chest.

"The hero who tried to knock off the dictator five years ago."

Rapidly, she calculated . . . five years ago, she was in Mexico City. Covering the student protest turned massacre. The most dangerous story of her career.

"The Greek was tortured in prison but never broke," Mulotti said. "Now the dictator's set him free." He drew himself up. "Oriana Fallaci covers war and rebellion and doesn't know this freedom fighter?"

She shot him a withering look. He addressed her with too little respect, this twenty-five-year-old who had not the slightest idea how to report. "Coffee break *finito*," she said, bulldozing past him to her editor's office.

Tommaso was leafing through the new issue with his keen, judicious eye. Lovely man, she had the same thought she always had, salt and pepper hair, impeccably dressed in a slim khaki suit. The kind of intellectual she respected, unpretentious though published, currently working on a new translation of *Alice in Wonderland*. She had become world-famous under his wing; she owed him a lot. Especially since he had the good sense to let her be the boss.

"Where's Mulotti going?" she said, crossing her arms.

"To interview him." Tommaso nodded toward the television on its mobile stand and circled his desk to join her.

She stared at the RAI news footage of a young man, thirtyish with jet-black hair, squinting outside a barbed wire prison, blinded by sunlight. His face quivering with pent-up tears. A woman in black, his mother, the newscaster said, rushed toward him and threw her arms around his neck.

Oriana felt her own throat constrict, watching the dissident's first moments of freedom. She observed the world with a literary eye, saw everyone as a character with a story, and she knew a deeply human scene when she saw one.

The TV footage showed Alexander Panagoulis sitting for a press conference straight out of solitary confinement, chronicling his torture with a composure she found staggering. Who was this man? They hung him upside down until his chest was paralyzed, making it impossible to breathe. Clubbed the soles of his feet with the *falange* until he fainted. He was used as an ashtray, cigarettes extinguished in his scrotum. Whipped with a metal cable. Head beaten on the floor.

"Those brutes." Her eyebrows drew together in three fierce

lines. "They're so cocksure they have the right to dominate others. To kick the shit out of us if we don't obey." Tommaso nodded, watching her wind up. She despised it more than anything, the smugness of those in power, convinced they were superior to "the peons." This is why she did journalism, to cut dictators, fascists, authoritarians down to size. To be the voice of the people. The humble, ordinary neighbors she'd grown up with. Her parents.

Eyes glued to the TV, she tried to detect the exact qualities in Alexander Panagoulis that allowed him to withstand such a hellish ordeal. Lucid and steady, he narrated the details of his assassination attempt, trial, sentencing, without pride, with an undercurrent of emotion that leaked through only when he ran out of breath, in the space before he took another.

"It's obscene. Dictatorship and torture in the country that invented democracy." She turned to Tommaso, making her decision.

"No one is immune," Tommaso said. "Spain, Portugal. It's a Mediterranean epidemic at the moment. We had our turn."

"I'll take the next plane to Athens to interview him."

"Mulotti is going."

"He will not." She threw her editor a steely glare. "I will go."

"What about Brandt? He took you eight months to schedule."

"I'll reschedule," she said. The German chancellor would have to wait. She would decide her assignments, not Tommaso or any ambitious young *stronzo*. *L'Europeo* was lucky she gave them her articles at this point in her career. She could sell directly to *Life*, *Look*, *The New York Times*. They were chasing her every day. "Miss Fallaci, can we reprint your Gaddafi interview, we pay three thousand dollars, four thousand . . ."

"And *60 Minutes*?" Tommaso said.

"First Athens, then New York," she said. The prestigious news program was filming her Friday in her apartment. "But

I've talked enough about Kissinger. I want to vomit when I hear *Kissinger*."

"He's saying it was the stupidest mistake of his career, saying yes to you."

"It was." She gave her smoker's laugh and Tommaso joined her. "He never read my interviews, he just wanted to be in my club of leaders." Her Kissinger profile had sparked a scandal in America, catching her by surprise, but then she'd lured Nixon's lap dog into saying some embarrassing things. "Look, I'm going to Greece. Haven't I got you enough publicity?" she said to Tommaso, motioning to the clips jamming his bulletin board. The names Fallaci and *L'Europeo* were plastered all over the Washington, Chicago, and New York dailies.

"You have." Tommaso watched her. She could read his puzzled expression. Why was she burning to interview the little Greek dissident when three months ago she had entrée to the White House and landed an international scoop? Because she was sick of big shots, sick of power. And something else.

The TV flickered with the young rebel's image. She was impressed by Alexander Panagoulis, and it had been a long time since she'd been impressed by any man.

"It was my idea!" She could hear Mulotti crying like a baby in Tommaso's office as she packed up her desk. "She waltzes in here and takes what she wants!"

Lucia walked over to help her get ready and they exchanged smirks. "I got you on the three p.m. to Athens," Lucia said.

"Good girl."

Together, they ransacked the archives closet for news clippings on the Greek hero, creating a file folder for her trip.

"Mulotti cornered me yesterday in the stairwell," Lucia said as they worked. "Why won't I go to the cinema with him? He pinched my behind."

"Knee him in the balls," Oriana said without looking up.

"I'm married."

"That makes you more desirable."

"I'm so proud of what they wrote about you in *Newsweek*, Oriana," Lucia said.

"One more reason to hate me." She peered into the newsroom at her sniggering colleagues eavesdropping as Mulotti continued his rant. Simpletons, she thought, so limited by their XY chromosome. Men were missing the extra leg of the XX chromosome that women possessed. It was a deficiency, for sure, she had studied biology. "When are you going to try writing?" she turned to Lucia. "You're not going to be a secretary all your life."

"My husband says I should stick to what I know."

"Your husband doesn't know what he's talking about," Oriana said. Her brow crinkled with seriousness the way it always did when she was thinking. "I cut the path, now take it. They'll start you out on this season's skirt lengths and dinner parties. How far you climb is up to you."

Back at her desk, she tucked the research folder into her voluminous Fendi satchel, loaded a fresh Maxwell cassette into her tape recorder, and stowed five backups.

"Nice article in *Newsweek*, Oriana," a few colleagues chorused half-heartedly as they saw her readying for the airport. Would it ever get any easier? She had always imagined once she paid her dues, worked herself to the bone, became the most famous journalist in Italy, they'd forget she had different genitalia and accept her. But no. They still saw her as a threat. Oriana was feared, not liked. Did she care? Of course. Everyone wanted to be liked.

Arms laden, she started to go when Mulotti came tearing out of Tommaso's office. "What is it you hate about me, Oriana? Is it my uncle?" His face loomed close to hers.

"Why would I give a damn about your uncle?" she fired back, even as her shoulders tensed. "No, Mulotti, it's because you're entitled, you're no Einstein, and you don't kill yourself to improve."

"Maybe someday I'll write as good as *La Fallaci*," he said, mocking her. "I'll make myself the star of all my stories."

"You little shit." How dare he criticize her work, with the exact lies her enemies slung at her. "You could never write like me. Not because you're less talented, though you are. To write like me, you'd have to be born poor, born in war, born a woman. Are you any of those?"

Her face was up against his, and she could see each layer of his long shag haircut. He had the easy sex appeal of spoiled rich boys, and she felt herself briefly caught in the net of his minty breath, his smooth cheeks edged by wide sideburns. She couldn't stand the man, but she wasn't dead. Shaking off his cocky allure and stepping back, she was besieged by envy, wishing she could *be* Mulotti, though she hated it for being true. How charmed his life was. How dearly she'd paid for hers. Was still paying.

"Tell me the truth, Oriana," Mulotti said.

"I always tell the truth."

"If the Greek were old and ugly, would you be flying off to meet him?"

"I'll bring you a souvenir keychain from the Acropolis."

The flight to Athens took two hours. She turned her back to the window during takeoff, sickened by the unnatural tilt of the plane, certain they would crash. Her seat belt was so tight, it gouged her belly, and she checked the pouch for a vomit bag, resolving not to use it.

Work. Sometimes, often, it was her only friend. She locked her fear of flying into a compartment, the same way she'd stowed her carry-on in the overhead with a shove and a click, and dove into news clippings about the Greek rebel. Devouring every word on her subject. Drafting questions on her notepad and redrafting, arranging their order. *Madonna mia*, he was a poet. He wrote poetry in prison, using blood for ink, a matchstick for a pen. Blood from his beatings. In microscopic letters, on onion-skin packaging from gauze used to bandage his wounds.

She dropped her head back, swimming with his image on TV. The steadiness of his voice as he recounted grizzly torture. His refusal to show any emotion when he felt so much. She knew this determination to be brave. She had witnessed it before.

The past descended on her with force, slipping in like breath, like shadow, the way it always did. She caught a glimpse of it, collapsing into the present as if it were happening now.

Chapter 3

1943

"Edoardo Fallaci. You're under arrest."

She was fourteen. Mamma was washing dishes and dropped one on the terrazzo floor. The two soldiers who kicked open their door were Italian SS, on the side of the Germans. They cocked their rifles at her father, but he went on calmly chewing his last crust of bread. He was a leader of the Resistance in Florence, but the enemy had caught him.

They could arrest Oriana, too, for the errands she ran for Babbo! The soldiers' shiny brass buttons and long tunics were terrifying to look at. She threw herself at her father's legs as they dragged him out the door. Dragged her, too, onto the landing, where neighbors peered out, and she knew she was caught, until one of the soldiers wrenched her fingers off and gave her a shove.

At last, she and Mamma were allowed to visit Babbo in prison. Villa Triste, Sad Villa, it was called. Run by Mussolini's right hand, Mario Carità, the most vicious man in Florence. But when they arrived at Villa Triste, it was a pretty, yellow building with white pillars on Via Bolognese, and in the entry foyer, a monk in long robes played a tall piano. Then she heard them, piercing screams from down the hallway. The thunk of a heavy crash and glass shattering. The monk leaned into the keys and played louder. But he was a man of the cloth. Why didn't he run to help? Later Mamma told her the monk played music to cover up the sounds.

She needed a bathroom. Her insides spasmed as she and Mamma followed a mean guard down to the basement. "Wait here," the guard barked, pointing his rifle at a rickety table with a shadeless lamp. Through the light of the weak bulb, Oriana made out the mass of men huddled closely on the concrete floor. The stench of pee and armpits and things she'd never smelled before made her pinch her nose.

Mamma bit her lip and set down the pot of soup she'd made for Babbo. Oriana felt her mother's dread seep into her, contagious. All around, men were passed out on the floor, snoring and groaning. An old man hobbled toward them. One of his eyes was swollen shut, puffed out like an egg and surrounded by purple rings. His wrists were bound with rope. A streak of blood dribbled from his mouth.

"Come closer," the man said. She looked into his good eye and at the same time recognized the voice. Cold panic. Mamma stifled a cry with her fist. "Don't worry," her father said, lisping through a missing front tooth. "If they send me to the camps in Germany, I'll try and jump the train."

Camps. The word brought a whoosh of relief. Oriana pictured boats and a pond. But something was off, because for the first time, she heard a waver in Babbo's voice.

"We can't stop fighting them." He pinned her with his lopsided stare.

A shiver shot up her spine, but Oriana nodded quickly. She knew who "them" was—the Germans who occupied their city. Her father watched her intently, one-eyed but stoic, and the lesson seemed to leap across a private passageway from him to her. The lesson she would remember all her life: You will be afraid. You must act anyway.

Oriana had wanted badly to visit Babbo, but now she

couldn't wait to leave. Couldn't stand to see his bare feet and saggy pants with no belt to hold them up. This wasn't the same man who had taught her how to hunt in Tuscany. On Sundays in the fall, Babbo would wake her before dawn with a cup of warm milk. The two of them would pack sourdough bread and pecorino cheese and creep through the darkened forest in Panzano, the village where he was born. Stealthily, their nostrils filled with moist earth and pine, they waited to spot a speedy hare with black-tipped ears. Then, with Babbo's hand steadying her rifle, Oriana raised it to her shoulder and fired. Together they let out a whoop if her shot was successful, but there was also guilt, too, as they bagged their limp prey.

The SS didn't execute her father. They moved him to a second prison, but nobody would tell her mother where.

The priest paid a visit. "Why don't I see you in church, Signora Fallaci?" He wagged his finger. "Now is the time you must pray."

"Go away, Father," her mother said, not letting him past the foyer. She did not shrink from his black robes or raised finger. Oriana felt her ferocity flare and surround them in the room. "I have no time for mass. Who knows if I'll ever see my husband again?" her mother said. "I've taken in sewing to feed this child."

Three months later, like a vision, Babbo was home, kneeling and opening his arms. Oriana flew to him so fast, she knocked him over, and they lay on the floor, giggling in an embrace.

That same week, Oriana was pulling on her navy dress uniform for school, sleepy eyed, when the air raid siren shrieked. "Let's go!" Her mother yanked her down five flights, her legs spaghetti, running to take cover inside the Duomo. A mass of frantic neighbors shoved through the doors and congregated on the cold marble floor under the soaring cupola as they'd been instructed. Instead of soothing church bells, a window shattered and the floor shook. The priest prayed on his knees, *Lord Jesus*

Christ son of God, have mercy on us. Women wept and rocked toddlers. Signora Liveri, still in her grocery apron, screamed at everybody to shut up and recited Hail Marys clutching her rosary. Even her pimply son, Nino, who was the dumbest in school, hung on to her skirt and bawled.

The chorus of crying set something loose inside her and she let out a sob, then another. *Stop*, her mother warned, pressing her nails into Oriana's palm. She couldn't stop. *Shht!* her father said, raising his finger to his lips, but all around them was wailing and begging and she knew they were going to die.

All of a sudden, the crack of an explosion. A bomb tearing off her face. She gasped. But no, her father's hand was in the air. Babbo had slapped her with all his might. "Girls don't cry!" His eyebrows slashed down with fury. Shame gripped her as she held her stinging cheek, and she looked to her mother for help, but Tosca cast her eyes down and said nothing. Babbo grabbed her by the shoulders. "Do you understand?" His gaze was rock hard. She nodded swiftly and finally his gaze softened. He patted her on the back.

It wasn't a slap, she understood. It was a lesson. Her parents were strong. She had to be strong, too.

Oriana turned away from the rattled priest and weeping neighbors and concentrated on the geometric pattern of the marble floor, circles and squares, green and red, telling herself the nightmare would be over soon and they could go home. *I'll count the squares*, she decided, and as soon as she got up to fifteen, the sirens did stop, just as she'd willed them to do, and the crowd cheered and moved toward the door. Joy sprouted in her chest as she clasped her parents' hands. She had flipped a switch, turned her thoughts away from danger and fear, and they had survived.

A few days later, Babbo met her outside. "I need your help," he said, and she felt a ping of pride, straddling her bicycle. They were partners again. She would do anything for him.

"Take this to Mannelli." He tucked a wilted lettuce into her basket. "I've cut out the heart." He parted the leaves to show her a rusted oblong object and told her its name, *grenade*. "Never touch the pin. See? Or let it fall."

She nodded solemnly in her plaid dress, pigtails swinging, and he smoothed the lettuce leaves back into place. Next, he sprinkled shriveled carrots and zucchini into her basket, as if she'd just shopped at the vegetable vendor. "I'll meet you upstairs." He gave her shoulder a firm pat. It was not Oriana's first time as his courier, but earlier she'd carried messages, scraps of paper rolled into her braids. A grenade was more important, her father said, it could *explode*. She and Babbo were in this together, battling the cropped blond heads that made her tremble all over the city.

"What if they stop me?" She didn't want to ask, but a little voice slipped out.

"They won't," he said. "You are only a girl. Remember, all Florence is behind you." Panic invaded her chest and she flushed, knowing her father saw it. "What did I teach you?" he said patiently.

"The only thing to do when you're scared is act," father and daughter recited together.

"Otherwise, you are paralyzed," he said. "Frozen. No use."

She gave a solemn nod and took off, pedaling across the cobblestones of Piazza del Duomo, down Via dei Calzaiuoli past the Medici palace. Store windows were bare. Only a few people scurried on the sidewalks, past the empty cafés and restaurants. Don't look, she scrunched up her insides, don't get caught. Soldiers in brown uniforms patrolled every corner. The ones she had to beat.

Out of nowhere, the air raid siren blared. She jerked the handlebars and swerved. Planes roared overhead, bombs fell in the near distance, pedestrians screamed and fled. Help! The Duomo and safety lay in the opposite direction. BOOM. Rubble and rocks spewed in her face. Another blast and Oriana was on the ground, the bicycle pinning her legs. The lettuce had rolled away! She crawled toward it, palms and knees burning. Gingerly, she picked it up and tucked it back in her basket. Swooning with relief. She hadn't failed. The carrots and zucchini were half-buried in dirt, but she collected them, too. Her knee streamed with blood. She rubbed it with the hem of her dress, wincing from pain.

Standing on the pedals, panting, she made it to Ponte Vecchio, past the goldsmith shops, to the far end—Mannelli! Never had she loved the brick tower so much. Once it had been a medieval pirate lookout but now it was her father's second home, Resistance headquarters for *Giustizia e Libertà*.

Heart banging, she cradled the lettuce up the spiral stairs to the second floor. Glancing up, she could see the hole in the roof where a German bomb blasted through last February, but she felt safe here in the cocoon of partisans. "Brava, Emilia," one called to her, using her secret name. Another pulled her pigtail. Her spirits soared. She had faced her fears. Done something brave. The feeling would be branded into her for the rest of her life: *I can win.*

"What do you have for us, vegetables for soup?" The pigtail puller, Carla, taught history at liceo, which Oriana would attend next year if the war didn't close it down. Carla took the lettuce and carefully handed it to the Rossini brothers, Nardo and Paolo, those handsome masons. Nardo winked at her, and she felt the warmth of being in this family, of working together for something important. They were laborers, socialists like her father, all banded together to save their city. Women fought in the Resistance, too, but no children came to Mannelli. Oriana was special, more serious than kids her age who hollered and chased each other outdoors. Now she kept her ears open and learned the Americans and English had bombed an outer neighborhood of Florence, to kick the Germans out, but the plan failed and hundreds died. Nardo cursed the Allies, but Paolo said the Germans were worse, and at least the Allies promised not to bomb the center and its art museums.

Her father strode in carrying a brown paper bag. A flurry of partisans greeted him and her skin tingled, hearing their respect.

"Babbo!" She flung her arms around him and buried her head against his chest. She blurted out her story about bombs falling and the grenade rolling away. "But I didn't stop."

"That's my girl." He ruffled her hair. "Now I need you to hand these out." He pulled out four pages stapled together. Big bold letters across the top said, MUSSOLINI AND HITLER MURDERERS.

"But . . ." She looked up at Babbo. "This isn't what we learn in school." In school she attended assemblies and stood at attention hailing Mussolini as the re-creator of the Roman Empire. She recited with fellow students, "The Duce loves children. God loves the Duce."

"This is the truth," her father said. "Only our newspaper tells it."

She felt a kind of shock, a trapdoor opening into the adult world of secrets. With his gaze, her father was telling her so many things. That he was sorry but he had to be honest. He had faith in her but she needed to grow up fast. *Non Mollare*, the newspaper was called. *Don't Give Up.*

"Hurry!" Her mother cracked open the door and pulled her inside. Oriana had finished passing out the newspapers to food shops along Via Ricasoli. ("Not the butcher," Babbo had said. "He's not with us.")

"They took Signore Otuni today," her mother said.

Oriana covered her mouth with both hands. The neighbor who gave her a peppermint stick on Christmas, who had a newborn. Everyone had wished his wife with her round belly *un figlio maschio*, may you have a male child.

"Life is brutal. Nothing but struggle." Her mother bit the inside of her cheek and moved to the stove, stirring. "The sooner you learn, the better." As far back as Oriana could remember, this was the lesson her mother had been urgent to impart, sometimes with bitterness, other times taking her to her knee. Don't expect luck or fairness. Keep your nose to the grindstone and try to survive. Oriana had absorbed this lesson well and didn't expect good things to come easily, if they came at all. But before the war, there had at least been dinner bubbling on the stove. Oriana was so hungry, she could practically taste her mother's ragu. She peered into the pot. Nothing but watery soup. Every afternoon, her mother took shriveled celery and blackened artichokes from the hollow refrigerator and boiled them for dinner.

"Don't sit by the window. Come here. Where is your father? He didn't get home until midnight last night."

Oriana shrugged. Her mother had no idea what her father asked her to do. Tosca's role was keeper of the hearth. When she first married, she'd been the maid in her in-laws' home according to tradition, until she and Edoardo scraped together money for their own rent.

Absently, Oriana scratched her knee. The scrape turned bloody on her fingers.

"What did you do? And your dress!" her mother cried.

Oriana noticed the tear.

Mamma pulled her into the bedroom and dabbed on Mercurochrome, which turned the cut bloodier. She slipped off Oriana's dusty white sandals, which were already too small, her toes hanging over the sole, and stood her on the lumpy bed where she and Babbo slept. With an expert flick of her fingers, Mamma threaded a needle and began repairing the dress she had sewn from scratch.

Oriana's attention swerved to the nightstand, to the red

leather book with gold lettering. "What are you reading, Mamma? Can I read it next?"

"Did you finish Jack London?"

She nodded. Last night she had devoured *Call of the Wild*, the story of Buck, the mistreated sled dog. It was set in Alaska and Oriana had never seen snow, but she understood on a visceral level that Buck was born to be free; his suffering was an injustice. Just like the suffering of the Italian people. On the living room sofa bed, Oriana dozed off each night gazing at the row of red leather spines in their glass-fronted bookcase. Her family's prized possessions. The classics her parents had scrimped for and purchased on installment. That contained characters who felt like friends, whom she missed when the book was over. Who lived on in her imagination.

"Yes, the *Iliad* is important for you to read next," her mother said. "You're lucky," she added, not for the first time. "I had no books at home."

No matter how many times she heard it, Oriana felt the weight of her mother's deprivation. Mamma adored literature as much as she did, but as a girl, she'd never had the pleasure of drifting to sleep with a book in her hands. Waking up early Sunday mornings and being transported to Russia or the English countryside, in an epic romance or adventure, while the rest of the household slept.

Oriana stretched her hand toward the *Iliad*, eager to begin, but Mamma seized her wrist. "Promise me. You'll go to university. Don't be an ignorant servant like me. Work, travel. Fly, fly!"

The misery that clouded her mother's face was different from Signore Otuni getting arrested and her father coming home late. It was the pinched look of someone who didn't like sewing or soup. Who had something burning inside she hoped to give her daughter. Or—the thought hadn't fully formed, it was a sensation—she hoped her daughter would give *her*.

Oriana nodded. She didn't understand how her mother could be this sad if she loved Babbo, loved her. She promised anyway.

This was her childhood, a rebel and a reader. When the war ended in late summer, a letter came to the house, the first ever addressed to her. Oriana sliced it open with a kitchen knife, the way she'd seen her father do, and raced over the page. It was from General Alexander of the Allied forces, thanking her for fighting the Germans. Inside the envelope was 2000 lire, discharge pay from the volunteer Italian Liberation army.

That same afternoon, she insisted on visiting Signore Oresti's store. Her mother protested, but Oriana made her sit and measure her foot and pick out low black pumps, and for Babbo, dressy brown lace-ups. Standing tall at the counter, she paid Signore Oresti with her discharge pay. Nothing for herself, only for her parents, a shiny new pair of shoes.

Chapter 4

1973

Greece was all sea. The country shimmered from above, so radiantly blue, it looked charged with electricity. Sprinkled into the ubiquitous blue were smooth brown mounds of tranquil islands. She knew the famous ones—Corfu and Rhodes, playgrounds of royalty and the yachting set, and private Skorpios, owned by Ari Onassis, who had managed to marry Jackie Kennedy—but there were hundreds more Greek isles, most unpopulated or dotted with fishing villages and sheep. The view was so mesmerizing, the neon blues of sky and sea, that even her fear of flying couldn't stop Oriana from staring out the window, her eyes stinging from the famous Greek light, which illuminated like stage lighting. She found herself wanting to dive into the calm see-through water though she couldn't swim and had never taken a beach holiday (or any holiday at all).

Poor Greece had suffered a military coup five years earlier. The land of Plato and Pericles was now governed by a bald dictator with winged eyebrows and a Hitler mustache. The dictator had imposed martial law and banned political parties, The Beatles, miniskirts, Tolstoy, the peace symbol, even Sophocles. But when Oriana landed in the stifling, one-room Hellenikon Airport, the only evidence she saw of fucking fascists was a smattering of soldiers with rifles slung over their shoulders. They were barely in their twenties, damn good-looking with profiles like marble statues, joking and laughing with one another. One soldier even leapt forward to retrieve her Samsonite from the rickety baggage claim. She looked into his good-natured face and thanked him. *Don't be brainwashed*, she wished him, resist. The Greek hero she would soon meet had deserted the compulsory army rather than serve the regime. Good for him.

Outside, the arid brown hills were serene and human scaled but spoke of the inability to grow anything except a few olives and grapes. Greece was the poorest nation in Europe, but its turquoise sea could have been a travel poster for the unspoiled Mediterranean.

Idiot. She leaned forward, ready to strangle the taxi driver when he couldn't find Aristofanos Street and they got lost on the winding dirt roads of Glyfada. The seaside hamlet where Alexander Panagoulis grew up was rustic, with big untamed properties and goats and chickens ranging free. Finally, when she couldn't stand the shot springs of the sweltering jalopy any longer, they pulled up before a yellow house. It was one story, built on piloti columns with an open-air car park underneath, though there were no cars, only bicycles, garden tools, and a rusted Vespa. The driver cried out and crossed himself, as relieved as she to be done with it, and she collected her satchel and tape recorder and stepped out.

The house was nestled in a large, verdant garden and rimmed by a white fence. Entering the gate, she cooled off briefly in the shade of a feathery palm and stepped onto a terrazzo patio extending off the car park. Rows of orange and lemon trees fragrant with fruit bordered the patio. The cicadas were beating out the lazy rhythm of an August afternoon. Above her, a wide veranda circling the entire house was crammed with people enjoying a noisy celebration. She had sent a telegram announcing her arrival but didn't have time to wait for a reply. She worried now that he hadn't received her message.

Climbing the stairs, she was hit by another jaw-dropping

view of the Aegean Sea, a halo of turquoise surrounding her, as if she were sailing on a ship instead of entering a home. She scanned the jubilant crowd. All the young men looked alike—short, dark and handsome. She couldn't find him.

The guests were sipping coffee in demitasse cups and scarfing down fried meatballs and yellow cheese. Talking with their hands and cackling. *Una faccia una razza*, she recalled the adage about Greeks and Italians—one face, one race. But no, these Athenian women wore flowered housedresses and had thatches of underarm hair, and the men wore undershirts with bellies poking out. The group more resembled southern Italians, peasants, loud and unrefined. Was she a snob? Of course, she was a Florentine, descended from the Renaissance, the granddaughter of Michelangelo, DaVinci, Galileo. Northern Italians had little in common with uncultured southerners, who were poor and tilled the fields for the padrone, killing each other over a sideways glance and drowning their food in tomato sauce. In her travels, whenever someone asked, "Where are you from?" (and they asked often, due to her accent), she answered "Florence," not Italy. It was a crucial distinction.

On the veranda, an old woman in black, earthy and square-faced with a gray bun, was serving food. His mother, Oriana recognized from the TV news. And there he was, surrounded by animated young peers clapping him on the back. He was physically attractive, but not in the typical way. He had a softness, a vulnerability radiating out from him that was magnetic, that she could feel from where she stood. Certain features were obviously appealing. The unruly ink-black hair. His eyes, a deep chocolate, the look inside them warm and wistful, gently welcoming you in. The right lid had a tiny scar above it, as did his lips, well drawn and generous. He wore a black polo buttoned to the top that made him look sweetly masculine.

As she was studying him, his gaze landed on her. He leapt up and greeted her with a tight embrace. Oriana was taken aback by his overheated body next to hers. He felt lean and muscular, like the soccer players she glimpsed on TV, and she wondered how he'd managed to stay fit in solitary confinement.

"I'm glad you came," he said. "Thank you." His voice pricked up the hair on her neck. It had a deep, persuasive quality, rich and resonant, that got under her skin. That arrived inside her like a coaxing.

She pulled away, but Alekos clasped her shoulders, squeezing her five-foot-one frame as if he would lift her. "For you." He grabbed a bouquet of red roses, limp and past their prime, off the table.

"*Grazie*," she said, getting caught in his eyes. The well-wishers on the veranda were boring holes in her skin, and her stomach was queasy, not from the plane ride or winding coastal road—she'd managed those just fine. The world leaders she'd interviewed had offered her coffee, drinks, cigarettes. Nobody had ever given her flowers.

"Is there somewhere we can work?" She scanned the packed veranda. "I leave tomorrow."

Not hesitating, Alekos took her hand and led her into the house with an inborn courtliness. He moved with smooth assurance, accustomed, she saw right away, to taking control. There was an unmistakable current between their palms, and she had just managed to avoid any vision of a wild embrace when he steered her into a dim room dominated by a full bed. Oriana averted her eyes from the ivory matelassé spread, but he found them.

"My mother's room is the quietest," he said.

His voice slipped past her defenses. A bedroom voice, that's what it was. A man who knew how to approach women, unaggressive, his charisma drawing you in. She glanced away to the icons of Mary and Jesus on the corner shelf, the burning frankincense that could choke an ox, the crocheted doilies draped over every inch of bureau and nightstand.

"Sit." He pulled a straw-bottom wooden chair to the nightstand. Oriana tucked her dress under her thighs, but the straw pinched her bare legs. Why had she worn a dress? She always wore pants. In fact, she'd bought the gauzy white dress with tiny violets yesterday at Laura Biagiotti, where she was a regular since the interviews put real money in her pocket. Alekos's trousers were deeply wrinkled, she noticed, his shoes scuffed and unpolished.

He settled on the edge of his mother's bed, across from her, his shoulder grazing the tacky Formica headboard. The look in his eyes was hopeful, expectant, but his cheeks remained sunken, his mouth downturned.

"You don't seem to be enjoying your party," she said. "Why, Alekos?"

"We still have a dictatorship, nothing's changed," he said. "Don't be surprised if they barge in and arrest me again."

Her hand froze in the middle of setting up her recorder. It was the kind of personal question she started with, to catch her subjects off-guard, but it hadn't worked. She was caught off-guard herself. Focus, she thought, lighting a cigarette. She had interviewed Gaddafi, for crissake. Who was this Alexander Panagoulis to rattle her? Some idealistic young gun who'd messed up his assassination attempt on Greece's dictator. He wasn't the dictator himself.

She smoothed her dress, woven of barely there cotton for summer in the Mediterranean, and gathered her hair to one shoulder. It was cool in his mother's bedroom, thanks to marble floors and sealed shutters, but she felt herself heating up.

He was a poet. She had idolized writers from the time she was a girl reading the red leather classics in her home. But there was another reason for her accelerating pulse. Ever since the Resistance, when her father enlisted her as a little partisan among the great partisans, courage and defiance were the traits she held highest. Would he sell out under pressure, abandon his convictions? Alexander Panagoulis passed her test.

"Look." He sprang up. He was good at that. They hadn't broken his stamina when they broke nearly every bone in his body. But he was young, she remembered, only thirty-four. A full decade younger than she. "I read this in prison." He reached under the bed into a green plastic suitcase and pulled out *Nothing, and So Be It*, with *Oriana Fallaci* bigger than the title.

It was her Vietnam book, a diary really, subtitled *A Personal Search for Meaning in War*. Of course, there was no meaning in stupid, cruel war, a fact she confirmed seeing the boys from the Midwest cornfields get their limbs blown off. Children playing with corpses as if they were toys after the Battle of Huê.

Alekos ran his fingers, slender and nail-bitten, back and forth across her book jacket. It was jarring to see herself sitting cross-legged in American fatigues and pigtails—in his hands. Did he notice her dedication to Pelou?

"You had the guts to criticize the Americans," he said.

"And the Communists," she said. "At first I was sympathetic. They invited me to Hanoi, and there I saw the worst totalitarian government ever."

"Left and right, it's all shit," he said.

"All shit. Tyranny can sprout from any side. I don't belong to any party."

"Neither do I," he said. "My party is freedom. Respect for the individual."

A spark of recognition passed between them, something inner, old, nothing to do with their earthly identities. She was disoriented. He felt as familiar as family, her twin brother.

Once more Alekos rifled through the green suitcase and held up *If the Sun Dies*, her collected articles on NASA space missions. She had eaten space food and inspected rockets and been in Houston the moment Neil Armstrong walked on the moon. "The Eagle has landed." What pandemonium in the control center, engineers cheering and crying.

"I went on hunger strikes to get these," Alekos said, stacking the books on the bed. She felt unmoored, imagining him living on sips of water just to read her. "Your books kept me company in my cage. How can I thank you?" He reached across the table and touched her cheek.

"I should thank you. I thank all my readers," she said, unsettled by his touch, refusing to show it.

"After I deserted the army, I went underground to Italy and began learning your language," he said.

He had hidden in her country? "Where?" she said.

"Brindisi." His eyes sank into hers. "In prison, I studied with a dictionary. Hoping we would meet."

"Let's begin," she said briskly, pressing her finger on *Record.*

Chapter 5

1973

For a moment, Alekos looked hurt. Then he lit his pipe and drew himself up with a new formality. A puff of cherry tobacco wafted between them.

Oriana felt a prick of conscience. He had flattered her with his roses and warm reception, and she had snubbed him. Normally, she didn't give a damn about being liked. Her job was to be *antipatica,* not *simpatica*, to ask daring, impolite questions that provoked her subjects into spilling their truth. Besides, what kind of game was the Greek playing? How much of a gentleman could he be if he single-handedly tried to blow up the dictator?

Basta. She checked the battery indicator to make sure the tape was rolling. He was throwing off her game. Oriana always felt her way with each interview subject, relying on a finely tuned emotional sensor to direct the conversation, detect truth and lies, strengths and insecurities, obsessions and motivations, like the psychiatrist she'd once intended to be. Nothing slipped by her. She registered each shift in tone, facial expression, body language, with a kind of intuition. Women's intuition? Maybe. For sure, women listened better than men. More likely it was her own unique gift handed out at birth. She could pick up a lot about a person just by being near them, without exchanging a word. Once the interview began, she poured herself into it, determined to connect, to dig through layers of public persona and get down to the hidden self. She asked astute questions, always deeply informed, and considered her subjects intriguing and cared about what they said. (Maybe that was the key—she cared.) There was nothing more fascinating than the complexity of human beings. And people wanted to talk. You just had to find a way to crack them open. Ultimately, she was so good at stripping subjects naked, at getting down to their souls, that often she felt embarrassed at the moment of exposing their innermost secrets. Because people without their secrets were often pathetic, demented creatures—the ones she despised, autocrats first and foremost. Or heart-wrenching figures—the ones she liked, Golda, for instance.

She already knew which category Alekos would fall into. He perched on the bed, polite and attentive, waiting for her to begin. She smoothed her hair. It was true what her enemies claimed: She used her femininity, but not in the dumb way they assumed. She would never sleep with a subject for a story. It was unethical. Instead, she used her face and figure to trick subjects into underestimating her intelligence, thus gaining the competitive advantage. She breezed into meetings wearing the latest fashions, the current shades of lipstick and nail polish, and always Joy by Jean Patou, the most expensive perfume. As a Florentine, it was in her blood to make a good appearance, *sempre elegante*. It wasn't her fault if men were lulled into assuming she was a delicate flower. When she hit them with a look of suspicion, a direct challenge, a snicker—*you must be joking*—they found out pretty quickly she wasn't harmless. It was a dance, her interview style, a seduction. She had invented many metaphors for doing interviews over the years. She was a midwife delivering the truth, a surgeon wielding a scalpel. Once in a while, if her subjects had an ounce of sex appeal, she imagined the interview as coitus, two bodies moving forward and back, penetrating each other deeper and deeper.

She wouldn't imagine coitus now. Cassette wheel spinning,

she looked squarely at him. "Alekos. You were the first to take up armed resistance against the dictator Papadopoulos. Why did you decide to act?"

"Love."

Her gaze skidded over his lips. What did love have to do with it?

"I love people," Alekos said. "I'll do anything for them." She was unprepared for the return of his warmth. "Look," he said, not formal anymore. "Papadopoulos is a criminal. He's mentally ill."

"All dictators are ill," she said.

"He insists he's saving Greece from Communists. Saving Greece by turning it into a police state." Alekos scoffed. "I hate violence, but sometimes you have to take justice into your own hands."

She glanced at his hands. Cut up, scarred, especially the wrists. They had kept him handcuffed for a year. "Tell me about the attempt," she said. "You wore a bathing suit, crouched among the rocks, waiting for his limousine."

"I made the two explosives myself and set them under a stone bridge. Five kilos of TNT each at a depth of one meter." He had a math brain, she remembered, had studied electrical engineering. "The problem was . . ." Alekos hesitated, his eyes crinkling at her. "A couple was having sex on the beach below."

She refused to be thrown again and gave a knowing scoff, as if sex in broad daylight was a nuisance in her line of work, too.

Alekos recounted his attempt the same way he had on the television news, matter-of-factly, without self-congratulations or posturing. The couple threw off his timing, he said. Worse, the fuse got tangled, he had to change position, no longer had a clear view. Finally the black limousine and its motorcade approached. He gripped the detonator. The limousine grew bigger. Big. He set off the bombs. But he heard only a small bang, saw only a puff of dirt and stones.

He sprinted down the cliffside and dove into the sea. His escape boat had instructions to leave by eight, no matter what. To make up time, Alekos swam ashore, then ran barefoot over the rocks to the tiny inlet where the boat was—just leaving, chugging into the bay.

Frantically, he scanned the rocks and found a microscopic cave. He contorted himself inside and tried to slow his panting. Did he kill the tyrant? A helicopter whirred in the sky. Police swarmed the cliffs, growing louder.

"Find him, motherfuckers!"

Through a fissure in the rock, he glimpsed the legs of a cop directly above him. "This area's clear," the cop yelled, turning away.

He'd escaped!

But the cop tripped. He landed on his hands and knees directly in front of the cave. "Come quick!" the cop shouted, pointing his quivering gun. "I got him!"

Uniforms attacked him from all directions, searched his genitals, his mouth. Shoved him into a car. "Who are you?" Branded him with cigarettes. "Talk, murderer! You failed in your little plot."

He failed.

They drove him to ESA, military police, interrogation division. Outside, an industrial fan whirred to cover up the screams. Inside, he was strapped naked to a cot with broken steel springs that bloodied his body. An interrogator straddled his chest, another clubbed the soles of his feet. "Are you sorry? Say it."

"I'm . . . only . . . sorry . . . I missed."

More beatings. "Who were your co-conspirators?" He was near fainting.

Hours later, a new uniform. "Leave him. It happens once in a million, someone won't talk."

Oriana studied the Greek hero intently as he finished his account. He looked normal, like everybody else. What was it, she still couldn't piece together, that gave him such guts? "How did you feel at your trial," she said, "when they sentenced you to death?"

"I wished I had more time, so I could do more for Greece." His face was fully open to hers. "Some of us are made for giving and not taking." A chill shot through her. *Alekos was giving.* Irrationally, she wanted him to give to her. He had the same noble spirit as her father, as the artisans and laborers who took up the Resistance for Florence. Who defied Hitler and Mussolini, sacrificing to save their country.

Alekos described waiting three long days for his execution on the blue and white island of Aegina. He began a chant, "Long Live Liberty, Down with Tyrants," and got the young guards to join him.

"Did you know the world was fighting for you?" In her file, she'd been surprised to learn that Lyndon Johnson and the Pope sent telegrams to Greece's dictator to stay the execution. Picasso and forty artists signed a petition. Italian workers organized a five-minute work stoppage for him.

Alekos turned on her a slow, blazing smile. "When I heard what you were doing, I felt less alone." He was conveying gratitude to her. But no, she looked away. She had not signed one petition, not read one of his poems smuggled out of prison and published in her own country, winning the Viareggio prize. She was busy flying to Mexico City to cover the protests of the 1968 Olympic Games.

"You didn't know me then," Alekos said, reading her thoughts. "It doesn't matter. We're together now." He slid his hand over hers.

She pulled away, staring down at her notes, exhaling a plume of smoke.

"And when they decided not to shoot you, Alekos, so you wouldn't become a martyr. How did you feel?"

"They never told me. Not for three years. Any morning, the guards could have come in and said, *Let's go. Today you die.*"

Their eyes met. She felt his harrowed waiting.

The moment was broken by his mother shuffling in with two demitasse cups on a silver platter. She served them coffee and biscuits and crossed herself before the collection of icons. Oriana studied the woman, her face dignified but full of hardship, her forehead an accordion of wrinkles. Athena had been the only person permitted to visit Alekos in prison and only once a month. She had stood up to his torturers, never crying, demanding a space heater so he wouldn't freeze in winter. She had smuggled out his communiqués about the regime's atrocities to the international newspapers and Red Cross. Lay spread-eagle in front of the American Embassy to implore President Johnson to save her son.

Now Athena opened the mirrored wardrobe and took out an officer's uniform, showing it to Oriana. "Yorgos," she choked out, brushing the shoulders on their wooden hanger.

"They killed my brother," Alekos said, a shadow coming over his features. Haltingly, he confessed that he'd pressured his brother to desert the army and join the Resistance. Yorgos, more rule-following and a captain, finally agreed and went into hiding, seeking asylum at embassies in Turkey and Syria, but he was refused. When he tried Israel, the authorities betrayed him and turned him over to the Greek government. He was arrested and shipped back, handcuffed to the bedpost in his cabin. Somehow, he "disappeared" between Haifa and Athens. His cabin was empty and the porthole shattered when the ship arrived in Greek waters.

"Every so often," Alekos said, "the coast guard calls my mother to identify a body. It's never him." He swallowed hard and she saw the guilt it still caused him, the disappearance of his only brother.

Athena returned her elder son's uniform to the wardrobe and shuffled out, her mouth a sorrowful line.

"And your father?" Oriana said.

"He died while I was in prison." A tear escaped the corner of his eye and he flicked it away. "Do you believe in a broken heart?"

She went perfectly still, immobilized by his losses. By the difference between her comfortable life and his.

Sighing deeply, Alekos recounted his five years in solitary confinement at Boyati Prison. His cell was like a tomb, built especially for him, five feet by ten feet, half-buried underground. A straw mattress on the floor, a bucket for a toilet. He described sexual tortures. An iron wire rammed up his urethra and heated to red-hot with a Zippo. Days of urinating blood.

"They had the right to execute me for my attempt, but not to be inhumane. I have scars all over my body." He lifted his polo shirt. "See? They stabbed me with a switchblade."

She winced at the jagged scar so close to his heart. Her gaze drifted over the rest of his chest, strong enough to survive everything they did to him. "How did you stay sane, Alekos?"

"I never stopped writing. Never stopped cursing, fighting back. Even when I was on my knees with sorrow."

He was on his knees with sorrow. She swelled up protectively. "And now this amnesty of Papadopoulos that's set you free, with three hundred other political prisoners? Does it give you hope?"

Alekos shook his head. "It's a charade. He pretends to be democratic, but he goes up for election alone. Only the Greek people give me hope. They're joining the Resistance, and one day, they'll overthrow him. *Under absolute despotism, it is their right, it is their duty, to throw off such government.* That's the Declaration of Independence. Not me."

His conviction created a buzz inside her and Oriana did something she never did, she gushed. "Alekos. As the founder of the Greek Resistance, you're a symbol of courage throughout Europe."

"I'm not a symbol. Please. And I'm not unique. They tortured thousands who had long hair or attended a rally. You think too much of me. I'm just a man."

She stared, stunned by his lack of ego.

Alekos stood. "A man who's eaten cold lentils for five years. Are you hungry? Let's see what Athena has fixed us to eat."

Chapter 6

1973

It was late and the well-wishers had gone home. Alekos held out her chair at the veranda table and scooted his own closer until the straw seats met. His mother had set out an array of dishes prepared by neighbors, and Alekos visibly relaxed in the company of family and two boyhood friends. He rubbed his palms together, digging into the feast.

"You like *tzatziki*?" He loaded yogurt dip onto Oriana's plate. "It has lots of garlic. You're not planning to kiss anyone?"

The corners of her mouth slid up, even as she tried to remain professional. She checked her watch, a man's style, bulky and black. Ten p.m. He had captivated her for hours with his intelligence, peppering their conversation with Dostoyevsky, Camus, Kipling, Christ. Even as he described hunger strikes, he spoke like a scientist, detailing the physical effects on the body of no food for thirty days. She leaned toward him. "I need to find a hotel for the night."

"Stay here." She laughed. "I'll take you to the airport tomorrow." He was serious. Alekos gave her shoulders a squeeze to settle the matter.

She stiffened at his touch. Her critics would have a field day, but the hour had gotten late. And she'd slept in far more dangerous places, including a desert tent with Palestinian guerrillas. She found herself relenting as Athena piled her plate with roast lamb and lemon potatoes, and the scent of potted gardenias wafted through the night.

Alekos entertained them with tales of his luxury villa at Boyati. He tried to escape once by fashioning a pistol out of soap, but the guards got so scared, he doubled over in hysterics and lost his chance. To get through the nights, he'd given "radio broadcasts" from a grate in his cell, mocking the prison warden for his monstrous case of hemorrhoids, his wife's sneaking around with a pack of lovers. Even the guards gathered outside for the nightly comedy. Oriana laughed at his stories—how had he kept his humor?—and Alekos joined her, their gazes meeting in a shared satiric streak.

He gave her plenty of warm looks over dinner but included others in his glance, Oriana noticed. Inviting her to sleep in his home was the famous Greek hospitality, nothing more. The two of them shared a commitment to social justice and a hatred of power when it was corrupt (and it was always corrupt). That was why she was staying.

At midnight, they resumed their interview in the living room, face-to-face in mahogany armchairs of yellow velvet, the seats covered in plastic. She set up her tape recorder on the end table between them, where there was only a dim lamp on. The intimate lighting was made more intimate by the fact that Athena had prepared the sofa with white eyelet sheets before padding off to sleep.

The only interview where she was surrounded by beds, Oriana mused. "Ready?" Alekos folded his hands in his lap. She pressed *Record*, her muscles loosened from the surprisingly good wine at dinner. "Tell me." Oriana paused for effect. "After all you've been through, Alekos, have you lost faith in humanity?"

"You don't understand me." He looked disappointed in her. "I'll never lose faith."

"But they stuffed a rag soaked in shit down your throat."

"The Greek military police are not humanity." His face went mild. "People are born good. Think of babies, how pure. My neighbors today, most of them poor, did you see the homecooked meals they made me?"

She noticed it again, the resemblance to her father, that same combination of tough fighter and a sympathetic heart. Oriana was jaded, yet somehow Alekos wasn't. He was far more forgiving than she.

"Don't be disillusioned." He read her easily. "I met so many good people in prison." He told her about the guards who sneaked out his poems. The woman who mopped his hospital room and sat beside him all night with her hand on his forehead, soothing him after beatings. Alekos blinked and looked away.

"You're crying," she said.

He wiped his cheeks, embarrassed, then looked straight at her, eyes welling. "I'm touched. Understand? Kindness touches me." She felt him crashing through her armor, this man with emotions, showing them to her. "Let's go to bed," Alekos said. She startled. He saw her reaction and grinned. "It's two thirty in the morning." He motioned to the sofa prepared with guest sheets.

They double-kissed on the cheek, making plans for the airport in the morning. Oriana spoke woodenly, mortified by her misunderstanding. Alekos lingered. Did she have everything she needed? Pillow, towels. Finally he backed out of the room and clicked closed the frosted glass door, his footsteps echoing down the hallway.

She kept her eyes glued to the door, half expecting him to burst back in. *I learned Italian hoping we would meet.* Did he want to go to bed with her? Of course he wanted to go to bed with her—he hadn't touched a woman in five years. Oriana was famous, she could be useful, with plenty of lire, too.

Stop. She had promised herself, no more stupid mistakes.

What would he be like in bed? Fast and greedy after years of deprivation, or slow and sensual? Surely Alekos had had a girlfriend before his arrest. *How many girlfriends* was more the question. There must have been at least one doe-eyed maiden who flew into his arms the day of his release. He had stayed up *with friends* until six in the morning, he'd said.

Enough. She could not survive another affair. Late at night, when she allowed herself, she was still licking her wounds from Pelou. Barely six months had passed since she stormed out of his hotel room in Madrid. She would never speak to that weakling again.

Love had been nasty with her. As high as she'd climbed in her profession, she'd been kicked low in matters of the heart.

Her cheeks burned to remember her first cut, Renzo Gori, a big editor now at *Corriere*. "You're the talk of the town," he had flirted with her at the Christmas party the moment they were introduced. When they danced, he ran his thumb along the pearls of her necklace, brushing her clavicle and sending shock waves to her toes. She was thirty, more famous than he but with far less romantic experience. What she heard in his *you're the talk of the town* was that Oriana might be successful yes, but she should make herself smaller, because what a man deserved, what he needed, was for the town to be talking about *him*. Gori was six years older, well born into a publishing family, and bedding a revolving door of women, she was crushed to find out. Lovesick as an adolescent, she wrote him bad poetry. *No other woman could care for you as I do / with all my heart and all my want to / the only man I could belong to.*

"You should wear your hair longer," he said. "Get your suits made by a seamstress."

"Do you like this green silk, Renzo?" She showed him a swatch of fabric. Green was his favorite color.

The more she clung to him, the farther he ran. Gori was

a correspondent in London at the time, and she was traveling back and forth to America for *L'Europeo*, so there was plenty of opportunity to convince herself that distance was the reason he couldn't see her. She wrote him desperate letters. *Wait for me, I'll come to you in a month. Don't replace me with another, or I'll fall on a dagger like Juliet.* He never answered. The humiliation still seared her, the night she flew to London and hunted him down at a press dinner. He shook her off, smoking cigars with his colleagues at a front table while she was left to scavenge a seat in the back. After the presentation, she wound her way back to him, only to find his chair empty and his colleagues glancing away with smirks. She followed their gazes to see Renzo ducking out with a blonde, his hand on her backless sequined dress.

The next day Oriana pleaded her way into his apartment, and after he fucked her, she cleaned it for him and made him a roast chicken. Her letters grew more frantic. *I want to quit my job, I'm bored with traveling and meeting celebrities, my profession means nothing to me. Yours is the important one. I want to stay home and have your slippers ready when you come home.* She showered him with a gold pocketwatch, silk pajamas, ulcer medicines from America. When she got pregnant, she was elated. If she behaved properly, if she were sweet and pretty, Renzo would marry her, they would be a family. Instead he wrote, *Are you crazy? I don't want it. And if you keep it, you'll never see your name in print again.* Her letters grew more pathetic. *Don't be angry. I'll see to it, but please find someone who won't kill me. Even if I'm punished and go to hell, I'll do it. I don't want to ruin your life.* Steeped in Catholicism, a part of her really worried she would go to hell, but anything for Renzo.

He didn't answer, ignoring her pleas to find a clinic. Her belly grew, but a woman could not be pregnant in the workplace—pregnant *and* unmarried, forget it. Anguished, she needed to take care of it fast, away from prying eyes. Abortion was illegal in England, same as in Italy, but she found an address. Alone, always alone, she made her way to the East End of London, to a dark, cold office. "Do you have the money?" the weary doctor said. She did. "Lie here and slide down." Her thighs trembled as they gaped open in stirrups.

When it was over, she took a cab back to the Normandie Hotel, weak with cramps, planning to hide for two days and recover. But she fainted on the sidewalk before she could get inside. Blood. Emergency surgery. "You might have trouble in the future," a different doctor said gravely.

For weeks after, Oriana could not eat or sleep. At *L'Europeo*, Tommaso assumed she was overworked and insisted she take medical leave. A doctor prescribed sleeping pills. She dreamed the baby died because she forgot to feed it. Renzo disappeared, severed from her completely. *I took care of it*, she wrote him. *Please, even if you've tired of me, see me one last night for my birthday*. On June 29, she turned thirty-one, flew to London, and waited anxiously by the phone. All night, she lay curled in the hotel bed, but it didn't ring. How could he deny this one request? The answer was like a black fog steamrolling over her body, suffocating her under its weight. She was alone alone alone. Ever since she was a little girl pedaling frantically to Mannelli, there was no one to help her, no one to hold her hand if she was scared. Every single thing she'd accomplished on this earth, she had to grit her teeth for, pretend to be tougher than she was. Now her tenacious shell crumbled around her. Her shoulders collapsed from the awful burden of appearing strong, of pushing herself forward, and she let them. She let her life rain down and fall apart.

At 4 a.m., she fumbled in her purse for the vial of sleeping pills and swallowed every one.

The hotel manager summoned her poor parents. Six weeks in the psychiatric hospital, her wrists tied to the bed with leather straps. She stared out the barred windows, shattered inside, where no one could see. Renzo didn't want her. No one wanted her. She was unlovable. Somehow she managed to keep it in the family.

Her mother spoon-fed her soup upon her release, and her father took her on walks, supporting her by the elbow, but the pregnancy remained her heavy secret. Four months of bleak numbness before she felt half sane again and could force herself to put on clothes and makeup and return to *L'Europeo*. Ultimately, it was work that gave her a reason to get out of bed in the morning and lifted her out of the fog.

This is who she was, formidable investigative journalist and fragile suicide attempter. Every woman was two women. At least two. The great lesson Oriana had gleaned from her romantic disasters: Once your heart became entangled with another human being, you were finished. Fucked.

Now this Greek hero with the fire pit eyes . . . she could almost hear him breathing down the hallway. He was damn attractive, she admitted it, with something familiar that tugged at her core. He had teared up in his mother's arms the day of his release. Choked up over the cleaning woman who soothed his forehead. Alexander Panagoulis had enough soul to last a lifetime, she would never be bored. She felt herself falling brain-first, she was cerebral, she couldn't help it. His conviction, the courage to act . . . a man with more balls than she had, finally. And his literary bent. Action is a duty, he'd said during their interview, poetry is a need. The way he emphasized "need" made her weak in the knees and belly and God knew where else.

As she tossed and turned, her gaze fell on the coffee table where she'd set her blue Samsonite, on the amber worry beads and saucer-size blue amulet painted with an eye. The evil eye she'd seen on her travels all over the Middle East. To ward off bad luck.

Merda. What was she doing sleeping on his rock-hard sofa?

Journalists were supposed to be impartial, but Oriana had never been impartial, she was too damn opinionated, and anyway there was no such thing. She didn't believe in objective reporting, only honest reporting, emotional reporting. A story was always filtered through human eyes, human experience—human bias, let's face it. Better to admit subjectivity, this is *my* view, as she did.

Enough, she would leave Athens in the morning, publish the interview, never see him again. Her insides wobbled. His Italian was impressive, despite the so-so accent, and his manners . . . the welcome bouquet, drawing back of her chair. Chivalry stirred her. She didn't give a damn if she was old-fashioned.

Footsteps. She hinged up in bed, staring at the figure on the veranda. *Madonna.* Through the sliding glass doors, she could see his silhouette against the railing, the red glow of a cigarette in his hand. He faced out to sea, but his energy was palpable, boiling and bottled up, and she clutched the sheet over her nightgown.

Maybe they should just do it and get it over with. After her catastrophe with Gori, she had sex without ties, like men did, because love hurt and sex didn't. She refused to let any man mark her, fashioning a thick wall around her heart. On assignment in Paris, Houston, or New York, she invited an actor, photographer or astronaut back to her hotel. Otherwise, after the day's mad dash for a story, the night had its way of reminding her that nothing much mattered and she was on her own in an uncaring universe. To avoid that agony, she buried herself in a stranger's arms. A few of her affairs lasted two or three weeks, but most ended by daybreak when Oriana didn't need anyone. She had her work.

Abruptly, Alekos turned, standing just outside her sliding door. Their eyes caught. Then he flicked his cigarette over the railing and disappeared down the veranda.

Bloody hell. She didn't need this. She fell back on the pillow, sliding her arm underneath and clutching it like an anchor, her whole center magnetized toward the Greek hero. When just last night she'd been mooning over—

She refused to even think his name.

Chapter 7

1967 to 1973

She was thirty-eight when she first landed in Saigon. Finally, her chance to be a serious reporter, to do what men did, risk their lives to cover the big stories. She had convinced *L'Europeo* to send her, the only female correspondent from Italy, but after she'd shown press credentials to the guards and checked into the hot, modest hotel, she stood on her balcony and wondered, *Now what?* The only action she saw was rickshaws dodging traffic, crowds of conical hats, jeeps with jolly soldiers on leave, and outdoor food markets. The Americans had given her permission to imbed with troops, but where were the troops? She got a tip in the hotel lobby from journalists hustling in and out: François Pelou in the French press office was the man to see, the expert on the fighting.

Map in hand, she rushed directly to Rue Pasteur, to the dilapidated building ringed by barbed wire, headquarters for Agence France-Presse. She showed her press pass to two armed guards and climbed a rickety staircase to a door with the handwritten sign *Do Not Enter*. She entered. The long, narrow room was crowded with desks belonging to photographers and journalists, everybody speaking French, a language she knew. "*Ou est François Pelou?*" she said. Someone pointed her past the clattering telex machines to the sole private office.

He looked up from *Le Monde* with a scowl that said, *Who*

the hell are you? The office was crammed with war photographs, liquor bottles, newspapers, a foam mattress on the floor. He slept in this filth? Pelou had alert blue eyes, gunmetal hair. "Yes?" he said without getting up.

She felt the immediate crackling of attraction. The classic looks, gruff façade, she couldn't resist a challenge. "Do you have a bathroom?" She went into the stained toilet and emerged with fresh lipstick and hair brushed.

Pelou rose and motioned her to a threadbare armchair. He had the kind of lanky build she liked. Briefly, she recited her credentials, but his expression didn't change. Clearly he hadn't read her work. "Where is the war?" she said. He told her it was in Dak To. "How do I get there?" A flicker in his eye.

At the commissary, she purchased American fatigues in olive green and a steel combat helmet, tightening it to the maximum to fit her head. Pelou had given her one piece of advice: "Never take off your helmet." The standard-issue boots were too clunky for her size five feet, so she kept her kid leather Trussardi loafers. Last, she picked up a canteen and knapsack, surprised by how natural it felt to outfit herself like a soldier. They made her sign a form stating the U.S. government could not be held responsible if she was killed. The last question on the form: *In the event of death, where should your remains be sent?* Fear landed in her gut, but by now she knew how to banish it with sheer will. *The Italian embassy in Saigon*, she wrote on the form and quickly changed her thoughts, flipping an inner switch.

The newsroom back home. How she'd badgered her editor to send her to Vietnam, insisting readers didn't give a damn about the technical aspects of M16s versus AK-47s. What readers cared about, what *she* cared about, was how it feels to point a gun, drop a bomb, lose a friend. War was senseless, proof of human idiocy, why did we do it? Oriana had grown up in war, it had left a mark on her, a trauma, and it felt like the question she was meant to tackle all her life.

"You're sure about this?" Tommaso had said, his expression unsure.

"Was I wrong about the astronauts?" she said, resolute. Nobody had believed a woman could "handle" the complexity of space travel, yet Oriana had read and watched documentaries, then flown to Houston to inspect a rocket, try on a space suit, interview John Glenn and Alan Shepherd. They were true heroes, those straitlaced, nice-looking, military men, but she tried like hell to find something engaging in their personalities. Finally she met one astronaut who was spontaneous and funny, Pete Conrad, who drank and sparred with her, and they grew close. Another one who had a wife.

"You weren't wrong," Tommaso said with a shrug, the one she'd grown fond of, that said it was no use arguing, she called the shots.

From Saigon, a military cargo plane flew her to Dak To. Squatting next to her was a TV reporter from New York, Bill-something, trembling head to toe. Oriana was scared, too, but she refused to show it. Fear was contagious; she could feel it flapping its wings under her rib cage. The TV reporter caught her eye, wanting to commiserate, she sensed, but the engine was deafening and it would do her no good anyway. Instead she stared out the plane's open door to the phosphorescent-green hills, willing her insides to settle.

Bravery, she had learned during the Nazi occupation of her city, didn't mean you were fearless. Only a moron wouldn't fear the brown tunics patrolling every neighborhood with rifles. Bravery was how you acted despite your fear.

The scene when they landed at base camp was chaotic. Fighter planes took off from the short airstrip with supersonic shrieks, lines of trucks with unshaved soldiers zigzagged through the jungle. Dak To was in a valley surrounded by tree-canopied peaks. It was June, ninety-five degrees and humid, and she was drenched. In the distance, the rumble of gunfire. The 2nd Battalion was fighting on Hill 1338, fighting and dying, rumor was. Tomorrow she would head to the front.

The lieutenant press officer escorted her to a tent and handed her a sleeping bag. "There's no bed. In a few days, a bunk should free up."

Fine, she didn't want special treatment. Rolling out the sleeping bag on the floor, she sat cross-legged and began to write in her diary. The diary she was planning to publish as a book.

Two young privates sprawled on a nearby bunk spoke grimly of casualties on Hill 1338. She eavesdropped, then introduced herself to Norman and Bobby, both twenty-three, and interviewed them. The boys had fought together in seven battles and saved each other's lives. They regretted volunteering and wanted badly to go home. "The only silver lining," Bobby said, "is that we met because of this war. Now we're brothers."

At sunset, a cry went up. "Clear for the dead!" She ran to the helicopter pad and watched choppers unload silver body bags. One hundred ten, she counted, arranged in a row, some with recognizable human shape, others flat. It was shocking and obscene and she held her breath from the stench.

A captain standing next to her bowed his head. "My God."

She introduced herself and learned he was a career officer. "Why do you do this for a living, Captain?"

His face clouded, and she saw that he asked himself this very question. He was a teacher before joining the army, the captain said. He liked to shape young people.

"But you're sending them to die, Captain." He lowered his eyes. "What do you feel when you lead an operation?"

"Fear," he said. "But I have to pretend for my men. *Don't be scared, let's go get them, forward march.*"

Dinner was served in the officers' tent. Spam and beans. She slid her tray down the line, feeling the stares of men at long wooden tables. Who would she sit with? Maybe she should look for Bill-something. An alarm bell shrieked. She dropped her tray. Officers bolted outside, and she ran like hell, too, clamping on her helmet. The sky turned red from enemy gunfire exploding over the airstrip. The Americans began shooting back. The war had come to base camp.

"Where's the bunker?" she screamed, spinning. "The bunker!" No answer. Out of nowhere, a man grabbed her wrist. In French, he yelled, "Come with me!"

They ran. He pushed her down into a bamboo-covered bunker made of concrete. It was crammed with young soldiers. One boy lit a match and stared. "It's a lady!"

The Frenchman still held her by the wrist. She was panting, trying to stay quiet, not wanting to embarrass herself or endanger the soldiers.

"Are you all right?" the Frenchman said.

She nodded. "Who are you?"

"Pelou told me to watch out for you."

Whiskey with Pelou at the Hotel Continental in Saigon. Her thirtieth day as a war correspondent. They had not slept together yet.

The hotel bar was set in a tropical garden of orchids and palm trees. They drank beer in cane armchairs under a striped awning and ate mango from a bowl. Her GI fatigues were stained with sweat and dirt.

Grimly, Pelou showed her a photo. His France-Presse had broken the story. The Vietcong had killed Ignacio Ezcurra, the Argentinian journalist who had recently become her friend. His body lay facedown in a pool of blood. "The moccasins." Pelou pointed to his feet. "That's how we know it's him."

She went pale. The last time she saw Ignacio at this very bar, they'd bonded over their inappropriate footwear, his moccasins, her loafers.

"The eighth journalist killed this year," Pelou said.

The next dead journalist could be her. Could be them. "The Vietcong are barbarians. They're not freedom fighters," she grimaced with disgust. Oriana had been on their side, people defending their country from outsiders, but no more. They had fired a rocket at a children's hospital two days ago.

"Man is neither angel nor brute," Pelou said. "Haven't you read Pascal?"

She shook her head, hating to admit it. Perhaps if she'd had the chance to finish university, like he did. She resented his note of arrogance, yet at the same time felt ashamed of the holes in her knowledge, what they exposed about her. The minute she returned home, she would devour Pascal.

Late that night, a knock at her hotel door. She opened in her nightgown.

Pelou held out a copy of Blaise Pascal's *Pensées*. "Catch up on your French philosophy."

It was heated. They had let it build for a month. He tore off her clothes and lifted her onto the bed. She didn't care that he was somebody else's husband. Marriage was a form of authority, and she spit on authority. They had met in a liminal place of no rules where only surviving mattered and being alive one more day, and she disappeared all night long in his arms.

Oriana had sworn never to lose herself in a man again, but in the morning, she watched François sleep, running her fingers through his prematurely gray hair, which gave men a seasoned air. Admired his chiseled jaw, fine straight nose. She could never be with a man just for his looks, but François saw journalism as a calling, like she did, to create more justice in an unjust world. He hated the insanity of war as much as she did.

Flashes of their lovemaking came back, how he'd hovered over her with long limbs, touched the place inside her that dissolved separateness. Freed her from the confinement of thoughts and words. He came with a cry, looking into her eyes, and she knew with sudden certainty he wasn't happy with his American actress wife. He would be happy with her.

Oriana returned to Vietnam seven times because she was madly in love and because the war went on. She jumped out of a helicopter and landed on something soft and gelatinous—the belly of a dead Vietcong. She grew weak with malaria, washed her face and teeth with a glass of water, peed outdoors. The petrified boys with crew cuts undid her. I HEARD AMERICAN SOLDIERS BEGGING GOD TO SAVE THEM, she wrote for *L'Europeo*. The boys entrusted her with phone numbers: "Please call my parents, my girl back home, let them know I'm okay." She called every one of them.

We are publishing a groundbreaking article, wrote *L'Europeo. Oriana Fallaci is the first Italian journalist to enter Communist North Vietnam.* In February 1969, she landed an exclusive interview with General Giap, commander of the Vietcong. The mastermind behind the Tet offensive that sent twelve hundred Americans home in body bags.

"How long will the war last?" she pressed Giap. "How many more of your people will sacrifice their lives?"

"As long as I need them to, even fifty years, until we are totally victorious," Giap said.

After the interview, his lieutenants handed Oriana three pages of propaganda she was "permitted" to publish; the general would deny any other reporting. She published his lies side by side with her actual questions and answers, recorded by her trusty Sony, so readers could see the hypocrisy of Giap and the Communists. The interview was reprinted in newspapers across

Europe and America and read by Kissinger, she was astonished to learn.

She became Fallaci, war correspondent. Her Vietnam diary became a bestseller, *Nothing, and So Be It*, published by Doubleday in America. Reviewers called it "profoundly moving" and her descriptions of fighting and death "the best written about the war." Holding it in her hands, smelling its fresh pages, she ballooned with pride. She had tackled humanity's greatest calamity and proven herself as good as any man, capable of weighty reporting.

Naturally, reviewers in Italy badmouthed her. She was "too personal" in her reporting, "too emotional." *Too female*, they didn't have the balls to say. She had put herself in physical danger and written with honesty. It was the best any reporter could offer, and it was a lot. Let them spend one day in her shoes, the critics, and they would cry and run home to their televisions and their sofas. Fuck them.

Her book had not even disclosed one of her most harrowing experiences. At two in the morning, with François still editing at France-Presse, she was dozing in the faded armchair beside his desk. Pelou's office had become her office. She liked eating C-ration meals with his team and drinking crappy coffee from the ancient machine. That day, she'd finished her weekly article early and telexed it to *L'Europeo*. She was bone tired and longed for her bed. "Take a gun," Pelou said. The guns and bullets were stocked in a cubby for journalists on night duty or those headed on risky operations. But Oriana didn't like holding a gun. The cold weight of it in her hand sickened her. "I'm fine," she said.

It was a humid night, long past the 7 p.m. curfew for journalists, and she could hear the distant rumbling of bombs. Her hotel was a three-minute walk away and she was wrapped in thought. Would she land an interview with the Vietcong whose diary Pelou had given her? Would he ever leave his wife?

She didn't see the jeep until it screeched to a halt and six drunk South Vietnamese soldiers poured out. In one chaotic moment they got her on the ground.

"I'm a journalist!" she cried, but they muzzled her, pulling down her fatigues, ripping open her shirt. She held on to her underwear, thinking nonsensically she could save herself if she didn't let go. The first one unzipped and lowered himself. She could feel his gun bulging against her hip. She knew stories of gang rapes: the last soldier's job was to shoot the woman in the head. Frozen with fear, she withdrew deep inside, observing the scene from afar.

"Hey! What are you doing?" Two American soldiers driving by in a jeep. She bit the hand smothering her and screamed. They saved her.

At home, she sank into the bath and scrubbed herself, feeling stained though he hadn't penetrated. The next day, she avoided Pelou. *Take a gun.* It was her fault for walking alone, being preoccupied. She never wrote about it, never told a soul, unwilling to draw attention to a vulnerability that was female. At every turn, she was bombarded with "women can't do this" and "women aren't good at that," and she refused to give them ammunition. Besides, only recently, Pelou had begun to praise her, *Brava Brava,* as she learned to do her job in the war. She erased the assault. It never happened.

He was everywhere in her book. *François promised to ask General Loan to let me interview a Vietcong prisoner . . . François asked me to bring back a bottle of Chianti . . . François escaped with his life today.*

To celebrate her book's publication, Tommaso and the director hosted a reception at *L'Europeo.* François flew in to be with her. It was impossible to keep the glow off her face, to keep from touching his arm.

"Who's this Pelou?" A member of the male den winked

at her. A second buffoon made three pumps with his fist in a gesture for screwing.

"Pelou's the best war correspondent there is," Oriana said. "You're jokes in comparison. Let me introduce you." She pulled him over and bragged about François's place in history as an eyewitness to the murder of Lee Harvey Oswald. Pelou was the reporter whom Jack Ruby elbowed out of the way to shoot President Kennedy's assassin.

That shut them up.

Five years. She and Pelou didn't stop, even when he was reassigned to Spain. In December of 1972, just after her Kissinger interview erupted in the papers, she flew to Hotel Madrid. "Come here, little one," Pelou said, his nickname because of her petite size, and because she deferred to him on war reporting. They fell into bed, and afterward, he raided the mini-fridge and they sat naked, feeding each other Iberian ham with their fingers.

"I was afraid you were too famous to come see me," Pelou said.

"Why?" she said, confused, then catching his meaning. The Kissinger scoop. "I'd never be too famous to see you." She ran her fingers through the sparse hair on his chest. Then, since he had brought up work, she said, "It's absurd, isn't it? The ugly little professor fantasizing he's John Wayne."

"Kissinger has always had a high opinion of himself. Nothing new," Pelou said.

It hit her like a slap. She'd expected him to admire the way she handled the bastard. That she got Kissinger to talk to her at all.

"I can't come to you anymore." The words tumbled out. They were meant to punish him, but unexpectedly she meant them.

"You're too famous. I knew it." He gave a weak smile. In the twitch of his facial muscles, she read jealousy, his little outpost in Spain.

The phone rang. "*Ma chéri*," he answered, looking straight at her, making sure she heard. His American actress wife. "How are you?" He leapt out of bed and pulled the cord into the bathroom. "Billy, what's doing, little man?" He shut the door.

She growled, jamming on her clothes. How dare he speak to that woman! He had been inside her not ten minutes ago. *She* wanted to marry him, goddamn it, *she* deserved to have his child. Oriana had forced herself to be patient, seeing Pelou only when he was free, showering him with gifts when they reunited—even a Mercedes Spider. He wrote her reams of blue airmail letters, calling her the most passionate woman he'd ever known, yet here she was relegated to the shadows. How much could Pelou love her, she faced the question squarely, if he couldn't get past his damn Catholicism, his guilt about divorce?

When he returned, the phone in its cradle, she was fully dressed, staring out the window with her arms crossed. He buried his lips in the nape of her neck.

"You need to decide." She spun around, poking her finger into his bare chest. "I won't be second choice. The end."

"The boy is young," Pelou said with a shake of his head.

"He's not even yours!" she said at top volume. Another voice inside her, more fragile, said, *Choose me, love me.*

Silence. François lowered his eyes.

"You lived through Vietnam, but you have no bloody balls!" she said.

"You came a few times and think you're an expert."

Something broke inside her. She saw his cowardice. His readiness to put her down. "I hate you. Don't ever contact me again."

On the plane ride home, she chided herself for choosing the wrong man, again. It was devastating when the blinders fell off, to see his true character. He didn't love her. Her eyes stung, thinking of her inane love poems and chasing him around the globe. Hadn't she known Pelou was married from the start, and what did it mean, that she waged a secret campaign to win him, hiding her great need, her jealousy of his wife? A sports car, for crissake. And the fact that shamed her most, made her feel abnormal, ugly, cheap: She had lost.

What was she, if she couldn't get a man? Not a woman at all.

"Maybe this is our baby." She remembered the night she murmured the words after he came inside her. He had gazed off in the distance, not answering. "Maybe I should adopt," she said, to cover the silence. They were both troubled by the begging five-year-olds who flocked them on every corner of Saigon.

"Now that's a great idea," Pelou said. "I know a woman who does charity. She can take you to an orphanage."

Oriana turned away quickly so he wouldn't see her face. His meaning was clear. François never intended to make a life with her. Oriana might write bestselling books and influential articles, but he didn't want a baby with her.

Enough, she thought now on the plane, swallowing back tears, the passenger in the next seat stealing glances. Pelou was a haughty Frenchman, beneath her in professional status. She would remove him from her brain. There would be no suicide attempt this time, no months of gloom. She was a long way from that pathetic girl, a war reporter now, sturdy and resilient.

What would she have done with a husband anyway? Pelou would have clipped her wings the moment the ring was on, demanding dinner on the table and his articles retyped. And a child? The darn thing couldn't walk for an entire year. Her life was already brimming with assignments and deadlines, adventures that were always there for her, that never let her down.

By the time her plane landed in Italy, she had devised a plan. She had lost, but there was still a way she could win.

The moment she walked into her apartment, she made a

nice package of his letters. *I miss you. I want to stay in bed with you all weekend. Hurry and come to me in Madrid.* She tied them with red ribbon and mailed them to his wife.

Chapter 8

1973

In the morning they mumbled *buon giorno* and squeezed past each other in the narrow hallway. Alekos looked boyish with his hair wet and slicked back, and she caught a whiff of clean glycerin soap. A scent she liked.

Oriana ducked into the bathroom and tested the lock to be sure before peeling off her nightgown. *Naked in his house.* Her thoughts looped back to last night, to his pacing the veranda. Why hadn't he come in—his equipment didn't work? No, she had a feeling it worked just fine. Probably he'd been doing it nonstop since his release.

The shower lacked pressure and she stood under the trickling stream, lathering herself with the pure glycerin bar, thinking, *This is the bar he rubbed all over his body.* She closed her eyes and imagined him barging through the door. Not stopping to remove his clothes. Joining her in the shower.

Crazy thoughts. She toweled off and dressed in bell-bottom jeans and white Lacoste polo. Eyeliner, frosted pink lipstick. She looked pretty. In the mirror, she studied her high cheekbones, deep-set eyes like a cat's. Did he find her pretty?

Alekos was drinking coffee on the veranda with four men scribbling in notepads. Greek journalists, she deduced, watching them hang on his every word. She wasn't the only one captivated.

He smiled warmly when he saw her. "There she is." He pulled out the chair next to him and poured her coffee. They were dressed like twins, he in jeans and a polo also, though not Lacoste. Proudly, he introduced her to fellow journalists, draping his arm around her chair. She leaned back, not quite touching, trying to ignore the charge between them.

The conversation was about censorship and how much the regime would allow these men to publish. "Don't be sheep," Alekos urged them. They asked about his torturers. "The sadists enjoyed it," Alekos said. "But there were good soldiers, too, who said, *Please Alekos, do as they say, we don't want to hurt you.*"

"What's next for you, Alekos?" a spectacled journalist asked with obvious worship.

"They say"—he turned to her—"I need a friend to reacquaint me with life."

"Excuse me." She pushed back her chair and fled downstairs to the garden, her vision clouded, nostrils stinging with pungent citrus. Twice she tried to light a cigarette and twice the matches snapped. Finally, on the third try, she took a deep puff and paced down a row of lemon trees. Their bark was painted with whitewash to keep insects away. She felt herself steadying under the cool branches.

"Don't go."

She turned. Alekos was standing close. She could see his chest rising with breath.

"Stay another day," he said.

"I've finished the interview."

"That's not why you came."

"No?" she challenged. "Why did I?"

Slowly, he ran his fingers down her bare arm, his look questioning but at the same time self-assured. She faltered for only a second, twisted out of his reach, and streaked up the stairs into the living room with its sofa and white eyelet sheets. Leaving the journalists' heads spinning.

Alekos was right behind her.

"I'm not interested in a fling," she said, hurrying clothes and toiletries into her Samsonite.

"This isn't a fling."

"Sharing the same views isn't enough."

"I agree."

"I live in Italy."

"That's a detail."

"I won't ever give up my work."

"I won't ask you to."

She spun around. "Don't you have a little girlfriend, Alekos? Someone who was pining for you, who will bake you a cake—"

"I love *you*!" His voice was so raw and sincere, she stumbled back. He grasped her by the shoulders, steadying her.

"You know nothing about me," she said.

"Isn't that you in your books?"

"Of course it's me."

"Haven't you ever read something that gave you comfort? Made you feel understood?" She didn't answer, didn't want to hear his next sentence. "I stayed alive because of you."

He kissed her, soft and then hard, sweeping away the nagging doubt that no one would ever love her, that she was too difficult, too smart, too independent. When it was over, she dizzily searched his eyes, ready to blurt *I want this, too!* but the look in those dark, sensitive pools stopped her. He understood so much about the world, about being human, his eyes said, but nothing that would save them. Fear seeped through her, the fear of losing control in the tidal wave pulling her toward him, of knowing it would cost her but she would do it anyway. She would do it anyway.

Alekos took her face in his hands and kissed her. She kissed him back, harder and hungrier. Oriana was no stranger to risk, she'd been taking risks all her life. He slid his hand up her shirt, slow, masterful. She pressed against him, feeling their bodies snap together like pieces of a puzzle, with no separation between them.

Wait. She wrenched away. What was happening? She checked her watch, holding up her wrist to show him. "My plane leaves in an hour."

They nestled in the back seat of the Citroën while his friend drove them to Hellenikon Airport, sultry air gusting through the windows. Alekos held her hand for the entire ten-minute ride. She let him. She let her heart surge with the possibility of everything beginning. Her skin, scalp, brain—everything buzzed with heightened sensation. He wrapped his arm around her, drawing her closer, his compact soccer body fitting protectively against her petite one. He felt solid and sure, yet seemed to contain an infinite, yielding center.

The electric blue coastline streamed by. "Was it nearby, your attempt?" she said, wondering where along the beach he'd seen the couple making love, set off his explosives, hidden in a microscopic cave.

"I'll show you next time. When are you coming back?" he said.

Her lips curled at his youthful eagerness. "I don't know, Alekos, I have to work."

"I want you to." He kissed her hand with confidence. She leaned her head against his shoulder and felt the start of an unburdening. He was a different kind of man. A man with backbone. She had wasted so much of herself on Pelou, too weak to leave his wife, a bystander in life, like all journalists were. It was easy to type "this is right" and "this is wrong." But to be willing to die for right?

They stopped at a red light. Outside on the rocky coastline, she spotted three giant letters graffitied in white. OXI. "What does that mean?" She turned to him.

"NO," he said simply. The word sounded new from his lips, a bolt up her spine.

Too soon, they arrived at Hellenikon, the backwater airport

ringed by parched brown hills, spectacularly positioned on the Aegean.

Alekos swung her bag out of the trunk. "I'll come in with you."

A plane roared overhead into the perfect blue sky. Reality flooded in. He was a baby, for crissake. How could she start an affair—to do *what* with him? There was no place for Alekos in her frenzied schedule, yet in the past twenty-four hours, she'd been rocked by the sensation that they were the same. They were meant to be together. This was her chance. "Don't," she said. "I'll wait in the lounge."

"The VIP lounge?" he said, amused. "We don't have one."

"*Grazie* for the hospitality." She reached for her suitcase.

Alekos would not let go. He drew her by the waist and kissed her. Oriana avoided public displays, accustomed to being recognized, but she was sweltering and light-headed and returned the kiss anyway.

"Promise you'll come back," he said.

"Go. Your friend is waiting." She motioned to the driver staring goofily out his window.

Alekos made a gesture and the friend reluctantly pulled his head in.

"Take care," Oriana said, wresting her suitcase from him. Alekos surrendered but wouldn't take his eyes off her, and she found herself in a tug-of-war with his gravitational pull. She gave him a firm handshake and turned to go, hardly sure where she was planting her feet.

"Oriana," he called out.

When she turned, he lifted both palms in farewell. She floated toward Alitalia with a fool's grin, the sound of her name off his tongue ringing in her ears.

Chapter 9

1973

Oriana lived in a grand Renaissance building in the center of Florence. Her apartment was lushly furnished with antiques and faced directly onto the Duomo, the marble cathedral with its soaring red-brick cupola that distinguished her city from far away. She had leased the apartment for one specific reason: It offered the same view of Brunelleschi's cupola that she'd grown up with as a girl, the same music of the church bells six times a day. The family had been forced to move to a lesser neighborhood when her father lost his job during the Nazi occupation. Home became a basement apartment with no sunlight, where she could only see feet walking out the barred windows and dogs peeing. Even at fourteen, Oriana knew her family had fallen, and she felt the shame of their worsened circumstances.

When the war ended, the Galileo workshop remained shuttered, and nobody would hire Babbo to make his cabinets and furniture. They had no money for food, so Mamma took in laundry from the American soldiers who stayed during the transition. The first day, two white sacks arrived on their doorstep. Mamma opened one and found four cans of pork and beans, a loaf of bread, and a jar of strawberry jelly. Salivating at such riches, Oriana rushed to help, untying the second sack. She peered inside, expecting to find the same American uniforms (green pants, khaki shirts) that neighbor women were hanging from clotheslines. But her mother's bag contained only dirty underwear, grayish-white, with a strange opening in front and brown streaks inside. "Don't they have toilet paper, the rich Americans?" she asked.

Tosca pressed her lips tight. She boiled a vat of water on the kitchen stove. "We can't wash these where we wash dishes," she said, lugging the vat to the tub. Tosca demonstrated how to hold each section of fabric against the thumb pad and scrub it by hand. "If only I'd been born a man," she said. Oriana saw tears in her mother's eyes and felt her frustration. Men didn't wash underwear, the message was seared into her brain, they did better things in the world.

Mamma sent her to Signore Peppe's to buy mozzarella for the family. "Just an ounce," her mother warned.

"Nothing else?" Signore Peppe leaned over the counter to show Oriana the speck of mozzarella in wax paper.

Her mouth watered at the salamis and prosciuttos hanging from the ceiling, but she shook her head.

"I'm not hungry," her mother said as they passed the mozzarella around the table that evening. "Eat, Oriana, you're too skinny."

Those years of poverty had ignited a fire in her belly. That's why she was so disciplined about work, revered it even. Work had given her pride and a name, elegant homes, clothes, jewelry—including an antique brooch from Napoleonic France. Oriana applied herself tirelessly and had no respect for those who didn't, who expected life to come easily.

Her desk was inlaid with mother-of-pearl and cluttered with manuscripts, photos, newspapers, and magazines. An Olivetti typewriter held center court. Next to it, a silver dish used as an ashtray, always overflowing, and beside it her Sony tape recorder. Oriana was among the first journalists to use the new technology, and initially she hated the bulky machine lurking like a spy, the clumsy microphone she had to hold. Very soon, though, she learned to ignore them, and her interviews took on the air of natural conversation, especially as tape recorders grew smaller and microphones became built-in. The famous were more inclined to let down their masks when she maintained eye contact and no longer glanced away to scribble in a notepad. With the cassette wheels spinning (only 90-minute tapes; the 120s jammed up), Oriana was free to pepper the high and the mighty with personal questions. *Do you believe in God? How often do you cry?* Once they began talking about themselves, she had them in her palm.

Listening back, she discovered that nothing captured the essence of a person like the live voice. The voice revealed nuances—a break in confidence, a note of embarrassment, a flash of anger—that even her careful notes and prodigious memory did not. The first time Oriana heard her own voice on tape, husky, ironic, brash, she had the reaction most people did: *That doesn't sound like me*. But the voice on tape *was* you, and if you listened closely, you would learn things about yourself that perhaps you didn't want to know. For instance, she smoked too many cigarettes.

She paced the living room in her white Frette robe, trailing a plume of smoke, too agitated to summon her usual concentration and begin typing. She had already transcribed Alekos's cassettes, lured by that bedroom voice into listening three or four times. Her own voice had nothing of the usual prosecutor, it was all smiles. She should be composing now. Instead she reread his two telegrams. *Come back. Still afraid?*

Please. What did he want, this adolescent who declared his love after ten hours? *Your books kept me company in my cage.* He knew her through her writing, big deal. What could he deduce from her interview with Yasir Arafat? Oriana had found the leader of the Palestine Liberation Organization to be an ugly little man with fat lips and a protruding belly. He vowed he would wage war for generations to destroy Israel and take back the land of his ancestors. "You want your people to keep dying. Did you ever ask what they want?" she said straight into his sunglasses. When the interview was published, Arafat sent letters to *L'Europeo* calling her a spy and threatening to punish her. Police in protective gear had to be summoned to open his love letters for fear they were bombs.

"Look at the danger she puts us in," her colleagues grumbled, as if it were her fault much of the world was run by maniacs.

Alekos had read *The Egotists*, her interviews with celebrities, the fluff that began her career. Some stars she liked, Ingrid of course, Clark Gable. Others were repulsive. Alfred Hitchcock had gloated with pride when she asked how he felt about his films inspiring real-life murders. "I like to be imitated," he said, his double chin jiggling. They met in his hotel room in Cannes, where he was premiering *The Birds*. He sat like a giant sucking on a cigar and said he never watched his own movies; he was too scared. The majority of actors were dumb children; he had no respect for them and was especially irritated if an actress got pregnant. Oriana had been a fan, but after meeting Hitchcock, she told him to his face, and told readers, he was a diabolical man.

Fellini, another disappointment. He had become world famous for directing *La Dolce Vita* and agreed to an interview, gushing over her: "Little Oriana, I love you so much, you're adorable." Then he canceled five meetings in a row and finally, after conducting the interview lying on his hotel bed, he demanded story approval because he was a great artist, a great intellectual.

"Go to hell," Oriana told him on the phone. He called her a bitch and a liar and swore to get her fired. The entire newsroom listened to Fellini's tirade booming out of her receiver.

"Christ, Oriana," a colleague said when she slammed down the phone. "That was Federico Fellini you just sent to hell."

"For a good interview, gentlemen," she said, feigning calm, "sometimes you have to make enemies. If you have balls, that is." She did turn it into a good interview, though Fellini was evasive and rambling. She got him to say he prayed, he didn't read books or see movies, and he deserved all the adulation he received.

The critics were right about one thing. Oriana Fallaci's reporting was dramatic, often biting, and always included herself. Why shouldn't she be in her stories? She made the rules. No one taught her how to write, she taught herself, conveying what she saw and felt, grabbing her audience with an immediacy that put them in her shoes. Readers loved to experience vicariously her search for Marilyn at Hollywood's chicest nightspots. Her *very* close friendship with astronaut Pete Conrad, Commander of Apollo 12 and the third man to walk on the moon. She had dined and danced with him (and more than that, which stayed off the record), and he had carried a photo of Oriana to the moon at her request, though he refused to bring her a lunar rock.

Readers even got a thrill from riding with her on the bombing mission in Vietnam where she came near death.

I am strapped into an A-37 cockpit, helmet on, respirator in my mouth, parachute secure. Captain Andy, a blond American fighter pilot, snaps the capsule closed. "Here you go," he says. I hear his voice through a microphone in my helmet. He hands me three vomit bags that I clutch in my lap.

"I've never had a woman fly with me," he says. We rocket up above the clouds. He places his finger on the red button. "We'll be vertical," he says. "Ready?" I nod. Of course I'm not ready. You'd have to be an idiot not to fear ripping through the sky at 500 miles an hour. But I am here to discover what a man feels when he bombs the life out of other men. Captain Andy has flown 273 missions. Our objective is south of My Tho.

We nose-dive down, slicing through clouds, trees, branches. The ground is coming up fast. Faster. I'm going to die! Flashing lights zoom up at us. It's the Vietcong firing maching guns. We're about to get shot down or crash into the ground.

Every muscle in my body tenses to one point. Tighter and tighter so I can prevent disaster until finally there is nothing I can do. I let go. Let death come. There's a wild moment of release when we're racing through the galaxy. But no! I don't want to die. I brake with my feet. Push the red button, Andy! Kill the Vietcong!

Thank Christ he pushes it. A napalm bomb drops out from beneath my wing. Like a long black bullet, it hangs in the air a split second before nosing downward.

Kaboom! It hits. Tiny figures run out of dugouts, flailing their arms. Human fireballs. Smoke.

"You did great," Captain Andy says, roaring up into the sky again. My relief is so great, I don't care about dead Vietcong. It's us or them. "If you need oxygen, press that button," Andy says. "We're going down again."

Eight swoops down. We kill at least thirty people. Take out the Vietcong post.

"You didn't need any." Captain Andy is impressed when we land. He points to the vomit bags still in my lap. "We did 8 gs." He means we accelerated eight times faster than the force of gravity. After 9 gs, the heart can't pump enough blood to the brain. You die.

"I'm stubborn," I say to Andy, high on 8 gs, on getting safely back to earth. The guilt will come later. I have come to Vietnam to write about the madness of war, but now I feel only the drunkenness of being alive. Of winning. "Will you write a letter stating I took part?" I ask Captain Andy.

"I can do better," he says.

At the base, he signs a certificate. "This is a true certified copy to confirm"—he fills in Oriana Fallaci—"has participated in a successful bombing mission with the U.S Air Force 604 Squadron Fighters."

I frame it the day I get home.

Her personal writing style now had a name in America. Tom Wolfe with his Ph.D. was calling it the *new journalism*. Big guys like Truman Capote and Gay Talese (she liked Talese, he was Italian) were writing articles with characters, scenes, dialogue—abandoning objective reporting and using their personal voice. But this was an old story for Oriana. She had always used her own voice, by instinct, not diplomas. Frankly, she didn't know how to do her job without spilling her heart onto every page.

She threw her legs over the desk and hit *Play*, drawn again to the way Alekos pronounced that one sentence: "The worst thing in life isn't to suffer, you know, but to suffer alone." She remembered how he pinned her with his dark chocolate gaze at one in the morning, the words delivered with undisguised vulnerability, an invitation from his lips. *The worst thing in life . . . to suffer alone.*

Hitting *Rewind*, she listened again to the exact timbre of his *suffer* and *alone*, her skin erupting in goose bumps. Had this political prisoner from Greece been able to *see* her? In his living room in Glyfada, between their stiff armchairs, his solitude had seemed to float up and link arms with her solitude. He had been lonely in solitary confinement. She was lonely, too. Her enemies called her a bigmouth, a ballbuster, even a lesbian because she wore pants. Outside she was hardened, yes, but inside, how did Alekos know this, Oriana was soft, she craved comfort from someone near. A cry bubbled up in her throat and got trapped there, since there was no one to comfort her—she had nobody. The brutality of the moment was what she imagined it to be like at death's door, and it made her double over and hug her waist.

It wasn't that she longed to be a wife. Her mother had traumatized her on that subject. *Don't be an ignorant servant like me. Work, fly!* But she had always assumed there would be a man in her life—and children. Somehow her mother had forgotten children, though no Italian could glimpse a baby without pinching its cheek and crying *bellisima.* Oriana had achieved success beyond her wildest imagination, but this was her greatest defeat—she had never borne children.

She thought of her pregnancy with Gori, how she offered to end it and his callousness, ignoring her pleas to find a clinic. The baby she subtly campaigned for with Pelou, who already had one and didn't want hers. The absurd weight she'd given their affair, as if tumbling in hotel sheets was any kind of bond. She remembered Pelou's hot desire after a separation, the way she'd rush into his arms and not see one trace of his wife or son on his face. The tenuous hope that she'd won him, that she was no longer the other woman who had to be satisfied with crumbs. Then later, Pelou would receive a call from home. Oriana would listen to just a few syllables before escaping into the shower, where it was hard, very hard in the rush of water, to stuff back tears.

She reread Alekos's latest telegram. *Fate brought us together.* He had nerve sending these communiqués, playing with her. He knew nothing about her. Yet he knew everything.

Allora. She parked herself at the typewriter and twisted up her hair. Her fingers hovered over the keys and released in a storm, crafting a stage play, that's how she thought of it, with crackling dialogue that built to a climax, one with surprise or punch. The more she quoted Alekos, the more she felt fired up by his political ideals, inspired to fight on his side, to be a soldier again. Thirty years ago, she'd been the perfect child partisan, delivering this fuse for a bomb, guiding these American prisoners to safety. But as a journalist jetting around the world earning big money, Oriana had settled into an insulated life. In hotel rooms, VIP lounges, palaces where she conversed with kings and was served by starched butlers (tea, crumpets, beluga caviar), she swelled with her own importance and grew detached from her activist childhood. In Vietnam, Cambodia, Pakistan, she witnessed the atrocities of war and turned jaded. Men are sick, selfish, there's no hope.

Alexander Panagoulis woke her up with his devotion to his people, his willingness to act instead of being resigned like everybody else. *Don't follow the crowd*, he'd said during their interview. *Be willing to say the emperor has no clothes. It's everyday people who change the world.*

Back and forth, between transcript and typewriter, she shaped his portrait. She could hear every syllable of her question and answer, as if she were watching two actors onstage, and she built the scene. Immersed herself until midnight, chain-smoking, not stopping for food.

Chapter 10

1945 to 1951

"Be the best in your class," her parents drilled into her, and she was, graduating high school early at sixteen. But Mamma didn't praise her. "You did your duty. You were lucky to go to school." Her mother's coldness made her shrink with embarrassment. Oriana had imagined a celebration, the family going to Vivoli for that rarest of treats, a nocciola ice cream cone. But Mamma only took her diploma and folded it into the wooden box on her bureau that contained their identity cards and birth certificates. Through her mother's pressed lips, Oriana heard one clear message: She'd better work hard, even kill herself working, because the chance to get an education past the fifth grade was one her parents never had.

"I want to be a writer," Oriana said when it came time to take university entrance exams. Only male classmates were sitting for exams. Female classmates were getting jobs in factories or getting married. Oriana wondered if *she* might be getting married, if she'd had a brother whom her parents could favor in the traditional Italian way. At night, she heard them whispering about where they would find money for university. "We have enough for one year," Babbo said. "After that we'll see."

Oriana dreamed of becoming a writer because her parents had taught her to treasure books, and nowhere had she felt more enraptured than in the pages of *Don Quixote*, *Madame Bovary*, *Romeo and Juliet*. From the first time she read a poetic phrase that captured a feeling she never knew she had, she wanted to do the same, because it moved her and made her feel less alone. Another reason she was drawn to literature: Writers lived on after they were dead. She knew this from gazing at the red leather spines in the glass bookcase. Kipling, Dante, Shakespeare, Alcott. She wanted to live on, too.

"Do you know how many years it takes to become a writer?" Mamma said.

"You have to live first. Have experiences," Babbo said. "Even then, who knows if you can earn money."

"Jack London was a waiter." Mamma's tone was ominous.

It was another bucket of cold water mixed with shame. Dreams were a waste of time, at least for a poor girl like her. Literature was for others. She could only admire great writers from afar. Oriana understood that Florence was in tatters, their city bombed by the Germans as they retreated, reducing buildings to rubble and blowing up every bridge except Ponte Vecchio. Food was scarce and jobs scarcer. Life was brutal, just as her parents bitterly repeated, and the sooner she accepted it, the better.

"A doctor," Mamma said. "That's what you should be."

Oriana was raised to accept her parents' decisions. She passed the entrance exam and enrolled at University of Florence, one of only two girls to enter the School of Medicine and Surgery. The day before classes, she rode her bicycle to Piazza de San Marco in order to orient herself to the grand buildings with arched colonnades. She gazed up at the imposing doors and a thrill went through her imagining the knowledge they contained, knowledge that would soon be hers.

"That's a real piece of shit," a boy called out, pointing to her bicycle. His was shiny and new. But hers had gotten her through delivering secret messages, through German checkpoints.

"Tomorrow is the *corridoio*," she told her parents. The

"corridor" was a hazing ritual that required freshmen to pay 500 lire to upperclassmen before they could register for classes. If Oriana didn't have the money, she would be forced to pass through a long tunnel of upperclassmen who would thrash her.

Babbo shook his head. "Is this what education has come to?"

But Mamma gathered loose change from the ashtray and went down to the corner, returning with five packs of Macedonia Oro. "Give them these," she said, pressing the cigarettes into Oriana's hands.

The next day in the courtyard behind the medical building, a dozen upperclassmen, all boys, formed the *corridoio*. Oriana lined up with other freshmen, taking up the rear, her limbs rattling when she saw that every student ahead had money to pay. Only she and a boy in raggedy pants were left in line. Her hand trembled as she handed the ringleader the Macedonia Oro.

"Good, this is what I smoke," he said. She melted with relief. "This one's got beautiful eyes," he said to his gang. She started to walk away. He hauled her back. "Where do you think you're going?"

It was a long, suffocating pile-on of brutes. She steeled herself to go fast, but one tripped her, another yanked her braid. Blows on the head, neck, back. She lost her breath. Croaked out awful sounds.

Finally she stumbled away, hyperventilating with tears, spinning to find an exit. Students in the courtyard snickered and pointed fingers. The beating was for her, for her family. They were less than, though Babbo had taught her, *Everyone is equal, no one is better than you.* Why did he lie? She could hear her parents worrying at night, how to pay the grocer, the landlord. Money was the great separator. From now on, she would get money. Never be humiliated again.

In anatomy class, Oriana memorized the parts of the brain: hypothalamus, pituitary, amygdala. She would become a psychiatrist, she decided, because she couldn't stand the sight of blood and she was a good observer of people, curious to know how their minds worked, what shaped their character and behavior.

Three months into her studies, her father nearly died in a car accident. He was on his way to a political rally with fellow partisans, preparing to run for office, when a truck smashed into them. Now Babbo slumped on the sofa at home in a partial coma, her mother feeding him with a bib around his neck. Oriana didn't need to be told. She dropped out of university.

"I'll get a job at *Nazione di Firenze*," she told her mother, her sense of being the breadwinner clear. The desire to be a writer had never left her, and *Nazione* was the main newspaper of Florence, the one her family read. But she got off on the wrong floor. A man at the first desk she encountered—suit, fedora, pencil behind his ear—peered at her over his typewriter. "This is *Il Mattino dell'Italia*. Are you lost, little girl?"

There was a roaring in her ears and she fought the impulse to run. The newsroom was small and frenetic, with papers strewn everywhere and men in white shirts and ties shouting into phones. She stood up tall in the pink poplin dress Mamma had sewn, which made her look even younger.

"I want to be a reporter."

The man leered at her. "Editor Cassavo's over there." He pointed to an angular man leaning on a corner desk, barking into a phone. He wore a double-breasted suit and puffed on a cigar.

Nervous, she waited for the editor to hang up, then made her way over. "I'm seventeen," she lied. "I finished *liceo* with superior grades."

Nico Cassavo sized her up and down. "I'll give you a test. Give me five hundred words on the new nightclub on the Arno. By tomorrow at five."

Nightclub? The word conjured up alcohol and sexual

escapades. But Babbo and the Resistance had taught her to face her fears. As the July sun set, Oriana hurried across the river into Oltrarno, the neighborhood where artisans crafted pottery and leather goods. Where Babbo had a job until Galileo workshop closed down.

At Ballare, the new nightclub a few steps from the grassy riverbank, she circulated with a school notebook, self-conscious in the same prim dress and flat sandals, her face scrubbed clean among the revelers. But she felt strangely comfortable, too, as an outsider looking in, with her ally the pen, on a mission to capture a story. She had purpose, and that purpose allowed her to forget herself, to act in a way she normally wouldn't. Nosier. Bolder.

Initially she jotted notes about the colorful lanterns, three-piece orchestra, drinks with paper umbrellas that resembled orangeade but were called *spritz*. The romantic pairs swaying on the outdoor dance floor, men in pleated trousers and narrow ties, women in wide-skirted summer dresses. Then she noticed something more interesting. Mothers tugging their daughters by the arm, lingering around the dance floor, sipping Coca-Colas. She watched one mother's sharp eye land on a young man with a crew cut and glasses. The mother elbowed her daughter closer and stayed two steps behind, biting her lip as her daughter took too long to speak and the boy moved away. Another mother watched smugly as her daughter twirled by in the arms of a roly-poly young man, throwing the girl a stern nod.

It struck Oriana that these mothers had also come to Ballare on a mission, to find husbands for their daughters. Protecting their virginity while at the same time maneuvering for a dance that might lead to marriage. It saddened her to see them practically begging for their daughters to be noticed. Her mother would never do that; she had raised Oriana to use her brain and excel rather than be chosen. Still, the mating ritual unfolding at Ballare was the part of the story that spoke to her most, the human element. The traditional mammas scheming on behalf of their daughters in this new dance club on a summer evening on the Arno.

Oriana made it the centerpiece of her story. On the kitchen table, she wrote in her neatest handwriting on five sheets of school paper. The next morning she handed it to the editor.

"What's this?" Cassavo flung it back without reading. "Don't you type?"

He pointed her to an empty desk, and she approached the machine as if it were a tractor. It took her eight hours to hunt and peck, using only her pointer and middle fingers (the way she would type all her life). She started over twelve times because of mistakes before she realized, glancing around the newsroom, there was a way to erase. The men used a little bottle of white fluid, and immediately she found the supply closet and got one for herself.

Finally, her article was perfect. Holding her breath, she handed it to Editor Cassavo and watched his expression as he read.

"Hmph. You'll be our new hospital and police reporter," he said, his eyebrows arched in surprise.

A paycheck and a job as a writer! The next day, her Ballare story ran in *Il Mattino*. The joy of seeing her words printed in tight columns zinged through her all day, and she ran home that evening cradling the paper in her hands. "Why doesn't it have your name?" her mother said. She was too new, Editor Cassavo had told her. First, she had to prove herself.

The following morning, Oriana arrived at the courtroom early to cover the proceedings, anxious to do her best. As soon as the judge spotted her in the back row, he growled, "Who let the kid in?"

"I'm a reporter for *Il Mattino*," she corrected him.

"This is no business for a girl," the judge said. The case was against a man arrested for masturbating on a park bench. "Get her out."

The bailiff ushered her out by the elbow, but she'd made a friend from a rival newspaper while waiting, a gap-toothed boy in a bow tie sitting next to her.

"Hey, Nino! I'll give you my good pen if you tell me what happens," she called as she was being thrown out. Two hours later, she met Nino on the courthouse stairs and he shared his notes, declining her pen and flushing with embarrassment. *Masturbator unzipped . . . took it out . . . two women screamed.* Oriana copied from his pad.

Cassavo grunted when she handed in her story. "Why the hell is a girl covering this?" Did her editor have dreadful urges, too? Oriana cringed, visualizing his privates. She had glimpsed her father's once, a tired worm poking through a slit in his pajamas.

Editor Cassavo stalked off but published her piece.

It was an uphill battle, but the war had toughened her, and her skin grew thicker every day. In addition to accidents and arrests, they let her do society news, human interest—whatever the men didn't want to do. Oriana got her first byline writing about the eight-year-old shoeshine boys on every corner of Florence and their will to survive, a scrappiness she knew well. Every day she pounded the pavement, visiting hospitals and police stations searching for a story, and every night she returned to the newsroom and typed it up, riding her bicycle home at one and two in the morning. Sometimes she caught a ride home with the three-wheeled truck that distributed the paper. "Oriana, you'll catch your death, this isn't work for a girl," Luca the driver would say when it was cold or raining. Her coat was thin and her wrists stuck out, and one night, she collapsed with fever the moment she arrived home. Her mother tucked her into bed with a cool washcloth on her forehead. "If only you could have stayed at university," Tosca said. She shook her head in a way that said journalism was inferior to medicine, that somehow Oriana had failed, and her parents had failed with her.

At *Il Mattino*, her colleagues were men in their twenties and thirties, and they treated her like the *ragazza*, the earnest kid whose head they patted. "This fucking guy won't call me back." One of them would slam down the phone. "Watch your mouth in front of the kid," another would say.

"I'm used to cursing." Oriana sat up straight. It wasn't true, her parents never used profanity, but she began peppering her speech with *porca puttana* and *che schifo*. Being the only girl was a role she'd grown accustomed to in medical school, and though a certain loneliness was her constant companion, she never questioned her right to be in the newsroom. She might be different, but that was fine, or rather she'd make it fine, by being a quick study and working more doggedly than anyone else.

When the men got on the phone for a story, she noticed the way they barked questions and spread their knees wide. She mimicked their confidence and threw her legs on top of her desk. She started smoking, coughing and feeling light-headed as she practiced in the bathroom mirror, but knowing she looked sophisticated waving a cigarette.

Her daily outfit was a pair of baggy black trousers that Editor Cassavo said made her look like a waiter. But as Oriana reached her twenties and had a few extra lire in her pocket, she began to wear makeup and bought a tailored skirt and jacket that accentuated her narrow waist and round breasts. Add to that a silk blouse, stockings, heels. Very quickly, male attention changed. "That's a nice lipstick you're wearing, Oriana, your mouth is like a rose." "Mamma mia, those legs, where've you been hiding them?"

It was a fact of life that women were catcalled on the streets, even swollen-legged grandmothers. Nobody questioned the prerogative of hot-blooded Italian men to comment on women's bodies. Ever since she was a toddler, her mother had taught her by example to ignore boorish behavior and hold her head high. If the remarks were especially vulgar, her mother would spin around and say, "Shame on you, young man. Would you talk to your mother or sister this way?"

Oriana alternated between ignoring her colleagues and telling them where to stick it. She was a lowly girl reporter and they covered national news, but someday she would be the best reporter in Italy, and they wouldn't dare treat her with disrespect. They would bow down and acknowledge her brilliance.

The five male reporters sat in two rows, and she behind them. They ribbed each other constantly, and having no brothers, she listened and learned their unwritten code. Men never showed weakness, so she learned not to show any either. Their conversation consisted mainly of one-upmanship: whose team won the soccer match, who knew the better tailor, who earned the most compliments from the editor. Keeping up with their banter, Oriana learned never to downplay her accomplishments but rather to boast about them with her hands on hips.

Above all, men competed on sexual conquests. The cockiest reporter was Vittorio with knife creases in his pants, forever combing back his pompadour. He was from an important family and met a different girl each night after work. Oriana was unimpressed with his class, since her father had taught her to reject hierarchy. Still, it was the first time that privilege was rubbed in her face daily. As for the girls who kissed Vittorio, they must be idiots.

"Oriana, when you gonna go out with me?" Vittorio said, leaning across her desk. "There's a Lana Turner movie at the cinema. You can strap your arms around me on my Ducati." He winked.

"I have to work, young man," she said. "And I wouldn't go to the cinema with you. I don't care how much money your family has."

His colleagues hooted.

"I'll be gentle with you, Oriana." Vittorio strutted up behind her. "I can tell if a girl's a virgin by how tight she is right here." He massaged her shoulders.

"Get your hands off me." She slapped them off.

The newsroom erupted in whoops and snickers.

Reddening, Vittorio swaggered back to his desk. "How you gonna get a man to marry you, being a ballbuster like that?"

"I don't want to get married, genius."

"She wants to be an old maid." Vittorio shrugged to his dim-witted audience.

No, she didn't. "Old maid" conjured up Signora Beatrice upstairs, who had bad breath and talked to her cat. But Oriana had taken her mother's warning to heart: Domestic life was a trap; a woman could only find fulfillment in the big wide world. And right now, there were more crucial matters to think about than slimy Vittorio and his wandering hands. Newlyweds Frank Sinatra and Ava Gardner were coming to Italy. The society beat belonged to Oriana, since the men had no interest. But this was big news! Before her colleagues could figure it out, she pounced on the assignment.

"You don't ask permission. You take what you want." Editor Cassavo gave her an impressed look that carried more than a trace of revulsion. He tipped his head toward the male den. "They're going to hate you for that."

Maybe, she thought, but she couldn't ask permission. The answer would be a big fat *No*. She hadn't asked permission from the Germans to sneak messages to the partisans. She hadn't asked, "May I work as an underaged girl?" Now that she'd elbowed her way into the newsroom, she was going to squeeze every drop of opportunity. If the men hated her for that, tough luck, she was too busy to care—she had to prepare for her meeting with *Francesco* Sinatra. She would ask if his parents spoke Italian at home in America and what he liked best about Italy, which cities and foods.

But when Sinatra arrived in Florence, he refused Oriana's request for an interview. He avoided all press, his entourage whisking him on private tours of the Uffizi and the David. Oriana could only trail the glamorous couple with a pack of paparazzi, craning her neck from afar. "Mr. Sinatra, why do you ignore your fellow Italians?" she shouted as the couple swept into the St. Regis for dinner with the mayor. Sinatra turned his eyes on her, and they were so blue, they stung, but he said nothing, ducking inside. The *Corriere* reporter beside her sneered. "Did you really think insulting him would work?" he said.

Dammit. How would she get her story? She reported the facts, Ava's furs and strapless gowns, Sinatra's suave tuxedo over his scrawny build. The private yacht they booked to sail the Amalfi coast. But Oriana also wrote what she felt. Sinatra was a disappointment. He turned his back on fellow Italians, who wanted only to give him a grand welcome home.

Oriana used what she'd internalized from literature: A good story featured lively narration, conflict and climax, and most crucially an insight into human nature. She was naturally perceptive, intent on showing what was beneath the surface. Her language was simple and direct. If Sinatra was rude to fellow Italians, she would say he was rude. In her mind, she was writing for her mother, for the Rossini brothers, those handsome masons at Mannelli. They had common sense, a wisdom about life that had nothing to do with education, and she didn't need to throw around fancy vocabulary to impress anyone.

She wrote in the first person, like the great authors who'd left a mark on her, Brontë in *Jane Eyre*, Proust in *Swann's Way*. She felt natural saying "I" and putting herself in the story, because she was there, after all, seeing, feeling, interpreting—*and no one told her not to.* Immediately, colleagues pounced. Who was she, a woman, to have ideas and opinions and be outspoken about them? To criticize the great Frank Sinatra?

She was a person with a brain, that's who. Oriana had started to develop her own style, though she didn't know it.

Chapter 11

1951 to 1955

"I'll go." She jumped at any assignment that got her on a plane.

I MET PRINCESS MARGARET'S GREAT LOVE, she wrote about Peter Townsend, the suitor rejected by the British monarchy because he was divorced. Captain Townsend was hiding out in Brussels to let his affair with Princess Margaret cool off, but Oriana tracked down his address and ambushed him at his front door.

"I am Oriana Fallaci from Italy, you must let me interview you!" she said, with the same boldness that had sprouted in her on dangerous courier errands. She was hungry to succeed but felt no fear, no inferiority, talking to a man who was virtually British royalty, or wanted to be.

Captain Townsend looked dashing in his riding clothes. He respected her tenacity, he said, but couldn't speak with her. "Is it true you've given up on marrying the princess?" she persisted. Captain Townsend confirmed it was true, but Oriana noted the way he clenched his jaw and gazed into the distance. The poor man was lovesick—he hadn't forgotten Margaret at all! In her article, she described his reaction exactly, the tightening of his facial muscles and far-off look, to tell the story, even when Townsend refused to give her one. Failure was not an option. She would have to see more keenly, think more creatively, to get what she needed.

Il Mattino sent her to London to write about debutantes and their exhausting schedule of seamstress appointments, finding an eligible escort, and rehearsing to curtsey before Queen Elizabeth. Oriana's sarcastic edge found its way into the story as she let loose her disdain for class snobbery. *It turns out rich girls in white wedding gowns must be supernaturally coordinated to execute the series of curtsies by which their entire future will be determined. I tried it myself and the queen would have easily spotted me as a plebian imposter when my feet got tangled and I tumbled to the floor.* Oriana provided step-by-step instructions so readers could try the back-breaking curtsey for themselves.

"Funny," said Vittorio, her swaggering colleague, his nose buried in her piece. "Who knew you had a sense of humor?"

"I speak to you, don't I?"

"Relax, Oriana. You're such a prude." He turned to the male den. "Maybe she's doing the business with some guy overseas, so she can come back here and play the Madonna." He made a gesture for intercourse, poking his finger in and out of a round O.

"I certainly wouldn't do it with you," she said, embarrassed to be in her twenties and still a virgin, but who had time? She had to be disciplined, pour all her energy into earning her daily bread and beating the Vittorios at their own game. Besides, she hadn't been swept off her feet like Catherine in *Wuthering Heights*, the novel that from girlhood had shaped her earth-shattering notions of romance. Sex was reserved for couples sick with love, and she hadn't fallen in love yet. Not to mention that, since infancy, she'd been breathing the air of a Catholic country with a church in every piazza. Men could cavort and screw their brains out, Oriana had learned practically from the womb, but she could never escape the taboo restricting her gender.

Il Mattino sent her to Iran. She was part of a press junket inaugurating the first Alitalia flights to Teheran. As soon as they landed, Oriana abandoned the group, got her hands on a black chador, and covering herself from head to toe, sneaked into Sepahsalar Mosque, where only Moslems were allowed. She took mental notes of the exquisite tile motifs on the eight minarets and dome, the men washing their feet, the women removing their shoes (she followed suit) to cross the vast carpet to a screened-off area out of view.

In the afternoon, Empress Soraya gave the press group a tour of the palace, including her private rooms. Oriana lagged behind, stealing a look inside her closet. The empress had an impressive collection of black lace and leopard print lingerie, a telling detail Oriana would use. Rumor had it Soraya, educated in London and wearing a jaw-dropping green diamond ring, was under pressure to produce an heir. The Shah would need to divorce her by law if she failed.

"Empress, are your frequent trips to France and Saint Louis for fertility treatments?" Oriana asked. There was no time to waste with politeness. Empress Soraya denied her trips were medical, claiming she traveled on holiday. Oriana reported her words exactly, but also the anxiety she detected in the woman's body language, her sad expression at the mere suggestion of children.

A new editor, Vito Bornello, enormous and greasy-haired, took over the paper. Oriana sensed immediately he didn't like her. He invited only men to his office for meetings and puffed out his chest when he addressed her, calling her *Signorina Fallaci*. She read him easily. He couldn't swallow her popularity among readers, the growing status of a woman.

Late one afternoon, Bornello summoned her to his office. Chomping on a biscotto, he demanded she write a story mocking the new leader of the Communist party. The politician was to hold a rally later that week.

Oriana stood very erect. "I'll go to the rally first, then decide what to write."

"You don't need to go. Don't waste time," Bornello said.

"I will go, or I won't write anything," she said. Every day, she killed herself to tell the truth, avoid mistakes. She could never write falsehoods. Her byline was sacred to her.

The editor wagged his finger. Beads of perspiration dribbled down his temples. "Listen, you. At my paper, you must decide if you're going to be a woman or a man," he said.

"A man," Oriana said without hesitation.

An hour later Bornello loomed over her desk, shoving severance documents in her face. "Don't shit where you eat," he said.

"I do shit. And since you're a glutton, you can eat it."

Where did she find the nerve? Her father, *We are all equals, no one is better than you. Non Mollare*, a paper speaking the truth. A grenade hidden in lettuce that could have obliterated her at any second.

Oriana packed up her desk, no longer the girl who got off on the wrong floor, who didn't know how to type. *A woman or a man*. She'd be whoever she goddamn chose to be. If fat editor didn't have any professional standards, she refused to work for him. All she had was her name. She had seen her audience grow, her stories get more important.

But now she was without a paycheck. Her safety net ripped away, she was once more gripped by the humiliation of the *corridoio*. Her family was poor, she was less than. Babbo was catatonic, he might never work again. The family survival rested on her shoulders.

The press club was located in Piazza San Marco in a grand palazzo opposite her former university. She had heard Vittorio and the male den crowing about how they'd joined to rub elbows with important editors. Oriana would go to the club and find someone to give her a job.

On the walk over, she passed the medical building with its

arched colonnade and the excitement came back, entering the lab where she dissected cadavers (it stank like hell), the lecture hall where the professor quizzed them on functions of the brain. Her life had taken a sharp turn away from science, and she felt a stab of regret for the academic life she was missing. But she switched her thoughts and crossed the piazza, buried her pangs under a thickened professional skin.

A discreet brass sign on the palazzo read *Club Giornalisti*. This is it, she stepped into the cavernous marble foyer. A concierge in a white jacket and bow tie held up his hand to stop her. "Men only," he said.

"I'm not here to join." She knew the rules. "I'm here to find my director. He has an important phone call at the office," she lied.

The concierge looked her up and down and reluctantly let her by.

Ahead, she glimpsed an elegant, paneled room with floor-to-ceiling bookshelves and chandeliers. The books called to her, but she made her way toward the brass bar at the far end. The room was thick with smoke and the drone of men in suits. Young and octogenarian, each one stopped in mid-sentence and gawked as she passed.

"A whiskey, please," she said to the bartender, also dressed in a white jacket and bow tie. Oriana had heard Vittorio bragging about twelve-year-old Scottish whiskey at the club. Two old geezers bellied up to the bar and glowered, chomping on cigars.

"I can't serve you," the bartender said. Then quietly, "Everybody's watching."

"I'll take two whiskeys," a voice said. Oriana turned to find a familiar face, but she couldn't place it. Nino! The boy who'd saved her at the masturbation trial. They toasted, and she nearly choked on her whiskey but was grateful to Nino for the second time. He had landed a job at *la Repubblica*, he said. She widened her eyes, impressed, because Nino appeared meek but wasn't. He was climbing the ladder. "Try *L'Europeo*," Nino said, after she recounted her firing.

"But it's national. They won't hire me."

"I've followed you," he said. "You're good. Better than me."

The next morning, Oriana marched into *L'Europeo,* the most popular weekly in Italy. This time, her dress was store-bought and she wore kitten heels. Seeing Ava Gardner in person had taught her to paint on a curl of eyeliner with a pronounced upswing, and she'd become good at it.

The newsroom was buzzing. A crowd of desks, clacking typewriters, clippings plastered on the walls. All men, of course. Three in a clump, smoking.

"Honey, get us some espressos."

"I'm a reporter, I'm here for a job," she said. The men gave her the once-over and she worried they could see her chest thumping. "Where does Tommaso Giglio sit?"

They sniggered, elbowing each other in their expensive-looking suits.

"I'll take you," the ugliest one said, letting his hand brush against her bottom. She smacked it away.

"Ooh. She likes it rough."

"What's going on?" A different kind of man stepped out of a private office. Gray flannel suit, elegant pocket square, intelligent features. Calm but firm way of speaking.

"This woman, Tommaso. She wants a job." The ass-toucher smirked.

Tommaso Giglio's eyes swept over her, not unkindly. "You're late for your appointment." He tapped his watch. "Follow me."

Bewildered, she followed him into his office. He motioned her to the black leather sofa and she sat up straight, remembering to cross her ankles. "I don't have an appointment," she told the truth.

He shrugged and folded himself into the swivel chair opposite her, and it dawned on her that he already knew. Tommaso Giglio had a fairness few men had, certainly not the orangutans outside, and she'd landed in it.

Encouraged, she opened the manila file containing her clips. He remembered her story on London debutantes. "Very entertaining," he said. Briefly, he flipped through her articles, then set them down on the glass coffee table. "Why did you leave *Il Mattino*?"

"Bornello, the new editor," she said. "You know him, of course. *Cretino*."

Tommaso Giglio fought a smile.

She recounted her argument with the editor. "I do shit, and you can eat it."

Tommaso Giglio widened his eyes. Assessing her one more beat. "What's your greatest strength?"

"I'm not intimidated by anyone."

She didn't stop to think, yet the moment the words came out, she was surprised at how true they'd become. A childhood of fear had burned off the fear. Delivering a gun to a British soldier in hiding. Eating scraps of paper with the names of partisans so they wouldn't be intercepted. Conquering the typewriter so her family could eat. If life was a never-ending struggle, as her parents had drummed into her, Oriana had learned to fight.

Chapter 12

1973

It took four days to file her story on the Greek hero. She was a painstaking writer. She wasn't the kind who believed every word from her typewriter was earth-shattering genius. Frankly, the beginning of any piece, the blank page, made her doubt and suffer. But if she persevered, if she didn't give up even when she was lost in the forest, she conquered the chaos of too many ideas with no center, no logical order, and mysteriously, the story wove together.

"Don't cut a word," she ordered Tommaso, who was speed-reading her piece, swiveling in his leather chair. Her interviews ran extremely long but too bad if the copy editor pulled out his hair, if she took up five pages instead of two.

"I never do," Tommaso said without looking up.

"That's why I'm still writing for you."

She asked Lucia, who sat outside Tommaso's office, to call a taxi.

"Lucia Lucia." Mulotti strode in late as usual. "This is for you." He held out a long-stem rose.

"She doesn't want you, Mulotti." Oriana snatched the rose and tossed it in the trash.

"The queen has returned." Mulotti gave her a smarmy look. "Was he as handsome as his picture?"

"Who?" She stared stonily.

"The Greek. Who."

She felt herself flushing. "He's got one hell of a character. Who cares what he looks like?"

"That means yes." Mulotti followed her back to her desk. "Where to now?" He plunked himself down on her Samsonite.

"Off." She shoved him off. "I'm flying to New York in two hours." She let the prestige of that city hang in the air. "I'm invited on *60 Minutes* by Mike Wallace. Of course I'll see a Broadway show. *A Streetcar Named Desire* with James Farentino."

Mulotti gave an impressed nod, pushing out his bottom lip. "My uncle told me you were the most elegant writer he's ever met. Too bad things didn't work out with you two. You could have been my aunt."

She let out a laugh, too shocked to do anything else.

"I'm living with *Tio* Renzo now," Mullotti said.

"This is a place of business, dear boy. I don't give a damn about your personal life. What assignment are you working on? That's what we talk about here."

"Last time I told you that, you stole it from me. I'm keeping my mouth shut."

She grunted. "So you do learn."

On the way to the airport, she grew more incensed, the scene looping in her mind. "*Tio* Renzo." The little insect made her skin crawl, dangling his uncle's name. What else did Mulotti and *Tio* Renzo discuss about her? Never had she uttered that man's name, not in ten years; she had banished Renzo Gori from existence. She skipped over his byline in *Corriere*, ignored the only book he'd ever published (she still kicked herself over that one), and avoided like the plague his lunch spot in Piazza della Repubblica.

She tried to change her thoughts. What to wear on *60 Minutes*. The impudence of Mulotti. How unashamed he was of the nepotism that got him into *her* newsroom. As for his uncle, she'd surpassed him by light-years in their mutual profession.

“Have you ever seen a lion roar?” Gori had loomed over her that first time.

They had met at a Christmas party hours earlier. He had looked so sophisticated in his three-piece suit, his hair slicked back, but seeing him stark naked, his chest was puny and his back woolly as a sheep. She would have preferred to continue drinking Negronis and dancing the night away, but he had hurried her into a taxi. His bedroom was fastidiously decorated for a bachelor with a massive sleigh bed, oriental rug, polished highboy. Only in the Palazzo Pitti has she seen such fine furnishings.

“You’re like a doll with those eyes.” He pushed her down on the bed. “But I hear you’re a tiger at work. Insatiable.”

She was twenty-nine but had not the slightest idea what she was doing. Romance, she knew, would sweep her off her feet, the way it did Elizabeth Bennet and Scarlett O’Hara. This must be it, the moment Romance was happening to her, she thought as Gori positioned himself on top. She waited for him to caress her face, confess his passion, but instead he grew distant, fumbling below. Was he in? She didn’t think he was in. It never occurred to her to learn about her body, she was too busy surviving, and now she was a blank slate he would fill in. Her muscles clenched as if demonstrating a mind of their own, to keep this stranger out, but he forced himself inside.

“Have you ever seen a lion roar?” He threw back his head.

It hurt like hell. He stabbed her with it six or seven times and let out a long whistle.

Now he would hold her. They would make exciting plans for the weekend. But he only rolled off and folded his arms behind his head with a bored grunt. “I can’t sleep with another person in my bed. I’ll call you a taxi,” he said. “Get dressed.”

Flustered, she obeyed. Dear Renzo had to get up early. So did she. This is love, she thought in the taxi, her genitals sore and dripping. Now she and Renzo would go to the cinema and candlelit trattorias. She stocked her refrigerator and planned on inviting him for a thick, rare steak. But Renzo didn't call. He didn't introduce her to his professional circle with a possessive arm around her shoulder. More anguished every hour, she called him, but he had a business dinner, a trip out of town.

For the first time, she understood why Catherine took to bed after Heathcliff abandoned her in Wuthering Heights to earn his fortune. Perhaps she wasn't good at sex, or her body was shaped like a stick—that's why he wasn't calling. She bought a push-up bra, a clingy dress, and went to find him at Cafe Gilli, his lunch place.

"What are you doing here?" Renzo jumped up from his table. She stared at his dining companion, a blonde in a pillbox hat. "You're interrupting my meeting," he said, pulling Oriana toward the door.

"I wanted to see you before I leave for America." She gave him her most alluring smile. "Can I bring you back a gift?"

He stole a glance at his table. "Come to my flat at eight."

He answered in a towel. "*Ciao*, Miss America. What do you want me to do to you?" He pinned her against the wall.

Love me, the voice inside her said. But what came out was, "Make love to me."

He rubbed himself against her. "You're begging for it."

She closed her eyes to disappear from his lie or maybe how he saw through her. All she knew about being a woman was that you needed to belong to a man. It wasn't enough to be a journalist, even the best journalist. Her mother, the ladies in the neighborhood, all were paired off. If Oriana couldn't get a man, this man, she would be a pitiful failure.

Renzo led her into the bathroom. Why not the bedroom? She stole a glance at his sleigh bed and saw tangled sheets, a pillbox hat on the nightstand.

"Am I the best you've ever had?" He lifted her onto the

porcelain sink. Wrested off her underwear, his pinky ring scraping her thigh. "Tell me."

She closed her eyes and nodded.

Chapter 13

1973

The Manhattan skyline emerged all at once as her checker cab sped over the Triborough Bridge. The lit-up skyscrapers made her slide to the edge of her seat, their strength and sophistication setting off inside her the odd thrill of being home. New York had swept her away the first time she visited twenty years ago, and when the money came, Oriana didn't have to decide. She bought a two-bedroom in the same building where she'd rented her studio. The news focused on the high crime rate of New York, its near-bankruptcy, but Oriana felt among her kind in the city. People rushing to work with frenetic energy like hers, who had ambition and curiosity and were never satisfied. The entire city striving for greatness.

As a woman, she felt particularly at home in Manhattan, since *career* was less of a dirty word here. Florence was decades behind in equality. A woman like Oriana was unnatural, domineering, she needed to be slapped down and put in her place. Why? Because she worked her ass off and didn't rely on a man to feed her. Because she used her potential, one all women were born with but few had the chance to nurture and let blossom. Her own mother had suffered from suffocated potential. It had made Tosca miserable. That was not going to happen to her.

She greeted Raul, the doorman of her glass tower on East 57th Street. He swung her Samsonite out of the trunk and she spun around to take in Tiffany on the corner of Fifth Avenue,

Rizzoli her publisher just across the street. The traffic zooming past, brilliant lights, hordes of pedestrians. Oriana had traveled the world, but only here did she feel so expansive, as if a geyser of possibilities had burst open in the deepest recesses of her being.

Raul ushered her into the brass elevator that always upended her insides, and she clutched the rail as she zoomed up to the fourteenth floor. The moment she stepped into her living room, she got the usual jolt from her head-on view of the East River. The picture window was all serene sky and water, cargo ships and tugboats floating by. She darted through the rooms, exhilarated to be back, to be reminded, *This is my wonderful American air-conditioning, my ivory wall-to-wall carpeting where I sink my toes*. How hard she'd labored and what proof that she'd arrived, to have a home in this great city. In her business, it was the English language that counted, American media that counted, and Oriana had managed to get her byline into all the great newspapers and magazines of her adopted country.

It was 7 p.m. and she was starving. She changed into a burgundy pantsuit and ran out to meet Ingrid Bergman at Mamma Leone's. Her statuesque friend had just finished filming *Murder on the Orient Express* and was on her way home to London.

"*Ciao bella*," Oriana said as they double-kissed. Ingrid was already tucked into their usual table away from the window, and when she stood, Oriana took in her broad shoulders draped in a navy silk blouse, the legs that went on forever in casual slacks and flats. Always elegant but natural, her Swedish friend. When Ingrid first arrived in Hollywood, she made headlines for not wearing a hint of makeup. *You're too tall to be an actress*, studios discounted her. *Change your name, pluck your eyebrows, don't eat so much ice cream.* She showed them.

"You're the beauty," Ingrid said, eyes sparkling with humor. "Scandal agrees with you. Tell me everything."

What a voice, Oriana thought not for the first time, so deep it could be a man's, sexy and full of authority. They ordered a bottle of Cristal and she told Ingrid about her Kissinger face-to-face, her invitation to *60 Minutes*. "You know Mike Wallace, he goes for the knockout." Oriana gave her smoker's chuckle. "I'm climbing into the ring with him tomorrow."

"*Brava*, Oriana. Everyone watches his program."

"Americans are intrigued at the moment. The little Italian lady who broke Kissinger's balls." They clinked glasses on that one, *cin cin*. "Kissinger was the worst interview of my career, by the way," Oriana said. "I barely got him for an hour."

"It's never the things you think will make you a star," Ingrid said. "Life is a constant surprise. You go with it, or you lose your chance."

"Yes, *Casablanca* was a disaster, you told me," Oriana said. "They couldn't decide which man you'd end up with."

"Bogie was so mad at the script changes, he stayed in his trailer," Ingrid said. "I didn't know who I was supposed to love. *Play it in-between*, they said, so I did." Ingrid was fifty-eight, but her earthy glamour had only intensified. Oriana felt utterly reassured in the company of her friend that a woman could be daring and unconventional and she wasn't "crazy"—she was perfectly sane. In fact, she'd never met a woman as clear-eyed as Ingrid. The world was crazy, not them.

They talked about their mutual love of New York, the riches of Broadway, Carnegie Hall, the exotic restaurants and boutiques. It was *the* great international city, they agreed, having both seen the world.

"How's Lars?" Oriana said eventually.

"Feeling neglected. I'm never home. Why am I doing this play in New York, that movie in Hollywood?" Ingrid said. "It's a stage in my marriages. They think I'm dependent, but when I start to spread my wings, the trouble begins."

They launched into their favorite subject, how hard it was for a woman to pursue her ambition and at the same time love a man and raise a family. "More than hard," Oriana insisted. "It's impossible for a woman to have everything." Impossible on the level of Greek tragedy, she said, of Sisyphus pushing a rock uphill only to have it roll back down and squash every bone. Take the rare female leaders she had interviewed, Golda Meir and Indira Gandhi. To fulfill their destinies, both were forced to sacrifice marriage for country. Golda welled up with such tears of regret when she spoke of splitting with her husband, Oriana offered to stop the interview. "I feel guilty when I delve so far into a soul," she said.

"I can't give up my work for a man. Or even my children," Ingrid said. "Maybe for a month or two, but then I can't breathe."

"You were born to be an actress," Oriana said. "I, a writer."

"But why should our roles be so confined? Why must we limit ourselves?" Ingrid said.

"Because we didn't make up the rules," Oriana was quick to answer. "A man can have everything because there's a wife at home cooking, making kids do their homework, buying soap. A man would never accept being *the wife*." The two of them shared a laugh imagining the men they'd known even boiling water for pasta. "Love is a pain in the ass for women like us," Oriana said. "It's distracting and time-consuming and often a disaster, but we can't go to bed with our work."

"I do. With my scripts," Ingrid said. "They don't disappoint me."

They laughed with gusto, each recognizing in the other the warring needs of being a woman and wanting a bigger life, needs they could do nothing about. Something else bound them together. Ingrid was an "adulteress" just like Oriana. Ingrid's affair with director Roberto Rossellini had earned her a red letter "A" for getting pregnant while both were still married. She was denounced all the way to the United States Senate floor in 1950, called a "schizophrenic" and "a powerful influence for evil." The traitors in Hollywood shunned her, so Ingrid said *the hell with you* and spent the next eight years with Rossellini in Rome. That was where Oriana met her, at the film premiere of *Stromboli*. She walked right up to the world's most famous actress and said, "A man would never be so demonized. It's outrageous how you've been treated," and they cemented their bond.

Oriana, too, had broken the rules, sleeping with astronaut Pete Conrad. She had sat at the dinner table with Pete's wife and kids, eaten pot roast, pretended to be just a friend. Then five years with the married Pelou. They were women with real bodies, real appetites. "Opportunity knocked and I followed my heart," Ingrid once said. Oriana had done the same, but she'd made mistakes, too. No mistakes, Ingrid was firm. Regrets were for things you didn't do, not for things you did.

Still, *I don't know how she does it*, Oriana found herself thinking at Mamma Leone's as she buttered her roll. Ingrid's marriage to Rossellini had ended badly; she had even lost custody of their three kids, plus a daughter from her first marriage. Two families broken, yet Ingrid still kept her equilibrium and had even married again. Lars was a theater producer, and now she *visited* her children between acting projects, or they visited her on Lars's island in Sweden. Oriana doubted she could ever be so modern. She was too Italian, too ingrained in the Catholic edict of no divorce, of the Holy Mother. Ingrid's own mother had died when she was three. Perhaps that's why her friend was so unencumbered.

"I admire you, Ingrid. How you move forward and never look back," she said now.

"I've cried my eyes out, believe me. I thought my choices would work out, but they didn't. That's life." Ingrid shrugged. "Do you remember what I told reporters the day Hollywood welcomed me back? *Ingrid, are you sorry? Would you do it again and run off with Rossellini?*" She imitated the reporters who'd flocked her.

Of course Oriana remembered, and she emphasized each word. "Only I decide how I live."

The waiter Nicola hovered for a second time, so they ordered spicy baked clams to start and the house specialty, osso bucco. (Never spaghetti and meatballs—Oriana had tried it once, a portion fit for a glutton and drowned in sauce.) Over dinner, Ingrid entertained her with the story of a wealthy socialite who was turned away at La Côte Basque for wearing a pantsuit. The socialite promptly removed her pants and sailed into the snooty French restaurant wearing only her jacket and blouse.

"Good for her. I wish I'd thought of it," Oriana said. Last year, she, too, had been turned away for wearing pants at Lutèce. "Ladies should be dressed as ladies," she mocked the restaurant's policy. "What does that mean? White gloves? Girdles? That's why we come to Mamma Leone's. We can come nude and they let us in. Like Pan over there."

They smirked at the rococo statue of Pan with his fig-leafed penis, the plastic vines hanging from the ceiling. The décor was kitsch, but they were comfortable here. Oriana leaned in, enjoying Ingrid immensely, even if they saw each other only once or twice a year. They were both creative beings who portrayed other people and other worlds, Ingrid with her face on the screen and Oriana with her words. The only difference was that Ingrid had managed a rich home life. Perhaps there was still time, Oriana thought, since she was fourteen years younger.

"You haven't mentioned the Frenchman," Ingrid said.

Oriana's expression soured. "I'll never mention him again." She downed her champagne and recounted the grand finale with Pelou in Madrid. "All over the world, people know my name, but in my private life, crumbs. So, I confronted him."

"You did well," Ingrid said. "Five years is enough to make up his mind. And if you want a baby—"

"Too late for babies." Oriana smothered a wave of envy. An image came to her of Ingrid at Santa Marinella, her seaside home with Rossellini, swimming with three giggling monkeys hanging off her shoulders. Oriana had been invited to lunch, and she'd waded next to the family, mesmerized by the scene. Maybe Ingrid was an absent mother (she was like a father!), but she was a natural one, too, joyful and at ease.

"A toast," Ingrid said, raising her glass. "Good riddance to the monsieur. To someone new." Against her will, Oriana pictured the Greek hero standing over the sofa with white eyelet sheets, heard his *Let's go to bed*. She lowered her gaze, a smile spreading. Ingrid missed nothing. "Tell me about him," she said, her voice deepening.

"There's nothing to tell," Oriana said. "I'm not going to do anything."

Ingrid let out a ladylike belly laugh. "As if we have a choice, darling."

On the cab ride home, her thoughts were hijacked by Alexander Panagoulis. The way he'd lifted his polo shirt to show her his scar. The kiss in the garden of orange and lemon trees. Her cab sped past landmarks he had never seen. Radio City, where she liked to catch a good western movie. The neon lights of Times Square, its news ticker flashing the day's headlines. The centrality of her profession in this center of the universe.

Christ, she dreaded the night. Oriana climbed into her canopy bed with nagging doubts about her nomadic lifestyle, tonight New York, tomorrow Bonn or Beirut. Chasing the big story had always seemed crucial, but recently, she'd watched a fishmonger in San Lorenzo wrap fresh sardines in an article she'd written for *L'Europeo* just that week. Once, she would have ranted that people were lazy asses, they didn't give a fig about staying informed. Now she understood that her hard work barely made a difference in people's daily lives. And the years were slipping by. All at once she questioned her priorities. What was it Ingrid had said . . . *When you're young, work is more important than family. But as you get older, your hunger fulfilled, things change.*

Things had changed. Oriana was at the peak of her profession yet plagued by an empty feeling. *Is this all there is?* Outside her bedroom window, in all those skyscrapers, those little boxes of light, people were hosting dinner parties and playing music and making love. She felt cut off, buried beneath the layer of earth where human beings connected. Her days were filled with cold machinery—tape recorders, typewriters, airplanes. And strangers. She delved intimately into their lives for a few hours, then moved on, allowing no one to penetrate hers.

Her bed in New York was queen-size. She had learned to scatter her books and magazines on the side where a man might sleep, and it comforted her, cluttering up the empty space. Tonight, *Fear of Flying, The Gulag Archipelago*, and *Time* magazine with Billie Jean King on the cover (Could she beat Bobby Riggs in the *Battle of the Sexes*? Of course.) failed to do the trick. What would happen if she reached her fifties, or God forbid sixties, and still had no one? Only her parents had ever loved her, and soon they would be gone. Like every Mediterranean, she was tied with an umbilical cord to her family and vaguely assumed she would make her own someday. But how did people do it, she had no clue. Ingrid said opportunities came to her and she said yes, without worrying whether it was wise or not. Well, that strategy had failed miserably for Oriana. She had picked the wrong men, suffered when they didn't pick her. Her thoughts grew twisted anytime she ventured into this gray area, and she shook her head to be rid of them.

To lessen her aloneness, she slid to the middle of the mattress, but even as she did, she imagined Ingrid in a see-through negligee, cozying up with husband number three. What was it about Ingrid—was she was more seductive? impulsive? pragmatic?—that allowed her to have many children, many men, when Oriana had none?

Chapter 14

1957

She was twenty-eight and flying to Hollywood, a fantasyland for most Italians. Poor Italy was just recovering from the war, half the south had yet to institute indoor plumbing, its standard of living far below most of Europe's. America was paved with gold in comparison, and nobody Oriana knew had stepped foot there. Only *she* had managed to propose a monthlong series of articles titled *Hollywood Through a Keyhole*. If she was stuck with society reporting, she was going to peer into the most glamorous society in existence.

L'Europeo sent her with four hundred dollars for expenses, and Tommaso knew an Italian-American couple in Beverly Hills who offered hospitality in a room over their garage. Her English was good—she was excellent with languages—but mostly book-learned, and she felt wildly out of place as her hosts gave her a tour of the manicured lawns and walled estates of Bel Air, the glossy boutiques of Rodeo Drive clogged with convertibles and platinum blondes.

What were movie stars really like? Loyal readers awaited Oriana's reporting, but she didn't know a soul in Hollywood, had not the slightest idea how to break in. She was the daughter of an unemployed carpenter, on the big stage now and feeling less than. From grammar school, she had pushed herself to be the best in her class, the best little partisan. She had to push herself once more. *The only thing to do when you're scared is act.*

Oriana had splurged on just one evening dress for her trip, a black Valentino sheath. With the help of Livia, her host, she went to Sebastian's beauty salon, got her hair set by Jayne Mansfield's hairdresser and a manicure in the latest shade of orange-red.

In her new dress, white gloves, and rhinestone sandals, she went to Ciro's on Sunset Boulevard, sat at the bar, and ordered a whiskey sour, which went down like lemonade. The nightclub was a celebrity hot spot, according to Louella Parsons, whose gossip column she now read avidly. Was that Natalie Wood on the dance floor near the orchestra? Oriana stared at the sequined teenager throwing back her long dark mane. She'd loved Natalie in *Rebel Without a Cause*, but it wasn't her. A handsome man approached the bar. He resembled Dean Martin, the nice Italian boy, but no, he was a waiter. Everybody looked like somebody, but not one star.

Farther down Sunset, she tried Mocambo, ordering a martini. Nothing. Martinis should be renamed rubbing alcohol, and what a sad excuse for olives. As a last-ditch effort, she went to Chasen's on Beverly Boulevard with its autographed photos on the walls and ordered a crabmeat cocktail. Delicious, but still nobody. Her first deadline loomed, and she was fast running through her allowance. If she failed to dig up stories, *L'Europeo* would send her home. Tipsy, Oriana turned over her dilemma as she chewed her last crab claw.

Celebrities were normal people who slept and ate and sat on the toilet just like she did. What else did normal people do? Grocery shopping? Maids would do that. The next day was Sunday. What did people back home do on Sundays?

She got up early, donned a hat and gloves, and attended mass at Church of the Good Shepherd in Beverly Hills. Victory. Lined up in the front pews were good Catholics Gregory Peck, Loretta Young, Jane Russell, and—what was his name? Ricardo Montalban. The stars were dressed in their Sunday best, bowing alongside husbands, wives, and children.

Oriana made mental notes watching the actors and actresses

sing *Holy God we praise thy name* and line up for Communion. She lined up, too. Every Sunday of her childhood, her parents had walked her down the long nave of the Duomo, and she'd stared up at frescoes of Vasari's *Last Judgement* to relieve her boredom until her neck ached. Her mother still attended church, but Oriana had stopped believing. Still, this host she would take.

The next day, she filed her inaugural dispatch from Hollywood, being honest with readers about her outsider status. She brought them along on her celebrity-spotting quest, from her defeats at fancy nightspots to her jackpot at church. Oriana hadn't landed an interview *yet,* but she could entertain readers with her dramatic eye. *Gregory Peck appears to be the most devout star with his nose stuck in his mass book. He towers above the congregation even when he is kneeling. What could he be praying for with such piety when he has everything? Including a closet full of custom Brioni suits Mr. Peck took home from our country after starring in* Roman Holiday. *He looks far more elegant than the gentlemen who surround him in their boxy American suits. Amen, Italian tailoring.*

Her Catholic readers ate it up.

No one would speak to her at Joseph Cotten's party. She had wrangled an invitation to his Pacific Palisades home through her hosts, but on a terrace overlooking the ocean, the stars chatted and admired the sunset but gave her the cold shoulder. Worse, everyone was coupled up. David Niven, that handsome blue-eyed Brit with the pencil mustache, spoke into the ear of a redheaded actress whose name escaped her. An enormous Orson Welles towered over his aristocratic Italian wife, Paola Mori. Even she ignored Oriana, refusing to look away from her fascinating conversation with songwriter Cole Porter, except to give her the shrewd Italian once-over. Was Oriana from the right class? Were her dress and shoes impeccable? No, dammit, she was not a contessa like Mori, and she had committed a fashion faux pas.

In her apartment over the garage, Oriana had fretted over how to dress—formal or casual, day or evening? She had discarded the clingy Valentino sheath at the last moment and decided on a safer ivory suit. The trendy blue eye shadow made her look like a clown, so she wiped it off, leaving just a trace. Fire red lipstick, thinly arched eyebrows. She pulled back to assess herself in the mirror. That should do it.

But now she was hot and overdressed, the women wore strappy sundresses, and her makeup was melting in the sun. A maid in a white apron served a drink called Tom Collins, and Oriana gulped her second, then had to pee. She wandered around the cliffside palace thinking it was a good thing Cotten, a stage actor who struggled in Hollywood, was cast by his buddy Welles in *Citizen Kane* so he could afford such luxury. Finally a second maid pointed her to the bathroom and she locked herself in. Celebrities were rude. What made her think she should come here alone, a nobody? She hated Hollywood and its artificiality and she would leave.

At the front door, the giant Orson Welles threw out his arms and blocked her. He had left his wife on the patio. Did he have a fetish for Italian women?

"Don't go," Welles said. "We're all hounded by press so we're a bit rude. You're from Italy, I hear."

"Florence." She thrust out her hand and introduced herself.

His wife was from an old family in Rome, Welles said. Did she know them? Not personally, Oriana answered in her snootiest tone, but she knew the name.

"Our fathers both fought in the Resistance against Mussolini," Oriana said, having done her homework. "But your wife is too busy to speak with me."

"We're jet-lagged. Just returned from Portofino," Welles

said. "Your country is gorgeous, like its women." Was he flirting? Who cared. Oriana saw her chance.

"Mr. Welles. I didn't come to Hollywood to ask the usual questions. I don't give a damn about who is committing adultery and who is divorcing whom." It wasn't the truth, she wanted those details, too. "How did they start their careers, how did they learn their art? That's what I want to know."

Welles looked into her eyes and seemed to grasp her intelligence. She grasped his. "You're not the typical society reporter," he said.

"You're not the typical actor–director–radio man," she said. The word *genius* was overused, but Welles fit the bill.

He boomed a hearty laugh. "Whom would you like to meet?"

That same week, she went on set with Glenn Ford at Columbia Pictures. He was filming a new western and was taking a break in a tall director's chair. She hoisted herself onto the chair next to him, and, tape recorder rolling, interviewed him about his service in the Marines and breaking into the movies. She was intrigued by the many professionals bustling around the set, so he pointed out the director and the cinematographer and explained what a script supervisor did.

ORIANA FALLACI: Who is your favorite co-star, Mr. Ford?

GLENN FORD: Rita Hayworth. She's really very shy, the opposite of the femme fatales she's portrayed.

Ford pronounced her name with adoration. Oriana had read rumors of their steamy affair while filming *Gilda* although both were married. She wondered with a pinch of envy if a man would ever express that kind of adoration for her.

"May I have that for my article?" Oriana cornered the publicity man who snapped their picture.

When her story ran in *L'Europeo*, she presented it in a Q and

A format to help readers imagine they were on the soundstage, too, eavesdropping on the conversation.

The issue sold out, but colleagues mocked her for posing in the photo with Ford. *Who does Fallaci think she is? Prima donna, sitting in the director's chair.* Jealousy, of course, but it infuriated her. How hard she worked, and how they tried to knock her down.

Glenn Ford provided an introduction to his pal William Holden, who greeted her in bathing trunks, lounging around the pool of his modern ranch home. "How about a swim?" he said as she appreciated his stunning physique.

"I don't have a swimsuit," she said, wearing the sundress she'd finally splurged for. Holden escorted her to a cabana with a drawer full of women's bathing suits. "Pick any one you like. Keep it." She was jittery about appearing in a swimsuit before the movie icon, but fascinated, too, to have landed in the lap of Hollywood luxury. She chose a red Chanel one-piece with a gold ring between the cups and the sales tags still attached. She imagined Audrey Hepburn shopping for these suits. She and Holden had fallen in love filming *Sabrina*, and he was ready to leave his wife, but Hepburn ultimately said no, because apparently he couldn't have children.

He sure looked virile enough, eyeing Oriana with approval as she sailed out of the cabana. She was not accustomed to performing her interviews half-naked, but she was accustomed to that look from Italian men, and she knew how to handle it. Smile, smile and move purposefully to the pool to get your work done. Holden followed.

She didn't know how to swim but refused to let on, wading in the aqua shallows as the suave Holden somersaulted off the diving board. He did two showy laps, then leapt out, shaking droplets from his hair, and offered her a whiskey. It was noon but she'd learned of his dependence on alcohol and managed to keep up, taking small sips of the hard stuff. They sprawled in lounge chairs and Holden's butler served them club sandwiches. The California sun was glorious, the chairs cushioned and tilted back. Bizarrely, it felt like the life Oriana was meant to lead. The life her mother always wanted for her. Work, fly.

ORIANA FALLACI: Mr. Holden, you won the Oscar for *Sunset Boulevard*, but initially Montgomery Clift was set to star and he pulled out. How much of your business is luck?

WILLIAM HOLDEN: All of it.

ORIANA FALLACI: What about talent?

WILLIAM HOLDEN: Luck first. When I was shooting my first movie, *Golden Boy*, I was so bad, the producers were about to fire me. If Barbara Stanwyck hadn't stood up for me and said, "Give him a chance," I wouldn't have a career.

Oriana studied Cecil B. DeMille's biography until two in the morning before arriving at Paramount Studios to interview the founder of American cinema. His secretary had given specific instructions, which she followed exactly: Arrive early, dress smart, ask polite questions.

In her Valentino sheath and pearls, she entered the executive building on the lot, and the secretary ushered her into the imposing corner office. DeMille greeted her with firecracker energy despite being almost eighty. She flashed her most bewitching smile, removed her gloves to shake his hand, and settled across from the producer-director at his desk, congratulating herself on landing the big fish. At that exact moment, her eyes landed on it, the framed poster of *The Ten Commandments* hanging behind DeMille's shiny bald head. His biggest blockbuster had just been widely released—but she hadn't seen it.

As her mistake was sinking in, he tented his hands. "So, my dear," he said, "what did you think of my latest film?"

Should she invent a vague compliment? Lying was against her principles. "I didn't see it yet, Mr. DeMille."

Silence. The executive secretary who'd remained in the room stared at her steno pad.

"See it tonight," DeMille said. "Betty will make a reservation at the Beverly. Come back tomorrow when she can squeeze you in." He dismissed her, though not unkindly.

Her cheeks flamed as she left the office. How could she slip up so badly, like an amateur? Never again. From now on, she would prepare even more obsessively.

The next day, she returned for a four o'clock appointment, relieved to be able to tell DeMille she very much admired his baby. "The anti-slavery message is moving. *Let my people go*. And Charlton Heston is a god."

DeMille tilted back in his leather wingback, toking on his cigar. "I cast him because he's an ancient Egypt buff. Rattled off facts at his audition." DeMille had made Heston a star.

"I like his voice," Oriana said. "I am a great analyzer of the voice."

"That's me doing the narration," DeMille said.

"I recognized you," she said. "Your acting training served you well."

"And God said let there be light, and there was light," he reenacted his voice-over.

"Bravo." Oriana clapped, humoring him.

The Ten Commandments had the biggest production budget of all time, DeMille said. The largest set ever built, the most extras ever used.

Biggest, most, best, she made a mental note of his speech. Fifteen minutes later, he escorted her out, his next appointment waiting. "See *The Ten Commandments* again with friends. Once is not enough," DeMille said.

Aha! He was carrying on the legacy of his father, a lay

minister, Oriana realized, hoping to spread the faith to millions. Sure, sure, she shook his hand. She liked this man who had given her a second chance, who sat atop the Hollywood food chain, but there was no way she could endure that four-hour Bible lesson again. MY FAUX PAS WITH THE FOUNDER OF HOLLYWOOD, her headline read.

One star eluded her, Marilyn Monroe, the very one Italians were desperate to know more about. Monroe had recently married playwright Arthur Miller, filmed *The Prince and the Showgirl* (addicted to barbiturates and forgetting her lines), and gone on hiatus, even wearing a disguise when she ventured out. No one knew where she was.

Oriana had loyal readers to appease and refused to give up the hunt. She went to La Rue on Sunset, home of the power lunch, and spotted Louella Parsons sitting alone in a much-desired gold booth (rather than the red booths reserved for the hoi polloi). Oriana froze, finding herself without the gumption to approach. But how could she squander this one chance? She squared her shoulders and made her feet move.

"Miss Parsons, I am Oriana Fallaci, a journalist from Europe and a great admirer. May I sit down?"

The gossip columnist stared frostily, assessing Oriana for an eternity before giving an imperious nod. By sheer coincidence, Miss Parsons had just vacationed in Florence. In fact, she'd purchased the woven leather clutch she was carrying on Via Tornabuoni. Oriana oohed and aahed over the handbag and promised to bring Miss Parsons leather gloves from Madova, the best, the next time she came to Hollywood. At that, Louella ordered her guest a martini, and Oriana recounted her travails in tracking down Marilyn.

"Do you know where I might find her?" Oriana said.

Louella smirked. "Why would I tell you?" She tapped her ashes.

Oriana realized her mistake. Obviously the prominent columnist wouldn't divulge her leads. Quickly, she changed tactic, leaning toward Miss Parsons with the deference one would pay a mentor. (If Oriana ever had a mentor, which she didn't, doing everything in this damn life by herself.) Louella Parsons was a force in show business. She could make or break an acting career or movie box office with just one sentence. A woman could wield *that* kind of power in journalism—Oriana saw living proof for the very first time. The woman sitting before her in this booth.

"Miss Parsons. How did you become the most famous gossip columnist in the world, carried in six hundred papers?" Oriana held still for the answer.

Louella studied her shrewdly, then seemed to decide she was worth the answer. "I tell the truth, even if it hurts," she said, waving her gold cigarette holder. "People fear the truth. That's my power."

But Oriana did the same—she told the truth! Emboldened, she resolved never to hold back, even if she was mean. Even if it hurt. She wanted to wield the same kind of power as Louella, the power of the pen.

The next day a miracle happened. Louella Parsons wrote in her column *Will the Italian newswoman ever find Marilyn?* Louella described Miss Fallaci as *the elegantly dressed Florentine with the musical accent who is turning over every stone to scoop her American colleagues, and she probably will.* Oriana's profile shot up instantly. She became "the Italian lady" in town. Still no Marilyn, but she had a story for her readers: I WAS CHASING MARILYN AND ALL HOLLYWOOD KNEW IT.

Chapter 15

1958 to 1964

Her grand adventure, *Hollywood Through a Keyhole*, ended too soon and Oriana flew home to Italy. Readers flocked to her byline. Her Q and A format was new and easy to read. It drew people in, giving them a front-row seat to her tête-à-têtes with the rich and famous.

Tommaso and the director were ecstatic at *L'Europeo*'s jump in circulation. The director increased Oriana's pay and offered her a contract to sign, her first. She floated back to her desk feeling financially secure for a change, the nightmare of the *corridoio* behind her, only to see some clown had pasted a photo on the wall. There she was with William Holden in her red Chanel swimsuit, posing on the steps of his kidney-shaped pool. *Cutest ass in the business*, they'd written in black marker, with an arrow pointing to her backside.

She ripped it down. Naturally the male den had to demean her. She was rubbing elbows with movie stars and they had never left the country. Even more galling, Oriana had proposed a new series of articles, *America Seen by an Italian Lady*, and convinced Tommaso to say yes and give her a bigger allowance. Still covering Hollywood, she added New York to her beat, widening her perch.

She fell head over heels for her new city. Forty-Second Street with its neon marquees and buttered popcorn, its adult peep shows tucked in not so discreetly. Macy's eight floors, where she rode the wooden escalators with panic in her chest. The *Saturday*

Evening Post and its heartwarming Norman Rockwell covers. The rare bookshops she entered like a church. A hot pretzel with mustard on the street.

Like any good transplant, Oriana constantly compared her two cities. She missed the sun on her skin in the flowered piazzas of Florence. The only sun in Manhattan was an orange ball reflected in glass skyscrapers. In New York, she had to be a tiger to accomplish the smallest task, for instance hailing a yellow taxi when on every corner she faced a competitor. It was kill or be killed in her adopted home, but Oriana had never backed down from a challenge. Besides, she wasn't a freak of nature in Manhattan, where thousands of women woke up every morning not to iron tablecloths or wash windows but to rush to work.

For two years, she filed a story a week from America and met so many famous people, fame no longer fazed her. Spurred on by Louella Parsons's advice, she let loose her irreverence, weary of celebrities and their privilege, the way society fawned over them. Her interviews grew more prickly and opinionated. If she didn't like a subject, she made it clear. Hugh Hefner, the founder of *Playboy,* who greeted her in pajamas in his Chicago mansion, was a hypocrite. He rejected American Puritanism but looked down on any woman who dared to be as promiscuous as he. Muhammad Ali was rude. In his Florida home, he devoured a platter of fruit and belched three times in her face. The final time was a long one, *Buuuurp*. "Do you think I came all the way to Miami to be insulted?" she scolded. "I refuse to interview you." She packed up, but he grabbed her microphone and flung it against the wall. Hearing the noise, three bodyguards rushed the door. Frightened, she backed out of the room, fleeing to her waiting taxi, but she reported her poor impression of Ali's behavior.

Oriana discovered she was good at telling the truth, even if it hurt.

A few stars she liked. Sean Connery was so friendly and down to earth, they went to see a movie together after the interview. To her astonishment, he stood on the long Manhattan ticket line like everybody else.

A small publisher came calling, eager to collect her celebrity interviews into a book. Her childhood dream! But when Oriana held *Seven Sins of Hollywood* in her hands, saw her name on the cover, and opened its new-smelling pages, she fell to earth. This wasn't the book she was meant to write. It was gossipy and insignificant. Yes, she'd been unflinchingly honest, unmasking each celebrity to reveal the true person, but by giving them *more* attention, she had only contributed to their absurd status. And now she would be associated with "women's stories" forever. The Brotherhood of Macho Authors had already declared her book "shallow." It hurt, but she knew the reason for the put-downs. Only those with a phallus could author books in Italy.

Ironically, *Seven Sins of Hollywood* sold like crazy and was translated into five languages, bringing more fame and money. The first thing Oriana did was set up a monthly deposit into her parents' bank account, so they wouldn't have to ask or worry.

If she intended to do serious work, she'd better start now, she decided. In New York, she rented a studio apartment on 57th Street off Fifth Avenue, a tiny closet for an exorbitant $270 a month. She had forgotten her fear of elevators and clutched the rail each time it zoomed to the twelfth floor.

Intellectuals and leaders, that's who she was keen to interview. "Then that's what you'll do," Tommaso said. She scoured the competition, the *Sunday New York Times Magazine*, *Life*, *Saturday Evening Post*, searching for examples of serious interviews, but to her amazement, nobody was publishing the long Q and A, which had become her signature. Nobody except *Playboy,* that is. Hugh Hefner had recently hired prominent writers to sit down with Martin Luther King Jr., Walter

Cronkite, Jean-Paul Sartre, Vladimir Nabokov, the Beatles. How that demon of sex, with a pipe in one hand and a bunny in the other, had hit upon a quality idea was beyond her. All of a sudden, serious people were reading *Playboy* for the articles. "The Playboy Interview" had become a mark of culture. Oriana felt pressure to hurry up and publish her own portraits before she was accused of imitating *Playboy*. What an insult that would be, since she was publishing her Q and A's *first*.

She met Norman Mailer in his native Brooklyn, taking an expensive cab ride in traffic and arriving thirty minutes late. His stately townhouse was exactly like the one she dreamed of owning someday. This one even boasted a pop-up view of Manhattan skyscrapers across the river. Luckily, Mailer was busy rattling ice cubes in his gin (he drank every night, her research revealed) and seemed oblivious to her lateness.

He had the kind of blue eyes that hurt to look into and a bullish sexual energy that demanded attention, like another person in the room. His hair was tightly curled, his physique squat and muscular, and his nose, broken from boxing, gave him a coarse look. Mailer had become famous at twenty-five for his novel *The Naked and the Dead* and had been playing the literary bad boy ever since.

"Want to see my study?" Mailer asked. He wrote in the attic and the only access was a rope ladder. Gamely, Oriana took off her heels and held her skirt close, knowing she was entering the lion's den. Upstairs, Mailer's study resembled a sea captain's roost with a dazzling river view and paneled walls packed with books, including engineering books from his four years at Harvard.

She switched on her tape recorder and asked him about the image of America in his work. His answers meandered. Capitalism was ruining America, people suffered from alienation, only the young gave him hope. All the while, Oriana watched him, trying to penetrate who Mailer really was.

"One thing I don't understand about you, Mr. Mailer," she said. "You say the times are violent yet you defend violence. You even stabbed your wife near her heart when you were running for mayor. How do you explain such behavior?" He had nearly killed the woman, been committed to Bellevue Hospital for psychiatric evaluation, and served probation.

"I like wives I can punch sometimes," he said, "and wives who punch me."

"Are you joking?" He shook his head as if he hadn't said anything revolting. "You seem to like being married, Mr. Mailer, though you believe in beating women. Why have you married four times?"

He spoke abstractly but finally said, "If I didn't have a wife, I would be out every night looking for one."

"I've heard you have many mistresses."

"Women are a sport I'm good at," he said, downing another gin.

Thus they arrived at the topic of sex, Mailer's fixation, and he veered onto who made better lovers, Italian or American men. Mailer puffed out his chest and argued the case for his countrymen. Christ, was he going to lunge at her to prove it? His lopsided blue eyes waited for the go-ahead. For an instant, she pictured rolling around on Miller's daybed, stained with God knows what. His aggression resembled a construction worker's, which she didn't find the least bit appealing. And Oriana never slept with her subjects, despite the fantasies of her detractors.

"Let's talk about President Johnson." She changed the subject, and to her relief, Mailer dropped his peacock feathers and followed.

One month later, Oriana flew to India to interview the Dalai Lama, a much more relaxing man. She met him in the simple wooden hut at the foot of the Himalayas where he'd fled after Chinese Communists took over Tibet. Even as a refugee, his eyes twinkled and his voice was cheery in the flower-filled garden where they sat. In the presence of this monk who meditated for hours, Oriana had the impression of being a battering ram, and she tried to calm her energy by slowing her breath to match his. Impossible, she was the opposite of him.

He seemed sad about being taken away from his parents at age two to become the leader of Tibetan Buddhism. Sad but resigned. "If I could have chosen my own destiny, I would have been a mechanic. Better yet, an astronaut on a rocket to the moon."

Oriana pictured the Dalai Lama in a puffy white astronaut's suit. This spiritual man was giving her a peek into his secret desires. It would be a strong reveal for her piece, the moment of gold.

People were fascinating. Since the days of burying her nose in red leather classics, she had been obsessed with peeling back characters' façades to uncover hidden motivations, fears, fantasies. Oriana had a knack for the serious interview, she was discovering, for drawing out the essence of a renowned writer, senator, religious leader. Figuring out what made people tick satisfied her in a way that was difficult to describe, as if she'd gotten one step closer to unlocking her own mystery. The one that said we were all riddled with contradictions, flaws, longings—all terribly human in the end.

The number one rule of interviewing, she decided: Never be boring. Oriana pushed herself to ask daring, impolite questions, to avoid clichés and ass kissing. Number two: Be alert and focused yet *relaxed* in your conversation, to put subjects at ease. You could not be nervous and conduct good interviews. Number three: Study every known detail about your subject, then put aside your notes and listen. If you shut up and gave people space, they would reveal themselves to you, deliver the golden moment. Number four: Prepare to be disliked. If you hit on a good rapport, fine, but if the encounter was uncomfortable or hostile, with arguing or shouting, that was fine, too.

With each interview, Oriana grew bolder, discovering her greatest skill was in asking the thorny, embarrassing questions that somehow didn't embarrass her.

L'Europeo's circulation jumped from 25,000 to 100,000. Tommaso offered her another raise. It was not enough. She wanted more. She could leave for another magazine, she threatened, when really she was loyal by nature and had no desire to start over in a strange newsroom. She liked belonging to a family, even if that family kicked her and pissed her off.

"Fine, let's go see the director," Tommaso said.

"What did he say about me?" she asked as they climbed the stairs.

Tommaso sighed. *"Do what you have to do, but keep that little bitch here."*

A red-hot fury swooshed to her head. "Your little bitch wants a raise," she said, marching into the director's office. "Equal to what Gianni Volpero makes." He was the highest-paid journalist at *L'Europeo* in Milan, and she'd wrangled the number out of Tommaso. "No," she changed her mind, "I want fifty percent more. And to republish my articles anywhere I like, keeping the profits."

The director agreed to her terms, laughing off his "little bitch" comment and calling her their *star reporter*. "Your writing is unmatched, Oriana, you're a true talent."

For a moment she was thrown. She hadn't expected to win so easily. Thank God she'd been demanding and expressed her rage. The director didn't hand out compliments easily, yet here she was, better than any man, the top earner.

Three days later, when news of her jaw-dropping salary had made the rounds, she opened her mail to find a caricature drawn in ink. It was a crude attempt at her likeness—almond eyes, curled eyeliner—plus a wart on her nose and a pointy black hat. The caption read, *The witch of Piazza Carlo*. Piazza Carlo Goldoni was the address of *L'Europeo*.

Her eyes blurred. She crumpled the drawing into a ball, that one gesture powering her legs to move. "Which one of you vulgarians sent this?" She hurled the drawing at the male den.

One of them opened it. "Oriana, *ma no*. We're friends. We would never do this." The others ducked and shrugged.

"If a man quadrupled circulation, you'd be licking his balls," she yelled. Briefly, she saw herself through their eyes, willful, successful, foul-mouthed. Nothing like their docile wives and mammas locked at home ironing towels, curtains, even their underwear for crissake. "Jackasses," she said, dripping with contempt. "I have to be a witch in this business, or I'd get eaten alive."

In November 1964, wearing her Valentino sheath and pearls, she interviewed Senator Robert Kennedy at the Carlyle Hotel, where he kept an apartment. She had mistakenly walked to the Pierre, confusing the two hotels, and arrived flustered, but she always set out early, and he was late. The Kennedy name was mythic in Italy, just as it was in America, and the assassination of President Kennedy had hit Italians hard, including her. She was buzzing with anticipation to meet the younger brother. Robert Kennedy had just won the Senate seat in New York and appeared poised to carry on the family legacy. She might be meeting the next president, she knew, picking lint off her dress and crossing her ankles on the gray tufted sofa. She pressed *Record* to check her battery indicator. Good, plenty of juice. Shit! The tape got tangled in the roller. Quickly, she ripped it out and popped in a fresh cassette. Thank goodness she always brought plenty.

"It's my nephew John-John's birthday," Senator Kennedy said, striding into the living room. "I've got thirty-five minutes before his party." She extended her hand, disappointed he was giving her so little time, though she would include this detail in her article, to show he had assumed the paternal role.

Senator Kennedy sat beside her on the sofa, so she had to turn fully sideways to see him, dizzied by his all-American good looks. To steady herself, she took in one feature at a time, the blue hooded eyes, sharp nose, rabbitlike front teeth. His arms were muscular in white shirtsleeves rolled up to reveal blond arm hair.

Fleetingly, she envied his wife, Ethel, who was near this handsomeness all the time. They had lots of sex, obviously. His libido was on display in the photograph over his shoulder that featured eight or nine children.

The senator was lousy at being interviewed, unlike his relaxed, witty brother. Robert was introverted, even blushing profusely, but underneath his exterior she sensed he was tightly wound, and if he exploded, watch out.

She couldn't break the ice. Probably his brother's murder had made him distrustful, defensive. There was a bodyguard in the room. She had already taken note of the four framed photographs of Bobby and the late president on the end tables and bookcase.

She persevered, asking Senator Kennedy the very questions people discussed behind his back. Was his ultimate goal to follow in his brother's footsteps and become president? No, he was happy being a senator. But his term would end one day. He was focused only on being a good senator. She showed him news clippings in which many criticized him and called him ruthless. "Do you know why?" she asked. He wasn't going to guess why people called him ruthless or any other name, he said.

Very soon, she asked the big one. "Are you afraid of being murdered, too?" Bobby was not, he insisted. Could they talk about something else? He blushed and stared at his shoes and, very soon, politely shook her hand, ending their appointment.

On the walk home, she berated herself for the lousy interview. Frankly, she was relieved to escape the man, he was so buttoned up, the encounter had been exhausting. Should she have skipped the assassination question? Absolutely not, readers wanted to know if Robert Kennedy worried about a fatal shot.

She hadn't extracted any news but began to analyze Senator Kennedy as if he were a character in a novel. He appeared deeply affected, even traumatized, by the violent loss of his brother. Afraid, with good reason, that he would be robbed of the chance to raise his own brood. The mantle of being a Kennedy weighed heavily on his shoulders. She felt moved, suddenly, by the choiceless younger brother.

Politicians, Oriana realized, were written about in a dry, boring way, but they were full of human drama. Birthday parties, photos of dead brothers, dynastic ambitions, complex motives to seek power. She would write about politicians in a new way, the way she wrote about actors and writers, using her Q and A signature. Nothing beat the Q and A for portraying the real person. By reporting dialogue word for word, she could reveal what was hidden in people's hearts. Some deep-seated truth. Raw emotion. Pressing need or desire.

Ever since Oriana broke into this damn profession, she'd been warned politics was too complicated for the female pea brain. Nobody would take a woman's reporting of hard news seriously, not when she had breasts to stare at instead. Oriana would prove the journalistic establishment wrong. She would cover politics the way she had covered every other bloody topic, better than any man.

L'Europeo published her Kennedy cover story with the headline AN ORIANA FALLACI EXCLUSIVE. The photo featured Bobby sitting close to her on the sofa, listening intently. She had asked the bodyguard to snap it with her own camera. Tommaso and the director took her to lunch to celebrate. It was exhilarating to be the only Italian journalist to land a Kennedy. To be the only woman to triumph on this scale, toasted with Negronis at Bernardo's, a watering hole for the all-male press corp.

When Oriana returned to the newsroom, cheery from cocktails and her turn away from Hollywood to more substantial subjects, she walked into a huddle of peers griping behind her back.

"How did she get Kennedy?"

"How do you think?" The speaker made a fist and slid it up and down near his mouth. "Oriana Fellatio." His audience snickered.

Their ridicule sliced through her professional skin. She who had never traded sex for a story, who worked like a dog. A lump rose in her throat but she stomped over to the fellatio gesturer. Got close to that filthy mouth of his. Her eyes narrowed with scorn.

"You do that with skill," she said. "You should give lessons."

Chapter 16

1973

In the morning, all worries about a personal life were erased by the urgent need to prepare for *60 Minutes* and know her stuff, no room for mistakes. Oriana dashed down to the corner newsstand on Madison Avenue to buy *The New York Times,* then sat at the Chock full o'Nuts counter with coffee and a corn muffin, catching up on American news like a student cramming for exams. Nixon accepted responsibility, but not blame, for the Watergate break-in. He was under pressure to release White House tapes. The American bombing of Cambodia was officially over, ending twelve years of fighting in Southeast Asia (for what, no one knew). The stunning technological feat called the World Trade Center had been dedicated by Governor Rockefeller. She flipped through the thick issue. The earth kept spinning and vomiting up stories, which meant she would never rest.

By 9 a.m., she was parked in her stylist's chair at Elizabeth Arden for a blow dry and manicure. Hurrying home to the full-length mirror in her bedroom, she decided on bell-bottom jeans and a navy Fila T-shirt with long sleeves. No pantsuits, she wouldn't try too hard. The face was a different story. She took care lining her eyes, making sure to curl *up* so she wouldn't look worn out, and applied frosted pink lipstick.

The shoot would take place in her study. She surveyed her leather chesterfield, Tiffany lamp, bookshelves lined with first editions of *Wuthering Heights, War and Peace, Call of the Wild.* She had an obsession with first editions, hunting them down at Argosy on 59th Street and trembling each time she laid her hands on one.

The mess of papers on her oak desk needed tidying. Hastily she straightened piles and hid pay stubs that were nobody's business. Wallace would grill her about Kissinger, of course.

What happened with Kissinger was this:

She arrived at 1600 Pennsylvania Avenue wearing a plaid blazer and flared pants, her tape recorder slung over her shoulder in its black case. The deputy press secretary, a tightly wound young man, escorted her down the blue carpet to the west wing, where she was impressed by the neoclassical architecture but even more by its pristine condition. Her beloved landmarks in Florence—Giotto's Tower, the Uffizi, so much older and grander—never had the money for such scrupulous preservation.

Henry Kissinger was Nixon's closest advisor, and he greeted her solemnly in his office wearing a dull gray suit and duller tie. He had granted her a rare interview just three days after receiving her letter. Oriana had no idea why, except her reputation had skyrocketed to the point where it was prestigious for heads of state to sit down with her. Kissinger certainly oozed self-importance. He must be craving to join her club.

Her neck was stiff with tension because she took her work damn seriously. She wanted to perform well. But she was not intimidated. Her father's voice, *No one is better than you, we are all equals*. As she shook Kissinger's hand, she gave him a skeptical look that said she doubted he deserved all this status.

The first thing the national security advisor did was turn his back and read a thick report, to assert dominance, she understood. Oriana settled on the chintz sofa and coolly offered him a cigarette. He declined and kept reading. How it triggered her fury when people acted superior. She lit up and gazed through the floor-to-ceiling windows to the Rose Garden. Then back at Kissinger's short, pudgy physique. What did women see in this alleged ladies' man? His eyes were blue but beady under heavy horn-rimmed glasses. And that droning voice could put you to sleep.

Dr. Kissinger presumed he was important because he held a Ph.D., because there were two phones on his glossy mahogany desk, red and black, and a dozen photographs on the credenza of him with Nixon. She wasn't impressed by any of it. In fact, she was disgusted that he sat in his fancy office deciding the fate of innocent soldiers and civilians in Vietnam.

At last, Kissinger put down his report and arranged himself in an armchair that towered above her.

She pounced, so he couldn't escape her again. "Dr. Kissinger, the cease-fire you promised in Vietnam has not materialized. Were you wrong, that peace was near?"

"I was not wrong. No." He insisted the war would end soon because the administration had decided so.

Spoken like a true imperialist. She bristled. Unfortunately for him, she'd witnessed firsthand the quagmire America faced in Vietnam. "Do you agree, Dr. Kissinger, along with so many Americans who protest the war, that nothing has been gained? Vietnam has been pointless?"

He nodded.

"Can you repeat? Do you agree?"

"Yes."

She held her expression still. It was the moment in every interview when she'd got gold, and it had come early.

The red telephone rang. Kissinger lunged at it. "Yes, Mr. President," he said. Two minutes later Nixon called again, then again, and it struck her the president was like a newborn crying for the breast of his mamma. Each time, Kissinger turned his back and murmured into the mouthpiece so she wouldn't hear.

Fed up with the interruptions, she jabbed him from another angle.

"Dr. Kissinger, you are routinely photographed at premieres and nightclubs with a different actress or heiress on your arm. How do you explain your reputation as a Washington sex symbol?"

Kissinger's lips curled for the first time. He was tickled. "My popularity stems from the fact that all the burden rests on my shoulders when I go to China, Russia, Vietnam. What will Kissinger say or do? Will he win? I am like a western hero who rides into town all alone."

"Western hero," Oriana repeated, masking her astonishment. She had met Glenn Ford and William Holden, real movie cowboys, and Kissinger was equating himself to them?

His boring voice turned defensive, as if she were not getting it. "The point is, I perform the job alone."

More gold. Kissinger was claiming he galloped around the globe conducting foreign policy *solo*, elevating himself above the president. She glanced at her tape to make sure it was rolling. Yes, thank God. His ego was digging its own hole.

The red phone rang. "Of course, Mr. President, I'll be right in."

Kissinger excused himself. She waited fifteen minutes. He hadn't even offered her a coffee. Thirty. She could wait all day if she had to. Once, at the Soviet consulate, determined to get a visa, she rang the bell at reception for two hours. Finally the frazzled consul came running out of his office. "Fine! Give me your passport. Here is the damn visa."

At the White House, she waited more politely, jotting notes about Henry's office décor, which she liked: simple and serene, lined with books, one modern watercolor above his desk. She wondered if Heinz, who was born in Germany and immigrated as a Jewish refugee, still felt like an outsider in America, as she often did, and perhaps this was the root of his solo cowboy bullshit. Annoyed, she checked her watch and got up to investigate, glancing left and right down the hallway. Kissinger was nowhere in sight. Enough of this disrespect, she would explore.

Next door was the Roosevelt Room, a brass sign read, with a mile-long conference table where the bigwigs likely met. At the end of the hall, this excited her, the press briefing room she saw on television. She slipped in and parked herself in the first row. The stage was surprisingly small, with the presidential seal hanging behind the podium. She imagined herself filing in every morning for a press conference, like Helen Thomas, the White House correspondent for UPI. What a woman. The press corps was all men except for Thomas, yet she'd earned a reserved seat up front and always asked the first question. She was a decade older than Oriana but had traveled a similar path: women's topics, society, celebrities. Thomas got her big break covering President Kennedy and now she traveled the world with Nixon. She was a fierce interrogator on Watergate. Blunt. Unrelenting. Oriana smirked. A witch.

The deputy press secretary poked his head in the door and told her the interview was over. Dr. Kissinger had left the building. Left? He had taken off with the president on Air Force One. They were already en route to Texas.

Rude. Oriana marched back to his office and packed up her tape recorder. Kissinger had been intent on dominating her, but now he was running away, she sensed, afraid he had said too much. From her point of view, it was a shitty interview, only the start of an interview, but it would have to suffice.

A week later, she published her profile in *L'Europeo*, and two weeks later, got it reprinted in *New Republic*, with the stipulation that the American magazine would not edit a word. They didn't. All hell broke loose. The Washington and New York dailies ran cartoons of Kissinger dressed like a cowboy in a leather vest, hat, and holster. Editorials eviscerated him: how bigheaded of Kissinger to see himself as the lone gunslinger of foreign affairs. Was President Nixon twiddling his thumbs while Kissinger rode into Moscow? Rumors flew that Nixon was livid with his closest advisor, cutting off access. Kissinger complained that Fallaci took him out of context. She fired back in the press that Kissinger was lying and she had tapes to prove it.

The controversy went on for weeks. It made her famous in America—she was "the lady with the tapes," she skewered Kissinger, adding another victim to her collection. Eventually, the scandal died down, and Kissinger and Nixon returned to being attached at the hip. What's more, Kissinger was promoted to Secretary of State. Oriana was not surprised. A psychiatrist could do a good study of that relationship.

The cameramen from *60 Minutes* ambled in with long hair and sideburns, fringed suede jackets, and T-shirts stamped with *Pink Floyd* and *Let It Be*. Oriana served them espresso on a silver tray while they shot footage of her Olivetti, American flag, cluttered desk. Wallace arrived twenty minutes after his minions. He was better looking than she'd expected, with shrewd black eyes, full lips, slicked-back hair. Dressed to kill in a charcoal suit.

"Nice to meet you, Miss Fallaci. You're so . . ." Wallace seemed surprised by her appearance, too.

"Small," she finished for him. "This is it." She threw open her arms, accustomed to people's astonishment at her petite stature. Some were forthcoming enough to admit that because of her big personality, they'd expected an Amazon.

Not Wallace. He admitted nothing, eyes shifting like a detective's over her study. They would not be friends, she sensed, probably because they shared a lot in common. Both had interviewed prominent world figures, including the headache-inducing ones like Arafat and Hussein. Both were determined to prove themselves as serious journalists. Wallace had been a game show host and a pitchman in cigarette commercials earlier in his career. She was called "nasty" and he a "prick" for their confrontational styles, their tendency to go for the jugular and elicit headline-making confessions. Before Oriana and Wallace came along in the 1950s, interviews of the famous tended to be puff pieces—"President Kennedy, tell us about the teas you've held at the White House"—and few serious journalists practiced the craft. She and Wallace had elevated the interview form, making it entertaining *and* newsworthy.

"Everyone's doing interviews today." Wallace seemed to follow her train of thought. "How do you feel about that, Miss Fallaci?"

"We started a trend." She scoffed. "They think it's so easy, you just turn on your tape recorder or camera and *voilà*."

They discussed the fact that *Rolling Stone*, *Life*, and *The New York Times* were showcasing the Q and A format—and *Playboy*, of course. Oriana told Wallace she had no respect for television interviewers (except him, she added cagily) because they had teams of researchers yet still managed to ask moronic questions. She caught herself, realizing Wallace was doing the chitchat so she would drop her guard. No way, dear Wallace. "That was not on the record, eh? Tell me when you begin."

"Fine," Wallace said, seeing her armor go on. He cut the preliminaries. "Make sure you get this," he ordered his crew, pointing to her Captain Andy certificate.

Oriana was not accustomed to TV cameras and glaring lights but pretended she was, sitting cross-legged on the chesterfield, defiantly casual. Ignoring the butterflies in her stomach, she intuitively got into character. Female character: She would be intelligent but not arrogant, assertive but not strident. It thrilled her that Wallace's enormous audience—she pictured Americans tuning in Sunday evenings in their living rooms—would know her name.

Wallace's makeup artist, the only woman on the crew, patted his face with powder. She wore a woolly poncho and tall lace-up boots and asked Oriana if she would like a little powder, too. Why not? Oriana closed her eyes, and as soon as the puff touched her cheek, she instantly felt more important. This must be the illusion Wallace suffered, riding in his limousine, pampered by staff, performing journalism for the cameras. Who pampered her? No one.

"Cigarette?" Wallace said. She accepted, leaning forward for his light.

Chapter 17

1973

"Roll it." Wallace snapped into his investigative persona, the smoke from their cigarettes swirling between them. "Miss Fallaci. You've become the most feared political interviewer in the world. You're very combative."

"It's my job. And a synonym for combative is courageous," she said pointedly, remembering to add the trace of a smile.

"You asked Yasir Arafat, *How many Israelis have you killed?* Colonel Gaddafi, *Why does the whole world hate you?* To his face, you called President Thieu of South Vietnam *an American puppet.* Miss Fallaci, do you do this to shock?"

"Not at all." She tossed her head. "These are my enemies who say this."

"You have enemies?" Wallace said.

"Oh yes. They even claim I alter my questions when I publish, to sound more *combative.*" She scoffed. "I am a woman doing a man's job, and in macho Italy, ooh la la, they hate me for that. They call me overly dramatic, a madwoman. Do I strike you as mad?"

Wallace chuckled unsurely. "I don't think so."

"Look. I do my interviews to study the bizarreness of power. Why do certain people believe they deserve power over the rest of us? It takes a certain type, no? Someone with self-regard for sure. I interview like a psychologist, to uncover their motives.

I want to understand what is hidden in people's hearts. Their story."

"But you put yourself in the piece. Your personality dominates," Wallace said.

"Just like you are in this piece, and you dominate." She fixed him with a disarming smile that didn't give an inch. "The moment you ask the questions, it's your show. I do it in print, where it's my show. Print is harder, no?"

Wallace winced. "I don't know that it's harder."

She reminded herself to soften. "Look. I am Oriana who grew up in war, my family was antifascist socialist, we were poor. I bring all that to the interview. I'm not a *tabula rasa*. Nobody is."

"Quite the contrary, you're very opinionated, very passionate."

"Come on, don't give me that *passionate Italian* cliché."

Wallace balked. "I mean you put your subjects on trial, you judge them, and not very positively."

"Of course I judge a leader. Does he treat people well or cause suffering?" Her thoughts were coming faster, her intensity showing. "I have emotions and opinions, yes. I was brought up to care about right and wrong. But I do try and understand those bastards who control our futures. Oops. Can I say *bastards*?" She covered her mouth with a sly gleam.

"We'll edit it," Wallace said. "Keep rolling. Miss Fallaci, your questions get very personal. You asked Kissinger, *How do you explain your reputation as a playboy?*"

"Because ordinary citizens want to know." Oriana pointed her finger at Wallace. "Don't you want to know who Kissinger really is? So I asked him. By the way, he said, *Women are just a pastime.*" She made a disgusted face.

"You don't back down from controversial issues." Wallace made a poor segue, but she answered.

"They should stop paying my salary if I did. Most journalists are thin-skinned and ask difficult questions at the end, when they're packing up. *Oh, by the way, did you execute five hundred innocent people and bury them in a mass grave?* I ask within the first ten minutes. I don't care about being liked."

"Neither do I." Wallace said it like a challenge.

She ignored him. "This need to be liked, women suffer from it. I don't. We all have different gifts." She flicked her ashes. "For me, every interview is a love story. We're meeting for a first date, getting to know each other. It's intimate and fraught. We might fall in love. Or hate."

Wallace widened his eyes. "You fell in love with Kissinger?"

"More hate, that one," she said flatly, dragging on her cigarette.

"What happened with Dr. Kissinger, for him to say you are, and I quote, *his worst conversation with any member of the press*?"

"I'm very proud of that, by the way."

"He says you misquoted him."

"That's a lie." She punched her thigh for emphasis, forgetting to soften. "I kill myself to be accurate. Journalism is an awesome privilege, to influence people's minds and often events. I take it dead seriously. And the machine records all, so there can be no doubt. I told Kissinger I would release my tapes."

"Did you release your tapes?"

"No, but perhaps I will let you listen." She leaned toward him conspiratorially. Flirtatious even.

"I'll take you up on that." Wallace leaned away. "Miss Fallaci, you started your career in the 1940s, in an all-male business. Was it hard for you?"

"Are you joking?" she said. Wallace stiffened. "It's still hard."

"You never married."

"If I married, I could never work and travel as I do. A man can come and go as he likes, because he has an obedient wife at home, but a woman has to choose. For us, family is a nicely decorated prison. You give up yourself." She felt a flash of annoyance at how much easier professional life had been for Wallace, who had gone through not one wife but two. "Frankly, I believe love is overrated," she said. "To paraphrase Marx, love is the opium of the people."

"Really? How do you mean?"

"Love is a fairy tale we tell ourselves to bear the pains of life."

Wallace reared back, more than a little repelled. "That's not something I've heard from a woman."

"I'm not your typical woman."

Hastily, he consulted his notes, seeming to lose his place. "You travel all over the globe covering war, Miss Fallaci. Are you obsessed with war?"

"My enemies again. You quote them well. Yes, I'm obsessed. Is there anything more tragic than war? War is a fact so I can't hide in my house, my conscience won't let me. And I don't fear dying. Do you?"

"I'm doing the interviewing here." He forced a chuckle.

"I forgot," she said, sensing his dislike, their unspoken competition. Wallace assumed he was in charge, but *she* was, of her image, of what she would reveal to him. "Death doesn't scare me because I've almost been blown to pieces many times," she said, "starting as a child in Florence. I fought Nazis every day. It was a trauma, but it toughened me up. If you fear death, you get paralyzed, you stay in your cozy home and do nothing. And I believe life is for doing something. I don't agree with Shakespeare that life is sound and fury signifying nothing. Sorry, William. I make sure my life signifies *something*."

They went on for an hour. She saw how her own subjects mistakenly assumed they were blah-blahing to a friend and hung themselves. She was too clever for that, but it was intoxicating to play the firebrand, the prominent interviewer being interviewed. Wallace was a good sparring partner. She could see why a reporter wrote, after the Kissinger uproar, "Oriana Fallaci is the female Mike Wallace." But they should call him "the male Oriana Fallaci." It was a thousand times harder to create drama on the page than the screen.

When the cameras stopped rolling, she let Wallace listen to her Kissinger tape, watching his eyebrows fly up. "So you'll tell your audience I was accurate in my reporting?" she said, pressing *Stop*.

"Will do." Wallace's eyes flashed with respect and, on its heels, envy. The envy aimed at her like a poison dart her entire career.

When Wallace left, she was buzzing. Was she good, did she say too much, how would he edit her? She'd murder him if she looked stupid or old. Wallace didn't like her, he had an inferiority complex, though he was the one with the big TV show. It shocked her that even in progressive America, women were not permitted to be anchors. They endured the same insults as Oriana: Women can't focus. They're only for decoration. They don't have the brainpower to handle serious news.

Bullshit.

The interview had made her ravenous. She crammed Baci chocolates into her mouth, the only food in the refrigerator, and called her parents in Casole. They fumbled onto the extensions she had installed just for this purpose, so she wouldn't have to repeat her news when she traveled.

"Are you in Bonn?" Babbo.

She explained she'd gone to Greece instead and now New York.

"Greece? Did you meet Alessandro Panagoulis?" Babbo.

The name brought him crashing back. Under the orange and lemon trees. *But I love you*. In the back seat fondling her hand.

Sì, sì, she'd met the man.

"We saw the poor boy on RAI." Mamma. "Like a Homeric epic, what he endured."

"I'm going to be on *60 Minutes*."

"What happens in sixty minutes?" Mamma.

Oriana explained.

"It's expensive to talk. Are you eating? Don't smoke too much. When are you coming home?" Her mother, who had urged her to *fly fly*, was constantly hoping she would return home.

"In two days. Or no—" Oriana checked her watch. "I'll catch the six thirty to Rome. I have a deadline," she lied.

Hurrying, she packed her Samsonite, unpacked just last night. Scanned the bedroom for forgotten items, the bedroom she had decorated by ripping out a page from *House Beautiful* and walking to Bloomingdale's. "I want this."

From the pocket of her Samsonite, she dug out his telegram. *I'm waiting for you.* She saw a flash of him in her canopy bed, saw herself on top.

The Alitalia lounge manager at JFK served her a decent panini while she read the *Times* in a caramel leather armchair. "Miss Fallaci, you've become the most famous Italian in America," the manager said.

"Sophia Loren is that," she said, thrusting her shoulders back anyway.

In the plane, she settled into her usual bulkhead seat and stowed the duty-free Larks she always brought from America in the overhead. After takeoff, she downed a Chivas. She wasn't going to do anything about the Greek. She was simply flying home a bit early. Following a mystifying urge to erase the Atlantic between them.

Tommaso dropped the latest issue of *L'Europeo* on her desk. On the cover, her name appeared in bold above the headline

MODERN DAY GREEK HERO. And there was the picture taken by his friend: the two of them on his veranda, both in polo shirts, sitting too close for strangers, vibrating with attraction.

"Good," Oriana said brusquely, even as she felt heat creep into her cheeks. "You didn't cut a word."

Tommaso was observing her closely. "When he comes to Italy, introduce me."

"He's not coming here."

In answer, Tommaso held out two square envelopes. Before he could hand them to her, Mulotti strutted over, and Tommaso swiftly hid them behind his back.

"*Brava*, Oriana," Mulotti said, motioning to her cover story. "I doubt the Greek would have invited me to sleep over."

"His mother invited me," she lied. The half-wit must have heard her chatting with Lucia.

"Sounds like you've fallen in love with your subject. Nothing of the confrontational bitch in this one." He put his hand on her shoulder. "That's what others call you, not me."

She had the urge to spit at him but shook him off instead. "Don't touch me. Panagoulis is one of the few who stand up to power, get it? What do you do?" She flipped to his byline. "Ah! A thrilling investigation of two tourists detained for entering Santa Maria Novella in hot pants."

Tommaso intervened. "Mulotti, give us a minute."

"I have a question for you, boss," Mulotti said.

"When I finish." Tommaso, always cordial, was firm.

Mulotti walked away, throwing peevish looks over his shoulder.

"*Stronzo*," Oriana said, hot with fury. "Why is he here?"

"You know why." Tommaso placed the two square envelopes on her desk. "These came while you were in New York."

She ripped open the telegrams. The first contained a poem inspired by her, Alekos wrote. She couldn't subdue a smile. The second announced he was in the hospital. Her hand flew to her mouth.

"What's wrong?" Tommaso said.

"Nothing." She stashed the telegrams in her satchel.

"How was *60 Minutes*?"

"Fine. It airs November. Mulotti's waiting for you."

She wanted Tommaso away from her desk so she could book the next flight to Athens. Beneath her relentless drive, the hard shell she'd built after her romantic failures, she was romantic in her bones. She had been waiting for a big love, a man to share her life with, who wanted her in the total, desperate way Paris wanted Helen. A man she could look up to—in her fantasies he would even teach her a thing or two, if there were something left to learn. Now here he was. A penniless Greek revolutionary who lived with his mother.

Chapter 18

1973

The taxi took Oriana straight to Evangelismos Hospital in downtown Athens. She lugged her Samsonite down the yellowed marble corridor, alarm pooling in her veins. Was Alekos hurt? Of course he was hurt after hunger strikes and beatings—he might have a collapsed lung or burst spleen. Did she really expect a tortured dissident to take her dancing?

The hallway was crowded with gurneys of ancient wheezing people. She found Room 282 and hesitated in the doorway. He was lying in a blue metal bed with his eyes closed, his thick hair vibrant against the pale green gown. Drawing near, she placed her palm lightly on his forehead.

He blinked his eyes open. "Finally you came." He kicked off his blanket and pinned her against the window. A warm beating chest. Kisses and IV tubes.

A doctor's booming voice and laughter. "Youth." Not just one doctor but three.

"They can't understand how I'm in one piece," Alekos said.

"In bed," the booming doctor ordered.

"Just tests," Alekos said, seeing her brow crease with worry. "I get a little tired when I walk, that's all."

"It's from being locked up," a doctor said. "They never let you out in the sun?" Alekos shook his head. "You'll gain your strength back soon, son."

"You two should have no problems." A second doctor winked. "He's healthy in that area. We're writing him up for the medical journal."

Alekos squeezed her hand as the doctors checked his vitals, everyone in high spirits. "Will you take a picture of us?" one of them asked Oriana, slipping a Kodak Instamatic out of his white coat. She snapped their picture embracing the hero.

When they were alone again, she pulled up a chair and gave him his gifts. The Zegna sport jacket she'd chosen first, matching it with a shirt and tie, imagining how refined he would look.

His smile spread as he fingered the fine linen, the supple silk. "You Italians and your style." He tore out a page from a battered notebook and thrust it at her. "I've dedicated my best poem to you."

Her breath caught. There was no better gift, and somehow he knew. At the top of the page, he'd written *a mia amata, Oriana Fallaci*.

"It's called *Voyage*," Alekos said. He read it to her in Greek, translating into Italian as he went along. His voice was even more velvety in his native tongue, each intonation landing inside her like a caress.

His poem described a ship on an endless voyage. The captain pursued a light in the distance and refused to drop anchor in any port. Alekos explained his life was the voyage, and he was the ship that would never drop anchor. The theme seemed to echo Cavafy's *Ithaca*; it's the journey that matters, not arriving at the destination. In a corner of her mind, the inkling of a warning registered, a poem that meant Alekos would never find safe harbor. Oriana shifted uncomfortably. But he was watching her expectantly from his hospital bed, certain she would understand him. And she did, intellectually. When had she ever rested in any harbor? Despite the tightening in her belly, she beamed at him like a kindred spirit.

His eyes grew damp when she showed him his interview on the front page of *L'Europeo*. "It will help the Greek people. Expose the regime. Thank you." He kissed her hand, moving his lips up her bare arm and making her shudder. She savored the rare gratitude for her reporting, and together they leafed through back issues of *L'Europeo* she had brought him. Alekos wanted to know the details behind each of her stories from the years he'd lost in prison. Astronauts landing on the moon, Nixon in China. He shook his head at the massacre in Mexico City, three AP photos shot in quick succession: Oriana standing, hit, injured on the ground. THE BLOODY NIGHT I WAS WOUNDED, the headline read.

"Did the bullets hurt?" he asked. "Were you scared?"

"I thought that's it, I'm dead." It was easy to sound offhand now, six years later, but she had been more than scared.

Alekos patted the bed next to him. She climbed in and he wrapped his arms around her. "Tell me."

She loved the way he listened, fully present. For the first time with a man, she didn't feel the need to diminish herself. "I was covering student protests on the balcony over Three Cultures Square," she began. "Ten thousand people were gathered below, and Manuel from Polytechnic had the bullhorn. He was making his anti-Olympics speech. The 1968 Games were about to begin, but I agreed with students. Why did the Mexican government spend millions on stadiums while its people went hungry?"

All at once, whirring in the sky. She recognized the sound from Vietnam. An army helicopter swooped down in circles shooting out green flares, lighting up its target. "Watch out, kids!" she said.

Eight armored trucks roared onto the Square. Soldiers in white gloves poured out, firing machine guns into the crowd. The helicopter started shooting. Manuel yelled into the bullhorn, "Everyone! Don't panic! Leave in an orderly fashion!" But the rapid fire drowned him out.

For a blurred moment, it was a movie. Bodies jerking in the air. Bayonets slashing into stomachs, decapitating heads. Soldiers stormed the balcony where she was standing. "Hands behind your heads!" Students shrieked. She was shrieking. A white glove grabbed her by the hair, stuck a revolver against her temple. "I'm a journalist!" The steel barrel was cold and hard. He was going to blow her brains out. *The only thing to do when you're scared is act.* She swayed with dizziness and crumpled to the ground.

The soldier moved off to continue the killing spree, but she had only pretended to faint. Bit by bit, she slithered on her belly toward the wall. Toward safety. Almost. A searing flame tore through her shoulder. Back. Knee.

Gushing blood. She was going to die here.

She fainted for real this time. Opened her eyes to two policemen bouncing her body down the stairs. They dragged her into a room flooded with water and threw her on a pile of corpses.

"I'm not dead." Her mouth was dry, her tongue not working, but she pushed to be heard. "I need an ambulance."

The policemen gaped. "The colonel doesn't want any ambulances."

"I'm a journalist. My embassy knows I'm here," she lied. "If you let me die, your colonel will be in trouble."

They exchanged a look, then moved her under a leaking pipe, snickering as rusty water dripped onto her face. Days seemed to pass. She was in and out of consciousness.

The ambulance arrived at last, but the first and second hospitals refused to treat her, their emergency rooms overwhelmed by victims with melted faces, arms and legs blown off, a pregnant belly torn open. The third hospital, French, admitted her. Emergency surgery. Doctors removed shrapnel millimeters from her spine, inside her knee and shoulder.

The next day, Oriana's hospital room filled with flowers and telegrams from home. Manuel from Politecnico was alive, thank goodness. A knock at her door. She hid her catheter under the sheets and said "Come in" to reporters and a TV camera. They told her hundreds had died in the massacre and thousands had been arrested.

"I was an eyewitness," she said into the news camera, propped up on pillows. "The police, the army, were violent. The students were peaceful."

"Señora Fallaci, aren't you afraid the authorities will punish you?"

"They'll have to cut out my tongue to shut me up."

Alekos squeezed her hand as she finished the story. That same day, she told him, she dictated an eyewitness report, and *L'Europeo* ran the story with a photo of Oriana in her hospital bed. Tommaso and the director embarrassed her with the caption *Oriana Fallaci tells the tragic story of the Mexican Olympics in which she played a heroic part.*

"So many people died, and they made me important," Oriana said. "But *L'Europeo* wanted to sell magazines. It drove my colleagues nuts. *La Fallaci exaggerating her injuries.* I survived a massacre and still they attacked me. Because I'm a woman."

"Because they're not real men." Alekos traced his finger along her jawline. "I wish we'd been together then." His voice was heavy with regret.

She had the same feeling exactly, she told him without words, her eyes searching his. "Why did you say *I love you* the day we met?" she asked.

"It was the second day," Alekos said, and a thrill went through her. He remembered. "Your courage," he said simply.

Exactly the quality she loved in him. "I'm not as fearless as you," she said.

He stroked her cheek. "How many journalists risk their lives the way you do?"

"The guys in my office go home at five. They take weekends off to go skiing."

"Exactly. That reminds me." He ripped the tape off his wrist and pulled out the IV. "You came all the way to see me. We can't stay cooped up here."

"But you're not discharged," she said.

"I am now." He pulled on trousers and the Zegna jacket she'd bought him, a handsome fit, and took her hand, striding down the corridor with a casual wave to orderlies and nurses. Outside on bustling Vasilissis Sofias Avenue, he jutted into traffic and hailed a taxi.

She watched him, giddy with relief. Alekos wasn't sickly. He was bold and virile and flouted the rules.

"Now we'll eat," he said, giving her shoulders a squeeze in the back seat. They dissolved into intimate laughter, back and forth, a duet spurred on by the pleasure of the other.

Chapter 19

1973

He took her to Psaropoulos, a fish taverna perched on the rocky coastline with outdoor tables facing out to sea. Psaropoulos was a hundred-year-old establishment where his family had celebrated special occasions and his band of friends still gathered. "We came here the night before my attempt," Alekos said.

"You dined out on fried calamari while plotting to blow up the dictator?" she said.

He shrugged and took her hand, leading her across the crunchy gravel patio to a table overhanging the Aegean. All eyes turned to them and she raised her chin, relishing the spotlight. Tonight, for once, Oriana wasn't making her entrance alone, and she felt her femininity aroused, her body humming. A man was taking the reins, the right man, younger yes, but strong enough to be her partner. The two of them, shoulder to shoulder, felt invincible.

As soon as they sat, a waiter rushed over and pumped Alekos's hand. Then a second waiter. A lively table of male contemporaries, shirts open, legs sprawled, sent over a bottle of wine. Alekos lifted his hand and mouthed *thank you*, then gave her a shy shrug. He was much more humble than she.

In the midst of the warm reception, the word "Communist"

rang out. She turned to see two well-heeled, middle-aged couples scowling toward their table.

Alekos looked down and busied himself with his silverware. "I'm not a Communist," he said, sounding injured. "Dogmas aren't for me."

"They call me a leftist, too," Oriana said. She had been raised a socialist but no more, political parties were rigid and corrupt. She believed only in democracy and civil rights. "We don't fit their labels," she said, "but we sure do stand up for freedom."

She glared at the snooty bourgeois who called him a Communist. Alekos had sacrificed his youth, and in return, these people treated him with contempt, the very people he fought for. *You ignorant, self-satisfied sheep. You sleep well with your money under the mattress. You don't even know when the dictator is fucking you. You bend over and say, "Yes, go ahead."*

She gave Alekos's hand a squeeze, signaling, *I am with you.* He had been forward the day they met, flirting and confessing his love, but now he grew tongue-tied and almost knocked over his glass. He gave the impression of dining with a woman for the first time, but Alekos had a magnetism that made that scenario far-fetched.

"You're quiet," she said.

"When I read your books, I felt I knew you. Now you're here."

The ripple they had caused upon arrival settled, and they became enveloped, just the two of them, on their own island. They exchanged stories of their childhoods. Alekos had lived through extreme poverty, like she had, and three authoritarian regimes—this wasn't his first dictator. His formative years had been jam-packed with rallies and rebellions. During the Nazi occupation of Greece, when Athenians were dying in the streets from starvation, his family fled to his mother's island, Lefkada, where they grew their own food. Oriana told him about her war years. "I didn't have any friends," she said, watching a bunch of kids kick a soccer ball at the far end of the taverna as their parents dined boisterously at the next table. She had been bookish and reserved, then Hitler's troops marched into Florence. The worst was the WOOO of the air raid alarm, the sound triggered her still. She told him about the day she broke down in sobs inside the Duomo and her father slapped her. *Girls don't cry.*

"He slapped you?" Alekos reached for her hand.

"It was for my own good. To toughen me up," she said. Then quietly, "I never forgot that slap."

Alekos shook his head with pity, as if he could see the girl in pigtails. But she was uncomfortable with pity and relieved when an old flower peddler in a headscarf approached their table. Alekos instantly reached into his pocket and bought the entire basket. He handed Oriana a red carnation, its stem wrapped in foil.

"What will I do with all these?" She flushed, moved by his gesture.

"You're right." He called over the flower peddler and returned the basket of flowers. She assumed he wanted his money back, but Alekos pressed it into her palm. The woman was so overcome, she kissed him.

Oriana tipped her head back and laughed, catching sight of the moon, a giant orange ball in August, ridiculous, sheer romance. The sky and rocks and sea of his country were elemental and exerted some kind of primal pull. She could feel herself being stripped down to her essentials, surrendering her inhibitions. The warm air teasing her skin. The convivial hum of people relishing food, relishing the night. The flickering lights of ships plying the water in the distance. Greece might be impoverished, primitive, yes, but there was something divine in its simple beauty. She didn't believe in the divine, of course, but she was transported *somewhere* by the balmy breeze tickling her neck. She wanted Alekos to touch her neck.

The fresh fish were displayed over ice on an antique wooden cart. Alekos ambled over and picked out a hefty red snapper for their meal. The waiter carried it to the kitchen to be grilled with olive oil, lemon, and oregano and served with a side of dandelion greens. First, for *meze*, they feasted on fried zucchini, grilled octopus, *horiatiki* salad. Alekos served her first, then attacked his own plate with gusto, the stomach shrinkage of his hunger strikes clearly behind him. She tried to keep up, the owner of a respectable appetite herself, but found herself focused on his well-defined lips, his tapered fingers. What he would do with them later.

The retsina wine tasted rough and resin-heavy but helped her to relax. After a few glasses, she forgot her Tuscan snobbery and decided it paired crisply with the grilled fish and night air.

Alekos clinked glasses. "*Oti agapas.*"

"What does that mean?"

"To whatever you love."

Oriana had booked a hotel room down the coast, but once more, Alekos wouldn't hear of it. "Hotels are for strangers. You'll stay with me." They strolled back to his house arm in arm after dinner. It was midnight as they rounded Aristofanos Street. Two policemen were staked out on the corner, two more across the street. Alekos threw them a mock salute. "Say hello to Papadopoulos for me," he said.

"What kind of amnesty is this?" Oriana shot the policemen a scathing look.

"It's a dictator's version of freedom."

"Be careful, Alekos."

"Let's make their night worthwhile." They had reached the garden gate and he swept her up in a kiss. Oriana had never been kissed before an audience and it made her feel absurdly young and carefree. She had manically circled the globe, rushing to war zones to understand what is humanity, what is life. She should have fallen in love more often, kissed in public more often.

They slipped through the garden of orange and lemon trees and upstairs to his boyhood room. The shutters were open, moonlight washing in, jasmine climbing over the veranda rail perfuming the night air. They sat on his single bed with the pine headboard and she watched his lips, readying her own, ready to tip back onto the narrow mattress. But he only took her hands.

"Don't leave me." His voice was thick and his eyes welled.

"I won't leave you."

"I'm so tired of being alone."

She felt the hot sting of her own tears, remembering how petrified she'd been riding her bicycle to Mannelli, with no one to ride beside her. An outsider at university, in the newsroom, with no friend to ease her way. Coming home to four walls nightly, more alone than she'd ever imagined she would have to be. So much heartache, if she let it, if she dropped her guard for one second.

He cried. She gathered him in her arms and ran her fingers through his hair, deep into its ropiness, pouring every ounce of herself into soothing him. Soothing both of them.

Without warning, the moment changed and Alekos lifted his face to hers, his cheeks wet. He kissed her. Laid her down on the bed and undressed her, drinking her in as if she were the most exquisite woman in the world. He wrestled off his clothes and made her heart thud with his eagerness. Murmured *agapi mou*, buried his lips in her breasts. Scooped her on top in a tight embrace, surprising her with a neediness for affection that matched her own.

What would Alekos be like after five years in the desert? Tender, giving, exposed. He took his time, moving his mouth over every part of her with tiny groans. Teasing alive her nerve endings in all the places she knew, and some she didn't. Behind her knees. Her toes. He parted her legs only last, only slowly, past the point where she was ready, making her cry out with wanting him. His eyes searched hers, hungry not for erotic release but for finding a way home.

She opened to him deeply. The shyest parts of her that had never opened up, not really. The way he touched her was the way she wanted to be touched. The way he moved was the way she wanted to move. She loosened, shed layers of defenses. Shrugged off her warrior shell and showed herself to him, her need for closeness, reassurance. Alekos had the same emotional makeup, she saw that now. For all his defiance, his brave face, he longed to be consoled, to lie safe in her arms. They gave and gave each other all the comfort they needed.

She expected him to fall asleep. She was accustomed to men retreating, and after all, Alekos had got his itch scratched after two thousand nights of deprivation. But they stayed pressed together with animal warmth, and she barely recognized herself, weightless and worriless. He nestled closer, a volcano of affection, his arms and legs locked around her. He did not let go. She was the one who fought the urge for a cigarette, the impulse to take cover in her well-worn shell.

"We'll be together forever," he said, facing her, their foreheads touching.

"People change their minds." She made one final move to protect herself.

"I don't," he said.

Fireworks in her chest. Somehow, she trusted this man she'd known less than a week. This beautiful man with the jagged scar too close to his heart. She traced her fingers over its sad, shiny surface, welling with the desire to give him the gift he'd just given her. To take care of him, the way she hoped to be taken care of.

Chapter 20

1973

Oriana had always known that she wasn't made for pleasure. Pleasure was for luckier or lazier people and she was meant to work. Less than a week by Alekos's side upended that perception and she saw herself in a startling new light. She deserved. She was gaining something she should have always had. The sky would not come crashing down if she loosened the reins of discipline she imposed on herself. If she indulged in life's enjoyments for once, rather than deprive herself, she would not be punished.

The days in Glyfada took on a holiday rhythm. Breakfast was fatty sheep's yogurt drizzled with honey on the wraparound veranda overlooking the sea. Alekos skinned fat purple figs and fed her sugary bites off his paring knife. Athena bustled in and out with piping hot bread and giant juicy peaches, and though her face lit up at the sight of her son, it dimmed into a more complicated expression for Oriana, one that seemed to say, *I just got my son back, only to lose him to her?*

After breakfast, swimming in the turquoise Aegean. The beach was a minute's walk from the house, and Alekos and his brother had grown up in bathing suits, diving off the rocks from Easter to November. Oriana didn't know how to swim. She was a city girl who crossed the Piazza Signoria daily and took the statue of David for granted. She envied Alekos's ease, the way the sea was a second skin.

He taught her. She slipped off her beaded cover-up, glad she'd splurged on the Missoni bikini, glad they had the virgin beach to themselves. Followed him into the crystalline water, which was colder than she'd imagined, with minnows weaving around her ruby toes.

"Don't wet my hair," she said. He wet her hair, then scooped his hands under her belly as she kicked her feet. Oriana didn't recognize the sensation of sudden lightness, the burst of joy that came over her, yet oddly she did.

"Put your face in the water and blow bubbles," he said. "Now turn to the side and breathe." She did. There was a whole universe of beach customs she had missed out on as a girl, but she was an excellent student and liked what he was teaching her. Liked the way she was opening up to him and the sea as a second skin.

Afterward, they collapsed on the sand, the Mediterranean heat unraveling muscles, slowing the mind, transforming her into the natural woman she was meant to be. Alekos dozed under the scorching sun with his hand on her thigh. Her affair with Pelou had been clandestine, but this man belonged to her in broad daylight. He made love to her and said loving things and promised to be her person.

"You would make a wonderful mother," Alekos murmured.

"What?" She turned her head but he had drifted off again. *Madonna.* Was he serious or dreaming? Children? They were moving fast, Alekos was fast. But she was forty-four, who knew if she had any decent eggs left. Where would they live? Not in his country, though it was stunningly beautiful. She told herself to relax, don't jump ahead, how lucky to find this man. Why couldn't she trust life for once?

They went to Oscar, his favorite café in Glyfada, and ate lunch alfresco in rattan armchairs. The first afternoon, the proprietor pumped Alekos's hand, calling the waiter to bring two ouzos on the house. "This boy did something great," he said. "He has Greece inside him."

After lunch they bought newspapers at the corner kiosk, where the one-armed veteran refused Alekos's money, then they bent their heads together at their table. It wasn't long before the Greek newspapers went berserk publishing photos of the two of them smoking and drinking at the café. Then some paparazzo caught them wet and embracing on Glyfada beach.

"*Merda.* They're turning me into Jackie O," Oriana said, smacking the paper.

"Jackie was nude," Alekos teased. The former First Lady had been caught by telephoto lens sunbathing au naturel on Onassis's private island.

"They won't catch me at that one," Oriana said. "No more untying my bikini."

"Fine," he said, trailing his fingers down her back. She laughed.

It wasn't so funny when gossip began flying in Italy. *Foto*, the rag that splashed naked girls on its cover, that tried to compete with *L'Europeo* but was only good for lighting logs in the fireplace, ran a blind item headlined FALLACI'S YOUNGER MAN. Her eyes darted over it. *Alexander Panagoulis is a dashing freedom fighter, and the moment Fallaci saw him on television, she stole the interview from a colleague and rushed to Greece. She spent the night on his sofa and from there it was a small step to his bed. It's true what they say, Fallaci uses feminine wiles to trap her subjects.*

Shit. How did *Foto* know she'd "stolen" the assignment from Mulotti? The answer leapt to her brain: The little bastard was leaking.

"What's wrong?" Alekos said, seeing her expression.

"Nothing." She regretted telling Lucia to forward her damn mail. "They're running their mouths about us in Italy."

"Let them." Alekos took the tabloid and folded it away. "Enough reading." He shot her a smoldering look that said he wanted her that instant.

In previous affairs, Oriana had grown bored with sex. The opposite was true with Alekos. All he had to do was glance at her, brush against her, and she snapped out of her cerebral habitat and became a liquidy, spongy self. It was an awakening in her forties, the way he took her outdoors, indoors, with soft insistence. The way he glued his body against hers, smothering her with affection.

The Greek sun was still potent in September and gave them plenty of time in bed during afternoon siesta. Alekos had a way of shutting off her brain and drawing her into a web of slow and easy caresses. He never approached her the same way twice, and she found herself stretching languidly for him on the sheets, shedding a layer of inhibition she'd always had. Giving herself over to him, following his movements. So this is what it feels like, she found herself thinking, to trust that a man is yours.

Afterward, he lit two cigarettes at the same time and slid one between her lips. She wrapped her arms around him, wondering if she really might become pregnant. Alekos liked to burrow close, his face in the crook of her neck, and she caressed his head, shoulders, back, spilling over with the urge to nurture and protect him. No man had ever allowed her to be this woman. Not Gori with his wolfish conquests, not Pelou with his ever-present if distant wife. Only Alekos wanted what she had to give, and she showered him with all her softness.

What kind of feminist was she? One who liked men. Women's liberation was the biggest revolution of her time, yes, but Oriana had been thinking and acting like a feminist long before there was a movement. She didn't march or protest. Her entire life was a *vaffanculo* to women's servitude, to suffocating gender roles. But she refused to be a fascist, to tell other women how to live: Don't like men, don't shave your legs. If a woman wanted to call herself Miss or Ms., it was her right. If a woman made beauty parlor appointments and dressed fashionably, as Oriana did, it was her right. That was why she approved of Gloria Steinem with the miniskirts and boots; she enjoyed being attractive, enjoyed sleeping with men. Steinem was focused on the big issues—equal pay, reproductive rights—not whether you burned your bra.

After siesta, there were three endless hours to fill before going out to dinner at nine, Mediterranean style. His parade of friends crowded the garden, chattering in Greek, excited to have him home. Alekos was their clear leader, galvanizing them to raise money and launch a new Resistance, and she felt a strong attraction witnessing his star quality and blazing idealism. But modern Greek bore no resemblance to the ancient *Iliad* passages she'd memorized in school, and she couldn't keep up with the conversation. Inevitably, she grew bored.

Alekos and his friends were easy to look at, all that hot-blooded masculinity filling the garden. In her profession, she was surrounded by men in suits, and the earthiness of these brick layers and pipe fitters was stimulating for the eye. They won her with their chummy good humor, bronzed chests, tufts of hair peeking out of their open shirts. Like the partisans of her youth, they were salt of the earth, solid and decent.

Still, the newspapers were filled with world events she was missing. Nixon had released the first White House tapes. Egypt, Syria, and Israel appeared set to go to war. Oriana felt the itch for intellectual stimulation and, she couldn't deny it, work. Journalism had seeped into her bloodstream from the time she was a teenager handing out *Non Mollare*. It had become a habit, a way of life, jumping on a plane to be in the middle of a crisis. Every morning she got up needing the news as much as coffee. Every morning except the past week.

As if she had communicated telepathically, Tommaso tracked her down.

"How'd you get this number?" She skipped the hellos.

"I'm a newsman."

"Did you see *Foto*?" Her blood began to boil all over again. "I use my feminine wiles to trap my subjects."

"Ignore it," Tommaso said.

"I can't ignore it! They attack me because I'm a woman."

"Because you're good."

"Wrong. If I were a man, they'd kiss my ass, not post pictures of it." She growled with frustration. "Mulotti leaked it."

"It could have been anyone," Tommaso said. "The entire office heard the brawl when you *stole* his assignment." He got a laugh out of her. "Fine, Oriana, I'll speak to him."

"Speak? I want him fired."

"You know I can't. His uncle and the director . . ."

"I don't give a damn if they went to university together or bed together. The director cares if I'm happy? If my name is on the cover selling magazines? I'm not happy. Tell him."

"Fine." Tommaso sighed. "Are you keeping your meeting with the Shah?"

"Why wouldn't I be?" she said. In truth, she'd been ignoring the looming appointment.

"I've saved the cover for you," Tommaso said.

"You can always send Mulotti."

"I'd have to show him where Iran is on the map." Tommaso paused. "Are you having a good time at least?"

"You wouldn't recognize me."

She hung up. Of course she would keep her appointment with the Shah. He was a reluctant subject but she'd finally twisted his arm to say yes three weeks ago. She had persuaded all the world's sonsofbitches to talk to her, sending letters that stroked their egos. "You are one of the most intriguing presidents/prime ministers/statesmen of today." If the letter didn't work, phone calls. A gift of Chanel No. 5 to the secretary. Only Fidel Castro had refused her, and Pope Paul VI. She was dying to ask the Pope, *Why is the church so enthralled with sex? Have you ever been in love, Holiness?*

Clutching her notebook, she returned to the patio, where Alekos and his friends were drinking their fifth coffees. At the pine side table, she began jotting questions for the Shah about his womanizing and his oil. It felt centering to engage her brain, to immerse herself in world issues. She could feel Alekos's gaze on her, proud and desiring. He would be slightly sweaty and smell like glycerin soap and cherry tobacco if she were to put her arms around him.

The friends left. Alekos fed her a slice of tangy orange from a tree.

"What are you writing, *agapi*?" He peered at her notes. "Is it your novel?"

She stared at him. During their first dinner at Psaropoulos, in the balmy air under the full moon, Oriana had confessed that, as a girl, she had dreamed of writing literature. Alekos remembered.

"I have to go to Iran." The words tumbled out. She didn't want to leave him.

"Iran?" Alekos looked crestfallen.

"Come with me," she said, reaching for his hand.

"You forget, I don't have a passport." It was her turn to be disappointed. "And the dictator won't give me one. Every day he plants a new spy at my door."

She could postpone a few days, stay with him and swim. But she found herself speaking. "I won't be long, two days."

Alekos grew quiet. "I have work, too." He strode toward the garden gate.

"Where are you going?" She trailed after him.

Alekos was already face-to-face with the policeman on the

sidewalk. "Tell that dog Papadopoulos he couldn't break me in prison," he bellowed. "He thinks he can break me now? I'll fuck you all!"

The cop said nothing, only snarled. Alekos marched back through the gate and pulled her inside. She opened her mouth to scold him—how stupid to provoke them—but no sound came out. This was what courage looked like, the realization hit her. Animal outrage, mad disregard for consequences. Courage wasn't words printed in one of her articles or books. It wasn't pretty.

"Come with me to Italy. We'll get you a passport. You can organize a new resistance. I'll help you," she said all in one breath.

"So that's your plan." His face darkened with mistrust.

"I don't have a plan," she said, stung by the sudden wall he'd erected between them. But he was right. Ever since rushing back to him at the hospital, barely registering in her consciousness, she'd imagined the two of them living in Florence, New York—never his country.

"I can't leave," he said. "Don't ask me to do that. Do I ask you to stop writing?"

I could stop, she almost said but didn't, aware she'd been on hiatus from the newsroom just ten days. Still, the interviews were exhausting. She no longer felt the compulsion to fly off to where news was happening. She had done it. The money was good, it was crucial never to be poor, humiliated that way again. But she had a fat bank account now.

"No," she said in answer to his question.

"I need you," he said. "Be my partner. My best friend."

The plea in his voice made it cruel, impossible to say no. "I will." Her shoulders relaxed, as if she'd laid down a burden. She had wanted a man, not a husband, a hero, not a coward. Here he was. From girlhood, Oriana had responded deeply to being needed. But not even her father during the war had made her feel so essential.

She gave in to Alekos's penetrating gaze. She didn't know how to do what he was asking. But no man had ever looked at her the way he was looking now.

"When do you leave for the Shah?" he said, telling her silently that he knew she had to go.

"Wednesday."

"And you'll only be gone two days?"

She nodded. "I have to get a ticket."

"I'll take you to Iran Air," he said. "It's on Ermou Street."

When she had finished grilling the Shah, Alekos picked her up at Hellenikon Airport and swept her up in a hug that made her forget what an insolent prig the leader of Iran had been.

They went straight to Oscar's rattan armchairs, and over ouzo and *meze*, she told him about the Shah's brooding face in the opulent palace salon. The bulletproof vest he wore under his custom double-breasted suit. The gold teacup, gold teaspoon, gold cigarette box studded with jewels. Persian carpets, mirrored mosaic walls that created a funhouse effect.

"Some call you a dictator rather than a king." Oriana had gone for the jugular.

"Only you say that! The press is full of immoral people!" the Shah yelled.

"Immoral people like me, you mean," she yelled back, "with my pants and red nails."

He was a maniac, she told Alekos. He said Iran could start a third world war over its oil. Of course he was a chauvinist pig. She mimicked him. *You want equal rights? You're not equal in intelligence. Where is your DaVinci, your Mozart? Women are for beauty, nothing else.*

"He said that to you?" Alekos widened his eyes. "Did you throw your microphone?"

"These are the insults vomited at me all my life," she said, "because I don't have a prick." She watched a ripple of understanding cross his face.

"I'm glad you're back. I want you to myself." Alekos slipped his arm around her and she leaned into him, the warm breeze feathering her hair.

"Alekos!" A clump of girls with impossibly smooth faces paraded over, begging for a photo. Two of them planted their behinds on the arms of his rattan chair. Bristling, Oriana moved out of the frame. Hours ago, she was drinking tea with the leader who controlled the global price of oil, and now she was an extra in this teenybopper scene. Finally, the girls trotted off. She remained quiet and lit a cigarette.

"You're not jealous." Alekos watched her.

"Don't be ridiculous."

"Don't be." His gaze turned soft. "I could have a hundred women."

"I could have a hundred men," she said.

"I only want you."

He crashed through her defenses. The waiter set down a gratis platter of sugary melon and she made her decision. Enough of running around the globe meeting maniacs. She had proven her worth. Even as some part of her itched to transcribe the Shah tapes—habit, habit—she decided not to seek any more interviews. She would stay with Alekos and be his best friend.

A worry snaked through her. The last time she'd been this ready to throw away work for a man, she had wound up in a sanatorium. But she was not the same idiot she'd been in her youth, believing she was not enough. This time, Oriana was older and wiser and knew she was plenty. This time, she was willing to trade work for something more precious, a full life.

The truth was, she didn't know of any woman who had managed to combine career and love. Not Ingrid, not Meir. Steinem didn't have a partner. There was no model for being a woman at the peak of your profession and a woman in love. One thing Oriana knew: To climb any mountain, you had to be stubborn and single-minded, devote yourself completely. *Choose.*

In bed that night, with Alekos's head on her shoulder, she had a flash of insight, or maybe she dreamed it. If this were the hero's story, she would have already slayed the dragon, grabbed the prize, and returned home to great fanfare. But in the heroine's story, it seemed, the journey repeated. The quest was not linear but circular.

A woman's work was never done.

Chapter 21

1973

The next morning Alekos woke her with kisses, already showered and dressed. "Come, *agapi*. You wanted to do some sightseeing."

Their taxi curved along the rocky azure coast, but he refused to tell her where they were going. "The Acropolis?" she guessed. She couldn't visit Greece without seeing the Parthenon, the ancient temple dedicated to Athena, goddess of war and wisdom.

"Stop here!" he said to the cabbie just before a stone bridge. The driver braked hard and skidded toward the cliff. One more tire rotation and they would tumble into the sea. "This is it," Alekos said, staring out the window, but she saw no temple or ruins. "The thirty-first kilometer from Athens to Sounion."

She snapped her head around. "Where you tried to kill the dictator."

But he was already out of the cab, bolting across the two-lane road, just missing a speeding car. Oriana chased after him. "What the hell!" she yelled as they huddled against the mountain, cars whipping around the bend. He didn't answer, glancing at his watch then down the road. In the distance, she saw black dots drawing closer. A motorcade winding toward them and she knew: the limousine carrying the dictator. He traveled the same road every morning, Alekos had told her. Three curves away. Two.

"Let's go back!" She gripped his arm.

One curve.

"This time I won't fail!" Alekos lunged into the road.

"Help me!" Oriana called to the cabbie, who was leaning on his door, smoking.

The cabbie sprang into action and wrestled Alekos into the back seat. Wild-eyed, Alekos twisted around to the rear windshield and watched the motorcade speed by, then dropped his head in his hands.

"You're Alexander Panagoulis!" The cabbie grinned with gold eyeteeth. "It's an honor, son, but listen to an old man. Stay out of prison. That shithead isn't worth it."

Slowly, Alekos raised his face to hers. "I'm sorry." His lip trembled. The spell that had seized him had broken, but she remained rattled, her breath coming in gasps. He had tried to attack the dictator again, with his bare hands for crissake, putting her life in danger, too. She was furious—what kind of idiot was he?—but the shattered look on his face made her hold back.

"Back to Glyfada," Oriana ordered the cabbie.

But they were already being followed. A blue hatchback revved up behind their taxi. They spun around in their seats.

"It's them," Alekos said, in a voice so calm, it raised the hairs on her neck.

"Who?" The cabbie gripped the wheel, nervously glancing in his rearview mirror. There was a photo of two toddlers taped to his dashboard, a large silver cross dangling from the mirror.

"Step on the gas," Alekos said. The cabbie did.

The blue car gave chase. Screeching around the hairpin turns high over the Aegean. *Bravo*, Alekos leaned forward, urging on the cabbie. The blue car streaked up the driver's side, maneuvering to pass. It was a narrow stretch with no guard rail, a perilous fall below. Oriana dug her fingernails into Alekos's thigh.

A loud, grinding bang. The blue car sideswiped them. They fishtailed toward the cliff. Oriana screamed and braced herself against the front seat, but there was no impact. The cabbie managed to find traction on the gravel at the last moment, skidding to a stop before the shear edge of the precipice. Oriana cried out with relief.

The blue car tore off. "They're gone!" the cabbie said.

Alekos clapped him on the shoulders. "You did it, my friend." He pulled a wad of cash from his pocket. "For you and the kids."

Oriana watched Alekos, his mysterious good spirits helping to draw oxygen into her lungs and at the same time making her livid. How could he be so reckless? The regime would destroy him—and her—if he kept trying to destroy them. As if to apologize, Alekos drew her protectively to his chest, and she let herself be consoled, surprised by the racing of his heart.

When they arrived back home in Glyfada, two more policemen were stationed at the corner, and a new spy with binoculars peered out the window across the street.

"Already," he said, casting them a dirty look.

"Of course," she said. "What did you think? The dictator would let you take a second crack?"

The moment they were safely inside the gate, she turned to him. "Come with me to Italy."

He brushed a stray lock from her face. "I can't."

Her tone grew icy. "I didn't come here to die on a mountain road."

In silence, they climbed the stairs and ate the stuffed tomatoes his mother set on the veranda table. His favorite, Alekos said, but Oriana could only roll the rice and meat around her plate, her mind churning.

With the cicadas keeping rhythm through the hot afternoon, they went to bed and somehow managed to find each other, weaving their bodies together. Urgent the first time, wanting to escape, soothing the second. Afterward, she tried to memorize the shape of him in her arms. Vulnerable, sweet, so different from the man on the thirty-first kilometer risking their existence. She pushed away the unsettling morning, feeling his head nestled on her shoulder, the warmth of his exhale in her ear. She tried to hold on to the solace that she now feared would be temporary. Relegated to the bedroom where they could hide from the world.

"Fine," he said.

She was dozing off and repeated dreamily, "Fine."

"Let's go to Italy," he said. Her eyes flew open. "I'm no good here. They've got me on a leash. I'll organize from your country."

"I'll help you," she said in a rush.

"You're somewhat well known, I hear," he said. She swatted his shoulder. "And there's some decent pasta, not the mush they cook up here."

Why the change? She didn't wait to find out. She flew to the phone, calling her travel agent to book tickets to Rome.

Chapter 22

1973

Paparazzi swarmed them at Fiumicino airport. "*Benvenuti*, Oriana! Introduce us to Alessandro. Do we hear wedding bells?" Alekos slipped his arm around her waist and she leaned into him with a girlish glow, letting their body language do the talking.

Marriage. The two of them had never broached the subject. It didn't bother her. They were a modern couple in modern times. Oriana had already considered herself a radical, and now the free love of the '70s made her even more disdainful of bourgeois institutions and religious fanaticism against "living in sin."

The new social norms suited her anti-authority disposition. She certainly didn't need permission, from church or government, to live with her man. Still, a little piece of her was stuck in her mother's generation, or a little piece of her mother was stuck in her. *Do we hear wedding bells?* The question unleashed insecurities. Maybe he didn't love her enough. Would he stay with her if she were just partner and friend?

They almost didn't make it out of Greece. The dictator's regime forced Alekos to jump through hoops for a passport, claiming his birth certificate had disappeared from city records. Finally, miraculously, passport in hand, they raced to the airport, but a horde of policemen blocked them at the gate, refusing to let them board. Phone calls zipped back and forth while she and Alekos tensed and fumed and all the other passengers filed onto the plane. "What's going on?" Oriana demanded. "We have passports and tickets, you can't hold us here."

Alekos quieted her. "I'll always be a thorn in their side."

At last, the Alitalia agent received a message on his walkie-talkie and hurriedly waved them through, and they ran onto the shuttle bus giddy at their getaway. As much as she hated flying, Oriana had never been so ecstatic to hurtle down the runway, to hear the wheels rumble and tilt up into the sky.

She had booked a suite at the Excelsior, the most elegant hotel in Rome, on Via Veneto, its most elegant street. She couldn't wait to take Alekos to the Pantheon, her favorite landmark, near Tazza D'oro, her favorite espresso, and at night the Jewish quarter for *carciofi alla giudia*. The Excelsior staff knew Signora Fallaci from her many stays between assignments, and they gave her the VIP treatment of fruit basket, wine, and flowers, all arranged on the coffee table in their living room.

"These are to welcome you, too." She showed Alekos the card on the bouquet, but instead of being pleased, he grimly surveyed the gifts, the Persian carpets and crystal chandeliers. He picked up *Corriere della Sera* from the coffee table. "PANAGOULIS IN EXILE." He read the headline with indignation and threw it to the floor.

"Don't pay attention." She hadn't considered him in exile exactly, but he *was* a political dissident. He was fleeing for his life.

"What should I do in exile?" he said. "Go to cocktail parties on the arm of Oriana Fallaci?" The way he pronounced her name stung. "Now I know why you chose me. I make you look like a real revolutionary."

"I don't need you for that," she said coldly. She chose him? He was the one who batted his eyes at her in his mother's tacky bedroom.

"You took me away from battle." He glared.

"Me! Papadopoulos chased you out! He tried to run you off a cliff!"

She ripped open her Samsonite for something to do, flinging notepads and clothes onto the green brocade sofa. Damn him. She had rescued Alekos from the dictator's goons, even paid for his plane ticket. Was he just like other men, wooing until he got his way, then tossing her aside?

"I shouldn't have come." Alekos paced, waving his arms at the lofty ceiling with its gilded fresco of cherubs and clouds. "What kind of champion of the people are you? Living like a queen."

"You don't like it, sleep on the floor."

He stopped, wounded, his eyes two pools of regret. "I shouldn't have told you I loved you the day we met. I didn't mean to drag you into my miserable existence."

I wanted you to drag me, she didn't say. Her empathy rushed in, and she understood that he was terrified of losing who he was. His Greece.

Alekos uncorked a bottle of Montepulciano and dropped onto the sofa. "I could take Italian lessons in exile. Learn to make wine." He downed two glasses in quick succession. Then three.

"Slow down," she said.

"You know the god of wine, Dionysus? He's the god of madness, too. And misfits."

"And ecstasy, no?" she said, trying to lift his mood. "Wait until you see my vineyards in Chianti."

He'd come to Italy before, he reminded her, when he deserted the army, but only to the south. Sure fine, he mumbled they could see the sights, but then he wanted to go home. When he'd finished the second bottle, he draped his arm around her and she helped him into the bedroom. He collapsed onto the horsehair mattress, pulling her down with him. Holding her in his arms.

Her mind raced, silently rehearsing how to convince him to stay. "I'm not asking you to give up," she said. "You can still fight."

"It's nice . . . I've never slept in such a nice room . . ." He passed out.

She wrested off his shoes and pants, her lips pressed together with disappointment. The moment she unbuttoned his shirt, she saw the zigzag scar on his sternum and swallowed hard, tracing it with her fingers, reminded of all he'd been through.

In the living room, she called her parents.

"How long will he stay?" her father said.

"Isn't he much younger?" her mother said.

She cut short the conversation. Not since her breakdown with Gori fourteen years ago had she told her parents of any man. Then, as she lay tied to the bed with leather straps, her parents had wrung their hands, knowing only that a man they'd never met had broken their daughter. From that day forward, Oriana's fragility in romance hovered between them, the unstated belief that she was better off sticking to work. It was a deficiency imbedded deep in her psyche. Even with Alekos curled beside her, sleeping off his wine, safe in Italy, she felt the familiar unease that she was no good at relationships. Obviously, she was deluding herself about finding happiness with this man. She had never managed to win at love. Therefore, she never would.

The best pizza in Rome was in Campo di Fiori. For lunch the following day, they sat at an outdoor table at Carbonara, surrounded by flower and vegetable vendors lining the piazza, and devoured a Margherita topped with anchovies and egg. It was early fall, and she wore a long suede jacket over bell-bottom khakis, a Gucci shoulder bag that hit below the hip, and aviator sunglasses. Alekos had pulled on the same wrinkled trousers from their trip. First order of business, she would fix his wardrobe.

She signaled over a newsboy and bought the latest issue of *L'Europeo,* and they bent their heads together, racing over her cover story on the Shah. ORIANA FALLACI EXCLUSIVE: THE PRICE OF OIL WILL GO UP, announced the headline.

"Your conversation jumps off the page," Alekos said. "You say what you want, you never back down. It's thrilling."

"It's like a play," she said, deeply flattered. "We start out circling each other. There's a spark and a fight. Suspense. Who will win? I win!" They laughed their intimate laugh. How lucky to have found this man who took pride in her talent. As she glanced back at *L'Europeo*, a tiny discomfort gnawed at her. Now that she was home, she'd better call Tommaso, tell him she was done with the interviews. "Why quit now, when you're on top?" she imagined her editor saying. Her gaze shifted back to Alekos, his black shock of hair, as unruly and noncompliant as he was. The tender way he was looking at her, making sure she was all right. Hell with it, she would put off the call. Why ruin the moment?

What about a paycheck? A different discomfort pinged her. Her parents depended on money she deposited into their account, and Oriana spent like a fiend, buying whatever she pleased and giving gifts. She would need more money.

"What's wrong?" Alekos said, seeing her forehead ripple.

"Nothing. Still hungry?"

They devoured a second pizza, this one topped with delicious, smelly Gorgonzola. Bellies full, Alekos dragged her from vendor to vendor in the square, insisting on buying her flowers, though their suite was full of them. He veered away from red roses, saying they were too common, and finally settled on twenty-four white as snow.

"They're pure and unmarred," he said, handing her the extravagant bouquet. "A fresh start. Like the one you've given me."

There was no better feeling in the world than being

appreciated. Her eyes welled, and she buried her face in the petals, wondering how she'd never noticed the beauty of white roses. They would be her favorites from now on.

Earlier that morning, they had bathed together in the claw-footed tub and groomed in the gilded mirror with the delicious novelty of being a couple, and she had avoided the issue. Now she saw her opening. "So we'll stay?" she said, looking up through the plump white buds.

He turned to soak in the historic piazza, the medieval buildings painted various shades of ocher. "Here? With you?" Breaking into a slow grin, he nodded.

Before she could react, a young couple in their twenties browsing the same stall approached. "Signora Fallaci!" the girls said. "I love you. I've read all your books."

"*Grazie*," Oriana said, shaking the girl's hand with both of hers. People who read her books filled her with gratitude and a rare humility. Where would she be without them?

"I want to be fearless like you," the girl said.

Oriana appraised her, an elfin thing with frizzy black hair and freckles. Her boyfriend stood dumbly, hands in blue jeans, while the passion of the girl made her appear ten feet tall.

"I'm not fearless," Oriana said, with the clear sensation she was speaking to a younger version of herself. "But I don't let fear stop me. I force myself. Understand?"

"I think so." The girl nodded.

"When you're scared, move, curse, try any action. Otherwise you are paralyzed, you turn inward, and fear eats you," she said. Her father's lesson. She was determined to give the girl the same gift he'd given her. Tearing a scrap of wrapping from her bouquet, she dashed off her autograph. "Don't be a good girl." She stared intently at her young admirer. "It's boring and you will lose. Fight."

They spent the afternoon strolling to St. Peter's Basilica and standing before Michelangelo's *Pietà* in the first chapel. The sculpture of the Madonna holding the dead Christ was behind glass ever since some nutjob attacked it last year with fifteen hammer blows. "Look at Mary's size," she whispered. "She's large, out of scale compared to the delicate Jesus in her lap."

But Alekos was already riveted. "His face," he murmured. "It's serene. He's surrendered. It's finally over."

His comment stopped her, because she had stood before the *Pietà* a dozen times but never focused on Jesus's face. She had focused on the tender way Mary held him. Her sorrow.

They shared a cigarette on the Spanish Steps, and Oriana pointed out the house where John Keats lived the last three months of his life, dying at twenty-five. "He wrote *Ode on a Grecian Urn* here," she said.

"That poem I like," Alekos said.

"Of course you do. It's about an ancient Greek vase."

"Stolen by the British Museum," Alekos said. "Do you know that bastard Lord Elgin took half the sculptures from the Acropolis and locked them up in that museum?"

"That's the story of half the world's treasures. Sacking and plundering."

She was in high spirits showing off her Rome, drinking from Fontana della Barcaccia, fountain of the ugly boat, from the one spout that was clean to drink from. Giving herself permission to play rather than be handcuffed to her desk—the world Alekos had opened for her in Glyfada.

Their last stop was Rizzoli, the three-story bookstore owned by her publisher. Usually she dropped in to check whether her books were facing out (to encourage sales) and how many copies were in stock. With Alekos, she had a different goal.

"Tell your manager Oriana is here," she said to the spectacled clerk behind the desk. He scurried away and the manager rushed over with double kisses. "Do you know who this is?" Oriana said. He didn't. With a flourish, she introduced the hero of the Greek resistance. "Give him a fountain pen to sign his books." The manager hurried back with a short stack of Alekos's poetry, *Others Will Follow*. "And restock," Oriana said as Alekos scratched his signature on the flyleaf.

The manager bowed his head. "I will order today."

Oriana darted to the aisle where Rizzoli displayed her books, six so far, with a silver nameplate on the shelf distinguishing her from other authors. "Writing about the moon was my big break," she told Alekos, running her finger alone the spines and pulling out *If the Sun Dies*. "I interviewed astronauts and proved I wasn't limited to women's topics. But this, no, I've forbidden more printings. It's not a serious book." She yanked all three copies of *The Useless Sex* off the shelf and stuffed them into her pocketbook. At age thirty, she'd been exhilarated to travel to Turkey, Pakistan, India, Japan, Indonesia, and four more Eastern countries, reporting on women's lives—and of course their subjugation, including child brides and the heinous genital mutilation. Her collected articles sold well, translated into eleven languages and excerpted by *Cosmopolitan* magazine, but her research was not in-depth, the reporting far below her current standards. The title still embarrassed her, *The Useless Sex*. There was nothing useless about women, but she and the publisher concocted it to grab attention and make money. "I'll never sell myself that way again," she said, cringing at the memory of her green, penniless self.

"You should publish a collection of your political interviews," Alekos said.

She stared. "How do you read my mind?" She had been considering a book showcasing those very interviews. "I would include yours, of course."

"Mine?" He ducked his head as if he didn't believe her.

What a beautiful, humble man. Beautiful but badly dressed. The boutiques around Piazza de Spagna were the most expensive in Rome and she took him straight to Brioni. "This would look good on you." She pointed to the mannequin in the window sporting gray trousers and a black leather jacket and headed for the door.

Alekos yanked her back. "I don't need new clothes," he said and stalked toward the fountain.

"Oh yes you do," she grumbled and followed.

The next morning, she was on the phone to Tommaso. "A collection of twenty of my political interviews." The idea had gathered steam in her brain overnight.

"Difficult to select which ones," Tommaso said.

"The most famous names. And Panagoulis, of course. Good idea, eh? Your hen who lays the golden eggs."

"Great idea," Tommaso said. She could imagine him swiveling in his chair with satisfaction since *L'Europeo* would earn a hefty percentage of her sales. "But *Interview with History*?" he said. "Isn't the title a bit grandiose?"

"What grandiose?" Oriana said. "There's no other profession that allows you to record history as it happens. That's why it scares me. It's an awesome responsibility."

"You, scared?"

"I give two thousand percent when I write, you know that. Exert all my brain and senses. I can't make a mistake. The truth matters to me deeply."

"Write that in your preface."

She grunted. "I will."

Did you tear Mulotti a new one? she was dying to ask. But she didn't need the aggravation and stopped herself with uncharacteristic restraint. Why give a damn about some rag's lies? *The moment Oriana saw him on television, she stole the interview from a fellow reporter* . . . That's right, and she would steal it again. Hadn't it been the luckiest of coincidences that she'd met Alekos?

Love was good to her for a change. She even had a book project that made her feel like herself again. Oriana called a meeting of her Rizzoli editors to discuss which interviews to include in the new collection, then did what she always did, followed her own instinct and decided for herself. In their suite, on Hotel Excelsior stationery, she drafted a preface that would tie the portraits together. What did world leaders have in common? Ego. Self-preservation. Abuse. She stated unequivocally that she abhorred power, that the only sane thing to do in the face of power was to interrogate and resist. *There's something abnormal about believing you should rule over millions of people. No one who craves power should have it. Abraham Lincoln said that to test a man's character, give him power. Well, the men I've met fail miserably. They don't have the character to command anyone, not even their dog.*

In the hours that she worked, Alekos reunited with fellow activists from his university days. They were Greeks now living in Rome and they greeted him enthusiastically at Sant' Eustachio for espresso. Yes it was terrible what was happening in poor Greece, but they had no time for rebellion, no funds to donate. Would Alekos join them for a dinner *festa* instead?

"They've moved on," Oriana said, looking up from her desk, tempted to add, *You should, too.* But she felt sorry, watching him flail, and she had promised to help, so she arranged a meeting with Sandro Pertini, the president of Parliament. Pertini had been sentenced to death by Mussolini himself, she told Alekos. "He's a true patriot, like you."

Pertini embraced Alekos, calling him "a man of rare integrity" and promising to provide assistance to Greece. But his help never materialized. He was out of the country, he couldn't be reached.

"These are the same politicians who championed me in prison." Alekos slammed down the phone. "Now that I'm not a symbol sleeping on a dirt floor, they have no time for me."

He was right. Nobody gave a damn. Attention spans were short. Deep down, though she would never admit it, she was a little bit pleased that Alekos felt lost, that she was the only thing he had. For the first time with a man, she wasn't the vulnerable one, the one in the weaker position.

Some newspaper reported that Fallaci's ten-year age difference with the Greek hero was unnoticeable. Vanna's beauty salon would keep it that way. She made an appointment for a haircut and manicure and left Alekos in Piazza del Popolo at Rosati's outdoor tables.

"You have lire?" she said, taking a crisp bill from her purse. He hesitated before stuffing it into his pocket. "There's a Caravaggio in the church if you get bored."

She returned with her hair freshly trimmed, nails the latest apple red, and a garment bag slung over her shoulder. Alekos was pacing nervously in front of the café. "For you," she said, handing him the garment bag.

He tugged open the zipper, recognized the clothes from Brioni's window, and shoved them back at her. "I won't be kept."

"Fine," she said, but it wasn't fine. "If that's how you feel. It was a gift."

"I don't want gifts."

"Lower your voice." He was embarrassing her. They were drawing stares. She was easily recognized. "Let's walk."

They returned to the Excelsior in silence. He stormed into the bedroom and slammed the door. She fumed. Alekos didn't want to live in exile, didn't want to be kept. Too bad. He should thank his lucky stars for the day he met her. She had saved him from the dictator and lavished him with Roman luxury, and instead of a glorious homecoming, he was turning it to shit.

On the coffee table, she glimpsed the newspaper photo of their arrival at Fiumicino five days earlier. Alekos tall and looming, his arm heavy around her, and she smiling and shrunken. Women always beneath their men, supporting characters.

Absolutely not, she was not liking this version of herself. She would meet with Rizzoli, move up the deadline of her book.

The bedroom was quiet. She listened hard, refusing to go in. After a minute, Alekos emerged wearing the new leather jacket and trousers.

"*Bello.*" She went to him, her muscles tense from fighting, her heart remaining soft for him. They stood for a long time in the embrace.

"I don't know why you love me," he murmured into her hair. "I don't have money or a job."

"I don't care about that."

He kissed her. Slid his hand under her blouse. All at once the balance shifted between them, and who was richer or more famous didn't matter. They dropped their clothes on the carpet. He lifted her onto the sofa.

"Come," he said when they were dressed again. "I want to show you something." He went to the balcony door and parted the curtain.

She peered out. Two men in dark suits and sunglasses lurked on the sidewalk, staring up at their suite. Her eyes shot to his.

"Plainclothes this time," he said.

Impossible. Was the dictator surveilling him even in Italy? Of course.

"You want to keep me safe," Alekos said. There was a catch in his voice, telling her that he was grateful, that he loved her, too. "But you can't."

Panic seeped through her, but she stopped it cold. *I can.* She saw a flash of herself as a child partisan, pedaling through

German roadblocks. A novice reporter, digging up stories in the rain, men assuming she was the coffee girl. How stubborn she'd had to be.

"I never give in." She leveled her gaze at him. "Like you. And I want to go to Casole."

Chapter 23

1973

The three-hundred-year-old country house was her oasis. Oriana managed to become almost serene in Casole. The rolling hills of Tuscany, carpeted with fir and cypress, the verdant vineyards that produced barrels of her own Chianti. She fell in sync with the seasons, bottling tomatoes in August, harvesting fat purple grapes in September with a kerchief tied around her hair. Finding a peace in the natural world that she never found in herself.

Casole was a sprinkling of houses tucked into the hills of Greve-in-Chianti, thirty kilometers south of Florence but another world. The countryside carried inside it the innocence of childhood, where her father had taken her hunting and her mother taught her to search out black truffles under tree roots in the forest, gathering them in her smudged apron. Oriana still remembered being allowed to use a special knife to shave truffle onto homemade tagliolini for supper, and the next morning onto poached eggs.

Her parents lived in the neighboring valley. She had bought them a farmhouse and installed an American washing machine that her mother never used. Her own house had three stories and a tower plus a more commanding view. The ivy crawling up the stone walls was fire-red in November. Her olives were ripe for picking, ready to be smashed by granite grinders and pressed into liquid gold. Casole was her perfect place, where she and Alekos could retreat from the world and be something unique. A couple.

They dropped their bags upstairs in her bedroom. It was simple but cozy and she had put her feminine stamp on it with a braided oval rug, rose coverlet, and collection of antique perfume bottles on the dresser. The moment Alekos set foot in the room, he altered the atmosphere, charging it with masculinity. It startled her, seeing him bounce on the double bed that had always contained her alone, testing it out with a grin. She liked him there.

On the train to Greve-in-Chianti, watching Alekos sleep, she had done battle with her doubts. Would he always have a target on his back, always be courting danger? Could they live together in her country? People weren't perfect, but always she expected them to be. That would have to change. If she demanded perfection in her relationship, the way she did in her writing, she would sleep alone.

The specter of returning to her former existence, typewriter-tapes-cigarettes, cracked open a cavern of loneliness. She had dropped her guard with this man and didn't know how to erect it back up again. My God, she was cooked. Alekos had become the person she sought all day long, his opinions, company, comfort. She had given herself to him, she was a fountain of giving: plane tickets, clothes, shelter. Now she gave him her hope.

"Tomorrow we'll walk the property," she said, immensely proud of being a landowner. Her house had twenty-three rooms, giving her the security she never had as a girl. Alekos followed her like a duckling, looking overwhelmed as she pulled sheets off furniture and threw open the green shutters for light to stream in. There were bookcases in every room, the books slanting every which way, well used.

"This is all yours?" He turned stiffly in the living room. "All these possessions?" He stared at the antiques she collected in the breakfront, nineteenth-century Murano glass pitchers in red, salt and pepper shakers in crystal.

Antiques brought warmth and character to a home, she said, remembering the frumpy furnishings of Glyfada, where he'd grown up. "They defy death, they're here for eternity."

Alekos nodded, his face tinged with doubt.

"These I made myself." She plumped up two needlepoint pillows of happy clowns on the red velvet settee. How oddly she'd been raised, her mother admonishing her to shun domesticity while at the same time steeping her in the domestic arts. Oriana had spent hours by Tosca's side practicing the difficult *punto tagliato*, the needle lace for decorating pillowcases and tablecloths. "For your trousseau," her mother had said each time she finished a new cutwork frill. The hand-stitched white linens were now on her bed upstairs, and in New York and Florence—her unmarried beds. Oriana appreciated the handiwork more as her mother grew older. She had learned so much about being an Italian woman from Mamma, mostly through osmosis, including how to treat a man. Food on the table three times a day, his clothes clean and laid out on the bed. Where is my toolbox, belt, cap? Her mother always knew.

The country kitchen featured an immense fireplace where farmers used to cook their meals. Oriana stepped inside it and spread her arms wide, demonstrating its size. Alekos watched, impressed, then took from the mantelpiece a large doll, blond and blue-eyed, and gave her a puzzled look.

"She's porcelain," Oriana said, smoothing Antonella's blue velvet dress. With that one gesture, the longing of her childhood swooshed back, watching the grocer's daughters play with dolls in the piazza because the family was rich. As soon as Oriana earned her first paycheck from *Il Mattino*, she walked straight to the toy store on Via Cavour. At sixteen, she was too old to play with dolls, but she bought Antonella anyway. "I never had one as a girl," she told Alekos briskly, but he saw through.

"We couldn't afford toys either." He stroked her hair.

She set the doll back and shook off the melancholy of the past, pulling him down the hallway. "Come see my study." It was a small, intimate room with a worn green carpet, soaring bookshelves, and a dark walnut desk littered with papers. Awaiting her was her black Olivetti, and next to it a half-filled crystal ashtray. She had the same model typewriter in every home. The machine was both friend and enemy in the long hours she spent wrestling with ideas. Finally, just as her brain was wrung out, she had the satisfaction of hitting the last carriage return, pulling the release lever, and yanking out the page.

"This can be your desk, next to mine." She cleared off a leather side table with claw feet. "You can write about the regime, I'll help you publish. The pen is mightier than the sword."

"I don't need a desk," he said, and retreated out the doorway. She followed him upstairs, where he sprawled on the bedcovers, hands behind his head, staring at the ceiling. "This is how I did my best thinking in Boyati."

"My country home reminds you of prison?"

"I need to raise money. Organize," he mumbled.

She shook her head at the maddening figure in her bed. Her Tuscan bed that he sparked alive, that even now, despite his mood, she wanted to climb into.

But the sight of her Olivetti had caught her. Leaving Alekos to ponder his next move, she padded downstairs to her study and fingered the keys. The very act soothed her. Writing was backbreaking work, but how much better the world's news bent to her will than the enigma upstairs.

On impulse, the phone was in her hand. "Tommaso, I'm in Toscana."

"When are you coming in?"

"My new book is going well. Thanks for asking."

"I need three thousand words on the abortion debate."

She hesitated. "I'll think about it."

"Think fast. They've made it legal in America."

"I read. I'm not an imbecile."

"Italy could be next," he said.

"Alert the Pope."

"I have three reporters clamoring for the assignment. Mulotti, too."

"You can't be serious."

"They're all former altar boys, staunchly against."

"I'll do it." She could almost see Tommaso's victory grin, having enticed her.

"I want to meet him," Tommaso said.

"Hmph. I thought it was me you missed."

As soon as she hung up, she threaded a blank sheet into the roller. Abortion was a Pandora's box, even a crack of the lid prompted tangled arguments to come shooting out. She found herself blocked, couldn't type a word. Too much anguish she didn't care to revisit and Alekos upstairs, so close she could practically feel him breathing.

In her daily bustle around Florence, she saw dozens of mothers walking children to school, and always it felt like a gut punch, witnessing the profound connection of a little hand inside a big one. These mothers were raising the next generation of humans. It was an important job, perhaps the most important, if you were lucky enough to get it. Oriana believed ardently in the miracle of life. She was pure Italian that way, the mother-child bond was sacred and she longed for a child herself. But nobody had the right to tell a woman what to do with her body. Certainly no man.

For years, her own pregnancy had lurked just below consciousness where she'd jammed it, excised along with Gori, but the memories swooped back with force. The hope she'd felt carrying Renzo's baby. How crushed she'd been when he didn't want it—*didn't want her*. Maybe he would love her if she obeyed and underwent the procedure. When it was done, she hobbled off the table, stuffed with gauze, imagining a smashed egg, that's how she pictured it, the baby scraped out of her with a bladed metal instrument. In the cab outside the Normandie Hotel, she reached for her pocketbook and saw blood pooled on the tan leather seat. *Her blood.* Hot, reeling, she opened the taxi door with a glance at the driver. Had he seen, should she tell him? It was one step to the sidewalk, two more to the entry. She regained consciousness with the doorman bending over her, confused by his red tunic and shiny brass buttons. Thinking it was a guard at Buckingham Palace.

Surgery. "You might have trouble in the future," the doctor told her in recovery and briskly left her bedside. The curettage, a nurse explained, avoiding the word "abortion," had been incomplete, and a second scraping had been necessary. "Trouble with what?" Oriana had asked, murky with anesthesia. "Scarring," the nurse said.

Now she stared at the blank sheet in her typewriter, kicking herself for accepting the assignment. Damn Tommaso, he knew how to press her buttons. She remembered the first issue of *Ms.* magazine published a year ago and searched for it in her stacks. The page was still folded, the stunning two-page declaration, "We have had abortions," signed by fifty-three prominent women, including Judy Collins, Nora Ephron, Lillian Hellman, Grace Paley, Anne Sexton, Susan Sontag—and Steinem herself, the magazine's cofounder.

Such a radical act. An army of women giving authority the finger and boldly asserting their truth to overturn an unjust law. Oriana had guts, but she would never expose herself in public that way. Her abortion felt as critical to cover up as nakedness on the street. Confessing an act so personal went against everything she'd learned about climbing her way up in journalism: She had to be a man, not a woman. Acceptance required that she disavow every female "weakness," from menstrual cramps to the catastrophic breaking of her heart to the visceral regret that she never bore a child. But wait, she thought, where were the men's signatures admitting *We Have Had Abortions*? Their sperm, their abortions. But no, men got off the hook silently and anonymously, while women bore the anguish and responsibility—and as if that weren't enough, bared their souls.

Sorry *Ms.*, but she would never confess to seeking out the dank office in East London. Didn't she have enough venom directed at her by media elites? Besides, Catholic Italy was more devout, more traditional, than America. Not to mention *la bella figura*, the Italian preoccupation with making a fine impression, not just in fashionable appearance but in reputation. This was not freewheeling America, where everyone was expanding their minds on LSD and reading pop psychology and letting it all hang out.

Although she couldn't imagine signing her own name, she admired the hell out of these women. The page included a "coupon," which readers were encouraged to clip and mail in with their names. "I have had an abortion," the coupon stated. It was a petition, really, to repeal the laws impinging on reproductive freedom. Oriana imagined the deluge of mail that must have poured into *Ms.* A million women in America had "illegal" abortions in 1971. Proportionally, just as many in her country and in Europe—maybe more.

Basta. She slammed closed Pandora's box. Tomorrow she would work on the article. Where was he? She listened. Still staring at the ceiling, probably. Her impatience flared. Why did she bring him to Italy, to her sanctuary in Casole—so he could sulk and ignore her?

"Mamma, we're here." She needed to hear their voices.

Her father got on the extension and immediately they began. Why didn't she tell them, they would have opened the house, brought fresh eggs and marmalade.

"Is everything all right?" A mother's omniscience.

"How does he like the farmhouse?" Her father.

"He's hiding in bed. Who knows," Oriana said.

"Still recovering, poor boy. Not used to large spaces. Casole will be medicine for his soul."

Her father was right, it hit her at once. Five years of solitary confinement had damaged Alekos. He *was* still recovering. In Glyfada and Rome, he had anxiously clutched her arm to cross busy streets, misjudging distances, veering too far left and right to avoid pedestrians. Indoors, he mechanically paced two steps forward and two back, still trapped in his cell. Since arriving in Italy, she'd been annoyed that Alekos wasn't deliriously happy, when she should have been compassionate—he was hurt, he needed her, patience.

In Vietnam, hadn't she learned too well the fragility of men? For every dutiful soldier who kept his sanity through the slaughter, she met a wrecked kid. She never understood which point became the breaking point, but soldiers broke all the time. The redheaded boy from Kansas was never far from her mind.

They had jumped out of a helicopter together onto Hill 875, and Jeff extended his hand to help her landing. "Ma'am," he said. "Are the rumors true? All the guys are dying up there?" He gestured uphill at the thick canopy of trees, his platoon's destination.

"No," she lied, knowing that Company A of the 503rd had been badly ambushed the day before. Fifty boys were dead. "You'll be fine."

It was November and eighty-one degrees, but she was chilled with perspiration trickling down her ribs. Jeff said a reluctant goodbye and headed off to join his platoon. Around her, soldiers were hacking out a landing zone in the jungle for air support. Others had begun their advance up the slope. Should she follow? Fear chewed her insides, and before she could decide, a whistle shrieked. She clamped her hands over her helmet and dove under a eucalyptus tree. Rockets and mortar fire. Fireballs shooting through the sky.

She spun around to see a burly soldier drooling snot and tears. "I can't, man! Don't make me go!" A comrade was pulling his arm, coaxing him to keep up with the unit, but the soldier had broken down. The atrocity of war made her turn away, what happens to men when they're ordered to kill.

Just as Oriana turned, she spotted Jeff with his red crew cut beginning the charge uphill. Good luck, she wished him, but her thought was obliterated by a rocket raining down on his platoon. Her bowels froze. When the smoke cleared, she staggered to where she'd last seen the boy, straight into a cloud of pink mist. Blood and bone oozed into her eyes and mouth, and she coughed and spit to get them out. Blindly, she looked around for the boy, then finally at the ground. Only his boots were left.

Alekos had never served on the front lines as a soldier, but he'd suffered shell shock. In Athens (she had tried to forget this incident), he had bolted upright in his sleep, shouting, "I'll make you piss blood, Zaharakis!" He had stared at her with terror, fists balled, believing she was the prison warden. She had calmed him in her arms, loved him more, seeing his fear. Casole would be a balm for his soul. She would make sure.

On the second morning, she dabbed Joy behind her ears and trailed it to the bed. "Our farmer's market is the best in Toscana." She leaned over him in her scoop-neck blouse, describing the delicacies they would buy. Balsamico sweet enough to drizzle over gelato. Prosciutto from pigs that ate only acorns.

"Acorns, eh?" He wet his lips.

She called a taxi and an hour later they were in Greve-in-Chianti, a medieval hilltown whose central square was actually a triangle, the cobblestoned Piazza Matteotti. The farmer's market took over Piazza Matteotti three times a week with long tables of fruits and vegetables, meat and fish, kitchen utensils, shrubs, even clothing—everything from underwear and housedresses to hunting jackets.

Oriana combed through mountains of purple radicchio, juicy tomatoes, leafy escarole, showing Alekos how to choose only the best and stuffing her selections into the net shopping bags he carried. They met Simone, the wrinkled blue-eyed farmer in charge of her vineyards, at his wine table, and he explained to Alekos the percentage of fat purple Sangiovese grapes required for Chianti Classico, the best wine in the region. Simone loaded Alekos up with two straw amphoras of his aged *Riserva*.

"You like *cotechino*?" Oriana asked, stopping before her usual salumeria stand. "*Cotechino* is my specialty."

"You cook?" Alekos said with surprise.

"I'm an excellent cook. In Italy it's a very sad home without aromas from the kitchen." She ordered a kilo of sausage, shaking her finger *No, No* when the vendor held up a string, pointing to the exact one in the case she wanted.

At the farmhouse in the afternoon, she brought out cushions for the wrought iron chairs and they relaxed around the mosaic-tiled table in the fading sun. The slate patio was framed by soft lavender, broom, and pink oleander. The vista was all rolling sienna hills dotted with cypresses and vineyards, with no other house in sight. Her favorite tree was the cypress, she told Alekos, because it stood tall and dignified, like a soldier. Oriana stretched her legs over the colorful table, but he roamed the garden, admiring the rosebushes and wildflowers. He was starting to like it here.

"You know the story of Persephone?" he called, gazing up at a pomegranate tree. "It's a symbol of fertility, the pomegranate."

"I know my Greek mythology. That thug Hades." She went to him. "Lift me up. November is their season."

He swung her up easily, she weighed less than a hundred pounds, and she twisted off a perfect pink globe. Then, hunting for a stone, she cracked it open, tearing apart the flesh and handing him half.

"You could behead a chicken." He looked impressed. "I'm sure of it."

"This I never tried."

He scooped out ruby pomegranate seeds and fed them to her, licking the juice off his fingers. Fertility. She watched the red juice stain him. Perhaps—she was careful not to wish too hard—she wasn't too old. They might still make a baby in Casole.

At dinnertime, he trailed her into the kitchen.

She donned an apron, tied her hair in a twist. "*Cotechino* is a Tuscan specialty," Oriana said, expertly slicing the sausage stuffed with pork and spices. "We serve it with polenta and lentils."

"I've eaten too many lentils for one lifetime," Alekos said.

"Mine you'll love."

He poured Chianti and they linked arms and toasted.

She darted to the stove and he followed, sniffing the aromas. "Stir this." She set him before a buttery polenta and he brought the wooden spoon to his lips, making a noise of satisfaction. She prepared the lentils. "You must use only red onions for this dish. Don't forget."

"I don't cook. You cook," he said, stirring.

"Because I am excellent and you are a disaster. Not because you have a penis."

He dropped the spoon and lifted her onto the farm table, sweeping aside brown paper packages filled with mortadella, peppers, olives. The wine had loosened her and he made it seem like the most natural thing in the world, her bare bottom against the weathered oak table, surrounded by food and sustenance.

"The polenta," she said, glancing at the stove.

"Don't. Worry." He focused on her alone.

It was fast and heated, and the moment they were done, they tore open the antipasti and devoured prosciutto with their hands. Hunks of parmesan. Crusty bread. The polenta had stuck to the pot, but so what, she would start over, they would eat at midnight. It was a revelation cooking together, the way Alekos stayed close to her all evening.

In the dining room, they ate by candlelight. For dessert, she had whipped up another Tuscan specialty, mini tarts stuffed with pine nuts and dried figs baked in the oven.

"You spoil me," Alekos said, his mouth full.

It's my favorite thing to do. Her whole body smiled back. Her mother was wrong. *Don't be a servant, fly fly*. Servitude was being chained to your desk, smoking sixty cigarettes a day and getting wrinkled. Her interviews lasted four to six hours and were so physically taxing, she often lost two or three pounds. Servitude was continuously having to prove yourself to resentful colleagues who wanted to see you fall on your face.

Tonight she relaxed in the coziness of the hearth, in domesticity and being a couple. Journalism with its austere demands, its lonely discipline, receded.

Later, as she drifted to sleep, his head on her shoulder, she had the clear sensation of being a girl. Skipping through the fields of Toscana, before the war. Her parents each holding a hand, lifting her up, up, off the ground.

Chapter 24

1973

In the morning, she woke to find him staring at the ceiling. Again.

"I have a new plan."

"Does it involve dynamite?" She yawned. "Or attacking the dictator with your bare hands?"

"You don't understand me." Alekos stormed out of bed. "You've never understood me."

"*I* don't?" she fired back. "Who the hell does?"

He yanked on yesterday's pants. "You want to lock me in your hotels and your villas."

"Poor thing."

"If I want to risk my life, it's my right. Even if I want to die, it's my right."

"Wrong." There it was. The chasm that would always stand between them. "You should appreciate life. Guard it. Life is precious."

"Not for me," he said. "Life is precious only if you fight. If you don't give in."

She kicked off the covers and stomped to the dresser, ripping a brush through her hair. "Are you sure you don't have a hero complex, Alekos? You're the only one who can save Greece?" There, she said it.

"I don't know any other way to live." His eyes pierced hers.

"Neither do you. You're always the center of what you write. Who's the hero?"

"It's *my* show." How dare he criticize her work.

"I decide whether I live or die."

"Fine. Die." She turned to march out but her feet got tangled in his dirty laundry on the floor. "Pick up your goddamn underwear!" Downstairs in her study, she flung herself into her chair. The man was impossible. Her heart beat wildly. He didn't care about living? *That meant he didn't care about her.* She couldn't win. How could she win against that? Everything was more important to him, Greece, the dictator, his flailing organizing. Well, she had important work, too.

The blank page in the typewriter taunted her. She let out a shaky exhale, the first one, it seemed, since their fight. Concentrate. No matter how many times she nailed it, the beginning of an article was always a crisis. Could she pull it off, was she good enough?

Fingers sliding onto the keys, she dove in, pushing herself until ideas and phrases bubbled up from she didn't know where. The mere act of applying her intellect unknotted her shoulders. *Roe v. Wade* had been decided on the basis of a right to privacy. Privacy, ha. Ludicrous in Italy, where three generations lived under one roof, screaming. She angled her head to listen for Alekos's footsteps. Wasn't he going to chase her and make up? She had the urge to yell some more and shake him to his senses, but she was also scared. Scared he would always be exasperating, scared he would leave her, the way every other man had disappeared from her life and ultimately been a mirage.

The half paragraph in her Olivetti was garbage. She pressured herself to do better, but abortion was too unwieldy a topic for one article. And there was her own messy history, which she didn't want to stir up. Straining, she listened for signs of life upstairs. Ambition leaked out of her, an unfamiliar sensation, and she dropped her hands.

The confession of Golda Meir came back to her. Oriana had interviewed the prime minister of Israel a year ago in her white stucco home in Jerusalem and been moved by her modesty and warm, earthy manner. Male journalists focused on her appearance, calling Meir ugly, but she reminded Oriana of her own mother, with her gray bun, black dress and pearls, and bowlegs. Meir lived alone, and since her housekeeper had left for the day, the prime minister herself served apricot cookies and coffee as they sat together in the living room and chain-smoked.

Oriana's early questions were about peace in the Middle East and whether they would see it in their lifetimes. Meir said no, and they discussed another possible war between Israel and Arab nations and her willingness to negotiate over the West Bank but never Jerusalem. Soon, unexpectedly, Meir opened up about her personal life. For the first time with any journalist, she spoke of "the heartache of her life." That was how this formidable world leader described the breakup with her husband.

"There is a type of woman who cannot remain at home," Meir said, eyeing Oriana. "Her nature demands a larger stage." A flicker of recognition passed between them. Meir was always attending political meetings, but her husband wanted her to live a quiet family life.

"Did you ever try to change, to make him happy?" Oriana leaned in, sensing wisdom she might glean from the older woman.

"I tried," Meir said. She left the kibbutz where she was thriving and moved to Jerusalem, giving birth to two children and attempting to be a conventional housewife. "I couldn't do it." Her eyes welled as she reached for another cigarette. "We separated."

Oriana felt a lump in her throat and lit up, too. It was an awkward moment when she delved so far into a soul, exposed vulnerability so openly, like a wound, but she pressed on. "Why didn't you divorce, Mrs. Meir, and marry a man more suitable?"

"People are not replaceable like old shoes. He was my first love. I met him when I was fifteen." Meir's face was unbearably candid. "A love like that never ends. Even though we couldn't live together, there was an unbreakable bond between us." Her voice caught. "We saw each other until the day he died."

The words had seared themselves into Oriana's brain. *A love like that never ends. Could not live together.* Even when she returned home and was composing the interview, she could still see the prime minister's deeply lined face, her doleful eyes. A phrase came to her that described Meir's predicament: the tragedy of love's not being enough. She congratulated herself for thinking it up even as she felt unsettled. The words had come too easily.

Now, for the third time, she listened for Alekos. Nothing. She trudged to the kitchen for espresso, always a high point. The Illy canister was in the refrigerator, and reflexively she scanned the eggplant and ricotta, wondering about dinner. She wasn't in the mood for big preparations. Fuck cooking.

"What should we cook tonight?"

She turned. Alekos was standing close, his chest rising and giving off heat. In the long moment before he kissed her, silently apologizing, confessing his need, she knew they would not be a tragedy, not be incapable of living together. Love would be enough, if she had anything to do with it.

In the evening, he built a fire. She curled into an armchair and watched him squat by the hearth to arrange logs. She liked watching him from this angle, the way he moved.

"Were you working on your new book?" he asked over his shoulder. Her mouth opened in surprise. "Earlier, I heard you typing."

"It's an article," she said.

"Make it a book."

Uncanny, his intuition. The way he picked up what she was grappling with. Abortion was too fraught to fit into the confines of a word count. The trials of being a woman deserved more attention. Journalism suddenly felt like a straitjacket.

"You want to write great literature," Alekos said, wiping his hands on his thighs and coming to her. "Get started."

"But literature is more difficult." Her forehead knit with worry. "In journalism, I tell the true story. I steal. I don't make up anything."

"You don't believe you can do it."

She shrugged.

He took her face in his hands, making sure she heard every word. "You have a voice like no other. A poetic imagination. No one is as good as you. Write your novel."

A wave of gratitude filled her. She had never known a man so sincerely on her side. It was one of the reasons she loved Alekos, maybe the main reason. He saw her essence and wanted what was best for her. But literature was daunting, and she had just found him. "It will take years to complete a novel," she said. "And who will make the pasta?"

"Don't give up who you are," he said.

Of course she wouldn't. She searched his face. Was he pushing her away? But she liked taking care of him, liked feeling essential. She was proud of her achievements, but she didn't want to stand separate from him. It made her feel insecure, as if she would surely lose him.

Alekos turned to the bookshelf, to her silver-framed photographs, his gaze moving from one to the other with undisguised admiration. Oriana with Robert Kennedy, Pierre Salinger, Paul Newman, Shirley MacLaine. The photos were proof that a woman could wrap her pretty little head around geopolitics, a carpenter's daughter could drink whiskey with Paul Newman and take a road trip with Shirley MacLaine.

"When you write it," Alekos said, "make this your author photo." He held up a black-and-white picture of Oriana in a headscarf. She was standing on a ladder in her vineyard, reaching her knife toward a cluster of ripe grapes.

"Funny," she said.

"Why not?" Alekos teased. "Because you gave up your Dior sunglasses to be one of the people?"

"What is it you have against looking and smelling nice?" She teased him right back. Yes, she was the offspring of socialists, but she appreciated the good things in life. She was not an idiot.

He picked up her real author photo, the one taken by Francesco Scavullo with her hair blowing back like a fashion model. "Caught in a hurricane?"

She leaned forward in her chair and slapped his backside, and they laughed with the intimacy that seemed to go on forever, that was present from the day they met. "At the photo shoot," she said, "Francesco kept snapping his camera and shouting *Brava, Oriana. Grande diva.* I felt stunning and desirable. What a ridiculous way to earn a living, these models. Maybe not so ridiculous. I'm tied to my desk shriveling like a prune."

"You are stunning." Alekos kneeled before her. "And desirable. Many, many women in one."

She felt the quick pressure of tears. A deep contentment, then its opposite, the sudden dread that life was too good and it would all end.

Alekos flicked open her blouse. She was bare beneath and he brushed her with his fingertips. Only he could do that, get her body to say yes before her mind knew he was asking.

Chapter 25

1973

Her two men. She watched her father and Alekos exchange a warm handshake in the gravel courtyard of her farmhouse, struck by the tableau they made: both brave patriots, selflessly fought fascism, suffered in prison.

Her mother double-kissed Alekos with wary admiration and Oriana read that tableau, too: Tosca anticipating the entire spectrum of misfortunes that could befall a woman in the roulette of mating.

Oriana had never introduced a man to her parents and felt self-conscious in the new two-couple configuration. "Go walk." She waved the men away. "*Babbo*, check on my new vines." Her father tended the earth since moving to Casole, patiently caring for his goats and chickens, vegetable and rose gardens. She relied on him to manage her property.

The men ambled into the fields, instantly linked in conversation. Oriana watched as they receded, two rebel fighters, her father shriveled, Alekos in his prime. The cycle of life, young into old. It mattered greatly what you did with your time.

Babbo was in his seventies. She had nearly lost him once in the car crash. She would lose him one day. The thought of being without her parents always carried with it its dark twin. *Who would love her?* She tried imagining Alekos with a shock of white hair and her own creased face beside him. Would they have the chance to grow old together? It seemed a version of the future never within her reach. Her father was fine-boned and fair like Oriana, her mother stocky and olive-skinned, but they had begun to resemble each other decades ago, facial expressions, phrases, rare laughter.

"He's handsome," her mother said as they strolled to the back patio and observed the men nearing the vineyards. "What will he do now?"

"He's not one to stop fighting." Oriana lit a cigarette.

"Will he stay in Italy?"

"We will. Together."

"You're working from Casole?" her mother said.

Oriana bristled, remembering her unfinished abortion assignment. "I'm bringing out a new book of my political interviews," she said, and then, "No, in fact. I'm not working. I'm tired, ever since I was sixteen. Airplanes, hotels. Money, furniture, jewelry. I feel nothing." She waved her cigarette, launched now, saying things to her mother she never had. Saying things to herself.

"You would feel differently if you were poor," Tosca said. "If you had a brood of children tugging at your skirt."

"But I don't have children," Oriana said, with blame.

Tosca toed the patio with her Ferragamo pumps, a gift from Oriana last Christmas. "Will you marry?" Bizarrely, her mother sounded hopeful, though she had raised her daughter to pursue less predictable goals.

"He is my partner," Oriana said. "We're two modern people. I don't want it. Neither does he."

Tosca looked confused, the era of flower power and love the one you're with was one she knew little about. Surely she understood that Oriana had been breaking the female mold since she was sixteen and hustled her way into the newsroom. Tosca never asked about the obstacles she faced in her profession, and Oriana never told her, assuming she had to fight her own battles. Instead, their ritual when Oriana returned from a trip to interview Indira Gandhi, say, was to sit down with espressos and clip a twenty-two carat gold bracelet onto her mother's wrist as a gift. Then Oriana would provide dispatches from India where women were in positions of power yet forced to undergo sterilization. Her mother listened with wide eyes, curious to know more about the world but perhaps not too much about her daughter.

But now Tosca was asking the very question paparazzi asked. Do I hear wedding bells? No, her temper flared. Alekos loved her, he showed his need for her every day, but they would not support a reactionary institution. Even so, insecurity crept through her. A mother's words, always powerful.

She threw her cigarette down and grounded it with her heel. "It's children that make a woman's life. Not marriage," Oriana said, unable to keep the edge out of her voice. Alekos made love to her constantly, but it was starting to sink in, she had probably missed her chance.

Tosca reflected briefly, then folded her hands and nodded. Her mother had done her best, Oriana knew, wishing she hadn't been so sharp, registering the sagging cheeks, the ever-grayer hair. Tosca had no way of knowing that a career would bring accolades but, ultimately, too much solitude. That no matter which path a woman chose, there was always a heavy price to pay, making her feel inadequate. A lesser person than she was born to be.

Where were they? Evening was falling, and Oriana squinted to make out their figures. The problem with solitude, she'd discovered, was you grew used to it, aloneness hardened into habit. She had never learned to get along with another human being. Never said, "I'm sorry." Never been able to forgive.

There they were. She strode out to meet the men, tucking herself between them and linking arms. "Let's go in, boys," she said. "Alekos will show you his poetry, Babbo. And we have *ribollita* for dinner."

She was nervous and drank too much Chianti at dinner, but she needn't have worried. Alekos held out Tosca's chair and filled Edoardo's glass, winning them with his sweetness and humility, the way he'd won her across the doily-covered nightstand in his mother's bedroom in Glyfada.

"You must visit Greece," Alekos said to her parents. "And stay at my home."

"We've longed to see the land of Homer," Edoardo said. "When democracy returns, not now. We can't do much at our age to show opposition, but this we must."

"God willing, it will be soon," Tosca said. "Will you return home?" she asked pointedly.

Oriana tensed. Naturally she wanted Greece to topple the dictator, but she'd carefully avoided thinking about that day.

"I will," Alekos said. "If she'll come with me." He gazed at her across the table.

"I'll come." The words poured out before she could think, *How will I work?* and *Athens is too backward*.

"Edoardo tried to run for political office after Mussolini fell," Tosca said, "but on his way to the rally, a truck hit him."

Oriana stared at her silverware. Why was her mother bringing that up? They never had, not in all these years.

"Signore Fallaci told me of his injury on our walk," Alekos said, his eyes welling.

"I remember sitting in that chair, utterly useless. I couldn't serve my country." Edoardo shook his head, choked with emotion.

Oriana was moved by her two men. Their tenderness, their capacity to be soft, still surprised her. Fierce fighters with sympathetic hearts. She relaxed fully, feeling the three people she loved form a warm knot around her.

"We read *Others Will Follow*," her mother said shyly to Alekos. "We were pleased when you won the Viareggio Prize. How did you learn of it in prison?"

"I didn't. Not for two months."

Tosca and Edoardo exchanged looks. "You must sign our copy," Tosca said.

"The title is perfect. The struggle doesn't end in one generation," Edoardo said. "You have followed me, and others will follow you."

"I hope so," Alekos said.

"He's written more poems," Oriana said, and to Alekos, "Show them."

"After dinner." Bashfully, he ducked his head. "Oriana tells me of your passion for literature," he said to her parents. "The red leather classics in your home."

"I selected what she should read," Tosca said. "Tolstoy. Dickens. Sophocles and Homer, of course."

"Reading was my education," Oriana said. "That's why I'm not impressed with degrees."

"She graduated *Liceo Classico Galileo* at sixteen with high honors," Tosca said.

"I was always pestering my teachers with questions, always correcting them when they were wrong," Oriana said. "They didn't like me."

"She earned an eight in ancient Greek on final exams," Edoardo said.

"Better than me." Alekos chuckled. "Now I want to teach her modern Greek."

He fixed her with a look, and she felt an electric volt jump across the table. "I know *alitaki, agapi*," she said, flushing, knowing her parents could see their attraction.

"Everything Oriana did, she did with excellence," Tosca said. "We didn't accept anything less."

"She always wanted to write," Edoardo said.

"You told me writers can't earn a living," Oriana said. "Mamma told me Jack London was a waiter. It frightened me. I lost precious years."

"You lost nothing," said Tosca. "Count how many books you've published."

"Journalism is not the same." Oriana traded looks with Alekos. "I come from a long line of stubborn Fallacis."

"It's not too late," he said, his voice low, only for her.

They said good night in the graveled courtyard. Alekos kissed Tosca and called her *Mamma*.

"We look forward to seeing you again," Tosca said, her expression eager. Her father patted Alekos on the back and promised to take him hunting.

When they left, Oriana plunked down on the stairs and lit a cigarette, buzzing with the evening's success. Finally she had a man to love, and her parents' approval. They seemed truly happy for her, and happy that someone had chosen their daughter. Strange, since they'd ingrained in her the drive to be somebody, not marry somebody. At a certain point, it seemed, parents changed their minds. Never mind. Tonight, Oriana felt complete as a woman and a daughter. Even so, just beneath the evening's surface, her mother's words echoed. *Are you working?* The unfinished abortion article weighed on her. Should she tell Tommaso to let Mulotti do it (good luck) and be free of it?

Alekos settled next to her on the stairs, nudging her with his shoulder. "Did they like me?"

"You know they did." He grinned. "You wooed them the same way you wooed me." She wanted to take him to bed, had wanted him all evening, the way he seduced her parents with his rock-solid integrity. She rearranged herself on his lap, facing him. "I have an idea."

He slid his hand down her cowl-neck sweater. "So do I."

The combination of cool autumn air and his touch made her shudder. "I'll get Rizzoli to publish your poems," she said. "A new collection."

"You would do that for me?"

She answered with a kiss. "And another thing. Let's go to Florence." *Are you working?* Of course she would finish the abortion article, tomorrow at the latest.

"But we just got here." Alekos looked confused.

The irony was not lost on her, that he was just calming down, adjusting to the rhythms of Tuscany and being a couple, and she wanted to pack up and run.

She tugged him to his feet, impatient to get him to bed. "I want you to know my city."

Chapter 26

1974

She found them the perfect hideaway in Porta Romana, the most elegant part of Florence. It was a spacious single room on the top floor of a four-story palazzo. The house, built by an aristocratic family and separated into apartments, was set behind a high wall and down a long driveway, on a large, wooded property that afforded total privacy. Oriana gave up her flat near the Duomo and leased the new one under a pseudonym, to avoid any risk of surveillance. They had found some peace in Casole, and she was going to keep it that way, sheltering Alekos from the dictator and his henchmen.

He visibly relaxed when he entered their little nest. The room had sky-high ceilings and glass doors opening onto a balcony with thick balustrades. They christened the balcony with prosecco their first day, and at night without clothes, holding on to the balustrades.

The days were idyllic, like the days of falling in love in Glyfada. The first landmark she showed him wasn't the Bargello or Medici museum, it was her girlhood home on Via Ricasoli. "See?" She pointed to the apartment window five floors up, just across from Brunelleschi's red brick cupola, icon of her city. "I had a perfect view when I was growing up. That beauty, that artistry, got inside me."

Next, they stood on the spot where she fell off her bicycle

when the mine exploded and the lettuce rolled away. It was ghostly quiet during the war, busy with trolleys and tour buses now, but she could still feel her panic as she ran to save the grenade. Alekos squeezed her hand with a sympathetic expression. It made her tear up, the merging of him and her hard scrabble childhood. She took him to Mannelli, the medieval stone tower rising above Ponte Vecchio. Resistance headquarters, where she learned to be a soldier. But now it was a gelateria and serving pretty lousy ice cream at that. She remembered how her heart thumped wildly by the time she reached safety at Mannelli, and euphoric with her success, she ran to meet Babbo on the second floor.

One night, her father recruited her to help hide boxes of *Non Mollare*, she told Alekos, in case Mannelli got raided. In pitch darkness, she and Babbo lugged boxes of newspapers to the vegetable garden behind their apartment building, hiding them inside thorny rosemary bushes. Just as they'd finished, three Nazi soldiers with peaked caps and pointed rifles marched into the garden. They were hunting for an escaped prisoner, one barked, had they seen anyone? No, her father answered calmly. Another German beamed his flashlight across their faces, and Oriana lost control of her bladder, hot urine streaming down her leg. Trembling, she shifted her foot slightly, to hide the puddle. A third soldier stamped toward the rosemary bushes and shined his flashlight, but she and Babbo had concealed the papers well. Then the soldier lifted the cover off a dry well in the corner. A man tumbled out, his arms and legs contorted, shouting *Don't shoot!* All three Germans attacked him with their rifle butts and kicked him across the dirt. She had never heard the sound of a boot stomping on a torso or ribs snapping. The man screamed and whimpered, and when he went limp, blood gushing from his forehead, they dragged him off. "Is he dead?" she asked her father. "Let's go," he said, biting his lip and staring straight ahead.

Not long after, on August 11, her family celebrated the end

of the war with all of Florence. Oriana showed Alekos where she was standing in Piazza Unita when the dashing American soldiers rode in with tanks and flags to liberate her city.

"Dashing, eh?" Alekos stuck out his bottom lip.

She ruffled his hair. "We saw them as saviors and cheered like crazy. They threw us chocolates. My mother taught me never to accept gifts from strangers, but she said I could have one. We had eaten only squash for months, and that chocolate was a river of sweetness."

There was one landmark she hadn't meant to show him, but in Piazza Carlo, a few steps from the Arno, her feet slowed. "*L'Europeo*." She pointed to the red-ocher building with the tall wooden door, the elegant stone archways over its windows.

Alekos watched her. "You want to go in. Go," he said with sincerity.

"No. I filed my piece, now I want to write a novel, as we said. Come." She led him away, but minutes later, on the cobblestone Lungarno Vespucci, when they passed a newsstand with the latest *L'Europeo*, she pounced on it.

Leaning on the parapet along the river, she tore through its pages. "*Porca puttana!*" There it was, her article on the Supreme Court decision in *Roe v. Wade* and the likelihood of Italy legalizing abortion. The first insult: *L'Europeo* had published her on page 10. Worse, she ranted to Alekos, they'd run her rigorous piece with a gossipy sidebar about which Italian actresses were rumored to have had abortions. By Mulotti, that hack.

"Tommaso, what the hell?" The phone was in her hand the moment they returned home.

"It came from the director," Tommaso said. "Circulation is down."

"Monica Ledo had an abortion? Who gives a shit! Don't put me on the same page with Mulotti again or I quit. He doesn't belong with me!"

She hung up. Alekos watched her. "I drive myself like a mule!" She hurled *L'Europeo* to the floor. "I become an expert on the history of abortion laws, the due process clause of the Fourteenth Amendment. The definition of fetal viability. Justice Blackmun's majority opinion. And look at the crap they run next to me!"

Oriana had never had trouble venting her fury, not in print and not in person. Frankly, anger had always been her ally, fueling her work. When she woke up in the morning and there was still injustice, still oppression of good people like her parents, anger made her fly out of bed to a new city or to the typewriter, where she could fight to make things better. This time, strangely, her rage over Mulotti lasted only a day and faded. The idea of tackling a novel had started to burn hotly and take up residence in her mind. And she and Alekos had a hideaway to decorate.

Although Oriana lived a nomadic life, her instinct was to feather the nest, to make a house a home. Now she climbed onto chairs to hang watercolors, unfurled a white shag carpet, arranged white roses on the coffee table. Alekos sprawled on the new camelback sofa, his feet on the table, and watched her creativity express itself in a different realm. "You have a talent for making me not want to leave," he said.

"Feet off the table." She shooed them off.

Hunting for antiques at Nenno, her favorite dealer, Oriana taught Alekos to distinguish seventeenth-century Renaissance, her preferred style. He ran his fingers over the woodwork, quickly adopting the new vocabulary. "Look at the marquetry inlay, the gilding." When they decided to buy the writing table, a drop leaf mahogany, he let her do the haggling. Oriana haughtily pursed her lips and cried, "*Ma, no, no,*" and marched away until Nenno capitulated.

For dinner they liked to stay home, dicing and sautéing side by side. Alekos tried to deviate from her recipes. "And if we add lemon instead of balsamico? Ah, remember the size of our lemons in Glyfada?"

She slapped his hand. "This is osso bucco alla Fallaci. Lemon will ruin it. Your mother puts lemon on everything." He gave a homesick sigh. "Fine, sprinkle it in."

After dinner, they cleared the dishes and bent their heads together at their new writing table. Alekos polished his Boyati poems, trying to recall even those he wrote in his head, and together they translated them into Italian, arguing over his made-up words that he insisted kept the rhythm. Afterward, she typed them up, stacking each new page into a manuscript. She had twisted a few arms at Rizzoli to publish a slim volume of his poetry.

"Use this as the title." She pointed to the last line of her favorite poem. *I write you from a prison in Greece.*

He angled his head. "You're right. That's it."

After two weeks of helping Alekos assemble his manuscript, she couldn't stay away any longer. While he napped one afternoon, she bounded over to Piazza Carlo and, the moment she entered the newsroom, got hit by a wave of belonging. This was her second skin, the din of phones and typewriters, the smell of cigarettes, carbon copies and men's cologne.

First order of business, she scanned the room for that scoundrel, that bone in her throat. Not at his desk. Fortunately for him.

"Where is he?" Tommaso peered over her shoulder.

"Who?" Briefly she was thrown, then the corners of her mouth turned up. "Look, Tommaso, I've decided to write a book about abortion. A novel really. I need six months' leave."

"Six months!"

"I'll give it to you to publish," she said. "In installments, which I hate."

"What will I do with a novel?" Tommaso frowned.

"You don't like making money from my name?"

"Fine. I look forward to reading this *War and Peace*." Tommaso paused. "I have an idea for a column Alekos can write."

"Two for one, is that your idea?"

They laughed. She had missed this refined man who was wise enough to let her be the driver. "I want to go to the press conference with Neil Armstrong," she had announced in July 1968. "Then go," Tommaso said, and the next day, she was on a plane to New York.

She would never forget sitting in the first row with heavyweight journalists (all men) in the CBS studio. Walter Cronkite was interviewing Armstrong by satellite, and the heavyweights had submitted boring questions about solid rocket boosters and starter trajectory. Oriana had no idea how a rocket went up, and she didn't care. For her question, she had printed three simple words, and suddenly Cronkite was reading them on the air. "This one is from Oriana Fallaci." He paused dramatically. He was good at that, Cronkite. "*Are you scared?*"

"Well, you know," Armstrong chuckled on the screen, "there's a surge of adrenaline."

"Who cares about adrenaline!" Oriana blurted out. "Tell us about fear, Armstrong, fear!" The heavyweights turned to stare. Good, let them. Cronkite had chosen her question.

Three days later, on July 20, she flew to NASA in Houston and, on a movie screen in the auditorium, watched Armstrong's boot emerge from the Lunar Module. He said his first words on the moon: "That's one small step for man, one giant leap for mankind."

She had found Armstrong dry and technical when she met him five years earlier, not showing one ounce of emotion for his missions. Yet he was the one who got everyone crying like a baby. Journalists in the auditorium, flight directors in the control room. She scribbled it all down in her notebook, the roar that went up, men in white shirtsleeves back-slapping and hugging. Elbowing her way through the long telephone line, she called in her story, describing the moon landing so that ordinary people—her mother—would understand. Armstrong and Aldrin bouncing around the lunar surface like kangaroos. Racing to collect rocks and soil in two hours before oxygen ran out. Armstrong planting the flag on the moon and making her throat tighten.

All summer long, readers devoured her space stories. *L'Europeo* created a copyright office just to sell her work. Six months later her book was out, *If the Sun Dies*. She was a moneymaker, liberated from female topics, free to pursue serious journalism—whatever the hell she liked.

"Wear this." Oriana laid a new Brioni suit on the bed.

"Shoes?" Alekos spun around helplessly. She found his tasseled loafers under a pile of newspapers.

She had never lived with a man. It was all new to her—sharing the telephone and overhearing conversations, sharing the bathroom and going with the door open. Getting him to switch colognes because she couldn't breathe with that awful Old Spice. Like her mother, Oriana took on the thousand details of managing the home, because she had no other example. At least twice a day she vented her frustration—crumbs, toilet seat, socks on the floor—but suddenly the happiest moment was unpacking groceries together. Drinking an *aperitivo* on the balcony while dinner simmered. Waking up in the same bed. The simple acts of domesticity. You couldn't overestimate their pleasure if you'd never had them. Maybe women tired of the routine. She might, but not yet.

"It's an honor." Tommaso greeted them in his glass and chrome office, shaking hands with Alekos. "All Italy has followed your trials." The glint in Tommaso's eye conveyed man-to-man respect. Oriana flared with pride and deftly connected the two through poetry. Alekos composed his own, but Tommaso had translated T. S. Eliot's *Alexandria Quartet*.

"Look what just arrived." Tommaso handed her a television reel off his desk.

"Why didn't you tell me!" She popped the tape into his TV monitor. The label read *CBS 60 Minutes*. "I've been hounding them."

"It just aired two days ago," Tommaso said.

Oriana hit *Play* and there she was on her chesterfield in New York with Mike Wallace. She looked pretty good, thank God. Feisty, sitting cross-legged. Ooh, she shouldn't have shown her teeth, they were a disaster from smoking.

At the sound of the television, colleagues trickled in, waving or giving her a nod before watching the screen. It wasn't every day that an Italian journalist appeared on an American news program. In fact, this was a first. Oriana could feel the air change and grow tense with their complicated reactions. Only Lucia brought in positive energy with her quick steps, giving Oriana a hug.

"Love is the opium of the people," she heard herself say on TV. Dammit, she wished they'd cut that part. She glanced at Alekos, but he wasn't buying her protestations.

"A colorful sound bite, the Americans call it," she said.

"Your *forte*," Tommaso said.

As she turned back to the screen, she caught Mulotti in her peripheral vision standing with his arms folded. Why should that toad share in her moment of triumph? Her mood worsened when she saw how Wallace concluded the interview. "Miss Fallaci allowed me to listen to her Kissinger tape," he told viewers. "However, I can't corroborate that she kept Dr. Kissinger's remarks in context, because the tape was fuzzy."

"Liar!" Oriana exploded. "Men in power stick together, covering each other's asses. You don't have to tell me."

Alekos took her by the shoulders and whispered in her ear. She calmed, giving him a grateful nod.

"How did you do that?" Tommaso said to Alekos, and all three laughed.

"*Tanti auguri*, Oriana." Lucia popped a celebratory bottle of prosecco and poured glasses.

Tommaso toasted. "To our number one reporter. You've given *L'Europeo* a worldwide reputation."

Colleagues raised their glasses. "*Brava*, Oriana. You held your own against Wallace." She could see their attempt to be happy for her, even as their human side cried, *Why not me?*

Mulotti strutted over and stuck out his hand to Alekos. "I was supposed to interview you when you got out of prison." Alekos wore a blank look as they shook. "Didn't she tell you?" Mulotti turned toward Oriana.

"You cry like a baby," she said. "Still."

"I'm glad you went to Athens," Mulotti said. "You haven't had an easy time finding a man, and now you've started a mythical love affair."

She got close to his face. "Watch yourself."

"I'm just saying you've had it rough since my uncle—"

"Back to work." Tommaso herded Mulotti out of his office along with the broader party.

"Very nice to meet you," Lucia said earnestly, double-kissing Alekos.

Oriana let the air back into her lungs, her head about to blow off. How much did Mulotti know about her lousy affair with his uncle? Had Alekos heard? "She reminds me of me," Oriana said to divert attention, jutting her chin at Lucia exiting the room. "Twice as smart as the men, only she doesn't know it. I did."

"Who's the jerk?" Alekos said in a low voice.

Oriana made a face. "Someone who should be bagging groceries."

"Time for business." Tommaso, having cleared the office, motioned them to the leather sofa. They discussed the spread of fascism in Europe, Franco in Spain, Caetano in Portugal. Papadopoulos, of course. Tommaso invited Alekos to pen a monthly column for *L'Europeo* about the Greek struggle.

"You believe the dictator will be overthrown?" Tommaso said.

"I believe in the people, yes," Alekos said.

"Will you enter politics?"

"When Greece is a democracy again. I feel it's a duty."

"You're serious?" Her brow grew deeply grooved. They had never discussed it.

Alekos shrugged. "It's a Greek word, 'politics.' It means the rights of citizens. And the voiceless still don't have rights. The least among us."

But the political machine will eat you for breakfast, she wanted to say.

"See?" she said to Tommaso, lingering behind as they left his office. "A man of principles. No talk. Just action."

The two of them regarded Alekos. "I see what you see in him," Tommaso said.

On the walk home, Alekos guessed, with his intuition and the dirty tricks of Mulotti, what she was hoping he wouldn't. "You were involved with his uncle?"

Treading carefully, hating to resurrect the past, she began with the bare minimum. Renzo Gori was an editor at *Corriere della Sera*. She had met him when she was twenty-nine and had not the slightest idea how to judge a man. "He wanted me for my name"—her tone was frosty—"and when he captured me, he moved on."

"He hurt you," Alekos said, taking her hand.

She pressed her lips tight, not wanting to go further, but

found herself speaking. "I thought that to be a woman, you needed to erase yourself. Devote yourself completely."

Alekos gave only the slightest wince. "You're devoted to me."

"I made a good choice this time." She squeezed his hand. A man I love, she didn't say, who loves me.

The novel was going well. She had invented a heroine, an unmarried woman who finds herself pregnant. Committed to her profession, she agonizes over whether to have the baby. An agony many women faced, Oriana knew. The idea grew out of her suffering with Gori. Carefully at times, uncarefully at others, she veiled truth as fiction and the story tumbled out.

The premise would be scandalous, she knew. To be pregnant outside of marriage was a sin in Italy, to consider abortion, a double sin. She was writing about a new, liberated woman whose focus was herself, rather than her family. A *selfish* woman, the ultimate insult to her gender. But Oriana knew most female readers would identify with the uncertainty that crept in when an embryo implanted in her uterine wall and began to grow hands and feet. Even her own mother had been wracked with misgivings. Not yet married to Edoardo and working her fingers to the bone as a seamstress's assistant, Tosca drank a nightly botanical brew to purge her unplanned pregnancy. "Many women did the same. But I threw the medicine away the first time I felt you kick," her mother told her. If Tosca could be conflicted about motherhood, how much more a modern woman who'd been ignited with ambition.

The Brotherhood of Macho Authors would have a ball condemning her novel. In their minds, literary fiction was the domain of men—only men could make shit up. Could Oriana prove them wrong and write honestly and profoundly about this most sacred of women's roles? That's what caused the knot in her stomach each time she sat at the typewriter.

Once, in *Look* magazine, she remembered, Katharine Hepburn had declared with trademark confidence that for women, marriage and careers didn't mix. "Careers and children, forget it." Oriana was determined to take on this most central female dilemma, the one she and Ingrid perpetually discussed, family or work, *choose*. But what if a woman wanted everything?

Everything, for Oriana, included the man bent over their writing table directly across from her. Alekos had finished his poetry manuscript and submitted it to her publisher, Rizzoli. For *L'Europeo*, he tackled his first monthly column. She was glad to help him translate, relieved he had a safe and productive outlet for his patriotism.

"I always envisioned myself as a writer." Alekos hunched over the page, biting his pencil. "It doesn't mean I'm giving up."

"Of course not."

"When Greece is free, I'll be ready for elections."

She dropped back in her chair. Mentally, she dragged herself away from the made-up world in her book, though she didn't want to. "Are you serious about politics?" she said, finally having the conversation.

"I'm not fighting for democracy so I can sit on the sidelines."

"But you'll need to live in Athens," she said.

He saw her worried expression and softened. "We'll go back together."

She didn't want to go to Athens. They were building a literary life here at their shared table. "But you'll have to get in bed with a party, and you hate parties. Parties require compromise."

"What are you saying? I'm no good at compromise?" He gave her a rakish grin.

It took a moment, but she grinned back. They were in her city, *bella Firenze*, and democracy in Greece was a long way off.

Chapter 27

1974

The box of books arrived at their Florentine hideaway. She had ordered fifty copies and bounced with excitement as Alekos knelt on the rug and slit open the package. His second collection of poetry, *I Write You from a Prison in Greece*, the title she had chosen.

Alekos stared at the jacket illustration, at his silhouette against a flame-red background. He ran his fingers down the rough, creamy edges and opened to the first poem, Oriana reading over his shoulder. At the end, it said this:

(Military Prisons of Boyati, 5 June 1971—After a beating)

She stared at the words in parentheses, so stark a declaration for the world to see. "I don't know how you did it." She knelt and took him in her arms. "I could never write in my own blood." He tried to speak, but his throat had closed up. "Come. It's a day for celebration." She handed him a pen. "Inscribe it to me."

He brushed the tears from his eyes. *Γιά σένα,* he wrote in Greek.

"What does that mean?" she said.

"For you."

"And how will I know *you* means *me*?"

"There's only one you."

Sweet days of writers' routines. Espresso on the stove in the morning, heads bent at their communal table. In the afternoon, trips to *mercato centrale* and whipping up supper. At night, a bit of television news. Often, Alekos liked to push the coffee table away and play Frank Sinatra on the turntable, taking her in his arms. *This is happiness,* she told herself, observing the dance as it was happening, trying to brand it into her memory.

They had managed to seclude themselves, find some peace in their little nest as the months ticked by and became almost a year together. At night, under the quilt, they still reached for each other. Often, she climbed into bed spent, wanting only to press their bodies close and fall asleep, but Alekos had a way of touching her that was unhurried and tipped her into a dream state. He waited for her, didn't push. Swept her up in a silky rhythm that primed her, her body more responsive than it had ever been. Each month, she hoped this would be the time he made her pregnant, and each month she wasn't, until finally she let it go.

She was writing intensely. The novel was more challenging than journalism because she didn't have a roadmap of truth to steer by, but she didn't let fear stop her, unleashing her imagination, embellishing her experience, feeling her way. He interrupted. To discuss Ennio Morricone, the composer who wanted to set two of his poems to music (a good development), or the latest news on the regime from his buddies in Greece. To persuade her to go for a walk. To kiss.

"I've had a breakthrough on the novel." She sprang up from their writing table one morning.

"*Brava.*" Alekos put down his pen, listening.

Oriana paced, waving her manuscript. "*Congratulations,* says the doctor after her pregnancy test. *Is your husband in the waiting room? I don't have a husband,* she says. He gives her a dirty look. She goes home alone, suffers her qualms alone. But here's the twist—she speaks directly to the child. *How can I bring you into this world, with all its violence and pain? What about my work, if I give you all my time and devotion?"*

"An honest book." Alekos quickly grasped her intention.

"Doubts that women are afraid to admit. While her boss and even the baby's father tell her to end the pregnancy."

"The father?" Alekos frowned.

"Yes, the father." *Always the father*, she wanted to add, stifling the memory of Gori. "Tommaso is making noises about my taking six months off."

"Do what you feel. It's your show, *agapi*."

"It is my show." She pushed her shoulders back. But if she took this sabbatical, she ran the risk of *L'Europeo* readers forgetting her. There was always a young hotshot ready to take her place. She had not scheduled any interviews but was finding it hard to disengage completely.

"I don't believe in abortion, by the way," Alekos said.

"I don't like it either," she said, knowing his soft spot for children. How lucky to find this man. And yet. "No woman wants an abortion," she found her voice. "She doesn't throw a party. But it's *her* decision." Besides, her book wasn't a moral lesson, is abortion right or wrong. It was about being human, fearing change. Ambivalence and doubt.

"Does she have the baby?" Alekos said. It seemed to matter to him.

"I don't know yet. This is the first line. *I knew instantly you were here, a new life within my own. My body already yours, forever entwined.*"

"Beautiful. Poetic. Make the entire book like that."

Alekos was psychic. It was exactly the issue plaguing her. The style of her writing was more lyrical than anything she'd ever attempted. Was it sentimental? She murmured the words aloud as she composed, discovering they had taken on a tone and music of their own. Was it any good?

"Let me see." Alekos extended his hand.

"No. I never show my work to anyone." She clutched the manuscript to her chest.

"I'm not anyone."

"Absolutely not." She buried the pages under a stack of *L'Europeo*s. The story was still forming, a mystery gestating inside her. Alekos looked hurt but she was adamant. She would not risk her creation, not even for him. "Let's talk about your poems." She changed the subject. "Why don't you find a Greek publisher? It's a crime not to be available in your language."

He blinked, her point sinking in. "It is! I'll find someone with the balls to publish me. That will really rile Papadopoulos."

Chapter 28

1974

When the news came, they sat glued to the television set. The Greek people were waking up. A group of disgruntled navy officers had staged a mutiny against Papadopoulos. The dictator managed to suppress it, but his hold was slipping.

Alekos squeezed her hand in the television glow. "Only a little while longer, we'll be able to go home."

Home? She churned with unease.

Late at night, she clung to him. "I don't want you to be disappointed, if the regime doesn't fall." It wasn't the whole truth.

"You don't want things to change." He stroked her cheek, reading her with ease. "But even if we stayed in Florence, we wouldn't be like this forever."

"Why not? My parents are growing old together. They even resemble each other."

"*Ta panta rhei.*"

"What does that mean?"

"Everything flows. You can't step in the same river twice."

"But I want to."

He kissed her forehead, her mouth. "You can't."

She lived with the dread that it would all end. This would be their last *passeggiata* along the Arno, last *Birth of Venus* in the Uffizi, last slow dance in their hideaway. Work came to her rescue, the publication of her best journalism in the book *Interview with History*. Sixteen provocative portraits of world figures, only two of whom she deemed worthy to be leaders, Golda Meir and Alexander Panagoulis.

Seeing her political interviews collected in one fat volume made her spill over with pride, joy, and not a small measure of disbelief. How the hell did she do it? It was the work she would be remembered by, she knew it in her bones. Never mind that the Holy Brotherhood would be loath to admit it. She wasn't expecting any backslaps of congratulations from them.

In the cover photo, she cut a chic figure in a black trench outside the Spanish embassy, her eyes narrowed with intensity and focused into the distance. Skimming the table of contents, she was astonished at the long hours of research and jetting around the globe she'd managed to pack in. The arduous drafting and redrafting until her portrayals were illuminating and told a human story, meeting her rigorous standards for truth and accuracy. How did she get Kissinger to talk at all? It seemed a miracle to her now. And Arafat, that terrorist. She had interrogated him about his penchant for bombing marketplaces and buses and asked why he wore dark glasses, as if he'd just had cataract surgery. Lucky he hadn't blasted her with that rifle slung permanently over his shoulder.

Oriana did a wave of publicity for *Interview* and attended the lavish launch party at the Grand Hotelet de Milan on Alekos's arm. She wore a one-shoulder Pucci gown he'd chosen, the saleswomen fluttering around him with cappuccino and biscotti. On her neck, a pearl choker he'd surprised her with from her favorite goldsmith on Ponte Vecchio.

It was the first time she had ever brought a man to a publishing party, and Alekos proved the ideal companion. He knew when to speak, charming at every introduction, and when to step back and let her be engulfed by well-wishers. It was one of the qualities she loved best, that he was masculine and commanding, yet secure enough to take a back seat to her accomplishments. The crowd knew the Greek hero, of course, pumping Alekos's hand and asking how he liked Italy and how much longer the dictator would hold on.

"Come with me," she said over her shoulder when publisher DeSantis stole her away to meet VIPs.

Go, Alekos mouthed. She fell in love with him all over again as he toasted her with his flute.

A few minutes later, when she checked on him across the room, Tommaso had found him. She wove back at the first opportunity, standing close and brushing his thigh. Alekos looked refined in his new Canali suit, and she had managed to get him to a barber. Let the VIPs come to her. The media and literary elites were whispering and shooting daggers anyway, tempted even in their evening clothes to tear her down.

"Champagne and caviar for one hundred. Not bad," she said, surveying the crowd and its raucous din.

"Rizzoli's putting a big push, expecting a bestseller," Tommaso said. "You have so many famous names. Kissinger, Gandhi—"

"Panagoulis," Oriana said.

"Doesn't have the same ring," Alekos said, ducking shyly. He had been moved, when the galleys arrived, to see his interview concluding her collection. A fat tear had splashed out of each eye.

"I'd rather spend three hours with you than any megalomaniac in my book," Oriana said. "They made my head burst into flames with their double talk. Ravenous for power. No empathy for their people."

"Sign it for me?"

She spun around to the voice. "It's already autographed," she told the intruder frostily.

"Inscribe it to me personally," Mulotti said, winking and holding out her book.

"Living dangerously, are you?" She took his pen. What to

write to be rid of him. *To an entitled dumbbell. A talentless prick.* Finally she scribbled *to Riccardo Mulotti.*

"That's it?"

"Don't push your luck."

"It's her best one," Mulotti said to Alekos and Tommaso, as if she weren't in the room. As if he were any sort of judge.

"Bye." She dismissed him with a wave.

He opened his mouth, gave a pathetic peep, and left.

"It's an insult he works at my magazine." She fumed at Tommaso. "Did you ever speak to him about—" She cut herself off, realizing her mistake. The last thing she wanted to do was bring up Mulotti's uncle Gori. She glanced at Alekos, relieved he was focused on a nearby table piled high with her books. Guests were picking up copies and leaning their heads together. "I can just hear them," she said, jutting her chin toward the table. "*How much does she make? She's already filthy rich. And to think, she's only a woman. Did she really say that to the CIA director? I hear she rewrites her questions to appear more ferocious.*"

Alekos squeezed her hand, telegraphing to forget them.

"The cover photo is *molto elegante*," Tommaso said. Blown-up posters of Oriana in her Burberry trench and sunglasses decorated the walls.

"It's not the photo Alekos voted for," Oriana said. "He likes me as a peasant picking grapes."

Their eyes crinkled over their private joke. "Here you're the 007 of journalism," Alekos said.

"That bastard DeSantis was planning to use a photo where I looked 103," Oriana said. "I made him do a new shoot."

"That bastard DeSantis is about to introduce you." Tommaso nodded toward the podium.

The publisher gave a stirring introduction about her status as Italy's most renowned journalist and bestselling author. She swept to the microphone, her skin prickling from the applause and Alekos's hand lingering at her waist.

"When I see my interviews collected like this," she said, "I understand why I need a vacation." Polite laughter. "It's been a frenetic five years chasing these men. All men, of course, only two women. People ask me, *Oriana, why are you so obsessed with power?* Because I was born during Nazi power, fascist power. And I learned early that we are at the mercy of a few demons like Hitler and Mussolini who rise out of nowhere to control us. Most leaders I interviewed in this book don't deserve their power. They're not special. And often they abuse it, exploiting the rest of us. Only rarely did I meet someone who deserves to be a leader. But this kind of person hates power as much as I do, and sees it as a necessary evil, one in which everyone deserves a voice."

She paused and gazed directly at Alekos. A ripple of whispers swept the room as the audience witnessed their bond. She wanted them to. Without Alekos, her book would have no heartbeat. It would be cynical, nihilistic.

"My parents couldn't join us tonight. My mother was feeling ill, but this book is dedicated to her. It was she who encouraged me to use my brain and participate in the wide world, she who believed women should not be confined to wearing aprons. She was disobedient, like me. And I thank her."

Only a sprinkling of titters. She rode thin applause back to Alekos's side. He was clapping with gusto. Clapping for her.

"Are you crazy?"

"I'll be back in a day or two." He was planning a clandestine trip to Athens using a phony passport.

"But that guy looks nothing like you," Oriana said. "He's got white hair."

"Papadopoulos will shit his pants. I'll show up unexpectedly."

"He'll arrest you, Alekos."

"I'm tired of growing fat in exile."

"Why don't you write about—"

"I've written. It does nothing. Journalists risk nothing."

She opened her mouth to argue, but he was right. Alekos was more daring than any journalist, including her. Words would never be enough for him. She felt a sinking in her chest. He could not be kept in a cage, even if that cage was gilded with the best food and art in Florence. "Fine," she said. "We'll buy a wig."

"What for?"

"You have to look a *bit* like the photo. And you'll stay just one night?"

With Alekos away in Greece, she stopped into *L'Europeo* to pick up her voluminous mail. Her desk was still there, good, not usurped, though she had decided to take her sweet time off to write the novel. She said a cool hello to her colleagues and threw him a lethal look, the boor on the phone.

Lucia had gathered her mail into a burlap sack, but now she hand-delivered one particular letter. "This one says *Personal*," Lucia said.

Oriana went perfectly still, seeing Pelou's handwriting on the blue airmail envelope, his return address in Madrid. "Send it back," she said, holding it out like a dead mouse to Lucia. "Forget it. I'll do it." Oriana stuffed the envelope into the sack.

"Did you see this, Oriana? I'm keeping watch, as you said." Hesitantly, Lucia retrieved a copy of *Foto* from the mail bag and opened it to a folded page.

Oriana speed-read the *Italy Is Talking* column. Another blind item, this one about her *Interview* launch party. The expensive champagne and caviar, the "authoress" caressing the Greek hero's thigh, the snobbish way she inscribed books, with nothing personal. *Fallaci has never married, though word is, there have been plenty of affairs.*

"Where is he?" She tore over to Mulotti's desk, smacking the rolled *Foto* against her palm.

"Oriana. *Sempre alla moda.*" He stood, arms out, pretending to admire her flared jeans and peasant blouse.

"I give people the benefit of the doubt," she said, her eyes narrowed into slits. "But if they kick me, I kick back harder. I crush them."

The three reporters at their desks stopped typing, shooting smirks at one another.

"Calm down, Oriana. What are you talking about?" Mulotti chuckled, touching her arm.

"Get your hands off me!" She slapped him away. "I know it's you feeding *Foto.*" She wagged the paper in his face.

"Is this why you're hysterical? But *Foto* sent a columnist to your party. A new blonde, Silvia something. How could you miss her?" He made a semicircular hand motion near his chest to indicate big breasts.

"Liar. I saw no one. It was you." Oriana pointed her finger in his face.

Smoothly, Mulotti collected his safari jacket from his chair and slung it over his shoulder. "I'm late for Club Giornalisti. Our director's being honored. Tommaso left already. Aren't you coming, Oriana?"

"I don't go to that dump."

"They don't admit women, I forgot," he said with an exaggerated slap of his forehead. "I'm thinking of writing a book, by the way. About car racing. Will you give me some tips?"

"Have you ever read a book, Mulotti?"

He smirked. "Just yours."

At home, she slammed her bulging mailbag onto the writing table. Mulotti was invited to Club Giornalisti, Mulotti was writing a book. All men had to do was show up and life unfurled a red carpet for them, no matter their qualifications. After decades of paying her dues, of driving herself mercilessly to research more, deliver more, the road had never gotten any easier.

Thank Christ that Alekos was in Greece and she could deal with this next aggravation in private. She dumped the mail onto the table and found the blue airmail envelope, turning it over in her hands. That spineless Pelou. For sure he knew about Alekos. Their return to Italy had been in all the papers. What did he dare write her? *Congratulations on your new love? Your new book?* Perhaps *Give me a second chance, I want you back.* Too late, weakling.

She refused to open it, flinging the letter on the table. Pride, but also self-preservation. She would never let him toy with her again. But before she could stop herself, she was opening the armoire, digging out the black-and-white photo she kept in a shoebox. There she was in a strapless cocktail dress at the press dinner in Saigon, demurely leaning toward Pelou with his aristocratic face and crisp white shirt, an invisible cord running between them. They had just rolled in the sheets in his peeling Saigon hotel room under the wobbly ceiling fan. She had given him a fresh copy of *Nothing, and So Be It*, her Vietnam book. Shown him the dedication, *To François Pelou.* Watched his lips slide up, flattered, then that flicker of envy, since Pelou had no book.

The blue airmail envelope tempted her back, and she held it up to the light streaming through the balcony door. Impossible to make out. Maybe he said, *Sorry for having tiny balls, for being too devout to leave my wife.* She imagined her reply. *Ending it with you was the best decision of my life. Now I've found a real man.* Pelou didn't deserve even that. She would return the letter unopened. It would show him he was nothing, zero. She threw it back on the table. Tomorrow, she'd buy stamps.

"I went to the Acropolis and pulled off my wig!" Alekos burst back into their hideaway the next afternoon. Waving his arms and telling her about goading the dictator, his eyes fell on the blue airmail envelope. "What's this?"

She grabbed it off the table. "Nothing."

But Alekos understood. "Another ex? How many men are we talking about?"

"He was just a colleague. In Vietnam."

Alekos nodded slowly, then snatched the envelope from her.

"Give me!" she said, her palm open.

He studied the name, the return address, his jaw tight, then handed it back. "French?" She didn't answer. "When did you break off?"

"Before we met."

"And still he writes."

"I'm sending it back. Unopened."

They faced off in silence, his expression more injured than angry, as if to say, *Can I trust you?* Her stance was more complicated: *I have a right* mixed with *Please don't ask me.* She didn't want to tell him about Pelou because he was married and it was a humiliation. Because she didn't want to jeopardize the only real relationship she'd ever had. Alekos admired her, needed her, they were partners—but he had Mediterranean blood. Intellectually, he knew she had a past, but rubbing his face in it was another matter.

"Pelou was my guide when I first went to Saigon," she said, carefully picking out details. He had let her use the telex machine at France-Presse to file stories and taken her on dangerous assignments with his staff. She didn't mention how many nights it was just the two of them in tiny noodle shops. How, when they disappeared into the faded elegance of his hotel room, the outside world ceased to exist. Saigon was a war zone, and they had survived bullets and bombs to live one more day. She didn't mention how she wrote sappy love poems and tried to steal him from his wife. How Pelou helped her become a war correspondent, maybe changed her life.

"Why did you break off?" Alekos said. She could see him wrestling to sound light. Wanting to know and not know.

"Pelou was a coward," she said. "I had more balls."

"Right," Alekos said slowly, regarding her with a cold, unnerving expression. "Difficult to find a man as strong as you are." He pulled her by the waist and kissed her. Abruptly he let go. Bending over the writing table, he jerked a pen across a blank page and thrust it at her. "Give him this when you return his letter."

She read it.

I am Alexander Panagoulis. Don't ever write her again or I can show you some of the nasty tricks I learned in prison.

She liked that he was willing to fight for her. She didn't like being told what to do. In a few steps, she was at the stove, holding Pelou's letter to the flame. "He's not worth the stamp," she said. The tissue-thin paper burned quickly, curling into ash.

Chapter 29

1974

Lethargic during the day. Queasy at night. The doctor confirmed what she already knew. She and Alekos had made a baby.

With her legs spread open in stirrups, the doctor asked for a second time, "Your age?"

"Forty-five."

He frowned, pressing on her belly with one hand, poking inside with the other. "Any previous pregnancies?"

"No."

Skeptically, he raised his eyebrows, but she kept her expression still. "Well," he said, snapping off his gloves. "You're old. You'll need to be closely monitored."

She buttoned her blouse in a stupor and walked home crossing against lights, narrowly missing traffic. She had stopped wishing for it, assumed her ovaries had surrendered. How would she tell him? On the turquoise beach in Glyfada, Alekos had murmured, *You will be a wonderful mother*. But men changed their minds about words said at the dizzying start of an affair.

For two days, she moved self-consciously, lost in thought, hiding her news from him: Your sperm has fertilized my egg and cells are furiously dividing inside my uterus! She chain-smoked, nervous for his reaction, waiting for the perfect moment. At supper, she covered her wineglass.

"No more?" Alekos said, ready to pour more Chianti.

"I'm full," she lied. There was nothing wrong with drinking during pregnancy, but a second glass would make her sleepy, and she was already feeling the evening seasickness come on. She pictured the embryo as a grain of sand with arm and leg buds floating in an amniotic sac, just as she remembered from the award-winning photographs in *Life* magazine. The photos were taken with microcameras in the womb, the first ever to record fertilization through birth. She searched everywhere for the issue, but dammit, she must have thrown it out. Alekos chattered on about a second clandestine trip to Greece. She watched his lips move, not listening, marveling at the fact that *three* now breathed in their hideaway.

The next night, she put on the red dress that never failed to get his attention, swept up her hair, and dabbed on Joy.

"You look beautiful, *agapi*." He set his newspaper on the sofa. "Do you want to go out?" She stood between his knees and raked the hair he refused to comb. "Tonight I'll take you to Emilio's and buy you white roses," he said. "I'll miss you when I'm in Athens. Let me get dressed."

"Wait. I want to read a poem to you." She nestled beside him on the sofa.

"What poem?" He settled back with anticipation.

"Sappho. Listen." Oriana opened a worn orange volume. *"Sleep, darling / I have a small / daughter called / Cleis, who is / like a golden / flower / I wouldn't / take all Croesus' s/ kingdom with love / thrown in, for her."*

"*Bello*. A rare fragment."

"Do you like the name Cleis?" she said.

"Yes, all the ancient names."

"Which one would you choose? Achilles? Artemis? Sappho?"

"I don't like Sappho, because in Greek we pronounce the

'p'—Sap-pho." He searched her face. "Wait. What are you saying, *agapi*?"

She gave a tremulous nod.

"My God." He got down on his knees, kissing and caressing her belly. They laughed their familiar laugh until he shed tears, and she did, too.

They were up until two in the morning, curled in bed in each other's arms.

"We'll name him Vassilis after my father," Alekos said. "If it's a girl, Vassiliki."

"What about my father?" she said.

"Everyone knows the firstborn is named for the man's side."

"Oh, do they?" She rolled her eyes. "I've always liked the name Valentina."

"It's beautiful. And starts with a V. Maybe Valentina," he tried it out.

"Not maybe. Yes."

"Can you imagine a combination of you and me?" he said.

Peals of laughter.

"I hope she gets your balls," Oriana said.

"Your brains," Alekos said.

"I've had to be twice as smart as a man. Otherwise they ignore you."

"She'll have your writing talent."

"No! Not chained to the typewriter. She'll be an actress."

"You hate celebrities."

"Ingrid Bergman? She's my friend. And Sophia Loren? Now there's a woman with a full life, a husband and two sons. What's better than wearing pretty clothes and pretending for a living?"

He lifted her nightgown and ran his palm across her belly. She felt aroused, protective, more complicatedly feminine than ever before. Her body had accomplished this miracle.

Eventually, Alekos drifted off, but she tossed and turned, her worries suddenly on parade. A baby. Would it be healthy? Could she be a mother and give up being *somebody*, or would she be like Golda Meir, constantly split in two? Fortunately, she had Tosca, who would be an enthusiastic *nonna* helping to raise the baby. But where? Her country or his? A child needed stability. It could not be carried back and forth like a suitcase.

They would find a way. She and Alekos were invincible together. She remembered the first time she had that sensation, on the terrace of Psaropoulos, their first dinner as a couple, walking in shoulder to shoulder, all eyes shifting to them.

Oriana could do anything she set her mind to. She would find a way.

Chapter 30

1974

Her breasts felt sore. Fantastic. Morning sickness came on in the evening, along with bone-tiredness. Good! Alekos bought her the book of *Life* photos by Lennart Nilsson, and they studied it together. By week six, the embryo had started to develop a brain, lungs, and a beating heart. She adored being pregnant. Maybe other women didn't feel this mountain of gratitude, younger women who were more fertile and had found partners more easily. But she did.

Oriana was humming along to Mozart on a small transistor in the tiny kitchen, drizzling oil on a rocca salad, when Alekos handed her a blue velvet box. "Open it."

Inside were two gold bands. Stunned, she searched his eyes.

"We don't need a piece of paper," he said. It was what she believed. He raised the smaller band to his lips, kissed it, and slipped it on her finger. A simple gold band without diamonds or fuss. She was moved by its starkness, the way it marked her. The way he wanted to mark her.

Mirroring him, she kissed the larger ring and slid it on his finger, realizing they were performing a private ceremony all their own. The first place Alekos put his hands was on her belly. She pressed her own hands on top, brushing away the small part of her that saw wedding bands and *maybe* wanted to call him "my husband." She imagined the two of them standing inside the Duomo reciting vows, but the notion of bowing to a priest and kissing his hand made her almost laugh out loud. Too bad civil ceremonies didn't exist in Italy—or Greece. But in marriage there was always a boss, and Oriana wasn't cut out for a supporting role. *I am the boss.* Alekos knew her well.

"Is this because of the baby?" she asked, holding up her hand with the glistening band.

"I've wanted to give you a ring since the day we met."

"Don't go to Greece," she murmured as they stretched awake the next morning.

"Fine."

"Fine?" She pulled back in surprise.

"I'm a family man now," he said with a shrug.

Instead of sneaking into Athens to agitate the dictator, he catered to her every whim, running out for nocciola gelato and leek frittata in a campaign to fatten her up, doctor's orders.

"Show me how to wash my socks," he said.

"Finally. I had to get pregnant." She showed him. His hands were like paws rubbing the fabric in the bathroom sink, spraying water on her as she shrieked.

He taped the *Life* photograph of a two-month-old embryo over the sofa. From the rocking chair where she curled up in the evening, she had a startling view of father and baby.

"Put your feet up. No smoking." He stubbed out her cigarette.

"The doctor said nothing about cigarettes. Don't break my balls." Touched, she lit up a fresh one.

Alekos came up behind her and spread his fingers over her belly while she simmered dinner on the stove. "Vassili. Valentina," he rehearsed.

The torment of her first pregnancy came on unpredictably. Watching his face warmed by candlelight at supper, she would be racked all over again by Gori's *Are you crazy? I don't want it.*

Lying in their cozy bed at night, she would have a flash of the cold metal speculum wrenching her open. *Aren't you going to put me to sleep*? The weary doctor had said only *Hold still* and jabbed her.

Now, ironically, she was in the midst of writing a novel about a pregnant woman, and she was pregnant herself. But everything had changed since those early pages. She jotted down new lines, new truths. *It's magnificent to grow another human being inside your body. An awesome privilege but also a fearsome burden. How do so many miracles occur without my effort? I don't want to make a mistake. I must take care of you already.*

Alekos picked up the phone to share the news with his mother. Oriana yanked it away, explaining there were three tricky months.

"My guys are fighters, *agapi*," he said. "Don't worry about that."

"Where will we live, eh?" She scooted next to him on the sofa.

"Glyfada, of course. He'll grow up in a bathing suit and I'll teach him to dive off rocks."

"I want her to hunt for truffles in Toscana."

"We'll come for Easter," he said. "And spend summer in Lefkada, my mother's island. It's green. And next door is Odysseus's Ithaca!"

"You're wearing a ring," Tosca said, her face lighting up, spatula freezing midair.

They were visiting her parents in Casole for dinner, and Oriana was in the kitchen helping to heap braised rabbit with pearl onions onto a platter while the men waited at the table.

"We're not getting married," she told her mother quickly.

"But you live together."

"Times have changed."

"Too much." Tosca shook her head.

Oriana was severely tempted to spill it. *I'm pregnant.* Her mother and father would faint with delight, typical Italian grandparents. They would adjust to Oriana's living together, just as they'd adjusted to her jetting to three countries in one week, sleeping in a foxhole, buying an apartment in New York.

After a spectacular meal—her mother should earn a Michelin star for her rabbit—they returned to Florence and took an evening stroll through Piazza Santa Croce. It was filled with couples pushing baby carriages and children streaking by with soccer balls and plastic pistols. Alekos kicked a stray ball back to its little owner, and Oriana imagined how tender he would be, teaching his own child that expert tap with his instep. She had never been good with kids, but tonight she waved at a red-cheeked girl whizzing by on her tricycle, and the girl waved back. She tried it again with a baby hinged over his mother's shoulder, and he clapped, his mouth a gummy O.

Pregnancy had changed her, she touched her belly, and the little *ragazzi* sensed it. Thank God she would not be a colossal flop in her new role.

As they strolled back to the hideaway, Alekos came to a dead halt. "Shit." She followed his gaze to a rowdy bunch of young men loitering at the bus stop across their gate. The bus stop that was always empty. All four had crew cuts and smoked cigarettes.

"I've seen that guy," Alekos said quietly, steering her by the elbow to their gate. "He was at the airport in Athens. Swastika tattoo." He patted his biceps.

She looked. It was true.

The pack stared as Alekos unlatched the gate.

"They're here for me," he said.

"No." She shook her head.

"I know the haircuts of ESA."

They stayed inside the entire next day.

"I told you not to go to Greece," she said, jamming a chair against the door, pulling down shades. "Don't provoke them. But no, you had to go."

He paced and talked mainly to himself. "If they wanted to knock me off, they wouldn't send kids. It's a message."

When they finally ventured out the next morning, the crew cuts had vanished. "We're free!" she said, but Alekos didn't answer.

The following week, they were walking home from a dinner of pappardelle with wild boar at a neighborhood trattoria. The four crew cuts were lined up on the brick wall, their legs swinging.

Alekos came to a stop.

"Ignore them." Oriana dug her nails into his forearm.

"Who sent you?" he shouted across the street.

"Fuck you, old man," the swastika said. His gang sniggered.

"Traitors! Tell Papadopoulos I'll be sitting in the first row when he goes before the firing squad."

"Tell him yourself," the swastika said. "He should have finished you off five years ago."

Alekos rocketed toward him. Oriana screamed, grabbing his sleeve. He jerked out of her grip and she lost her balance, falling facedown. Her belly impossibly splayed on the concrete.

The crew cuts whooped and scattered.

"My God!" Alekos knelt beside her. "What did I do?" He helped her sit up. Together they ran their hands over the baby.

"I'm all right. I fell in slow motion," she said. The hormones of pregnancy had loosened her joints.

"Forgive me." He helped her stand, trembling himself. Down the winding driveway home. "Please forgive me."

The bright red stain appeared the next morning along with a thudding backache. Oriana lay stiff on the examination table while Alekos clutched his temples and paced. The doctor delivered the news, placental abruption. Alekos went ashen.

"What does it mean?" Oriana willed herself to remain composed.

"If you stay in bed, the pregnancy might be viable," the doctor said. "Avoid all activity. All emotion."

"How can I do that?" Oriana said.

The doctor shrugged. "We shall see."

At the hideaway, Alekos fluffed pillows and settled her under the covers, his eyes damp.

"It's not your fault," she said, patting the bed.

"It's all my fault." Carefully, he climbed next to her. Forced her to do nothing but lie still.

"But Alekos, I'm only brushing my hair."

"I'll brush it for you."

"I'm only reading a magazine."

"I'll read it to you."

He covered her belly with kisses. Oriana let out a heavy sigh and fingered his hair. She had wanted this baby too much, that's why fate was screwing her. Life was brutal, nothing but struggle. A different unease snaked through her, but she batted it away, turning to Alekos, to the *Life* book he was leafing through with a hopeful expression.

"This is ours," he said, pointing to the translucent fetus at eight weeks, one centimeter long, oversized head with spidery blood vessels and what resembled a faint smile. "The baby's strong now," he said with forced brightness. She nodded, wanting to believe it.

He left her alone only to patch meals together. "I overboiled the spaghettini," he said, forking up strands of mush. "The bistecca is a little burned, I'll eat that part." She loved him for it. While he was out shopping for groceries, she jotted new lines for her book. *Don't leave me, child. I was wrong telling you life is trouble, life is harsh. There is so much joy. A beach in the Aegean, a meal with the one you love, a kiss.*

Before dawn the third day, Oriana hobbled to the bathroom.

"What is it?" Alekos vaulted up in bed.

She locked the door and sank onto the toilet. There was blood. Too much blood.

He shouted to be let in.

She sat for a long time, tears blocking her vision. Alekos banging down the door.

Chapter 31

1974

She carried the baby for one more week, refusing the procedure. Maybe it wasn't dead, what did goddamn science know. Until the doctor threatened her with septicemia.

There were drugs to knock her out this time, and when she woke up, Alekos was holding her hand. Newborns wailed in the nursery down the hall while she stared at the wall, numb and monosyllabic. *No, it didn't hurt. No, I'm not hungry*. Only when he went home to sleep did she let the tears go, one hand covering her mouth, the other on her still-round belly.

What was effortless for most women—the girl in the pink nightgown on the other side of the curtain, the one with the delirious husband smoking a cigar—was impossible for her. The suffocating burden of failure. Of a mistake she made long ago that meant she could never be a woman. He had scarred her permanently, the weary doctor with his gouging blade. How foolish she'd been fantasizing about a daughter with her blue-gray eyes, running free in the piazza with playmates and five dolls, ten dolls. A childhood she never had.

Enough. She tried to stop her thoughts. Would he stay with her, Alekos who had a soft spot for children, now that she was deficient? But she could love him exclusively. She had worried how to divide her attention, partition herself off into segments. They could be a literary couple. No mind-numbing days of sterilizing bottles and cleaning cereal off the floor, no nights in the piazza exchanging meaningless chatter with housewives and chasing a tricycle. Tosca had warned her, it was no life. And yet where would she be without her mother's love?

Tears burned her throat as her roommate, Pink Nightgown, squealed with delight, her newborn wheeled in by a nurse. It was swaddled in a striped blanket, crowned by a blue hat. Puffy slit eyes, a squashed face like an insect.

Oriana was not going to clean shit from diapers; she was going to live a big life. Author a book about maternal ambivalence, whether to bring a child into this rotten existence.

She never blamed Alekos. The blow that there would never be a person that they made, gathered around a Christmas table with capon and tortellini soup, made her cling to him tighter. He had made her feel like a woman in the deepest recesses of her being. The only love she was ever going to have.

She saw this version of the future, the two of them bent over their writing table, going on holiday to Sardinia, and convinced herself. Writer and partner, not mother.

A woman had to choose.

Alekos settled her on the sofa with espresso and cigarettes. "What else can I bring you?" His gaze fell on the *Life* photo he'd taped to the wall, a fetus in utero sucking its thumb. They had grown fond of calling it "V," but now he lunged at it and ripped it down. "Everything I touch turns to shit." He knelt on the rug and buried his head in her lap. "I'm sorry you're with me."

She stroked his hair, quieting him as his shoulders heaved. "Shh."

Eventually, he lifted his streaked face. "Why don't you ever cry?"

Because *girls don't cry*. Because after the evening in the hospital when she had let go, something had gone numb inside.

Alekos stared, waiting for an answer. She heard herself

speak. "It's not your fault. I've miscarried once before." The lie was unplanned. As soon as it left her lips, she wanted to reel it back.

He winced with surprise. "When?"

"With another man." The words sounded vulgar, even to her ears.

"The Frenchman?" he said stiffly.

She didn't answer.

I don't believe in abortion, Alekos had told her. How could she tell him the truth? He would judge her, leave her. It was her damn business anyway. The fleeting image arrived, the sweetness with which he'd kicked the soccer ball back to the little boy in the piazza.

"Why didn't you tell me?" Alekos said. She didn't answer. He pulled away from her, standing and pacing. With one furious motion, he kicked an ottoman across the floor.

"Because of this," she said. "Your reaction."

He went to the cabinet and poured a glass of Chianti, downing it in one gulp and pouring another. She wanted to stay and make everything better, but she was tired, very tired. It was like moving in slow motion, the floor made of tar, as she took refuge in bed.

In the morning, Alekos lay huddled next to her. She was terrified he wouldn't be.

"We'll try again," he said huskily.

She nodded, knowing they would never be a family.

The book poured out. *Letter to a Child Never Born* would climax in miscarriage, not abortion. The mother would decide after heavy soul-searching that she wanted this baby, but it would die because she chose to go on a business trip, putting herself and her ambition first. The child would speak for itself. "Mother, I don't blame you. I understand your need." At the end, the woman would die, too, as punishment for her selfishness. From sepsis.

Oriana attacked her typewriter keys. Released from painstaking factual reporting, she interwove dreams, memories, personal agonies into the narrative. The writing was lyrical, just as Alekos said. It also saved her life, the blank page there for her every day, where she could deposit her longing, rage, grief. Gori wormed his way into the story, but she got her revenge. He became the cruel, abandoning father, while Alekos, with his affection for children, was nowhere. She invented a courtroom scene in which the pregnant heroine was put on trial, judged by her parents, lover, boss. In their testimony against her, Oriana laced in all the vitriol directed at her as a "lady reporter," the too little respect eked out to all women by the patriarchy.

One afternoon, returning from the hairdresser and a quick errand to buy typewriter ribbon, she caught Alekos red-handed.

"How could you kill that poor mother?" he said, standing at the table holding her manuscript.

"I'll kill whoever I want to kill." She snatched back her pages and gave him a shove. He laughed. She shoved him harder, surprising them both with her ferocity.

"If you stop being mad at me," he said, "I'll give you a gift."

"What gift? I don't want any jewelry." She waved dismissively.

"A line of poetry," he said. That got her attention. "Let the mother live, and I'll give you the last three words of your book."

"What's wrong with my words?"

"They're too sad. There's no optimism. We can't survive without optimism."

"What three words?" Curiosity got to her.

He pronounced each word slowly, for emphasis. "Life never ends."

She hmphed and crossed her arms. You're wrong, she

thought. Life does end. An essential part of me ended in metal stirrups. Outside a London hotel. It keeps ending.

"You like it." He kissed her. She raked her fingers through his hair, roughly. Punishment for reading. He touched the thin silk of her blouse, tentative, questioning. She led him to the sofa. Their first time since losing the baby. Urgent, she peeled off her clothes and pressed his hand where she needed him. A flicker of understanding passed between them, and he wasn't tentative anymore.

In the evening, she edited her manuscript with Alekos hovering over her shoulder. Keys clacking, she crossed out the heroine's last words and tried his more hopeful ending. *Life never ends.*

"Not bad," she said. "The words look right, muscular on the page."

"It's true, you know." He swiveled her chair to face him. "Life keeps going. Giving us another chance." She widened her eyes to hold back their fullness. "And something else," he said, his lips grazing hers. "I like working together."

"Don't ever read my manuscript again," she said, her tone far gruffer than she felt. Then, with a light shrug, "So do I."

The end came all at once. In April, Greek students at the Athens Polytechnic rose up against the dictator. At their hideaway in Florence, they glued themselves to the television news, cringing and cursing as police in riot gear clubbed students to the ground. On the second day of protests, the youths broke into a chant. "Pa-na-gou-lis!" Oriana shrieked and pointed to the screen, where students at his former university had printed Alekos's photograph on placards. They hadn't forgotten him. But Alekos only swallowed and stared.

"Papadopoulos will send in the army," he said with a certainty that chilled her. He was right. On the third day, at four in the morning, military tanks crashed through the university gates. Valiant students refused to retreat. They were mowed down, murdered in the street.

Alekos dropped his head and sobbed.

The massacre at the Polytechnic created a public outcry. The dictator fell. Greece became a democracy again.

"We'll go back," Alekos said as they toasted with prosecco on the balcony, though it was difficult to celebrate, knowing what democracy had cost. Twenty-four students dead.

Everything in Oriana wanted to argue, *I don't want to go to Greece, it's better here in my country*. But Alekos wanted her to return with him.

She gazed at him and nodded, because she knew she would.

Tommaso took her to La Bussola for a farewell lunch. The old-world restaurant on via Porta Rossa was a midday gathering spot for big cheese journalists that Oriana strictly avoided, because they had shown her no friendship and who had time to waste on lunch. But Tommaso insisted La Bussola had the best *bistecca*, and she'd forgotten how elegant the place was, with its long marble bar and vaulted brick ceiling.

"I'm translating poetry again because of you," Tommaso said at their soft-lit table. "You and Alekos with your books. I'm moving like a snail through Lewis Carroll."

"You're one of us," Oriana said. "The few who don't assume every phrase we dream up should win the Nobel. You sweat. It makes a difference."

They sliced into their thick Florentine steaks that extended past their plates and commiserated over how excruciating writing was. Even with the upheaval of moving to Greece, she was making herself nuts doing a final edit on *Letter to a Child Never Born*.

"Let me know when to schedule the excerpt," Tommaso said.

"It's sacrilegious. I'm not sure anybody will want to read it."

"You always touch people, Oriana."

"Why?" She really wanted to know. "I'm a poor girl without university, why do readers like me?"

"You write out of emotion," Tommaso said, without having to think.

"Oh yes, I'm a *passionate Italian*." She scoffed. "That's what the Americans call me. A *passionate woman*, my critics here say. Either way, it's not a compliment."

"I'm losing," Tommaso said, putting down his fork. Oriana eyed him and put down hers. "The director wants more bikinis, more gossip. Circulation dropped the moment you took your sabbatical."

"You miss my dead seriousness?" Oriana said.

"I hope you're coming back."

She didn't answer. Tommaso nodded hello to two big shots from *L'Espresso* at the next table. *Ciao, ciao*, she did the same, then lit her cigarette, signaling the end of the niceties.

"I always wanted to be as good as them." Oriana waved her hand. "Now I want something else."

"It hasn't been easy," Tommaso said. "But you've been up for the fight."

"I'm tired."

"You, force of nature? If you're tired, there's no hope for the rest of us." Tommaso promised she could choose any assignment, fly anywhere, work as often as she liked.

"And the bikinis?" She squinted at him through a coil of smoke.

"Let me worry about that."

Tommaso was right about La Bussola—it was a damn good steak. As they left, the voice assailed her, nasal and thin. A voice she could never have stomached. She turned toward the short figure in a fedora, the lithe woman clutching his arm. Entering as they were exiting.

"Renzo." Tommaso shook his hand.

She froze. Ten years had passed but everything came speeding back, the too-coiffed hair, shifty eyes, aura of liking himself too much. What the hell, this wasn't his usual lunch place. Had she conjured him up, writing a book about a pregnant heroine, a rejecting father? With every paragraph, she had despised Gori all over again.

He had gone gray. Gold-wire glasses, weak chin, stockier frame. They avoided greeting each other. The air was icicles in August. What had she seen in this dandy with zero virility? His girlfriend stood a head taller than him, her face blank, as if bored by her own beauty.

"My nephew's learning a lot from you," Gori said, clapping Tommaso on the back. "You know young people these days, no discipline except for nightclubs. I'm trying to show him the way since his mother died . . . my sister." His voice cracked.

"I'm going." Oriana turned her back to show she couldn't care less about his loss. She double-kissed Tommaso. "My plane leaves in an hour. Alekos is waiting."

"Congratulations on your book, Oriana," Gori called after her. "Impressive collection."

"Go fuck yourself," she said, loud enough so he would hear.

Chapter 32

1974

All at once, her young rebel was running for Parliament. She hadn't expected to like it so much. Alekos campaigned with simple posters stamped *Social Justice!* and *Freedom!* and raised only a few drachmas for his campaign coffers, but he inspired the hell out of her, jumping into the race. Obviously she mistrusted politicians, but Oriana revered democracy, the only system of government that respected human beings, even if it wasn't perfect.

Alekos held a campaign event in Athens that moved her deeply, a press conference with the guards at Boyati who helped him survive. In a houndstooth blazer and tie, he perched on a sofa at the national newspaper association surrounded by four strapping young men spilling onto its arms. All had been teenage soldiers who served at the prison and now sported long hair and sideburns, turtlenecks and jackets. Oriana was struck by the handsome picture they made, Alekos like a soccer coach huddled with his devoted players.

"Dionysis Stamos treated me with compassion and love." He introduced each former guard the same way, leaning into a cluster of microphones on the coffee table. When he got to Yorgos Morakis, his voice grew gravelly with emotion. "Yorgos Morakis served an eighteen-month sentence for helping me escape. He lent me one of his uniforms and I made it out, until my cousin turned me in for a reward." Another guard, he said, Stelios Loukopoulos, was ordered to beat him but refused, until they beat him, too.

"The crimes of the junta are much bigger than what they inflicted on me," Alekos said. "They hurt these kids, brainwashing them and forcing them to be inhumane."

As the election grew near, Alekos made speeches at Greek churches and in town squares, and she stood in the audience, captivated by the way he could be sweet and humble one moment, commanding and fiery the next. But all at once, Alekos had a new campaign chief, new allies, a new role to absorb him. He was not fully hers anymore. Within a week of watching him tackle his work, she badly missed her own.

"I'll stay and proofread my galleys," she said in the garden of orange and lemon trees in Glyfada, the typeset pages of *Letter to a Child Never Born* on her lap.

"But I like you with me," he said, circling behind her and massaging her shoulders.

"And my deadline next month?" She fanned her galleys at him. "The copy editor is illiterate. He's made a hundred mistakes. Look, he's changed my paragraph break. Ruined my meter."

A new rhythm of being together had to be found, and a new rhythm wasn't easy. Life's trick, as soon as you had mastered one stage and felt the slightest bit secure, a new stage came along and knocked you back to being a fumbling novice.

As soon as Alekos left the garden, she missed him. There was Athena, on the balcony in a housedress and slippers, sweeping the daily dust from dirt roads. Soon she would wash and iron her son's shirts. Oriana waved.

She had booked a hotel room a few kilometers down the coast, but Alekos rarely wanted to sleep there. After the election they would find an apartment, he promised. She began escaping to the Coral Hotel herself, strutting naked in the room and soaking in the tub. She needed a manicure. Did the place have a salon? Forget it. It was a basic two-star, the best Glyfada had to offer. At least her balcony faced the sea.

Wrapping a towel around her hair, she pulled the phone outside and called Tommaso. He would not be pleased.

"I'm almost done with the book," she said.

"Then I'll schedule the first excerpt," Tommaso said.

"I gave it to Rizzoli."

"What? But I assigned you this story."

"*I* made it a book. The dilemma of being a woman. Having ovaries *and* aspirations. The impossible choice we face." Dead quiet. "Look, Tommaso, it's literature. It can't be sliced into installments like salami." *I'm in charge*, she was thinking, *I decide*.

"What do you want me to say?"

"*Congratulations, Oriana*. It's something unique, it's not for *L'Europeo*."

"Fine. Congratulations." Tommaso sighed. "Are you ready for an assignment?"

"Alekos is running for Parliament," she said, meaning no.

"The American Society of Newspaper Editors called. They've invited you to speak in New York."

"Yes!" She jumped off the chair. "They'll pay my expenses, of course."

Alekos was crestfallen. "But the election is ten days away."

"I'll be back in a week," she said, sure but unsure.

His friend drove them to the airport. They nestled in the back seat, riding along the electric blue coast the way they had over a year ago when she came for the interview. But it was October now, not August, the air through the windows cooler, the sea a darker, more ominous blue.

"You'll write your speech on the plane?" he said, fingering her hair, and she knew he shared her unease.

She nodded. "I'll wake up those Americans with my passion." Her bluster felt hollow and she leaned her head on his shoulder.

It was clear when they said their goodbyes at passport control that their days of being inseparable were ending. No more shopping at mercato centrale or making love on the farmhouse table. No more bending over the same desk, being writers together in their nest. Oriana wondered what new phase was next. In the corners of her mind, a worry rose: She was a failure at long-term relationships and now she was flying off.

New York welcomed her home as it always did. The Waldorf Astoria was the height of elegance, heads of state stayed at the Waldorf, and she was invited to stay there, too. It was one thing to be Italy's most famous journalist, quite another to fill a ballroom with American newspaper editors who paid money to hear her speak.

The boozy luncheon was filled to capacity with suits and thick with cigarette smoke. She was diminutive at the podium but stood on a riser and made her voice boom, discussing the Watergate burglary and the importance of investigative reporting and speaking truth to power. "You Americans say I badger my subjects, I'm abrasive. Thank you for the compliment."

Applause. She was right to come to New York, to be on this stage. During the question and answer, a gangly man in a boxy suit asked, "Of all the giants you've interviewed, Miss Fallaci, who was your worst interview?"

"I don't recall many giants, most were piglets." Laughter. "Baby Doc," she said decisively. "Who succeeded his father in Haiti. He was a butter boy, when you inherit privilege but have no balls of your own." More laughter. "He refused to answer my questions, vomiting propaganda. *This is a waste of my time*, I told him and walked out."

"Have you ever been in danger?" a bow-tied gentleman asked.

"In Vietnam and Mexico City, I almost died. And there's

always a thug with his rifle pointed at me, inside or outside the room where I'm interviewing. His message is clear. *Touch my master and I shoot you full of holes*." She could see mouths drop and paused, scanning the ocean of men. "Let me ask you a question, American Society of Newspaper Editors. Where are the women?" Mumbles and stares. "I'm disgusted by my own press club in Florence," she said. "But in America, I thought I'd find progress. Do you accept female members?"

More mumbling. A shaking of heads. "No," called out a beefy cigar smoker at a front table.

"Your loss." She stared him down. "I've met all the world's leaders, and frankly women are more intelligent, more hardworking. Far less arrogant and greedy."

"As soon as you hire a woman, she gets married or knocked up," the stinking cigar smoker said.

Oriana shot him a murderous look. "I've never done either. And I've never missed a day of work because of my period or a hysterical breakdown. Women are tough. You would be afraid, if you knew how tough." She paused. "Maybe you're already afraid."

Ingrid met her at Mamma Leone's at their usual table. Her friend had just won an Oscar for *Murder on the Orient Express*. Smiling, smiling, Oriana congratulated her and suppressed a bubble of envy at the fullness of her friend's life—husband, children, *and* prizes.

"Lars and I are getting divorced," Ingrid said as soon as they'd ordered veal scallopini.

"What happened?" Oriana reached for her hand. All at once, it was easier to be a good friend with the confirmation that even Ingrid got screwed by fate.

"He grew tired of my absences and found someone new."

Ingrid shrugged. "I love him. I love all my husbands. Lars will remain my friend."

How did she do it? Oriana marveled. Was it her cool Nordic blood that allowed Ingrid to move on after every disappointment? Emotional pain didn't seem to shred her the way it did Oriana. "You'll have a new man as soon as you want one." She squeezed Ingrid's hand.

"I'm not sure I need one. I used to, I lost my parents so young." Finally a wrinkle of sorrow around Ingrid's eyes. "The truth is, I've always had the sense I belong to show business."

Oriana nodded, knowing full well the allure of work, the greatest love she had ever known before Alekos. Today's speech at the Waldorf had reminded her how much she missed it.

"The children are fine," Ingrid said. Oriana felt another wave of jealousy. She had resolved not to mention the miscarriage, it was too upsetting, and she'd never told Ingrid about the abortion. "Every time I see them, they're taller," Ingrid said. "I feel guilty leaving them for months, but not guilty enough to stop."

They shared a meaningful glance and toasted with Chianti. A part of Oriana held back, caught in the irony of Ingrid's bearing more children than she had time for, and she being denied even one. Life was not fair. It wasn't exactly breaking news.

It was Oriana's turn to share, and she told Ingrid about Alekos. "He's the only man who's ever wanted me."

"I doubt that."

"It's true. And the first time I've lived with a man."

"And you've discovered?"

"We are their mothers." They broke up laughing. "The notion that women are the weaker sex, that we depend on men to survive—it's a myth," Oriana said. "It's men who fall apart without us."

"It's serious, then?" Ingrid pinned her with those deep-set blue eyes.

"He's younger."

"Good for you."

"A rebel with a cause. I try to calm him down, but people don't change. Do they?"

Ingrid shook her head. "Not for me."

"He's running for Parliament in Greece."

Ingrid looked impressed, then angled her head and her expression changed. "And what will you do in Greece?" she said with her usual forthrightness.

Oriana told her about *Letter to a Child* and writing literature. "Alekos is the one who said *do it*. But when I was wrestling with a chapter, he interrupted. *Will you read my speech? Can you sew this button? I'm hungry.*"

They laughed and talked over each other with examples of male neediness. Then Ingrid leaned in. "Can I give you some advice? Don't give up too much of yourself, so that a part of you is dying."

Oriana shifted in her chair, dodging her friend's warning even as heat rushed to her face. Maybe she'd already given up too much of herself for Alekos, or maybe she would. But she couldn't turn back now. Her feelings didn't work that way. "I'm not," she said to Ingrid, sounding defensive even to her ears. My relationship is going to succeed, she thought, even if you failed three times. "Are you here doing a play?" she changed the subject.

Ingrid fingered her napkin. "I came to see a doctor." Oriana froze in the middle of tapping a new cigarette from her pack. "You shouldn't smoke," Ingrid said, and then, "I'm not telling anyone."

Oriana dropped her head toward the table as if she'd been punched. Briefly, Ingrid explained she'd found a lump in her breast, but there were therapies. Cursing with frustration, Oriana assured Ingrid she would be fine, New York had the best doctors. Even as she consoled her friend, a wisp of shame clung to her from her earlier bout of envy, as if she'd somehow brought on this catastrophe. When they stood to go, Oriana threw her arms around Ingrid. "Call me if you need me," she said. "Wherever you are, I'll come."

The next day, she said goodbye to Manhattan skyscrapers, Walter Cronkite on CBS at six thirty, and Barbara Walters, who had finally done it, climbed her way from "Today Girl" reciting the weather to the first female co-anchor in news. Walters was still not permitted to ask questions of serious guests until her male co-anchor finished his. Even in America, women's rights took one step forward, two back. The inane commercials made Oriana growl at the set. Wives in aprons apologizing for burned meals. Stewardesses saying "Fly Me" with innuendo that meant fuck me.

In the bulkhead seat to Athens, her thoughts looped back to Ingrid. Nobody survived cancer, and her friend had put off treatment for a year to do a play in London. Dear Ingrid was only fifty-nine. If Oriana were to be invaded by the same devil at the same age—she smoked three packs a day—she had fourteen years left.

At Hellenikon Airport, she hurled herself into Alekos's arms and took him straight to the Coral Hotel. She pushed him down, tore open his shirt, moved her lips down his chest. The concept of sex as a life force had never made sense to her, but suddenly it did. She wanted to erase sickness and death—she was going to die!—and escape into the solidity of muscles, skin, bone.

"I missed you, too," he said, his body following hers in the tangle of sheets.

Two days later, Alexander Panagoulis was elected a member of Parliament.

"I want you with me," he said on his first official day. "We're debating the future of the monarchy." He led her by the hand through a private side door into the grand Parliament building.

It was originally built as the royal palace and had marble floors and walls, the same Pendelic marble that built the Parthenon, Alekos said.

Oriana negotiated the narrow spiral staircase to the spectators' balcony. Parliament was called to session. Alekos stood out with his youthful carriage and shock of hair among the fat, balding politicians who filled the semicircular room. He had joined the Center Left party, a bunch of independents, he said, who were least like a party.

After a boring half hour, he strode to the podium in his charcoal Armani suit (a new designer, she'd taken him shopping before leaving Italy), his hair neatly trimmed by a barber. Buzzing with pride, she leaned over the balcony rail.

"King Constantine rolled out a red carpet for the colonels, and he never condemned the killings. He should stay in exile forever, never see Greece again." Alekos had previewed his speech for her, and now his voice poured through the speakers, a natural. Almost overnight, Alekos had evolved into a statesman. He was a long way from the rebel in a bathing suit on the coastal road. But the longer Oriana watched him on the floor, the more she saw that politics, with its compromises and corruption, would never be a good fit. He jabbed his fist in the air, demanding to know why it was taking so long to arrest the dictator and his colonels. He crossed his arms, boiling with indignation as career politicians blathered on that justice takes time.

Still, Alekos was optimistic that Greece was a democracy again and he could play a role in his country's comeback from the abyss. Having a happy partner made her happy. Oriana had wielded the upper hand in Italy—her homes, her money—and now their relationship shifted. Alekos was a member of the ruling class, he had influence and a salary. Men needed productive work to make them feel like men. She remembered his anguish over exile when they first arrived in Rome, and realized how diminished he must have felt when she was the only thing he had.

He took her out for a celebratory dinner when the Greek people voted to abolish the monarchy. A second dinner when the dictator and his colonels were finally arrested and imprisoned on a remote island. They toasted at Psaropoulos, where they'd eaten their first meal together, the sea lapping below, crescent moon shimmering above. Alekos spoke with great feeling for his country, and it never failed to move her. A man who could love like that could love Oriana as deeply as she'd always needed, but never wanted to admit.

"*Che brutto.*" She wrinkled her nose at the torn vinyl chairs, the rickety table masquerading as a desk. For his new office, Alekos had leased a one-bedroom apartment in a residential building four blocks from Parliament. "I'll ship a few things from Florence," she said, studying the living room where he would work.

Alekos brightened. "Maybe a desk from Nenno's?" he said, conjuring the days of shopping at their favorite antique dealer, furnishing their hideaway.

Oriana took charge of decorating the new office on Kolokotroni Street. From Nenno, she ordered the new MP an antique desk, and from Milan, a black leather swivel chair and modular sofa. On the walls, she framed his beloved preamble to the U.S. Constitution, *We the People . . . in order to secure the blessings of liberty . . .* On the new bookshelves, she stocked Alekos's book *I Write You from a Prison in Greece*. The Greek publishers he'd approached had passed, so once more she had persuaded Rizzoli to bring out his collection, this time in his language, and purchased a hundred copies. "You can sign these as gifts to your constituents," she said.

She enjoyed feathering the nest, but this time she had an

ulterior motive. She had no intention of spending another night with his mother.

"We can sleep here." She led Alekos down the hall to the bedroom across from a small kitchen.

"And give up the sea?" he said. "The garden in Glyfada?"

"You'll be close to work. Wait until I finish. You won't want to leave."

He hired his longtime friend, Kostas, as office manager and interviewed perky young girls for secretary. Oriana rejected a cousin's neighbor with long legs and rosy cheeks for being inexperienced. When Alekos started to debate, she cut him off. "You haven't worked in an office. I have." Finally, she approved a no-nonsense matron named Nia, a longtime government employee nearing retirement.

"She's going to need a wheelchair," Alekos said and they dissolved into their private laughter. "You love me, don't you?" he said, pinning her against the wall and kissing her.

With his new status and confidence, he wanted her all the time. In his suit when he walked in the door after a day in Parliament. In the middle of the afternoon, between meetings. "I've got ten minutes," he would say, coming into the bedroom, where she was doing the umpteenth review of her galleys.

Oriana had transformed the homely beige box into a sanctuary with a Persian rug, nineteenth-century wall tapestry, and slim writing desk for herself. Across from their giltwood rococo bed, she had hung two framed photographs side by side, ten-year-old Oriana on her bicycle in a checkered dress, and ten-year-old Alekos standing on a plastic-covered sofa with his hands on hips. Would they have flirted the way boys and girls instinctively did or been friends? she wondered, studying the photos. Bookish and reserved, Oriana would have been dumbstruck by Alekos's wild nerve. The traveling back in time didn't work, of course. She would have been twenty when he was ten. Still, she knew with absolute certainty he would have captured every molecule of her attention.

Chapter 33

1975

Everything changed, slowly then quickly. Alekos spoke wherever he was invited, crisscrossing Greece. His people embraced the returning hero, including a flock of females who brazenly threw themselves at him with lipstick-stained kisses, phone numbers, invitations to dinner. Oriana accompanied him whenever she could, staking out her territory. Together they attended honorary feasts with mayors and councilmen, where whole lambs were slaughtered and roasted in a row of spits. She learned to do a simple circle dance that was part of the festivities, three steps right, kick, left, kick.

Very soon, she grew tired of tagging along from province to province. Alekos had a professional life, a life separate from hers. In March, she flew to Milan to deliver her galleys of *Letter to a Child Never Born* to Rizzoli. Five months later, her book had an impressive print run of two hundred thousand. News of her controversial subject was spreading and advance sales were strong. Her first work of literature would be translated across Europe.

"Why can't you come to the launch party?" She pressed her toes against Alekos's shins as they stretched awake in the morning.

"We're voting on expelling NATO bases Tuesday."

"But everyone misses votes."

"I don't." He pecked the top of her head and headed for the shower.

"Fine," she said, but it wasn't fine. She remembered the launch party for *Interview with History*, how her joy had doubled with Alekos by her side. Now the press would gossip: Where was Fallaci's hero? Had they broken it off?

At Milan's Grand Hotel, Oriana made sure to look her most elegant in a Valentino spaghetti strap and Alekos's gift, the pearl choker. Publisher DeSantis gave a glowing introduction about her entry into fiction with a groundbreaking novel for modern times, and she clicked to the podium in her heels, poised for the barrage of reviewers.

"Oriana, is it you in the book? Were you pregnant with Panagoulis's baby?"

"I've said it's fiction. Would you ask Dickens or Tolstoy these stupid questions?"

"*Corriere della Sera* began its review with Ugly, ugly, ugly."

"Maybe they were looking in the mirror."

"Did you ever have an abortion?"

The shiny ballroom, shimmering chandeliers, everything swirled and collapsed in on her. The voice was revoltingly familiar. She scanned the crowd and there he was, arm raised so she would spot him.

"No." It took all her will to let the word boom in the air. Thank God her parents hadn't arrived yet, and Alekos was in Athens for his vote. Remaining composed, she turned her back on Mulotti, that sonofabitch.

"Oriana, are you a feminist?" Thank Christ, a new hand.

"I don't like labels," she said, forging ahead. "But if it means women deserve the same rights and respect as men, I've been a feminist before there was the word. Don't be frightened, I don't hate men." A few sniggers. "I've worked beside men all my life. Once in a while, they helped me, but more often I helped myself.

Some think it's a disadvantage, but I'm glad to be a woman. I've had to work twice as hard, but it spurred me to get better."

"Your book supports abortion." Another genius.

"Wrong. The issue is not black and white. That's why I've written literature, because literature, if it's any good, illuminates the grays of life."

"But the woman in your book rejects being a mother."

"Anyone who thinks that is a fucking idiot. The heroine has ambivalence. She's human. Did you read it? No, I didn't think so. Read so I don't waste my time."

She stepped down from the podium steaming with indignation. So limited, these men, so narrow in their experience yet they passed judgment with absolute authority.

Where was that snake? But Tommaso was making a beeline toward her, holding out a champagne flute. "Don't let him ruin your night." Tommaso's expression said it was her business, no one else's, whatever decisions she'd made about maternity. Damn right. He had never gone near the topic of children with her, though he'd spawned two of his own, relieved, she assumed, that his star reporter wasn't reproducing and could keep up her moneymaking output. Oriana remained tight-lipped on the subject, pretending to be beyond such ordinariness. To fit into the male-run world, she'd learned to deny any otherness, including her own biology.

Thank God for champagne. She downed it. This *was* her night, Tommaso was right, the hell with Mulotti—for now. She had scaled a new mountaintop, one she'd set her sights on as a girl. Novelist.

"The critics read only excerpts, and still they jump down my throat," she said to Tommaso.

"You'll have the last laugh," he said. "Rizzoli is already planning another print run. I just spoke to DeSantis."

The news caught her by surprise and she surged with

confidence, vindicated by her readers. She had followed her instincts, written *Letter* from her soul. *Oh, Oriana, you're so emotional.* Yes, because real people, not these chromosome-challenged Neanderthals, were full of emotion. Intense, aching, confounding emotion.

The snobbish Milanese were giving her the eye, speculating about Alekos. *He must be the asshole father in the book.* No, he wasn't. Tommaso escorted her to the cultural attaché, university professors, scions of Italy's publishing families. The high and mighty who chafed at her success because she didn't have a degree, came from a no-name family. Italy was as much a classist society as it was patriarchal, but she was winning. *I don't write for you, you haughty tight-asses. I write for simple people who have more intelligence, more nobility. My parents.*

Tosca and Edoardo arrived late by train looking flustered and out of place. She swooped toward them and pulled over a waiter with his tray of drinks.

"Alekos?" her father said, scanning the crowd.

Oriana explained tightly he had a vote in Parliament.

"We're so proud he won the election," Tosca said. "How long will you stay in Athens?" Beneath her mother's genuine affection for Alekos, and her wish that her daughter see the world, was the real question: *I miss you, Oriana, when are you coming home?*

She missed her parents, too. The thought of being home in Florence and Casole made her ache. "DeSantis, you remember my parents." She lassoed over her publisher. He was overjoyed to be launching another Fallaci title so soon after *Interview*. She could see his pupils ringing like cash registers.

With her parents momentarily occupied, she moved to an empty table nearby. Her heels were killing her. She sank into a chair and rubbed her blisters while the party peaked around her.

"Nice trick, disguising your life as a novel."

She snapped her head up.

"You had an abortion," Mulotti said. "You killed my uncle's baby."

She jammed on her shoes and stood ramrod straight. "You don't know what you're talking about."

"*Tio* Renzo was drunk one night, we were having port and cigars. He was reminiscing about you, bragging, really. He read me your letters. You were obsessed with him." Mulotti smirked. "Did you get ahead, sleeping with him?"

"I was the one ahead, you sonofabitch."

"What shocked me was the way you lowered yourself. It's not the tigress you show to the world." Mulotti reached into his breast pocket. She felt stricken seeing her handwriting. "*I'll quit my job to wash your underwear*," he read in a mocking tone. "*I want what every woman wants, to stay home and take care of her man*."

Her cheeks flamed. She made a grab for the letter but it ripped, she managed only a corner, and he slid it into his pocket victoriously. The party dropped away and it was just the two of them, blood booming in her ears. "How dare you."

"Too bad you never got *what every woman wants*. Always the dirty mistress, never the bride."

She wound back and cracked her palm against his cheek. A collective gasp from neighboring tables. Heads turning. Mulotti's jaw hung open for the briefest second before he cackled.

"What do you want?" she stopped him cold, her stare menacing.

"An apology."

"I never apologize."

"For cutting off my balls."

"You flatter yourself. I couldn't care less about your balls."

"You talk tough. But you tried to kill yourself, poor thing," Mulotti said.

She went silent. Stunned.

"Your last letter to *Tio* Renzo was written on Hotel Normandie stationery," he said. "I'm a better investigative reporter than you think. The hotel manager who found you unconscious still works there."

The room blurred. She stumbled to the vestibule and into the restroom, locked herself in a stall. Shaking with rage and something more intolerable. Fear.

Mulotti would ruin her. Spill her most excruciating secrets to be gorged on by her enemies. She would be ridiculed, condemned. *Fallaci killed her baby and tried to kill herself. Fraud, hypocrite. Fallaci is weak.*

Everything she had built.

Already the Milanese at the party were in a frenzy over the slap. The night—*her night*—was a debacle. Surely her parents were searching for her this minute. She could hear their anxious concern. *Oriana, did you really hit that man? Who was he?*

Tosca still attended Sunday mass, still believed Catholics went to hell for their sins. Her sin, abortion. And Alekos, how would he understand? She had told him a bald-faced lie—*I miscarried once before*—in the wake of losing the baby. When she had the chance to tell him the truth.

Enough. She let out a long trembling breath and squared her shoulders. Unlatched the bathroom stall and checked her reflection in the mirror, wiping her finger up at the corners of her eyes to fix her smudged liner. The noise of guests stuffing themselves with hors d'oeuvres engulfed her as she swung open the door.

The secretary led her in, the same giraffe neck who was draped on his arm when they collided at La Bussola. Renzo Gori was a top editor at *Corriere della Sera* with a private office. Marching in, she glimpsed his slim book displayed on a bracket in the center of a glass conference table. Gori's exploration of social class in

Italy had propelled him swiftly through the journalistic ranks. His book had been adopted into the university curriculum, she'd heard through the grapevine. He would be earning royalties for decades.

Gori greeted her with arms wide, as if nothing ugly had transpired between them. The double kiss, overpowering cologne. "Sit down, please." He settled behind his desk, the power move she recognized, swiveling in his leather wingback. "Donatella, bring us some coffees." The secretary clicked away, but not without a possessive glance, the essence of suspicion on long legs.

"What a nice surprise. Cigarette?" Gori flicked open a monogrammed silver lighter. His hand trembled. He would be fifty now, with a definite paunch, and he seemed to have shrunk in height, or was he always so insignificant? No ring on his finger. A string of women, Donatella only one of them, high-heeling it back with their coffee.

"Close the door," he said gruffly when she'd finished serving.

As soon as they were alone, Oriana attacked. "Your nephew has my letters."

Gori winced, taken aback. He cleared his throat. "Impossible. I keep them locked in my credenza."

"I'll talk and you listen," Oriana said, and she recounted every detail of how Mulotti accused her and sabotaged her launch party.

"I heard something about a slap," Gori said, his Adam's apple bulging. "I had no idea why."

"Of course you heard about it! All Italy heard," she exploded. "Why would you read him my letters?"

"I had a bit to drink one night," he said, tipping his chair back as far away as it could go.

"Why would you save them in the first place?" Oriana

demanded, and her meaning was clear: you treated me like shit, why would you care?

Gori shrugged, but his embarrassed downward glance gave her the answer. He had saved her letters because she was Oriana Fallaci. She had become famous since he kicked her to the street.

A new worry seeped through her. Gori would publish her letters in a chest-beating memoir. *I fucked Fallaci.* No way, Mr. Big Editor. "Your nephew is leaking to *Foto*."

He looked dazed for a moment. "Riccardo wouldn't jeopardize his job or—or our reputation."

"Oh no?" Her tone was blistering. "You are implicated if he prints anything about the abortion."

Gori lit a cigarette and gathered himself. He exhaled with a sudden cool. "Wrong. I never told you *go to such-and-such clinic*."

Her head burst into flames. How differently she saw him now, sleazy, feeble, how he revealed himself. "And I never told anyone about your one and only book," she said, motioning to the holy relic displayed on his conference table. He squirmed. Oh yes, she'd come prepared. "You couldn't get two sentences on the page. I want my letters back. Every single one of them."

They locked eyes, each having played their cards. Gori looked away first, fidgeting with pencils on his desk, straightening the already straight row. "I'll talk to Riccardo. He was racing cars before I got him into *L'Europeo*. Mostly crashing."

"You don't talk. You get." She watched his face twitch as he calculated how to handle her. She'd always been too much for him. In their first year "together," while she was in the throes of believing he was her sun and moon, Oriana had taken his incoherent draft, his mess of notes, and doing research herself, written his damn book—then secured a contract with her publisher. She had come up with the title *Anxieties of Social Class in Post-War Italy* and centered its thesis around the split between the north, which had aristocracy, industry, and a burgeoning middle class, and the south stuck in poverty. Gori was born rich. He could never have written with such insight. His main contribution had been rubbing her shoulders in his study and picking up pasta *del giorno* from the corner trattoria as she typed late into the night.

Now his tone changed. "How are you, my dear?" He came out from behind his desk and leaned against it, his knees touching hers. "I always tell people, *Oriana has the most elegant way with words.*"

He waited for her response, and when it didn't come, he said, "I always regretted how things ended with us." He bent toward her and she let him, even tilting up her chin. When he was almost on her lips, she sprang up, knocking him back and sending his phone flying.

"You must be joking," she said. On her way out, she spun around, dead serious. "My letters."

Chapter 34

1975

Often in her career, though she would never admit it, Oriana had been a little bit thrilled by war, murder—all the world's problems—because she could forget her own. A few days later, when she was back in Athens, the news was big: The dictator's trial was finally beginning. She got them into Korydallos Prison, to the courtroom in the basement, with press badges from *L'Europeo*. Sitting at the long table of journalists with Alekos, her crisis with Gori and his nephew receded.

"Look at him." Alekos glared at Papadopoulos not twenty feet away. The dictator was bald, eyebrows twitching, his chin held high with arrogance. He stood before the judge but refused to answer any of his questions. "He's not sorry at all for what he did to Greece," Alekos said with disgust.

The trial lasted a month, but in the end, justice reigned and the dictator was sentenced to death by firing squad. Alekos swept her up in a hug the moment the verdict was announced. But hours later, as they toasted with his friends in the crowded office, the new *democratic* prime minister pardoned the dictator, commuting his sentence to life imprisonment. The news blared on television and riots broke out in the streets of Athens, the people apoplectic. Why the pardon? Oriana couldn't understand. Because, Alekos explained calmly, there were still fascist elements in the army, and the new prime minister wanted to placate them to avoid another coup, this one against him. Oriana banged out the story for *L'Europeo* on her typewriter. She wasn't taking assignments, but this was major news, and she happened to be in Athens.

The torturers of the regime were put on trial next, and Alekos was called as a primary witness. He approached the bench with resolve and dignity and testified about the falange, suffocation, the lighting of his urethra on fire. He lifted his shirt to show the judge his scars. In the end, the two officers who led his barbaric treatment were sentenced to seven years. But Zaharakis, the prison warden who beat and humiliated Alekos daily, who yanked out his pubic hair and confiscated his pen and paper, was set free. He was absolved for "merely carrying out orders against an aggressive prisoner."

At home, Alekos wept. She drew him a bath and lathered him with soap. They had waited so long to see the dictator punished, to see Zaharakis rot in prison, but even as she rubbed a loofah over his shoulders, sharing his defeat, she felt exhausted by it all. Listening and supporting, the same problem over and over. How much was she expected to give? Ingrid's warning rose up in her memory: *Don't give up too much of yourself, so that a part of you is dying.*

Work. She needed a new project to consume her, now that *Letter* and *Interview* were out in the world. Love, she realized with a latecomer's arrival, was not the panacea she'd imagined it to be. At times, she couldn't reach Alekos, he was preoccupied with his country's tenuous recovery, and she felt as lonely as before, lonelier even. Nights under the quilt connected them, but in the day, they drifted, the space between them widening, the one she'd thought so permanently erased with their first kiss. In the end, it seemed, she had only herself to rely on. The truth of being a couple was that nothing got easier. No other person could save her, make her feel fulfilled and secure around the clock, not even her partner.

She called Tommaso and began accepting assignments. Jetting back and forth to America, Oriana covered Nixon's resignation, two assassination attempts on Gerald Ford, New York City's bailout from the brink of bankruptcy. Now was the time to buy the townhouse she'd always coveted, but why, if Alekos could never come? The American consul general in Milan had refused him a visa in accordance with Article 212, "Because Mr. Panagoulis, you were in prison for the attempted assassination of the leader of an organized government."

"Organized government? Is that what you call a military dictatorship?" Alekos had bellowed. He hoped to visit Washington to thank Senators Javits, Kennedy, and Fulbright for protesting his execution.

"Mr. Panagoulis is the founder of the Greek resistance," Oriana had argued with the consul general, all the way up to Ambassador Volpe, without winning.

He traveled within Greece, and she traveled, too. Sometimes, when she was across the Atlantic in New York, she imagined Alekos speaking in some outpost village with a pretty young thing by his side. The worry could eat her up if she let it, but mostly she chose to believe that he handled his independence the way she did hers, with loyalty. She was a liberated woman above sexual jealousy, or at least she tried to be. Alekos called every night when he was away, and she called, too. Transatlantic calls were obscenely expensive, but she could well afford the luxury.

After her trip or his, they craved each other's company and went straight to Psaropoulos, where he had so much to confide in her. She poured out her news, too, but the romance of their favorite restaurant, the al fresco breeze and starry sky, always got her reminiscing. "Did I ever tell you how many times I listened to your voice on the interview tape when we first met?" she said.

"Tell me." Alekos settled back, the flattery easing him.

She slipped off her pump and ran her toes up his leg. "You had this quality to your voice that was undressing. Hard to resist that voice."

"You were a shameless flirt when we met," he said.

"Me!"

He reached for her under the table.

They never ran out of things to talk about. He should do something for women, she urged. He had discovered the perfect case, he said, a friend's sister who earned half the salary of her male counterparts at the National Bank of Greece. He would propose a new law for equal pay. Yes! she said. It could be his signature effort.

Some nights, as they ate grilled fish under the moonlight, the question would prick at her. Should she tell him?

Lucia was still forwarding her mail to Greece, along with that weekly trash *Foto*. She had told the young woman to keep an eye on Mulotti, but so far, no more blind items, thank Christ. Gori must have reined in his nephew, for the sake of his own reputation as a mighty author; he couldn't give a damn about hers. He had her letters locked in his credenza and waiting for her, Gori said when she called to badger him.

In a back compartment of her mind, she buried the chaos he and his nephew had unleashed on her. Why ruin the intimate dinner that she and Alekos rarely enjoyed anymore? Each time she opened her mouth to tell him about the pregnancy, the choice she'd made and the aftermath, she closed it again. It was so much easier not to tell him. So much easier to forget.

A few days before Christmas, Alekos won the Omega Prize for his collection *I Write You from a Prison in Greece*.

"It's the same prize they gave Jean-Paul Sartre." His eyes pooled.

"I told you!" She shook him by the shoulders. "Didn't I tell you, get published in your own language?"

The award ceremony was held at the Louloudis Theater. Oriana chose a white Etro gown for herself and a charcoal suit and black tie for Alekos. She bought him twenty-two-carat gold cuff links to mark the occasion.

"The poetry we honor tonight was written by an extraordinary man in extraordinary circumstances," the judge opened the program. "In the poems written at Boyati, Alexander Panagoulis shares with us his patriotism and his pain. Tonight is a tribute to his literary achievement but also his undying dedication to democratic ideals."

Whistling and applause. Alekos ducked his head and took the podium.

"If you've ever tried to write on toilet paper, you know it's not easy because the paper tears." His shy smile. Voice like silk. "On the rare occasion they did give me paper, I wrote in such tiny letters, to save space, my poems were often illegible when they were smuggled out. Whatever the warden found, he destroyed. Still, I wrote every day. It was a way to keep from dying of loneliness, and to offer something for Greece."

A stinging in her throat. The image of him all alone.

"I had only my imagination for solace and escape," he said. "Poetry gave me a place that was mine, a place I could be free."

Standing ovation. Oriana stood with the crowd. Alekos won her all over again.

Always, he wanted to hear music. They went to his favorite nightclub on a rooftop in Plaka, the old quarter of Athens. The club with the stunning view of the Parthenon, columns uplit, and a live bouzouki band.

"For you." The singer motioned to the two of them as they sat at a front table and a new number started up.

"It's a love song." Alekos leaned close and translated the lyrics. *Make up the bed for two. For you and for me. Let's embrace like we did in the beginning. So all will be renewed.*

Oriana beamed at his sharing of the words, at the public acknowledgment of their bond. They ate grilled octopus and drank retsina, but when the band took a break, Alekos turned to her with a feverish look and dropped his voice.

"Guess what I said to Rigas today before all of Parliament."

She went still. Now what.

"You know who he is, the Minister of Defense," Alekos said. "He's a junta sympathizer. I said, *I demand to see the military police file on my brother. I have a right to know how he died.*"

"What did he say?"

"*Dear esteemed colleague. My aide hasn't been able to find the file.* What a load of shit," Alekos said.

Every muscle in her body tensed, recognizing his new obsession. "You think this Minister of Defense was involved in Yorgos's death?" she said.

"He's a rat. Rigas collaborated with the colonels. He's collaborating still."

"Alekos, you have no proof."

"I'll get proof." His eyes burned into hers. "I'm going to break into ESA and steal Yorgos's file."

"They'll shoot you!" she cried, forgetting their surroundings.

He wanted to leave. She followed him out of the club, down the stairs into the cobblestone lane. The lonely hunch of his shoulders was new. Alekos's posture was normally vital and upright, and it ignited her sympathy. His brother was gone, the body never found, Alekos carried a tremendous sorrow. But where would this latest crusade lead? Against a minister, for crissake.

At home, she followed him down the corridor, but Alekos stopped short, and she collided into his back. When she regained her balance, she saw it: the black skull and crossbones spray-painted across their door.

"I told you," Alekos said, shoving his key into the lock.

"Someone wants to hurt you." Her knees were weak as she trailed him into the apartment.

"The dictator's goons aren't gone. They're masquerading as democrats now."

"Listen to me, Alekos," she said. "I have money."

"I don't need your money."

"We can hire protection."

"I can't be protected."

"Then I can't be with you!" She hurled her pocketbook at him, and he caught it with one hand. It all rushed back to her, the car chase along the cliffs. The crew cuts. The baby.

"You're scared," he said, seeing her expression and softening.

"Only an idiot wouldn't be scared."

He drew her to him and she went, closing her eyes, trying to find calm in the warm thudding of his chest. But it was impossible. Her own heartbeat skittered, getting confused with his.

"Don't be afraid." Alekos tilted up her chin. "I'm a member of Parliament now. See the important office?" He gestured at the desk and shelves she had so lovingly arranged. "By the way," he said. "Will you buy me a car?"

Chapter 35

1975

He was like a kid, hopping into every model on the lot, falling in love with a Fiat 132 in neon green. She turned up her nose at the ugly color but Alekos insisted it was beautiful, and besides, it was the only one in stock. Oriana hated cars. Her father had almost died in a car accident, and as a result, she'd never learned to drive. But it was impossible to say no to Alekos, who swore he needed it to find his proof. Besides, she had a weakness for giving him gifts, and she liked the size of this gift, that she was a woman who could afford big gestures.

The *primavera*, Alekos nicknamed the new Fiat, claiming it was green like spring. He was an excellent driver. She watched him expertly shift gears through Athens traffic as they drove home.

"When did you learn to drive?" she said.

"Thirteen."

"You get your license at thirteen in Greece?"

"Who said I waited for my license?"

He became obsessed with his brother's file, scheming to break into military police headquarters. "Guess what! I found out there are the minutes from the investigation of the ship captain. The one who was supposed to bring Yorgos back," he said.

"Yes, yes, the ESA files," Oriana said, her eyes glazing over, taking a bite of the pasta all'Amatriciana she'd made them. She had wanted a quiet evening at home, but did the conversation always have to revolve around him? Was she expected to cheer on every pursuit? "Alekos, did you ever consider that Yorgos might have drowned trying to escape? Maybe he smashed open the porthole himself?" There, she'd said it.

He put down his fork. "You can't believe that."

She didn't, not really, knowing the beasts of the dictatorship. Why did she say it? To shake loose his fixation, get him back to his bill for equal pay. "It's a possibility we have to consider."

"No we don't. No more thoughts. Please." He picked up his plate and disappeared into the kitchen.

Mercifully, *Ms.* magazine invited her to write an article on the theme *Why I Never Married.* It was the outlet she needed, a place to deposit her jumbled feelings. One minute she adored her man and wanted to pour herself out nurturing him, the next she wanted to scream at the top of her lungs that he was interrupting, draining, suffocating her.

She drilled deeply as always into the assignment. Why had she never married? Because no one ever asked her. She wouldn't write that. Instead, she wrote:

I was not raised with the fairy tale of finding a prince. My mother was a frustrated woman of unfulfilled potential, and she showed me that married life requires sacrifice and can be a prison. A woman must erase herself and her dreams completely. As a result, I never fantasized about wearing a white wedding gown. I fantasized about belonging in the wide world, first as a student, then as a writer. Forging my path as a journalist, where nobody wanted me, made me strong, too strong for most men. When I finally did meet my equal, a man who wasn't threatened but was proud of me, we didn't need a piece of paper. We were partners not only in bed and in cooking dinner, but partners of the soul, which is stronger than any paper.

The most I expect from a romantic relationship is that we keep each other company through life's twists and turns. Being madly in love fades, but we still make a meal together, still bring aspirin in sickness, still support each other against enemies. And here I must be honest. Even when we find a partner who fits us, we cannot forget to be independent. For instance, as I write this article, I am completely alone. No one holds my hand. I do.

As she wrote, she tested her ideas. Were they true? Yes, the best we could hope for in life was good company. Would Alekos be hers through this crazy, beautiful life? She wanted it badly. She also prized her independence. One thing was clear: In Italy, she and Alekos had enjoyed a rare bubble of togetherness, but since returning to Greece, more and more, she belonged to herself and he to himself. Separate work meant separate lives.

She jumped at a call from Rizzoli.

"I have to go to New York," she said, the moment he turned his key in the door.

He set his briefcase down. "Oh." He looked more disappointed than usual that she was leaving.

"My books are selling so well in Europe, they want to publish *Interview* and *Letter* in English! I'm meeting with an American publisher."

"Good news." He turned away, loosening his tie.

"I told them I can do my own translation, but they want to hire the best." She paused, watching him. "Will you be all right?"

"It's your *work*," he said, giving it weight. Alekos never told her what to do. It was the only scenario she could tolerate, a man who respected her will, her decisions.

When the morning came to catch her plane, she clung to him in her usual pattern, wishing she didn't have to go, blaming herself for leaving. But New York welcomed her as it always did. It was November and the windows of Saks and Bergdorf Goodman were already decorated for Christmas. A giant snowflake shimmered over the intersection of 57th and Fifth, a block from her apartment. Chic women breezed by in capes, furs, and platform boots with thick square heels, swinging shopping bags from Tiffany and Chanel. The long sweater coat that Oriana wore was just starting to appear in boutique windows. It delighted her that Italian fashion was ahead of New York's.

A gay rights protest blocked the entrance to Central Park. New York was ahead on that, for sure. Men held hands and marched with signs that read *Stonewall* and *I Am a Homosexual.* At Grace's Market, she ordered buffalo mozzarella at the counter and her jaw dropped. Standing next to her was Greta Garbo in a cloche hat ordering chicken parmigiana. Oriana didn't say a word, respecting the star's privacy, but they bumped into each other at the exit, both struggling to open umbrellas.

"After you, Miss Fallaci," Garbo said, holding the door.

Stupefied, Oriana mumbled, "Thank you," and hurried down the rainy avenue. Had she become so famous in America that the reclusive actress knew her name? Always, she'd felt a kinship with Garbo, because she had turned her back on Hollywood at thirty-six to move to New York, travel in Europe, and live on her own terms. Increasingly, Oriana felt a similar urge to say *basta* after climbing the ladder of journalism. Garbo! She couldn't wait to tell Ingrid. They often gossiped about her fellow Swede, another woman who shattered the mold and did what she pleased. But Oriana was reluctant to call Ingrid. She was a lousy friend and hadn't checked in—maybe the cancer had spread. She was relieved when the maid said Ingrid was in London.

In a brownstone on East 48th Street, she met with Liveright, her new American publisher. They had published Hemingway! She was following in the great author's footsteps as he, too, had started as a journalist. Coincidentally, Oriana had interviewed Mary Hemingway, wife number four, in her Manhattan penthouse just after his death in 1961. For the first time, Miss

Mary, as Hemingway called her, had admitted that yes, Ernest shot himself that July morning in Idaho. Until then, the widow had maintained he was cleaning his gun and it fired by accident, so Oriana got a scoop. Now here she was ascending the same curved staircase as not only Hemingway but T. S. Eliot, Gertrude Stein, James Joyce, Eugene O'Neill.

Liveright had the reputation of being progressive and undeterred by political controversy. No wonder they wanted her. She was in the right house. Her new editor, Tim Daly, was tall with huge hands, a Harvard degree, and a bottle of gin on his desk. He offered her a drink and they toasted. He wanted to showcase the "provocative Fallaci style," he said. Would she write a short commentary to introduce each interview?

"Why? The interviews stand on their own," she said.

"Our readers are . . ." Tim Daly trailed off.

"Uninformed, you don't have to tell me. Fine, I will do the history lesson. Who the leaders are, their importance. Where we met, their behavior. My honest impressions."

Fourteen commentaries. It was a heart attack assignment, but she began straightaway on the plane back to Athens, jotting in her notebook. Golda Meir, modest, earthy, washed her own dishes. A suspicious thing happened after their six-hour interview. Oriana's tapes were stolen from her hotel room. *It appears someone doesn't want us to talk*, Meir said when Oriana called in a frenzy, *so we will talk again.* Meir invited her back the very next day.

In Athens, Oriana settled at her Olivetti in the bedroom and suddenly she was herself again. It was easier to be in harmony with Alekos, to shrug off the ESA files, stock toilet paper, serve espresso, when she had put in a productive day crafting sentences, sharpening ideas, nailing down truths. When *Interview* was published in English, she would not be an important Italian journalist, she would be an important journalist, period.

Chapter 36

1976

While Alekos was in Parliament, Oriana sat on the sofa and privately scoured the latest issue of *Foto*. The tabloid was so pathetic, filled with "B" actresses in fishnets and crooked businessmen in cigarette boats speeding around Lago di Como. The standards of journalism were falling, nobody had to tell her that. Sex and money were being stuffed down readers' throats. Seriousness was going out of vogue. She refused to go out of vogue.

Her eyes swept over the *Italy Is Talking* column and suddenly the page shook in her hands. A blind item. *What famous woman would have traded her career to wash a man's underwear? The same one who tried to kill herself when he broke off their affair.*

She was on a plane to Florence the next day. Alekos offered to come along since Parliament had adjourned for a religious holiday. No need, she convinced him, she'd be reviewing a boring matter of royalties with Rizzoli and would return straightaway.

In their Florentine hideaway, Oriana paced with the phone in her hand. "What do you mean *a meeting*, Donatella! Did you tell him who was calling?"

She demanded Gori come to her this time. He arrived with a shopping bag from a tobacco shop and gave her a double kiss, which she accepted like a marble statue. Reaching into the glossy bag, he handed her a stack of worn, ivory envelopes. She opened the first to make sure. *Renzo dear, I live only for you.* The slant of her handwriting unleashed cellular memories. The tears she'd shed on the stationery, copying her pleas onto a fresh sheet when the ink blurred. The hope she'd harbored, licking the envelope and affixing the stamp, that these would be the words to convince Renzo to love her.

"I don't believe the leak is coming from my nephew," Gori said, crossing his arms.

"You don't believe?" She cut him with her stare. "Are you calling me a liar?"

"Anyway, I told Riccardo to watch his step or I'd send him back to Padua."

She locked the letters in a cabinet, then turned to him at top volume. "I kill myself to make a name and you jeopardize it with your drunken carelessness! Invading my privacy with your dummy protégé! Why did you keep my letters?"

He sighed and his stance changed, his arms out to her. "Why do you think? I was in love with you."

She burst out laughing. "You can do better than that." He was a terrible actor.

"Oriana, I have nothing to gain here," Gori said.

"Don't you?" she said. "Maybe someday you'll have the talent to write your own damn book, what Fallaci was like in bed, how you screwed her and she mopped your floors."

"I would never."

"I'll set my lawyers on you." She had no lawyers. "Speaking of gain, your nephew is taking kickbacks from *Foto*." She showed her full hand. Gori slumped into a chair. That gem Lucia had seen Mulotti open a manila envelope at his desk. He thumbed a stack of lire, stuffed it hastily into his safari jacket, and tossed the envelope away. When he cleared out for his three-hour lunch, Lucia picked the crumpled envelope from his trash and found a note inside: *Riccardo, keep up the intelligence.* On *Foto* letterhead.

Gori read the proof she dangled in his face. She could see him calculating how this would reflect on the family, publishing aristocrats born into leadership positions they didn't deserve. "Ungrateful shit," he muttered. "I'll cut off his legs."

Oriana loomed over him, wedging herself between his knees, so close their breath mingled. She pinched him by the chin. "I want his balls, not his legs."

They heard it simultaneously and turned, the tumbler in the lock, the door swinging open.

"Alekos!" Oriana said, reeling back from Gori.

The boyish eagerness faded from Alekos's face. He had given her the gift she always wanted, chasing her, surprising her, being unable to live without her. Now he stood in their hideaway with a jarred expression.

"This is Renzo Gori. From *Corriere*," she rushed to say. "We had work."

"What kind of work?" His stunned gaze shifted between them.

For once in her life, Oriana had no reply. Alekos gave her a ruined look and slammed the door behind him.

Piazza Santa Croce. Boboli Gardens. Cafés along the Arno. She searched in all their favorite places. Maybe he'd taken the Alitalia flight back to Greece. Please no. Last, exhausted, she peered into the doorway of Café Greco. A three-piece orchestra was pumping out Italian pop music, a girl singer onstage in hot pants and white boots shaking her long, lustrous hair. She batted her doe eyes at a patron at the front table. He lifted his glass to her. She watched Alekos watching the girl with a familiarity that was unmistakable. She could feel him physically cut off from her in a way that was excruciating.

For a long time she couldn't move, then she forced herself to weave around tables. Alekos looked up, nonchalant, as if expecting her, and motioned to a chair. Empty wine bottles littered the table.

"I don't want to stay," she said, lighting a cigarette and needing one hand to steady the other. Bracing for his *I don't want you anymore. I want her.*

But Alekos threw lire on the table and led the way out.

"Who is she?" Oriana said hotly on the cobblestones, unable to hold back.

"I met her at the break. She's half-Greek." His voice was hard. In this game of betrayal, he seemed to say, they had each made their move.

They crossed the Arno in smoldering, hurt silence. Ponte Vecchio, so familiar to her, Mannelli Tower with its childhood memories and bad ice cream, swam at a remove. *I'm not young enough, not Greek enough, not musical enough,* the tape looped in her brain. Images assailed her. Alekos screwing the singer in her dressing room. Standing her up by the mirror and sticking it in.

Veering off the sidewalk, she vomited into the bushes.

At the hideaway, she told him everything. How she debased herself with Gori when she was young and unbearably naive. The botched abortion, the reason she could not bear children. Sleeping pills, bed with the leather straps. Mulotti's threatening to expose her.

"I'll kill him," Alekos said. "I'll kill them both." His protectiveness blazed forth like a physical object, a sturdy net she could fall into, that would catch her if she fell. She had always been deprived of this one thing, ever since her father had sent her in schoolgirl braids to outfox the Nazis. She had never had someone to protect her. Always, she'd survived by her own wits. Now the rescue Alekos offered felt miraculous and foreign, soothing and impossible all at once.

"I took care of it with Gori," she said out of long ingrained habit, relying only on herself.

"You can't trust him," Alekos said, shaking his head. She could see him thinking strategically, problem-solving, on her side in a way she hadn't dared hoped. His eyes were two wells of compassion and made her own sting. He was right, of course, she couldn't trust Gori. But Alekos couldn't fix this. So much of life, her life anyway, had to be done alone.

An idea came to her. She could take control, preempt Mulotti by writing her own article, confiding *I Had an Abortion* to the world. It would hurt her parents. She had plenty of fuck-you's in her but not Steinem's, not on this topic. Why should she be pressured into disclosing her personal life? It should be her decision. She was firm on this, *her* love affairs, *her* body, *her* mental and emotional upheavals. It didn't make her any better or worse a person than Steinem, morally inferior or superior. She was simply exercising the right all women had, or should have: free will.

Alekos held her in his arms, and she tried to escape into his body heat, the scent of wool tweed mixed with a freshly pressed shirt. "I was weak with Gori," she said, pulling back to look at him, unable to remain in his solace. "If they find out, they'll bury me alive." She suffered no illusions. Men were flawed but forgivable, permitted to indulge in a galaxy of sordid affairs, gaffes, behaviors. But not women. Women had to be perfect, superhuman—and if they were, they'd be slapped down for that, too.

Alekos brushed a wisp of hair from her cheek. The shame she felt was not about abortion. Thousands of women in Italy had abortions—and premarital sex, for the Pope's information. No, the shame was groveling to cook Gori's dinner and polish his shoes, her desperation to throw away her career and be his helpmate. She had molded herself to please him, panted like a doggie for approval. Tried to end her life, for God's sake. A line came to her from her recent speech to the American newspaper editors at the Waldorf. *I've never missed a day of work because of a hysterical breakdown*. Her enemies would feed on her like crows.

"You've never lowered yourself," she said to Alekos. "Even in prison you never broke. You don't know what it's like to feel ashamed."

A shadow crossed his face and he brought his lips to her ear. In solitary, he whispered, he had just one friend, a cockroach. Chestnut brown, bigger than his thumb. He used to feed it crumbs and talk to it for company. Why, Oriana searched his face, had he never told her? She hadn't understood his desolation and she never would. No wonder Alekos would never kill a spider but cupped it in his hands and set it gently outdoors. One day, he continued, the guard caught him petting the cockroach, and the bastard burst out laughing and squashed it under his boot. Alekos wept. The guard roared even louder. That night on his straw mat on the cement floor, Alekos decided the next time they shaved him, he would steal the blade and slice his wrists. He had never wanted to give up, not even when he was emaciated during a hunger strike and could see death over the next wave. But that night, he wanted to evaporate off the earth. He couldn't fight anymore.

"I do know." Alekos wrapped his arms around her and kissed the top of her head and it was all said. It was not her fault, there was nothing to be ashamed of. She could tell him anything.

They were partners.

Chapter 37

1976

In the director's office at *L'Europeo*, Oriana milked the moment, dramatically presenting the handwritten note on *Foto* stationery: *Riccardo, keep up the intelligence*. The message accompanying a fat wad of lire.

"You lazy piece of shit," Gori ripped into his nephew, spit flying from his mouth. "Your mother was right, God rest her soul, you would put her in her grave. You won't put me."

Mulotti looked ready to blubber. He cast his last vile look at Oriana. "You never helped me."

"You never helped yourself." She stood beside the director, hands on hips, glaring at the two interlopers from across his desk.

The director ordered Mulotti to pack up and leave that same day. "Go back to horse racing or whatever the hell you were doing. You won't work in journalism again."

Downstairs in the newsroom, Oriana handed Lucia an extravagant box tied with gold lamé ribbon. Inside, a mink stole to celebrate their victory. Lucia draped the gift around her shoulders in disbelief, swirling her fingers through the sleek fur, thanking Oriana profusely.

"Thank *you*," Oriana said, giving the young secretary a penetrating look. "You're smart, Lucia. What are you going to do with your life? You could go to university."

Lucia lowered her gaze. Her hand went to her belly.

"No." This time Oriana was the one in disbelief.

The young woman nodded, red-cheeked.

"Ah," was all she could manage. She felt a rush of envy, inadequacy, embarrassment for trying to advise a girl who had surpassed her into a realm she knew nothing about. A calmer, more generous feeling followed that *yes*, this was the right path for a woman like Lucia, beautiful inside and out.

"You've done well," Oriana said, meaning it mostly. She couldn't help envisioning the promising young woman in a scene of thwarted potential, up to her elbows in greasy pans, a man and child demanding to be fed.

"Oriana, I've always wanted to ask," Lucia began shyly, glancing away before pressing on. That's what she liked about this girl, she pressed on! "At what point did you make up your mind to have a profession rather than a family?"

"I didn't decide." Oriana flicked her ashes and tried to keep her voice from wobbling. "It happened."

A wrinkle passed over Lucia's brow. "But you're happy."

Oriana traveled back to the night she and Alekos strolled across Piazza Santa Croce, watching children streak by in their gleeful games. Fantasizing about the little soccer player or tricycle rider they would raise to be a fighter, to take risks and never back down.

Lucia was watching her, waiting to hear that of course Oriana was overjoyed with her profession. That any path a woman chose was blissfully fulfilling.

"You should have two or three," Oriana said, squeezing the girl's hand. "Just keep the *bambini* away from this." She folded the mink into its elegant box. "Maybe you'll name one after me."

The next day, she was at her typewriter, hair in a messy bun, puffing on fifty cigarettes a day. Hammering out her last commentary for *Interview* and her American publisher. She and Alekos had celebrated her ass-kicking of Mulotti with prosecco and a toe-curling session of lovemaking. Now he was back in Athens and she was submerged in precious solitude, the only way she could write. She wasn't cooking, wasn't speaking, didn't know if it was day or night.

The big-name translator hired by Liveright had done a decent job, better than her own English, which was not Shakespearean, she had to admit. She would earn her place as a master of the Q and A, a pioneer of her own Fallaci style. Interrogations, not conversations. Audacity and opinions. No such thing as objectivity, people—get that through your heads.

Her commentaries were blunt and hard-hitting, how she really viewed these world figures. One essay remained, Alekos. The public knew they were partners, she would need to slip in that detail for full disclosure, but how to sum up Alekos? So far, she'd written, *Politics is only one of his abilities. By nature, he is a poet and artist. The common thread through all his endeavors is human dignity no matter what the cost.*

Laser-focused at the typewriter, she reread her words. Not bad. The phone clanged.

"I found the documents!" Alekos said, pleased with himself.

"What? Where?" She was still in her solitude and had trouble catching up.

"ESA. The secret police. A girl unlocked the office for me," Alekos said.

"What girl?" A heavy tension filled the line as she pictured the singer in Café Greco, remembered how cut off he'd been from her.

"Her boyfriend was there, too," Alekos said. "He helped me."

The word *boyfriend* brought instant relief, though she hated it for being true. "Did you find Yorgos's file?"

"No, but I found enough. I'm going to expose Mr. Rat Minister for being in bed with the dictator."

"The Minister of Defense? But how, Alekos?"

"*Ta Nea* will publish the classified documents. I've arranged it with Yannis Zogradis. He's the only journalist with any balls."

"When?"

"Tomorrow. Pack your things?"

"I have to work."

"Please. I need you with me when it happens."

I need you. It was all he had to say. She packed up her manuscript and returned to Athens on the evening flight. Alekos had been in Parliament just one year, and he was about to unmask the most powerful minister in Greece as a collaborating fascist pig.

Ta Nea was an afternoon paper. They drank espresso and fidgeted on the sofa, waiting for Alekos's exposé to be splashed across the front page. At ten thirty, the telephone rang. He spoke rapid-fire Greek. Oriana slowed her breath, sensing it was not good news. After two long minutes, he banged down the phone and shoved it across the desk. *Ta Nea* had canceled publication. The publisher had backed out due to "national security concerns."

"Cowards! They bought him or spooked him." Alekos paced like a caged animal. "I'll find someone with spine to publish the documents."

"You will," she said, not at all sure, wishing he would let it go.

With the back of his hand, Alekos brushed away tears. Despite his courage, his insane courage at times, beneath it all, he was dangerously soft. "You don't know what it's like to always lose," he said.

She opened her arms. *Remember?* her expression said to him, and when he curled on the sofa with his head in her lap, she smoothed his hair. *Remember just last week, when my enemies tried to destroy me? We're partners.*

Three days later she woke with a start. She was catching a plane to New York in a few hours to meet with Liveright.

"I don't want to leave you." She kissed his forehead and lingered there, as if checking for fever. As if she could dodge her responsibilities and stay in that place.

He was affectionate as she packed her Samsonite, gathering up her hair and nuzzling her neck. "How long will you stay away this time?"

"A week," she said and saw his face fall. "Do you want to read what I wrote about you?" She brought him the pages from her desk.

In her commentary for *Interview*, Oriana told the story of meeting the Greek hero on his veranda. *We admired each other's honesty and convictions, and that led to my returning to Athens to see more of him.*

"I had to send you three telegrams," he said, glancing up. "You were scared of me."

"Damn right. And you were swept away by me."

They shared their intimate laugh and he went on reading.

Alekos can be warm and humble one moment, difficult and immovable the next. Though he's known for his political struggle, his natural state is that of an artist, and like all artists, he will never fully realize what he envisions in his imagination.

Anxious for his reaction, she clicked her Samsonite open and closed.

"You call me *difficult*," he said, handing back her pages.

"You're not?" She tipped her head.

"We're the same."

"Stubborn past the point of reason?"

"You're an artist, too," he said.

"We'll grow old at the same writing table," she said.

He didn't answer, his expression growing distant.

Disappointed, she glanced at her watch. "I have to go." She pressed against him, drinking in his glycerin soap and cherry tobacco scent. She should have stayed one more day, but no, she never missed a deadline.

In New York, she delivered her manuscript to Liveright. Tim Daly, the editor with the Harvard degree, called her introductory commentaries "blunt and unsparing, a blast of fresh air." The glint in his eye told her it would sell like hell. She returned the look: *Good.* He summoned art directors so Oriana could approve the cover design with her name above the title. Publicity people so she could schedule interviews with *Time*, *Newsweek*, *Life*.

In the evenings, she returned to her skyscraper on 57th Street, buzzing from the productive meetings and energy of the city. Outside her picture window, toll ships plied the East River, gearing up for America's bicentennial. On TV, Walter Cronkite soberly reported that a bomb had exploded at the TWA baggage claim at LaGuardia Airport. Eleven people were dead. It was not the airport she used, but the incident hit close.

His voice. She needed to hear it. Greece was seven hours ahead, but she called anyway.

"I tried *Eleftheria*." Alekos skipped the hellos. "They won't publish the documents either."

"Too bad," she said impatiently, pulled back into his existence. Had he heard about the airport bombing? What bombing, he said, and launched into a tirade against the corrupt Greek press.

"If you're interested in my news," she interrupted, "I told the cover designer to use that photograph of me picking grapes. The one you like." He grunted at her joke. "Did you go out tonight?" she said. Alekos always shared details of where he went and what he ate, but he hadn't offered anything tonight.

"I'm going out now," he said.

"It's one in the morning."

"I'll call you tomorrow."

Click. Where was he going? She stared out her picture

window at the lights of the 59th Street Bridge. It was only six, and the night stretched out ahead. She refused to dwell on him any longer and dialed Ingrid. The maid was evasive. "I know she has cancer," Oriana said. "Where is she?"

Sloan Kettering was seven avenues east. She stopped to buy flowers from a shop in the lobby.

"I don't give a damn about visiting hours," she said to the desk clerk and barreled into the elevator without a badge.

Would Ingrid be thin or bald? Oriana braced herself in the doorway. But her friend still radiated natural beauty, though with more lines on her face, more tiredness. She was propped up in bed wearing a silk robe and reading *Vogue*.

Oriana gave her an awkward hug, glancing down at her chest, not wanting to hurt her.

"They're lovely." Ingrid fingered the bouquet.

The room was drowning in floral arrangements. Dammit, she should have brought books or Baci chocolates. "You had surgery," she said. "Why didn't you tell me?"

Ingrid shrugged. "I hate to bother people with my personal problem."

Oriana put her hands on her hips. "Did they cut off one or two?"

Ingrid giggled. "Ouch. The stitches. One."

"Let me see."

"It's bandaged. I haven't looked." Ingrid's expression clouded. "When I woke, I knew from the doctor's face. I felt sorry for him. Can you imagine, the awful job of telling a woman she's amputated?"

Oriana kept her gaze steady. "You're beautiful. And it's none of anyone's business. When do you go back to work?"

Ingrid brightened. "I start *Autumn Sonata* in three months. With Ingmar Bergman."

"Good. What is it about?"

"I play a celebrity pianist who constantly leaves her daughter to tour." They exchanged knowing looks. "I suggested a line to Bergman for my character. *I'm always drawn toward home. But when I get there, I feel trapped. It's something else I need, out of reach.*"

"*Bello*. Did he accept it, the great genius?"

"Eventually. Oh, I argued about many lines." Ingrid gave a small smirk and dropped her head back. "The daughter hates me. It's a depressing script."

Oriana squeezed her friend's hand, the dilemma of being a woman who wants everything uniting them even with cancer in the room. It struck Oriana this would be a personal movie for Ingrid, who'd been estranged from her eldest daughter for years. Yet she was diving into the role with typical bravery, like the great artist she was.

"Tell me," Ingrid said. "What are you doing in New York?"

Oriana filled her in on the American editions, promising Ingrid that if the books sold well, she would buy a townhouse in Manhattan, and why didn't she buy one, too; they could be neighbors. "In the theater district." Ingrid smiled weakly. "We can walk. And I can get us into rehearsals."

A nurse entered with a reprimand about visiting hours. Oriana insisted on one more minute to say goodbye.

"You're coming to Toscana this summer, Ingrid. Bring the kids," Oriana said with forced confidence. "Don't you always say you miss the warmth of Italians?" Even as she uttered the invitation, her mind filled with the terrible possibility of never seeing her friend again.

"I've had a good life." Ingrid said, reading her thoughts. "Better than any I could have imagined."

Oriana gave her a careful hug and blinked back tears. It wasn't possible, this stunning icon, this giant of a woman. She had felt a sisterhood with Ingrid from the day they met, reassured that a woman could live a different life.

Alone in her apartment, Oriana paced and chain-smoked. How long did Ingrid have? Even Fallaci didn't have the nerve to ask. She had a cold premonition that her own demise would come from this devil, too, but it didn't make her throw her pack away. This thing called a lifetime wasn't so long, after all. Her love with Alekos would be brief, they had met so late.

He called the next day sounding energized and upbeat. "I'm meeting with a small newspaper tomorrow that wants to publish," he said. "Small but with big balls." They laughed. "Tell me about your meetings," he said sweetly.

She recounted that she and Mr. Harvard, after much debate, had agreed on a subtitle for *Interview*: *A Superlative Journalist's Portraits of Power and Dissent Around the World.*

"You are superlative," Alekos said. "Am I dissent?"

"The definition."

She spent her remaining days in New York rewriting jacket and catalog copy because some imbecile in the ad department could barely form sentences. At night she longed for Alekos in bed, but she didn't call. Sometimes, loving was easier from a distance than loving in person.

He called, sounding harried this time. "Can you take a taxi from the airport? I can't get you."

"Fine," she said, but it wasn't fine. Why did she buy him the damn car if he couldn't give her a ride?

Returning to Athens, she lugged her suitcase into the creaking elevator and unlocked the office door. It was noon and Alekos was still in his bathrobe, staring out the window and gulping a beer. Was this the busy schedule that kept him from picking her up? She was so mad, she couldn't say hello.

He turned and she saw that he was unshaven, with dark circles under his eyes. “No other paper will publish the documents,” he said.

“But you found a small one . . .”

He shook his head miserably. “I failed. Again.”

Chapter 38

1976

She wasn't failing. Every one of her dreams had been hard-fought and won: a man of her own, *Interview* and *Letter* selling briskly in America, Mulotti and every other macho enemy out of her hair. But it was impossible to be happy with an unhappy partner. Alekos was floundering. They were out of sync. She had to help him.

Forget about nailing the Minister of Defense, she urged him, focus on equal pay or introducing your country's first anti-pollution laws. "You want to save Greece," she said, on a rare weekend stroll along the beach in Glyfada. "Start here." She pointed to an empty Coke bottle bobbing in the crystal Aegean.

They could visit New York, she suggested, try again for a visa.

"I'll never go, not if Ford himself invites me," Alekos said, embittered by the rejection.

"It's Kissinger who blocked us. He hates me," Oriana said. "But I'll go around him." She could not imagine a life together that didn't include her adopted city. She was intent on showing Alekos her river view, the Greek diners on every corner. They could go to poetry readings and music clubs in Greenwich Village.

Amherst College in Massachusetts invited her to speak. Her profile was high in America with *Interview* and *Letter* earning good reviews. The topic was perfect for her, *Journalism and the*

Resistance in Europe. Amherst would pay an honorarium and all expenses.

"Come and go as you please. You're good at that," Alekos said, trudging home from Parliament. He no longer carried a briefcase, no longer wore a tie.

"It's my *work*," she said, repeating the point he'd once made.

Alekos shrugged. "Go. I won't tell you what to do. There's no ownership here."

It hit her like a slap. His detachment, the belittling of their bond. "Where are you going?" She watched him head for the door.

"You're not the only one who's busy."

The door slammed. Alekos rarely returned to Parliament in the late afternoon unless there was a vote. If he thought she would chase after him, forget it. She was angry and uneasy and tried to find steady ground at her typewriter, drafting her Amherst speech. Pecking at the keys instead of attacking in her usual storm. Rather than what to say to those fine undergraduates at that fine institution, her thoughts looped back to Alekos. Three years. The longest relationship she'd ever had. Why was she leaving? He wanted her by his side, and that request, even that demand, had always pleased her and made her feel secure. But what was she supposed to do, pass up the opportunity to speak in America? Inconceivable.

He didn't return until eight that evening, holding out a snow-white bouquet. She was still at her desk, staring at her meager sentences. "What's this for?" she said. Unbidden, the image of the girl singer with white boots invaded her brain.

"I've been thinking," Alekos said. She braced herself. "I don't need a newspaper. I'm going to present the documents myself. In Parliament."

"Oh!" She exhaled with relief. Just politics, Alekos fired up with a new plan.

"On Monday, I'll take the podium," he said, pointing his finger at his imagined opponents. "Why, Mr. Prime Minister, did you choose Rigas as Minister of Defense, a man who collaborated with the junta? Who was a spy. Who covered up the murder of my brother."

"You'll make enemies, Alekos."

"Stop." His face went mild. "Be on my side. You're my only friend."

The plea in his voice. *Be on my side.* "How can I help?" she said instinctively. It didn't matter that she doubted the wisdom of his plan or that she had a speech to write or a plane to catch.

He kissed her with urgency. "I love you."

"I love you, too." She had never meant it so much or believed him so much. The moment stretched, holding inside it something they were never able to communicate. How blissful and wrenching it was to care.

Alekos moved first. He pulled two blue files from his briefcase. "The documents."

"Tell me." They were in this together.

"I want you to hide a copy," Alekos said. "If something happens to me—"

"Nothing will happen to you."

"You'll try and publish them."

"I don't know what they say."

"Later I'll explain each one." He got quiet, running his hand along her slim desk. "Remember how happy we were in Florence, the two of us being writers together?"

She nodded, the pressure of tears building.

"Was I wrong?" he said, rueful.

"About what?"

"Thinking I could make a difference. That everybody counts and nobody should be mistreated."

She shook her head. "You're not wrong."

"Stay," he said cupping her cheek. "Don't go to America."

Mentally, she began drafting her telegram to Amherst. *I am sorry to inform you that I am ill.* Not a telegram, better to call the dean personally.

Out loud she said, "I can't cancel with Amherst at this late date, *agapi*. It's unprofessional." It wasn't the whole truth. "I'll be back on May fifth."

"May fifth." His face held only the briefest disappointment.

"Will you be all right?" she said. "Speaking out on the Parliament floor?" She wished she could be there to cheer him on, to catch him if he fell.

"I'll tell you everything by phone."

In bed, they sealed their bodies together. Somehow her pending speech in Amherst and his in Parliament, separating them on different continents, had added weight to the evening, a reminder of the shortage of time.

"Don't forget about me," Alekos said, their foreheads touching on the pillow.

"I won't. Even in America, in a restaurant, I think, *What would Alekos order*? Steak and baked potato with sour cream."

"I don't mean America," he said, tracing his fingers along her collarbone. "Did I ever tell you? You've been the love of my life."

The only words she had ever wanted to hear. But not this way. "Why speak in the past, Alekos? You still love me. You better." She laughed, trying to get him to join in, but he didn't. "We need a holiday." She tried again to lighten the mood. "Let's go to Ischia when I return."

"If I were dying, what would you say to me?" he said.

"Stop." She propped herself up to stare at him. "This is silly. Besides, I'll die first, I'm a couple of years older."

"A couple, eh?" He finally grinned and she swatted his shoulder. "Tell me," he said, serious again. "People give eulogies when it's too late." He rolled onto his back and shut his eyes.

"I don't like this game," she said, but he remained rigid, arms folded at his chest. Words that were her trade ricocheted in her brain. *I never believed a man could love me the way you do. You've changed my life forever.* But no words came out, until she heard herself say, "What a warrior you are." Alekos blinked his eyes open in surprise. "You've lived your life to the maximum. Left your mark. Done everything possible that a man could do."

His cheeks grew damp. Somehow, she had intuited what a man like Alekos would want to hear. A man who had known only struggle and never winning. He took her in his arms. For the rest of the night, they clung to each other, speaking the rest silently.

Chapter 39

1976

Amherst sent a limousine to meet her at Logan Airport in Boston. The college was the epitome of the ivory tower with white-pillared buildings and rolling green lawns. It reeked of money and privilege. Crossing the campus, she felt pangs of envy, having missed out on her own education, and at the same time instantly at home in the rarefied atmosphere where important thought was taking place. The students looked relaxed and self-assured with their guitars and Frisbees, unisex long hair, work boots and flannel. She watched a group sitting cross-legged on the grass as a bearded professor led the class. How lucky they were to study here. Did they realize their good fortune? Probably not.

She followed a winding path studded with Carter and Ford signs staked into the grass. (Carter would win in November, she predicted. Ford had screwed himself by pardoning Nixon.) With each step across the green, she was flooded with visceral memories of her own eighteen months at University of Florence. For a disorienting moment, it was teenage Oriana hurrying to anatomy lab to dissect a cadaver. The stink of formaldehyde had her near fainting, but in entering the colonnaded building, she'd had the sensation of walking on hallowed ground. The red-brick buildings of Amherst radiated the same intellectual power she'd tasted briefly, the only kind of power she could stomach. The kind of power, she realized, she'd been pursuing all her life.

Students and professors crammed the amphitheater lecture hall for her speech, some even sitting on stairs. "A journalist's job is to be disliked," she projected from the podium. "The more conflict between me and my subject, the better the interview. You Americans are obsessed with being friendly, but a good journalist should never be nice. She should be a pain in the ass, brazen and persistent and stirring up trouble. Resistance means saying a very simple word: No. *No* to the absurd misinformation and evasions you will hear. You must practice saying *No* in the mirror. If the powerful don't answer the question, say, *You are avoiding my question.* If they're incoherent, say, *Your answer makes no sense.* If they're ridiculous, say, *You must be kidding.* Why? So you can deliver truth to the people. The truth that Power always tries to hide, so we can be puppets, and they can pull the strings."

When it came time for questions, the *bambini* shot up their hands.

"Miss Fallaci, when did you know you wanted to be a journalist?"

"I was born during Mussolini fascism, when real journalism didn't exist, only propaganda. But I was lucky. My father asked me to distribute an underground newspaper, *Non Mollare, Don't Give Up*. And I got to read that newspaper. It told the truth, and I wanted to do the same."

A girl with a beaded headband raised her hand. "Miss Fallaci, I want to be an investigative reporter and do interviews like you."

"Forget it, you can't do interviews like me. You would need to have my parents, my childhood. My belly ache from hunger during the war. Understand?" The girl nodded unsurely. "You must do interviews like *you*. Bring yourself into it, what you notice and wonder. What you love and hate."

During the wine and cheese reception, she signed books and looked into the wide eyes of the students, realizing she was their age when she broke into journalism, though not as innocent. You grew up fast when bombs rained down on your city. Still she liked these young people, their curiosity and idealism. She would have made a great professor, lighting a fire under them. Making them mad enough at injustice to jump into the fight.

At the quaint inn on Main Street where Amherst was hosting her, she sprawled on the bed buzzing with the evening's success. Alekos would have made fun of the king-size mattress, patting the vast space between them and pretending he couldn't find her. He was driving her crazy with his plan to expose the minister, but she couldn't change him.

In fact, she was practicing a new skill lately, the key, it turned out, to lasting relationships: letting things go. Her job as a journalist was to challenge people, grill them, *never* let things go. The whole point of her career was never to overlook anything, but love couldn't survive such scrutiny. She was learning to forgive.

Ravenous, she scanned the room service menu. There was the rib-eye steak Alekos would order. What time was it in Athens? Too late. She called anyway. He picked up on the first ring, wide awake.

"Did you get the documents?" he said.

"What documents?"

"The blue files. I mailed them to you for safekeeping."

"But we locked them in the armoire in Athens, remember?" she said. "We went over them."

"Oh. Yes."

"Alekos, are you all right?" He had a razor-sharp mind, never forgot a detail.

"I'm tired, that's all. Not sleeping well."

She yawned, exhausted from jet lag, too. "Maybe you should postpone your address to Parliament."

"At night, when I drive back to Glyfada, two cars follow me. A red BMW and a pale one."

"Two cars?" She tensed. "But why sleep in Glyfada? Why not stay downtown?"

"I can't sleep in our bed alone."

"Alekos, listen to me. Have you told anyone about your plan to present the documents in Parliament?"

"What's going on with your American students?" he said. "Do they know where Italy is? Thank God it's shaped like a boot."

The next morning, the dean of Amherst invited her to stay an extra day and meet with students from the campus newspaper. She accepted, enjoying the back-and-forth with these budding young journalists. They had studied her interviews and had big goals of being hired by *The New York Times* and CBS after graduation. She admired the rigor of their operation—publishing a daily paper was no small thing—and the fat budget that paid for the latest in IBM electric typewriters, though she would never trade her manuals for such a beast.

During her free afternoon, she went straight to the three-story Amherst library. What she would have given for access to these shelves as a girl. The library carried *Interview*, it carried *Letter*! She curled into a club chair facing the green and spent the rest of the day reading political journals, literary criticism. Wishing she could be here the next week for a reading by E. L. Doctorow, a campaign stop by Jerry Brown, the young California governor, both events promoted on posters.

The phone jangled her awake at midnight. "It's me!" Alekos said. "When are you coming? It's May Day, a holiday weekend. We'll go to the country for roast lamb."

"I'm in Amherst, remember? I fly to New York tomorrow. We have a date for May fifth."

He hesitated. "Oh. Right."

She sat up in bed. "Alekos. What's wrong?"

"Every May Day, we went to my father's village." She heard the hitch in his voice. "There's a white chapel hidden in the olive groves. A big picnic and dancing."

"*Agapi*, should I change my flight?"

"Don't change. We'll go to the country another day. We have time for holidays, yes?"

"And Monday you'll address Parliament?" she said.

"I'll be the star of the chamber. They'll be cheering me by noon." He sighed. "I need to review the documents with you, in case something happens to me."

"You did that already. And nothing will happen to you. Alekos, you sound odd."

"I have to go. See you on May fifth."

Click. Something was wrong and she couldn't see his face, his expression, to figure out what it was or how to help him. She had put an ocean between them to pontificate in academia over bad wine and cheese. Nervous, she packed her bags and tossed and turned the rest of the night. Alekos needed her. He always needed her.

She landed in New York the following day, Friday, April 30. Streaked around the apartment repacking her Samsonite. Rang his office. No answer. She caught the evening Alitalia flight to Rome. Threw back a Chivas and tried to read the newspaper, stuck on the same paragraph.

Ach! She heard a gasp and twisted around to the row behind her. Unmistakable. The sound hung in the air—but the seats were empty. Alekos, she knew right away, his timbre and pitch. But it was impossible, she hadn't heard right.

Hurry, dammit. She wanted to blink herself to Athens. This was what happened when you didn't put loved ones first, when you had a life of your own that was demanding and fascinating and you felt split in two. Hurry, dammit. She hated planes.

This time, she would stay with him, comfort him. Drive to the country for roast lamb.

Chapter 40

1976

At Fiumicino in Rome, she hurried out of customs, annoyed by the flurry of reunion hugs clogging the aisle. She consoled herself that in three hours, after connecting to Athens, the hugs would be for her.

The air changed. She had the fleeting sensation that someone was indeed waiting to greet her. She scoured the faces behind the security rope and there he was . . . Tommaso. What the hell was he doing here? Her feet slowed.

He met her with a grave face. She put up her hand, a wall against his next sentence.

"Let's sit." He touched her elbow.

The blood drained out of her. "He's dead."

Tommaso wet his lips. "There was a car accident. Early this morning."

"They killed him."

"The facts are few. The newspapers don't print on May Day—"

"I don't need facts. He was to present his proof to Parliament on Monday."

"Proof?"

Alekos is dead. Alekos is dead. The moment she was coming to him, boarding her flight from New York. The gasp in the airplane. *Ach.*

She watched Tommaso's mouth move, his voice muffled, she was trapped behind glass. "No." She lurched numbly toward the gate. Tommaso held on to her elbow. "Get me an earlier flight to Athens," she said to the gate attendant, gripping the counter with trembling fingers.

"You're already booked on the next flight out, Signora Fallaci." The attendant recognized her.

"Seat me away from other passengers." She jammed on her sunglasses.

"Let me see if I can change your seat." The attendant clicked keys.

"Don't see. Do it."

On the plane, she hid her face against the window, chain-smoking. A boulder strangling her esophagus. Her mind a jumble of their last calls. *Two cars follow me. I mailed you the documents.* He was anguished, alone. She could hear it now. Why couldn't she hear it then?

His friends met her on the tarmac, Elias ashen, Tasos whimpering into a handkerchief. She had last seen them in their tile layer's clothes, toasting with beers in Alekos's office. Reporters swarmed as she descended the aluminum stairs. For a moment, time collapsed, and the cameras clicking were that day she and Alekos arrived triumphantly in Rome. Briefly, she tasted again the glow of being a couple, of bringing the Greek hero home. But it was not that day.

On the car ride into Athens, his friends gulped back sobs and she pieced together the shadow of a story. Friday night, Alekos had dined with a couple from Australia, political supporters, Mr. and Mrs. Nolis. He took them to Psaropoulos. *Where he took her on their first date.* After dinner, he insisted on driving them all the way downtown to the Hilton, where they were staying. In his *primavera*, the damn car, neon green.

He was driving back to Glyfada along the coastal road.

Almost 1 a.m. Two cars screeched out of the darkness. One hit him in the rear, the other sideswiped him. Alekos lost control. He flew off the road and smashed into the wall of a Texaco station.

Oriana shut her eyes. He had told her on the phone, *At night, when I drive back to Glyfada, two cars follow me, a red BMW and a pale one*. Why didn't she hire a bodyguard, board a plane that instant? She saw a flash of his assassins chasing him. Alekos petrified. Then hitting the gas, saying, *Fuck you all!*

Chapter 41

1976

The hospital morgue was frigid. Blue with fluorescent lighting. She stood facing the wall of eight metal doors in two rows. The orderly bent down and pulled the handle of the lower left.

His body slid out, naked on a metal slab. Oriana knelt. Purple bruises covering one eye and cheekbone. An autopsy scar swerving from neck to navel, his torso sewn together with grotesque black stitches. A gash in his right thigh was so deep, his leg dangled from the bone. Where was the blood? No blood. The doctor had said Alekos's liver burst into nineteen pieces. His heart exploded on impact.

The orderly left. She touched his hair, shivering from the blast of refrigerator air. The jet-black hair, the body she knew so well. She touched his hand, impossibly icy. Summoned the nerve to squeeze it. How? How did this happen? She spoke to him. *I should have stayed, Alekos. Come to you sooner. I didn't do enough to protect you.*

The face she loved. Ghostly white with frost on his eyelashes. She made herself study it, the noble forehead, scar over his eye and lip. He was only thirty-six. Was this the boy they found so dangerous? She remembered only sweetness.

Goddamn you, Alekos. Why couldn't you leave the bastards and their dirty secrets alone? She knew the answer. They would have murdered him anyway. Alekos had made his choice, hero and martyr. But not hers.

His gold band. She slipped it off and exchanged it with her own, a different promise for all eternity. His blue lips. How many kisses had they shared? Midnight and morning, pecks and penetrating. It was her last chance to kiss those lips that cried, "But I love you!" on a sultry August afternoon.

They were drained of all passion. Stone affection. She stumbled to her feet and punched open the swinging doors of the morgue. Doubled over, gulping for air. Telling herself, *Don't faint, don't faint.*

Kostas, the office manager, timidly touched her shoulder. He had driven her and waited, his face slick with tears.

"I'll fly out private investigators!" She turned her blurred gaze on him. "The best in Italy!"

Kostas drove her home into the deafening silence of the office. The absence of Alekos's greeting, *Agapi, are you home*? His navy sport jacket with gold buttons hanging lopsided on the chair. His chewed-up pipe in the ashtray. Her legs, detached from her hips, propelled her down the hallway. He had not been sleeping in town, he said. Their bed was made. Sloppy, but made.

They would never lie in this bed again.

She picked up his crumpled shirt from the floor. Folded it onto the chair. Unlatched the shutters and shaded her eyes from the relentless Greek light. She circled to his side of the bed, ran her hand over his pillow. A stray black hair. She picked it up. Long. Alekos needed a barber. She flapped her hand to release it, fleeing down the hallway, pouncing on a cigarette. "*Non è vero. Non è vero.*" She held her temples.

On the sofa, Kostas cleared his throat. Startled, she remembered him. "He asked me to go to the country," she said.

"I insisted he stay in town for the holiday," Kostas said. "Attend a labor rally." They traded wrecked looks.

"Tell me." She huddled next to him on the sofa, hugging her knees.

Hesitantly, Kostas began. There was an eyewitness, a taxi driver named Skoulikaris. He was riding directly behind Alekos and saw the crash. He and his passenger ran down the embankment to help. "The *primavera* was crushed. Alekos was thrown into the back seat. Blood . . ." Kostas swallowed and motioned across his chest.

"Was he alive?" Oriana forced herself to ask, the journalist's question.

Kostas nodded. "He tried to speak. *I am . . . they were . . .* The taxi driver rushed him to the hospital. From the rear seat, he heard Alekos say, *My God. My God.* Three small groans. Blood trickled from his mouth. He turned his head and was gone."

Gone. The word landed inside her like an ax.

Kostas dabbed his cheeks with a crumpled handkerchief. "Last week, something happened. He asked me not to tell you—"

"Tell me." She clutched his arm.

"We were sitting outside in Vari eating lamb. You know the grill Alekos likes. A car slowed down and the driver yelled, *You're a dead man, Panagoulis!*"

"It's a plot," she said.

Kostas cast his eyes down and nodded. "He was getting phone calls. *Watch your step or else.*"

"I'll tear them to pieces!" she said. "Assassins. Thugs."

He asked if she wanted water or coffee and, with a hunted look, stood to go. They double-kissed with a clumsy embrace, and Oriana was struck by his frailty, though Kostas was a hefty man. He was one of Alekos's loyal band of friends, a devoted follower. He had never been strong on his own.

The quiet was petrifying after Kostas left.

Bed. She crawled under the covers, staring at the filthy blue sky. The sunlight mocked her—the shutters should be sealed forever. Eventually she made herself do it, roll over to Alekos's side. Press her face into his pillow. It was there, his scent, cherry tobacco, glycerin soap, the Missoni cologne she'd convinced him to wear instead of that awful Old Spice. She hugged his pillow. Circled her arms around Alekos forever and never, one last time.

In the corner of their bedroom, a pair of suede slippers, her gift last Christmas, awaited his bare feet. His nightstand was strewn with drachmas, tobacco tin, worry beads, pens, all waiting to be crammed into his jacket pocket. It was four in the afternoon, Alekos's time to bound in the door from Parliament. *I'm home, agapi! Good, you're here!* She strained her ears for him. A void. Only the refrigerator hum.

It could not be. Her head shook left and right on its own.

Alekos had never been freed from prison, not really. *I'll always be a thorn in their side.* Her own pathetic hopes came into focus. Suit shopping in Rome, *cotechino* in Casole, being writers together in Florence. She had devoted herself to keeping him well fed, well dressed, sheltered in their nest. A futile attempt to keep him safe, to cling to him a little while longer.

It was always going to end this way. He had tried telling her. Yet they had given themselves completely, on the beach in broad daylight and under the quilt with a full moon. That unforgettable evening in Florence when they watched children streaking across the piazza, his hand on her belly, daydreaming of their own. It could have easily gone that way. But life with its sneaky dark recesses, its hairpin turns, had other plans.

No. The simple joys had never been within reach, not really.

She squeezed his pillow to her face, slipping one arm underneath. Something pricked her fingers. She sat up. A folded paper with his handwriting. For her! She opened it. Her heart sank.

He had written only one word, *Socrates*, and below that *The hour of departure has arrived, and we go our ways, I to die and you to live. Which is better, God only knows.*

Her mind reeled back to the Greek philosophy she'd learned in school. Socrates on trial for corrupting Athenian youth, his defiant defense to the jury before drinking hemlock. *I to die and you to live.*

Alekos knew. She heard his voice on their last call. *I need to review the documents with you. You did that already, Alekos, you sound odd.* He knew his murderers were getting close and she didn't understand, didn't lift a finger to help him. Amherst. New York. Her precious reputation. Work. She had even fantasized that Amherst would grant her an honorary degree. Dr. Fallaci. She curled into a ball and let out a wail, but the tears would not fall. They got stuck in her throat and behind her eyeballs.

The phone trilled and she jumped. Her parents talking at once. The news on RAI. Yes, it's true. No, don't come. Her father had a cardiologist appointment later that week. Why, what's wrong? Don't cancel. Don't come. Oriana could sense her mother wringing her hands as they hung up, she might as well beg, "Don't swallow pills, Oriana! Don't lose your mind!"

Alekos is gone. Alekos is gone. She pulled the covers over her chin. *Action is a duty*, he'd said over and over. Why had she never been a duty, love never been a duty? She had wanted more. She had wanted everything. Children and Sunday dinners and growing old together. Not for you, Oriana. You will not be Aphrodite lying down for amorous evenings or Hera warming the hearth. You will be what you've always been, Athena, goddess of war and wisdom, born with helmet and spear.

She was lacerated by what they'd done to him. The severed leg, exploded heart. But the main lament sneaking in and out of her consciousness was not about Alekos.

It was this. *Who will love me? How can I go on?*

Who chose the glass-covered casket, she could not be sure. One more dagger in her heart. Mourners gawked as if he were a plastic mannequin in a store window. She had placed an arrangement of pure white roses over his folded hands. Hands that were never at rest, that sliced the air to make a point. Guided her limbs with soft insistence.

In the teeming Mitropoleos Cathedral, his mother stood beside her, hand on the casket, bent with misery, burying another child. She had asked Oriana to dress him. "Please. I can't." Oriana nodded. She would do this final thing for Alekos, it was hers to do. The church had a back room. A deacon helped. Charcoal Armani suit. Hermès tie she bought for his birthday last July. Fingers through his hair until the deacon handed her a comb, the one Alekos never had use for.

She had tried so hard to keep him safe, but he had slipped through her fingers.

The newspapers announced PANGOULIS MURDERED and THEY KILLED ALEXANDER SO HE WOULDN'T SPEAK. Thousands of citizens clogged the streets and streamed by the coffin to pay their respects. He was laid out on a white sheet embroidered by his mother, sprinkled with red rose petals. At the foot of the casket, a handwritten sign posted by his friends. *In 1968, Alexander Panagoulis was sentenced to death because he searched for the truth. In 1976, he died because he found it.*

The Greek Orthodox ceremony was endless. Athena rocked and keened. Oriana felt tears threaten but she pushed them back, blowing them through her nose into a tissue as if she had a cold. The priest in gold vestments waved his censor with choking frankincense. Hands flew up, making the sign of the cross. She did nothing, perspiring in her black trench. Dark glasses not dark enough. No eyeliner, no lipstick. Face fallen.

"We'll see each other May fifth," Alekos had repeated, like the refrain of one of his poems. May fifth, the day of his funeral.

Chapter 42

1976

"I need a forensic expert to examine his car." She was on the phone to Tommaso.

"I'll get you a name. What do the police say?"

"What those in power always say. *He was speeding at 120 kilometers, he lost control.* Guess what? They haven't returned his agenda. Because in it, he'd marked the date of his confrontation in Parliament."

The fierceness in her voice was not at all what she felt at night, twitching in their Athens bed with insomnia. The worst came after she dozed fitfully, and her eyes flew open toward dawn, and she was suspended for a moment in the blankness of not knowing—before the avalanche flattened her all over again.

The Italian examiner she hired found no mechanical problems with Alekos's *primavera*. She applied her journalistic skills to scrupulously retracing his last hours, interviewing witnesses, Australian dinner guests, waiters at Psaropoulos, where he had his last meal.

"'Stomach contents snapper, calamari, dandelion greens, white wine,'" Kostas read from the autopsy report.

The exact meal they'd eaten together on so many starry nights. Unpredictable, what would stab her. "How much wine?" she said.

"Blood alcohol below the legal limit."

"That's good," she said, exchanging a look with Kostas that said nothing was good. "I want to see Skoulikaris again."

They spent hours with the taxi driver who had witnessed the crash and rushed to Alekos's aid. "Two cars, are you sure?" Oriana said.

"Positive," Skoulikaris said. "A red BMW and a gray Peugeot."

A dozen more witnesses reported seeing two cars to the police. One even testified that the drivers were hand signaling, as if plotting together. Two cars, a dozen witnesses agreed, until mysteriously they all changed their story: one car, only one car.

A week after the crash, a Thanasi Steffas from Corinth came forward, the owner of a gray Peugeot. He told authorities he'd been driving along Vouliagmenis Avenue and been forced to brake suddenly. Alekos, riding too close behind, slammed into his Peugeot and flew off the road. Why didn't Steffas come forward earlier? He was shaken. Why did he flee the scene? He was in shock.

Oriana dispatched the Italian investigator to examine Steffas's car, and the investigator found it was dented on the front bumper *and* rear. Steffas said *coincidentally*, he had been shopping for machine parts for his manufacturing business on the retail level of Alekos's office on Kolokotroni Street *the morning before the crash*.

"Coincidentally?" Oriana said to Kostas. "The police are fucking idiots if they believe that. He's an assassin. He was watching Alekos for weeks."

The police charged Steffas with homicide due to negligence and leaving the scene of the accident. At most, he would serve ten months. Two days later, the official government investigation concluded that Alexander Panagoulis died in a car accident.

The press hounded the family for a statement. Oriana, Athena, and Kostas sat together on the veranda in Glyfada surrounded by the brilliant blue sea and sipped coffee and wrote. The veranda where Alekos had scooted his chair closer, saying, *Stay, I want you to*, after their interview. The feeling of his overheated body next to hers came rushing back as she gazed over the rail into the garden of orange and lemon trees. Why couldn't it be that day?

Instead they strung words together, evil, nonsensical words, and Kostas called the press and Athena read the statement.

Since the investigation has failed to turn up mechanical problems with Alekos's car, and his blood alcohol levels were within legal limits, the family does not accept that he died in a car accident. We believe his death was a criminal act. We will do all in our power to find the truth.

Oriana did what Alekos asked. She met with journalist Yannis Zogradis and the two of them bent over the blue files. "Alekos was planning to speak in Parliament on Monday, May third. But May third never came," she told Zogradis. He had found proof that Minister Rigas was covering up the murder of his brother. What's more, Rigas acted as a bridge between the military junta and the new democratic government. He aided the colonels. "Here are the documents. Yes, you can quote me," Oriana said.

Minister Rigas was quick to refute her claims, stating, "I consider a foreign journalist's accusations to be those of a desperate, injured woman. I will not address this matter any further. Parliament is the only forum in which I will speak. But I have nothing more to say. Nothing."

Got him. Oriana felt a sliver of satisfaction watching him flail, for a moment reliving her inquisitions of a long parade of fascist pigs. Desperate woman? I'll show you.

But she didn't show him. Zogradis's newspaper again refused to publish the documents in the name of national security. Oriana took them to the judge in Alekos's "accident" case and there they languished. The consensus was that the documents proved nothing about Rigas's ties to the dictatorship. The consensus, naturally, of those hanging on to power for dear life.

Chapter 43

1976

She returned home to Florence. Tommaso asked to meet her at the press club. "I need to see you outside the office," he said.

For years, Oriana had refused to bestow her presence on that male bastion, even as a guest, but in her frame of mind, nothing mattered, and she didn't bother to argue with Tommaso. She walked past the arched colonnades of University of Florence, where she had been a bright-eyed student eons ago, and crossed to the palazzo with its discreet brass sign, *Club Giornalisti.*

The room was packed with bombastic men in suits. She plowed toward the brass bar, ignoring the stares that measured her up and down. What was she wearing, what was she earning, was she really in mourning?

Behind her, she heard a clap, then another, building into the unmistakable crescendo of applause. Some asshole VIP must have just arrived. Curiosity made her glance back toward the doorway. Every single pair of eyes was trained on her, and something more surreal: The members who had shunned her were raising glasses.

She kept her expression still and moved toward Tommaso at the bar. He, too, was holding up his drink. "For you." He handed her a whiskey and clinked glasses. "They've changed the bylaws to let you join. The first female member."

"I'll think about it," she said. The applause went on. Her

skin became rough with goose bumps, a thousand reactions competing inside her. The always gratifying sense that she'd won, shown these old geezers and young punks. Resentment, because their acceptance had come too late, after too many insults. The numbness that dwarfed all other feeling, because he was gone and she had no one to run home to and share her news.

The room finally quieted. The members were waiting for some kind of response. With a nod, she raised her glass. "Salud," was all she said.

"How are you holding up?" Tommaso asked, when the members had turned away and it was just the two of them.

"Fine." She waved away his concern. People asked, but what could you tell them? You were dead inside, you were missing a limb. You spoke aloud to him and every minute expected his call, his touch.

Tommaso swallowed hard. He had an airiness to his personality, it was much lighter than hers, and she knew immediately it was bad news about *L'Europeo*. "I didn't want to tell you on the phone," he said. "The director is out. They're bringing in Barto Temeli. He's going after wider readership."

"You mean stupider," she said. "Temeli's illiterate. Let me guess. Naked girls on the cover."

"They're pushing me out," Tommaso said.

She banged her glass on the bar. "If you go, I go."

"Don't decide anything now." Tommaso put his hand on her shoulder and shook his head. "Poor thing. You've been through hell." Oriana flushed, never wanting people to see her vulnerability. But it was Tommaso, and she let him see.

It took three tries to fit the key in the lock, with one hand steadying the other. Their Florentine nest in the woods. In every corner, Alekos breathed. In the bed where they made their child. In the bath where he soaked like a duck. At the stove where they simmered their pots. *Should I add lemon, agapi?* She felt his voice prickle her skin, saw him lift the wooden spoon to his lips and slurp greedily.

Air, she needed air. The balcony. She stepped outside and tried to breathe in the peace of the wooded property. They used to call it their private park, where they drank prosecco and watched the sunset and read. But their paradise of cypresses and pines had taken on a deserted, menacing air. There rose in her an ocean of remorse. She hadn't appreciated every minute together, hadn't cherished him enough. Alekos had been obsessed, volatile, needy. She had longed, at times, to be left alone. What to do now, with her vast, ominous freedom?

Hating herself, hating everything, she trudged inside for a cigarette. The sight of their empty bed made her double over and hug her ribs. As a journalist, she'd written reams about death, seen soldiers blown up in war, vaporized into a mist of pink blood and bone. But it turned out she knew nothing about death. She was totally unprepared for it. You could only understand death when it ruined you personally, when it stole the one you love. *The one who loved you.*

She paced and smoked and sat gingerly at the table where the two of them had been writers together. A stack of *L'Europeo*s leaned messily against her typewriter. Cover stories with *Oriana Fallaci* in boldface. She had driven herself relentlessly, worried she might miss a point, make a mistake, didn't have what it took to be the best. Now she shoved the magazines to the floor with the jolting realization that journalism was finished for her. Topless models on the cover, Tommaso being pushed out. She didn't want any part of it.

And yet. Work had always been her purpose. Her stability. Center. She fingered the keys of her Olivetti. Held on to the carriage with both hands, as if it were a buoy that would save her from violent waves.

It was what she had left.

You want to write great literature, get started. He had given her even this. *Don't forget about me.* The book came to her whole and inevitable, a knowing spreading through her veins. She would tell Alekos's story. The bathing suit on the coastal road, prison, Parliament, documents. Murder. She would put herself in the book, as she always did, two people who found each other, who cared about truth and guts and doing the right thing. She would tell Alekos's story so that people would know he fought to make their lives better. (*People are born good!* she could hear him say.) So she could stay with him a little while longer. So instead of losing, Alekos would finally win.

From the office in Athens, she had taken his Dunhill lighter, most-worn clothes—and a photo. Now she placed it next to her typewriter. The silver-framed photo of that day, the two of them huddled around the doily-covered nightstand in his mother's bedroom, tape recorder at her elbow. She in a white dress, glowing, talking with her hands, he in a black polo, grinning with his eyes downcast. The moment.

She positioned her hands over the keys. Shut out the world without him. Took a shuddering breath. And began with a dedication in his language.

Γιά σένα. For you.

Chapter 44

2003

The book is in her lap. She runs her hand over its elegant silver jacket that never fails to please her, the stark purple letters spelling out A MAN.

"Sign it for me?" the producer says.

"I don't know how I wrote this." She shakes her head. "I lost Alekos and eight months later my mother. The two people who understood me best." Her throat clogs even now. "I was in a fog, a depression. I forced myself to work, I'm a tough cookie. But inside I was wrecked."

To Dennis Brady. She inscribes the title page with her Mont Blanc pen. *Who came to me with white roses.*

"Three million copies in twenty languages." She cradles the book a moment longer before giving it up to him. "I did publicity, even *The Today Show*. Only *Ms.* didn't review it." She is still riled by that insult. "They claimed I gave up my life to be with a man. Wrong! I was always working. And Alekos was the one who encouraged me to write literature. Not just because he said *you can do it*. Because he loved me, and it gave me the confidence to be myself. I was complete. Someone cared. He did that for me."

"I get it." The producer nods.

"You do, eh?" She sees that he does. Maybe he found a better match, after the divorced wife. "Look, dear. If I ever say yes to this movie, you should know one thing." She lights a cigarette. "The actor playing Alekos can be taller, sexier, I know your tricks in Hollywood. But he *must* have his voice." From the side table with the Tiffany lamp, she takes a paparazzo photo of the two of them exiting customs in Rome, 1975, she in tinted aviators and a long suede coat, he in a black leather jacket. "To this day, I can look at his picture." She wipes off a speck of dust. "His shirts—I even made a lady's blouse out of one at the tailor and I wear it. But there's one thing I cannot do." The next comes out haltingly. "Listen to his voice."

The interview tapes. She has preserved Alekos's cassettes in a cushioned jewelry box from a Beirut bazaar, locked them away in a cabinet. Howard Gotlieb, her curator, is not getting those for the Oriana Fallaci Collection. Those stayed with her. Gotlieb is calling day and night, archiving her work at Boston University. She imagines journalism students of the future donning white cotton gloves and pawing through her letters, photographs, notebooks, manuscripts. Listening to her tapes stored on specially humidified shelves. My God, how to decide what she wants public, and in which boxes they hide? For months, she has imagined tying up her work in a perfect bow, but the ends hung dangerously loose. The pain of life's to-do list, you could not get through it in the end.

"Should you be doing that?" The producer points to the brown cigarillo she's puffing on, that she orders by the case from Nat Sherman on Fifth Avenue.

She blows a plume of smoke. "Don't break my balls." Then, "She's lucky, your girlfriend, if you watch over her like this. I was never lucky. Some women aren't."

"That's not true," he says. "In many ways you've had more luck than anyone. Everything you've accomplished."

"I could look at it that way."

"Why don't you?"

"Because we never do. I'm human."

"You're right," he says. "We never appreciate what we have."

All afternoon, she has practically written the damn script for Mr. Hollywood—Fallaci's one chance at love, how happiness was stolen from her—but there is one detail she has omitted. That when she wants to twist the knife just a little deeper, she asks herself: If Alekos hadn't met his assassins on a dark coastal road, would they have stayed together?

There is no answer to that question. Death made it unanswerable. Alekos will be hers forever, and she his. It riles her when some know-it-all claims that *Oriana Fallaci was more enthralled with the hero than the man, the symbol rather than the reality.* What they missed, these parasites, these nonentities, of all the men she had given herself to, only Alekos never left her.

He has become the 450-page book with the stark purple title. The faded photograph of seventies fashions. The memorial stone she engraved for him in Allori cemetery, next to her parents, *Rest in Love* (not peace, Alekos never wanted peace). She can conjure up mere traces, but it had happened to her, the safety of an embrace, the unburdening of a secret, the warmth of a shared meal. Memory has gone to work embroidering over rough patches, as it always does, leaving her with the words and images that are comforting to keep. We make our dead into what we need them to be in order to go on living.

She has lived another thirty years without him. Good years, many of them, she didn't curl into a ball and give up. Never.

"Would you like to hear about my Khomeini collision?" she asks Dennis Brady.

"Sure." He leans forward in his easygoing way.

In 1979, as an independent journalist, she landed a rare interview with Ayatollah Khomeini, the new Supreme Leader of the Islamic Republic of Iran. He had reinstituted the veil for women and the laws banning music and alcohol. He called

America "the Great Satan" and was eliminating political opponents and ethnic and religious minorities to purify the new theocracy.

"Here." Oriana opens a drawer under the coffee table and hands Dennis Brady the *Sunday New York Times Magazine*, where her profile ran. She keeps multiple copies, curled and yellowed, and takes one for herself. "It's like a movie script, my Q and A, it's dialogue. See? Two characters. The eighty-year-old cleric in brown tunic, white turban, bushy beard. And me, the western journalist. Wearing this."

She takes a cashmere throw from the chesterfield and drapes it around her head and shoulders. "Out of respect for Moslem tradition, I planned to see Khomeini with a black Gucci scarf over my head and my mother's black shawl covering my shoulders. But my interpreter warned that it wasn't enough and lent me his wife's chador. A black tent, head to toe, only my face showed. No nail polish, makeup, perfume. No shaking hands if he doesn't. And no cigarettes—that one killed me.

"The setting is the holy city of Qom, small house, immense Persian rug, no furniture. No shoes. I'm kneeling in front of Khomeini holding out my tape recorder to catch every brilliant word—he was intelligent, in fact. He's sitting cross-legged staring at the rug, never me. Three guards, his son, and my interpreter cluster around us on the floor."

Oriana's early questions for Khomeini had been about the killing of Kurds and public executions of homosexuals, prostitutes, drug addicts, and adulterers. A pregnant eighteen-year-old accused of adultery had been murdered by firing squad while her lover was punished with lashes. Khomeini defended his right to cleanse society of "gangrene" and evil ways. His winged eyebrows collided. Was he the new dictator of Iran, she wanted to know, ruling by fear? No, the people loved him. He was tired, he wanted Oriana out. But she wouldn't leave before this.

She reads aloud from the interview. "*Imam, I must ask about this chador I was instructed to wear before I could see you. Why do you make women hide under this black cloak that makes it difficult to walk?*"

"*If women are not covered, their shape bothers and distracts men.*"

"Uh-oh," Dennis Brady says, following along in his magazine.

Oriana continues reading. "*But, Imam, even in chadors, you forbid women to attend university or have a profession. They can't enter a hotel or even a public bathroom, which are only for men. Where do women urinate, Imam? Don't they have the same biological need as you?*"

Here she grows furious, pointing her finger as she reads his response. "*You westerners! Islamic custom is not your concern. Don't wear it! The chador is not for promiscuous women, anyway. It's for pure women.*"

"At this point, they all cackle at my expense," Oriana tells Dennis Brady. "Khomeini, the guards, even my interpreter. No respect. So . . ." She reads again. "*Thank you, Imam, for your permission. I will take off this stupid medieval blanket right now.* And I rip off the chador and fling it to the floor." Oriana does the same with her cashmere throw, hurling it at Dennis Brady's feet.

He cracks up in amazement. "Holy shit. What did Khomeini do?"

"He gasped at my bare head and neck. Then he jumped up and ran away. Oh, but I got him back the next day. I didn't budge off that rug for two hours until his son got him to agree. It goes without saying I returned only with my Gucci scarf, my mother's shawl."

After Oriana published the interview, Khomeini made a hate speech against her. His followers tore her photograph down the middle and plastered her severed face on posters all over Teheran.

The scoop landed her in the news again. Harvard invited her to give a seminar to its Nieman Fellows, professional journalists given the opportunity to study (lucky bastards). Oriana had never been to Harvard, so she accepted, but the fellows were irritating and focused on her celebrity rather than her skill. Did she like her fame or was she embarrassed by it? Naturally she liked it, she said, it was recognition for hard work, but fame posed an obstacle to interviewing, too.

It was true. After the Khomeini-chador commotion sped around the world, top news outlets wanted her byline, but she couldn't land a new interview subject. World leaders were reluctant to meet with Fallaci, afraid she would cut them down to size. She would. In the end, she decided enough of journalism and, for the second time, ended that phase of her career.

Writing *A Man* had made her suffer, but time made her forget, and she went into isolation again in the 1980s to write *Inshallah*. The 800-page novel was backbreaking, a mini *Iliad* about Italian soldiers in Beirut, with complicated characters and plots that she transferred from her knotted brain onto a white board to keep them straight. She toiled in her Manhattan study from eight in the morning to six at night, nourished only by coffee and cigarettes. When stuck, she cursed her head off and did needlepoint (yes, needlepoint, that most ladylike of arts). In the evening she watched news, felt a twinge over world events she was missing, then went to bed dreaming sentences, composing even in her sleep.

Inshallah was published in 1990 with a gold jacket this time and her name in giant letters. No more books, she promised herself, books required too much sacrifice. She would rather cook, shop, walk around the city, but this was not her lot. From childhood, she had learned to face reality, to cope with what is. And so she submitted to the brutal loneliness of writing a new book, this one about her ancestors. Researching, making notes. Another ten years.

September 11, 2001. Eight a.m. A coffee at her desk, dressed and ready to work. Drawn to the television by the eerie silence of the city. The instant the second plane hit the World Trade Center, she called her policeman friend from the neighborhood. "Get me a permit to go downtown. I need to see what is happening." She was seventy-two. The policeman tried but failed. How to take action, to be useful? She had only the television with its unspeakable images. And her typewriter.

In a torrent of shock, outrage, grief, she banged out a four-page story for *Corriere della Sera*. A wake-up call to the West that Osama bin Laden had declared war. Because the West enjoyed freedom of speech and worship, freedom to drink, dance, and love whoever it wanted. Those who insisted on accepting extremist terrorism in the name of tolerance would be responsible for the end of Western civilization. She went further. Too far? Maybe.

Newsstands in Italy sold out of a million copies in four hours. The people were with her. Then her publisher turned it into a book.

"What about this one? You don't want to buy it?" She brings Dennis Brady the slim copy of *The Rage and the Pride* from her bookshelf. Red cover, gold letters. She prevailed upon Rizzoli to design it in the image of the prized classics of her youth.

"My movie won't get into anything controversial," Dennis Brady says.

"Then you won't have a very good movie," she says. "Even if you give them a lot of sex, Oriana and Alekos in bed, critics will say yeah, she was pretty good when she was young, but then came September eleventh. You don't want controversy, but I'm full of controversy." She pauses, studying him. "You haven't read it."

He looks sheepish. "Only a few headlines."

"Just like my loudest detractors." She shakes her head. "Nobody does homework these days. I did tons of homework. Here." She presses the book into his hands. "Read beyond the sound bites. Many don't like what I say. Many agree. I'm open to debate."

Dennis Brady tucks the thin red book into his messenger bag (she doubts he'll read it), and his face tightens with calculation. Ah, time for business. The lanky youth engrossed in her love story gives way to the angling salesman. "I brought a contract." He pulls it from his messenger bag and slides it across the table. "If we put *A Man* into development, we would pay you a hundred thousand dollars for the rights—"

"Money doesn't tempt me. I hate money." She steals a glance at the contract. Why has she told him her story, then? If he were a good interviewer, that's the question he would ask. Because, Mr. Producer, I'm at the end and I want to make some sense of my life. Show you I've lived a big, non-banal life. Maybe to set the record straight. In recent condemnations of "Fallaci the once-great journalist," some charlatan wrote that Alekos and I were estranged when he died. Can you imagine, presuming to know my business?

Out loud, she says only this, her voice husky, taking back the copy of *A Man* and cradling it in her lap. "When you suffer three years to give birth, you don't give up your child to strangers."

"We'll pay you two hundred thousand," Dennis Brady says.

"No." Everything about that *no* is fierce. The story must remain hers, if it's to be her story at all. The one she needs. From the start, she's been the keeper of her own image; a woman must be or they will walk all over her. "You can't present my portrait." She gives no reason, no apology. "Only I can do that. I decide."

The producer turns his palms out with a shrug, accepting defeat more easily than she would have predicted. Irrationally, she feels let down that she won't collaborate with this good-natured young man. Being on a movie set was fun . . . she remembers sitting with Glenn Ford in director's chairs at Columbia Pictures. She hasn't had enough fun.

Dennis Brady slides the contract back into his Prada bag with a disappointment that comes over him late, that is obvious to her now.

"Come back when you're in New York and we'll have cigars," she says. "Call my assistant at Rizzoli, the one you drove crazy." She shoots him a sly smile. "Maybe I'll say yes, you never know."

"I'll take you to lunch next time," he says. "That little place on Madison, Sant Ambroeus, do you know it?"

"I know every Italian restaurant. It's decent."

A wave of sympathy passes between them, each knowing there will be no next time. Time has run out, though not for him. He will be on earth a lot longer than she. It's only then that it hits her full force, though it has been in the air since she opened the door for Dennis Brady, making an exception to her *Go Away* sign. He is the same age as Alekos when they met that summer day in Glyfada, but something more. He could have been their son. A son comes running when you need him. He tapes up boxes and mails them to Boston University. Visits for Sunday spaghetti and meatballs. Takes you to the doctor and holds your hand. Manages the business with your publisher. The heir to everything you hold dear.

"It's late." She ends it there. Pushes off the bench and leads him one flight up to the front door, resting at every step, drained in the afternoons. Trying not to grimace with pain.

"Take care of yourself," he says when they reach the foyer, placing his hands gently on her shoulders.

"Don't worry about me. I have a stubborn determination to win. You should teach your kids this."

"I will. If I have any."

"You must! Have I taught you nothing all afternoon?"

"My wife died," he says out of the blue, with the same bluntness she has admired from the beginning. "She was always telling me *this book would make a good movie*. I was always . . ." He falters. "Busy with other stuff."

Her heart goes out to him. Poor boy. She has been way off target, presuming he's divorced. *How?* In the old days, she would have asked, but why do that to him, why risk tears?

In the next second, she knows how. The image of a blue vinyl recliner floats up between them, the drip drip of "treatment" that made her days hell. "Same war against the bastard?" she says. He swallows hard and nods. She sees into him, the many superhero movies he produces that don't mean a thing.

He bends to kiss her goodbye. Their conversation has taken her so far back, but now she sees all that is coming toward her, and she doesn't want to. Of course she's afraid of death. The last man she might ever speak to is about to kiss her cheek when she inexplicably turns her head and his lips find hers. Tender, warm, brushing lightly on the surface. It's only a moment before they pull apart, and he or she, it's unclear, mumbles *Oh!* and the other chuckles awkwardly, but she is reawakened to human touch. Consoled by someone near. Then his hand is on the doorknob and it's over. *Don't go!* She nearly grabs him by the lapels, but of course she doesn't. She has a lifetime of practice, what to do with her fear.

"Bye." He holds up his hand in a shy, lingering wave before bounding down the townhouse stairs onto East 66th Street.

Chapter 45

2003

The moment he is gone, she seeks refuge in her study and enters into an invisible cloud of the producer's citrusy cologne. She closes her eyes and inhales deeply. A foreign scent, not Alekos at all, but he is all around her in the room.

They want to make a movie about us, agapi.

Will you let them?

Don't be crazy. He's young, like you.

Did you fall in love with him, too?

A little. She laughs. Then hesitates. *Do you ever think about him?*

Her, Alekos says. *She would have been twenty-eight.*

The child they made together.

Life didn't give me this, she says. And after a long pause, *I chose my life, didn't I*?

You chose me, Alekos says. *You knew I was trouble.*

I was looking for trouble. They laugh their private laugh, playing off each other. *They built a statue of you in Athens*, she says. She hasn't talked to him in a while.

Come on, he says. More laughter.

Outside the Polytechnic.

I don't believe it. This time he's touched. *How do I look?*

Mad as hell. Pointing your finger at the bad guys.

Sounds about right.

For decades, the Greek government refused to acknowledge his act of heroism. *Everything changes*, she says.

I don't, he says. *You're stuck with me forever.*

And then it ends. He's gone, or she lets him go.

She approaches her typewriter and stares at the half-written page, worrying about which words come next and whether she'll have time to finish. A new truth sweeps over her. She has coveted this artistic life of being a writer ever since she was a girl, no matter how much she complains about her monkish existence, sweating over every sentence.

Everything that happened to her, she wanted.

Basta. It has been an unproductive day and she needs to chain herself to her desk or else 6 p.m. will come and she will hate herself. The book awaits. Her isolation is like a crown of thorns she puts on every day. She has disconnected from society. The story is about her family, and what a family she comes from, rebels for generations, especially the women, always defying convention, disobeying the rules. What gave them the guts? Necessity? Genetics? It is her lifelong pursuit, to understand what makes some people cowards and others courageous. But her ancestors' saga is far away. She can't concentrate. The letters in her typewriter are black squiggles, her eyesight shot by afternoon. The fucking metastasis has caused lesions on her optic nerve.

No eyes, but she has ears.

The boxy black tape recorder is still in its cabinet. As the machines got smaller, she did her interviews with a microcassette recorder, but this was the one she used that August day in Glyfada. The cassette label in her handwriting is faded. *Alexander Panagoulis, Greek Hero*. She stares at it for a long time, her pulse quickening, before slipping it in. Old habits come back, the way she presses *Play*, careful not to break her red fingernail.

The worst thing in life isn't to suffer, you know, but to suffer alone.

His voice, rich and velvety, cuts to her soul. The stoicism that she copied from her parents—*girls don't cry!*— falls away. She deserved a man. A child. The tears break through. She was wrong about family, that it makes you conform, it makes you feel trapped.

It was good to have people near.

"I'm scared," she says into the silence of the room. There is no answer.

How has she ended up so alone? Her decisions line up before her. All her life she's been brave, but she's been cowardly about this one thing: giving up her freedom. She has spent her life being ambitious, being on a mission. Work, fly. The honest fact is she's never fully directed her energy toward husband and children. The minute you are one thing, you cannot be another. We can't have everything. She couldn't anyway. Maybe someday, women would harness the astonishing potential of having brains *and* a womb. They could scale every mountain in the heroine's journey, be tenaciously driven, the best in their fields *and* limitless, nurturing mothers. They wouldn't have to choose between being somebody and loving somebody. They could have both, like men.

Oriana didn't believe it. Anyway, not for her. She was born too early, chose a profession too dangerous, with too much travel.

At least she has made an effort, left a mark, *done* something while she was here. She is the author of her own story. Of course she has paid a price. The world is not kind to women who step out of line. Who take what they want. Starring, not supporting, roles. Women in charge.

Enough self-pity. The afternoon with Dennis Brady has made her sentimental, it has made her weak. Where is that invitation? She finds it buried in a pile of mail, checks her watch, calls her assistant at Rizzoli. "Tell Salerno I'm coming."

"But you said—"

"I know what I said. I changed my mind."

The Regional Council of Tuscany is honoring her with the Medaglia d'Oro, the region's highest award, in exactly half an hour. The ceremony is being held at the Italian consulate in New York, to make it convenient for her to attend, but she has told council president Enrico Salerno she cannot, it's a distraction from her book, *Please accept it in my place.*

Climbing to her bedroom on the third floor, she stops and groans on every step now that no one is watching. Oh, Ingrid. She thinks often of her friend, lost two decades ago. How did you face it? Summoning her willpower, she reaches into the closet and prepares herself. Black velvet skirt and sequin top, Loro Piana cashmere cape with mink border. Hair in a chignon. Black eyeliner, freshened up.

Her assistant sends a car and she arrives at 690 Park Avenue without a speech or even notes, unheard of for her. A wave of excitement breaks out in the stately ballroom as Oriana makes her entrance. Three hundred people in black tie, the spumante flowing. Salerno rushes over to greet her, thanking her profusely for coming, handing her a drink. *Do you need to sit down?* No, she doesn't.

Jubilant, he takes the podium, knowing his event has instantly become more significant. His opening remarks pay tribute to an extraordinary Tuscan internationally admired for her courage to speak out against oppression and ask the difficult, urgent questions of her time. A woman who witnessed history as it was happening, whose opinions still make headlines and spark debate. Who has sold millions of books translated into twenty-three languages.

Listening to his introduction, Oriana feels an unexpected

swell of gratitude that clogs her throat. After twenty years as a recluse, out of the public eye, she has forgotten the exhilaration of being the honoree, the star attraction. Suddenly Salerno is gesturing toward her amid explosive applause. It's her cue to sweep to the podium, and she makes sure to walk tall and hide her excruciating back spasms. Salerno presents her with a gold medal, and pins it on her cape.

"You want to give me awards, others want to censor and sue me," she says into the microphone. "But I am used to life's contradictions." Dramatic pause. "You are giving me this award because I am dying." Whispers and gasps. "It's true. But don't worry, I accept." The audience joins in her raspy laugh. "People always ask me, *Oriana, what are you most proud of?* I'll tell you, it's simple: my guts to tell the truth. I say what I think. And I've always denounced fascism wherever I see it, because too easily we can lose our democracy and our freedoms."

The applause is unending. Her smile extends past her cheekbones. She keeps her remarks short because it is late and she doesn't have the energy she once did. Because by now, everything she wanted to say is already in print. Except "Thank you." She catches a glimpse of the consul general, cultural attaché, business and political big shots all clapping for her. It has taken eons to win the respect of men who labeled her *crazy Fallaci, bitchy Fallaci*, but never *expert Fallaci, a leader in her field*. The snubs hurt. And of course they made her better, drove her harder to succeed.

This evening is different—everyone is with her. She steps off the podium into a bevy of toasts and congratulations. A celebratory din reaching fever pitch.

Later, she will take a taxi back to her townhouse, alone. Tomorrow morning, she will park herself at the typewriter, alone. There will be plenty of opportunities to review her life and doubt her choices. To drown in what-ifs. What if she had chosen a career more conducive to family? What if her child with Alekos had survived? What if she had left Amherst one day sooner?

Tomorrow morning, she will muster whatever stubbornness she has left to bear the burden of her final days.

Tonight she lets it wash over her, the chorus of "*Brava*, Oriana . . . so much admiration . . . your legacy . . . writing changed my life." They like her, the crowd clinking glasses, air-kissing, posing for pictures. She basks in their recognition of who she is. Artist, writer, the identity she has obstinately pursued from her poor girl's beginnings. That she depends on like oxygen. Words, her first love and last.

This is family, the thought strikes her, feeling the glow of people circled tightly around her, the packed ballroom. It isn't like everybody else's, but it is hers.

A weight falls away. What she should have done but didn't, her mistakes, her damn sorrows. She lets go, brimming with the sensation that life has been good to her. Full. More than enough. Why doesn't she always know it?

Tonight, for a moment, she has no regrets.

Author's Note

My fascination with Oriana Fallaci began on the remote Greek island of Folegandros while waiting to catch a ferryboat back to Athens. It was the 1980s, and I was browsing in a dusty souvenir shop along the harbor when my eye caught the only paperback in English, *A Man*, spinning on a carousel. An hour later, on the sun-drenched deck of the ferryboat, I started to read that story of Oriana and Alekos, and it has never left me.

Oriana Fallaci is little known in America, though she was a pioneering woman in journalism, and I hope to introduce her to a broader audience. I endeavored to stay close to the historical record while creating a work of fiction and imagining the characters' inner lives. Some historical facts are unknown. For example, it is not clear whether Oriana had an abortion or a miscarriage during her first love affair. Another example: there is no proof that Alekos was murdered by political opponents—though it is widely believed, including by Oriana herself. On occasion, I shifted dates or chronology slightly. In rare cases, I invented a character, the most noteworthy being Mulotti, based on the fact that Oriana repeatedly stated she had enemies in her business.

What started narrowly in my mind as a star-crossed love story expanded into a novel about Oriana's life and career, from childhood to her peak in the 1970s, after which she largely retired from journalism. At this peak, Dick Cavett introduced her on his talk show as a "legend," and Walter Lippmann called her "the best reporter in the world." I wanted to explore how she built such a reputation from humble beginnings, without a university education, and despite so much sexism, and how she defied the rules to redefine the art of the interview—along with her dramatic and often painful personal life. Underneath it all, I was riveted by her courage and wanted to understand what accounted for her guts, not only in becoming a war correspondent but also in standing up to powerful figures and simply using the word "no." There is a clip of Oriana on *Charlie Rose* in which she disagrees with his statement with an assertive "No, no, no, no, no." It is a master class in not letting anyone explain things to you.

Oriana Fallaci's own books were invaluable sources: *A Man*, her moving memoir of Alexander Panagoulis, written in the three years immediately following his death. *Interview with History: A Superlative Journalist's Portraits of Power and Dissent*, a collection of her interviews with world leaders that Christiane Amanpour has said should be required reading for all journalists. The book is still in print under the title *Interviews with History and Conversations with Power*. In addition, *Letter to A Child Never Born*; *Nothing, and So Be It: A Personal Search for Meaning in War*; *The Egotists*; and *The Rage and the Pride*.

I am grateful for these additional sources for my research: *The Oriana Fallaci Collection* at Boston University's Howard Gotlieb Archival Research Center. Diving into manuscripts, letters, clippings, notebooks, and even greeting cards was some of the most fun I've ever had. Listening to Oriana's original interviews on cassette tape and hearing her pointed questions in her smoker's voice brought her fully to life. *Oriana Fallaci: The Journalist, the Agitator, the Legend* by Cristina De Stefano, a relatively recent and insightful biography for which De Stefano was given access to Oriana's personal records by her heirs. *Oriana Fallaci: The Woman and the Myth* and T*he Unmasking of Oriana Fallaci*, both biographies by Santo L. Aricò. Uniquely, Aricò interviewed Oriana in person and was her authorized biographer until she decided (characteristically) to renege and maintain control. *Alexander Panagoulis* by Kostas Mardas, the sole biography of Alekos, available only in Greek. *Oriana Fallaci: I'll Die Standing on My Feet* by Riccardo Nencini, a remembrance of conversations with Oriana during her final days. *Oriana Fallaci: The Rhetoric of Freedom* by John Gatt-Rutter and *Interviewing the World's Top Interviewers* by Jack Huber and Dean Diggins.

Television interviews with Oriana on *The Dick Cavett Show* and *Charlie Rose* were enlightening to watch, as was her brief appearance in the documentary *Mike Wallace Is Here*. Interviews with Oriana in print media, including *Playboy* and *Rolling Stone*, were enlightening to read.

The settings of *Oriana* are very real to me. I grew up spending summers in Sounion, just a few miles down the coast from where Oriana first met Alekos at his home in Glyfada, Greece. The Parliament building where he served and the Vouliagmeni Road where he died are familiar Athens locations. Over the many years I lived in Manhattan, I speed-walked down Oriana's block on the Upper East Side many times. Rome was the site of my honeymoon and feasts with the wonderful Oresti family. A research trip to Florence, Oriana's hometown, greatly enhanced my ability to envision her there, both as a child riding her bike to Mannelli Tower and as an adult in love.

Acknowledgments

THANK YOU.

To you, the reader. Nothing happens without you.

To Lori Milken and Joseph Olshan at Delphinium Books, for being independent and publishing what you like. Jennifer Ankner-Edelstein for pulling Oriana out of the inbox and giving her life. Colin Dockrill for the evocative cover. Elizabeth Shreve and Tina Andreadis, I'm so lucky to have you on my side.

My heartfelt gratitude to Arianna Huffington, towering role model for us Greek girls. Laurie Albanese, historical fiction fellow traveler, for generously showing the way and assuring me it was all okay. Alice Elliott Dark, you've always been so kind, and I wish I were your student.

Jim Gianopulos for meeting Oriana in Manhattan on May 5 and bringing her white roses. You are the charming producer.

Janis Hubschman, for motivating me to take writing seriously since our grad school days; you are a constant source of stimulation and you've made me better. Professor Jim Nash for your wise and affirming feedback and the most impactful course I've ever taken—creative nonfiction. Our writing group is a haven.

Lisa Kauffman for reading more than anyone I know, being supportive through every hurdle, and feeding me. Beth Hart for your attraction to the story from day one and your faith. Angela Beekers-Uberoi, photographer and artist, you enhance everything.

Cristina Matera, for the gynecological facts and a precious, lifelong Italian-Greek friendship. James Gardner, for the many times you told me I was in the middle of the ocean and couldn't turn back. Nausica Stergiou for the balcony, especially when we're all on it. Vicky Moraitopoulos and Sophia Pappas for tracking down Alekos' biography and sending it from Athens. Kaia Heimarck and Chip Gibson for going to bat for me early.

Gina Panettieri, Susanna Porter, Genevieve Gagne-Hawes, Amy Berkower, Leslie Wells—for your efforts, notes, and much-needed shots in the arm.

All of you inspired me and made me feel less alone. You gave me the courage to keep going. The truth is, I have far less courage than the woman I wrote about, which must explain (at least in part) my decades-long fascination.

To friends who helped get the word out: Jim Windolf, Chris Bonanos, and Zoe Gardner. Deanna Leodas, Mark, Melina, and Xander Schmidt, making movies with you has been pure pleasure since the days of Breakfast Lunch Dinner. Cathy Bartzos, Jen Lieber, Chris Hart, Frank Santopadre, Franco D'Alessandro, Todd Harris, Elizabeth Neukirch, and Watchung Booksellers, nurturers of our community.

My family. Parthena and Yorgos Rubis, who became Bertha and George when they immigrated to America, thank you for my childhood, my values, and the warmth, fun and love we grew up with (all-night parties and poker games, too). You took us to Greece, which wasn't easy with a family of five, where I fell in love with your birthplace and found this story. Pauline and Sophia, my sisters and best friends, we will always be three. I miss you so much, Dad and Soph, life is diminished without you. Isabella,

Ruby and Paul, gathering warms my heart, and raising our families together has been a gift.

Yanni, my husband, thank you for being an artist and giving me the discipline to be one, too, through your example, even though I'd rather be socializing or swimming or watching television or doing anything but (re)writing. Kassandra, my daughter, for sharing my elation when we opened The New York Times to see my byline, and more recently when we opened the box of arcs that was sitting out in the rain. I am in awe of your sharp editorial eye and our uncanny mind meld. You're a better writer and thinker than I am and will help the world. I love you up to the gods and back.

They say that writers are often compelled to explore the same theme over and over again. So one final acknowledgment to the movies that shaped me at the Linwood and Lee theaters in New Jersey while I was growing up. I can still remember standing dizzily outside the strip mall, eating the last of my Milk Duds, after seeing The Way We Were. The image of Barbra Streisand's palm on Robert Redford's cheek was seared into my middle school mind, and I was stunned with emotion, wondering why? why did they break up? After that came Out of Africa and well, I've carried the imprint of strong, independent, unstoppable women—and their love stories—all my life.

About the Author

Anastasia Rubis has been published in *The New York Times*, *Huffington Post*, N*ew York Observer*, and literary journals. Her story "Blue Pools" was included in the anthology *Oh, Baby* published by Creative Nonfiction and edited by Lee Gutkind. Another story, "Girl Falling," was named a Notable Essay in Best American Essays. She co-wrote and co-directed the short documentary *Breakfast Lunch Dinner: The Greek Diner Story*.

Anastasia earned a B.A. magna cum laude from Brown University and an M.A. from Montclair State University, where she was an adjunct professor of English. Early in her career, she was an advertising and public relations executive in Manhattan. She and her husband live in New Jersey, where they raised their daughter, and she spends summers in Greece, where her parents were born. *Oriana* is her debut novel.